COYOTE

COYOTE
a mystery

Brian Brett

thistledown press

National Library of Canada Cataloguing in Publication Data

Brett, Brian
Coyote / Brian Brett.

ISBN 1-894345-53-3

I. Title.
PS8553.R387C69 2003   C813'.54   C2003-911121-0

Cover photograph *Coyote* by Daniel J. Cox/Natural Exposures
Cover design by Brian Brett
Book design by J. Forrie
Typeset by Thistledown Press

Grateful acknowledgement is made for the permission to quote from *Animal
Liberation*, Peter Singer, Avon Books, 1975. Permission granted by the author.

Thistledown Press Ltd.
633 Main Street
Saskatoon, Saskatchewan, S7H 0J8
www.thistledown.sk.ca

Thistledown Press gratefully acknowledges the financial assistance of the
Canada Council for the Arts, the Saskatchewan Arts Board, and the
Government of Canada through the Book Publishing Industry Development
Program for its publishing program.

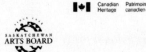

"It was not a lie — but it wasn't truth all the same. It was something . . . One knows a downright lie. There was not the thickness of a sheet of paper between the right and wrong of this affair."

"How much more did you want?" I asked . . .

— *Lord Jim*, Joseph Conrad

It was a dark and stormy night,
And villainous brigands, large and small,
Were gathered 'round their campfire bright,
When their dark master arose and said:
Antonio, tell us a story:

And Antonio arose and said:
It was a dark and stormy night,
And villainous brigands, large and small
Were gathered 'round their campfire bright,
When their dark master arose and said:
Antonio, tell us a story:

And Antonio arose and said:
It was a dark and stormy night,
And villainous brigands, large and small
Were gathered 'round their campfire bright,
When their dark master arose and said:
Antonio, tell us a story . . .

— Anonymous

SO, YOU WANT A STORY?

Everyone wants a story. They tell me this going down the dark roads of the city where the televisions flicker behind a million closed drapes, in crowded coffee bars while the hookers stroll past the windows, when I'm sunning on the wharf at the local swimming hole.

Since I'm a writer this is what they say:

"I've got a story for you to write. I've lived it all."

Even when I'm weak, when I'm wondering why I ever wanted to write. Even my friends.

"Just tell the truth," they say. "But it should also be a story."

So what do they want? A mirror of their own lives? Or a story?

A tale of love? That's almost always first — the foreplay needed to perpetuate our species.

Adventure, naturally. Thrills.

And murder. The threat that stains our nerves and our genetic imperative to survive, or so our brutal history tells us.

Murder is a natural business, unlike economics.

Strychnine grows on trees, and money doesn't.

Love and murder need a living landscape, though, so most don't ask for the city. They want mountains and fields and forests and memories — the way it used to be . . .

But what do you want? What could a story tell you, especially when you already know more about suffering than anyone deserves?

You don't want a story. You want an explanation.

Alright, I'll give you an explanation, only we'll call it a story. I'll give you love and murder, and the ecology of life as we know it — you and I — awkward and out of tune with the world — angled like arrows entering water. You know that.

That's why you walked away tonight with your request floating behind you.

For your twisted body — almost invisibly gimped and reaching for the grave — I'll make you a twisted story full of new journeys and odd questions.

It might ask why a rock isn't as important as a person.

Sometimes I ask myself that.

If I'm going to tell a story, I want to find the truth in it, even if the truth, when we reach it, is like a bird flown away.

I'll give you murders and lovers and birds and rocks — enough to delight any child whose disease makes him think like a man.

But first we have to go down a winding road that leads to the water.

1

Encounter at a Treehouse

THE SUMMER OF 1993, DAMP AND COOL AT FIRST, NOW HOT
AND DRY, had seared the hillside. Hundreds of black
crickets like tiny alien invaders ricocheted through the
dried grass.

Brian paused on the trail and wiped the sweat off his
forehead. Too much sweat. Too much whisky. The older
he got, the fatter and the sweatier.

He'd never seen so many butterflies. Monarchs.

An old man on the ferry had insisted that Artemis
Island was the Monarch's graveyard. "They come here to
die, he confided, "on the last, unspoiled island in the
world." He could have been talking more about himself
than butterflies. Brian guessed their abundance was due
to the lack of pesticide use by the local organic gardeners.
Nevertheless, it was a good story, and probably lured a few
tourists to the sole resort on the island.

He began walking again. Then, to the left of the trail,
a patch of wild strawberries. Surprised by this discovery
so deep into the heat-stained summer, he knelt and tasted
a few of the tiny berries. Like most good things, they were
addictive.

There was a pile of junk ahead — old automobiles, a
ship's propeller, other odd items — rusted and rotting.

And a woman's red shoe perched atop a stack of old saw blades overgrown by nettles. Where did that come from? Signs, coincidences — they repelled, yet fascinated him. His heart felt slack and odd inside his chest.

No wonder the lady at the store by the ferry terminal gave him a queer look when he asked for directions. "Charlie is an unconventional man," she said, "but he's one of us and we like him." She beamed as if remembering something. "If you take the High Road, his driveway is the lane after the Denison place. They got their name on a mailbox so you can't miss it. He don't have his name on his box; not much mail, I suppose. You can also take the Low Road, which curves the long-way-around." She was a striking woman with a skinny yet horselike face. Her narrow frame was adorned with globular breasts bound only by a tight white turtleneck, nipples pointed straight at him. "It'll be open for another few days before they rip it up for roadwork. Then you'll be stuck with that steep stretch from the ferry to the High Road." She paused for a moment, sizing him up.

Deciding he was a sympathetic type, she asked: "Do you want to sign our petition? That chute needs fixing before someone gets killed. We've already had a couple of cars go sliding sideways into the ferry line-up. It might give the tourists a thrill, but I don't want anyone parking on my cash register."

He glanced at the mess of signatures. "I don't sign petitions."

Her lips tightened. She wouldn't be half-bad if you put a bucket over her head. At least it would cover her horsey face and prematurely grey hair — top-knotted with a peacock feather slung over the shoulder.

Hey, man-child, this Brian sounds twisted. A bucket? And why is he named Brian? Am I playing games with you? Am I presenting an uglier version of myself? What the hell kind of story is this? It's the one you asked for. Go down to the water.

Despite his rudeness, she forced a smile, determined to retain the natural grace of an islander towards a visitor. "Whatever. If you take the Low Road, his lane is the one before the Denison place, so if you reach her mailbox you've gone too far. He's one hill past Jake's farm, which you can tell because there's always a sheep or cow running loose. All the roads here are the same road, they only have different names in different places. Keep on driving and you can find anybody."

Her instructions gave Brian vertigo.

Outside the store, a white peacock fanned its enormous tail on a piling. The bird made him think of his mother's nutty friend, Mrs. Dunham, who kept a small white feather in a golden casket on her dresser, claiming it was from the dove Noah had released on the ark.

The store's corner window was punctured by what appeared to be small bullet holes, with another petition taped beside them —this proprietor was a busy woman. It demanded the retraction of the Young Offenders Act, claiming that kids could get away with murder nowadays. That made him smirk.

There was a bulletin board, too. FOUND: EAR-TAGGED ROMNEY RAM ON THE HIGH ROAD. NO. 346B. JAKE SAYS IT ISN'T HIS. IF THE OWNER DOESN'T SHOW UP SOON, IT'LL BE MUTTON STEW. The florid signature said GUMBOOT JOE.

Beyond the store was a carnival-like cluster of ragtag stalls and foodstands — a market for displaying pottery, candles, spirit-catchers, crystals, carvings, organic vegetables, and all the other goods Gulf Islanders make or cultivate.

A strange boy was dancing on a blanket. He was skinny, anorexic with a curious pixie face — as if he were an Irish fairy inflicted with giantism — human sized. His dancing was oddly graceful.

Brian got into his car and drove down the Low Road.

Keep on driving. So much for that advice. When he'd finally found the unnamed mailbox it was too rough for a jeep, let alone a Miata. He parked the convertible behind a patch of blackberry brambles before the lane petered out, and walked up the trail.

It faded into a meadow of parched weeds and thistles. Not far ahead were the burnt remains of a cabin.

There was a plaintive honking near the trees. Another peacock. They were everywhere. It unfolded its tail feathers, almost seven feet high, as if it were guarding a treasure — the head angled suspiciously. Then it strutted into the cedars.

Halfway across the meadow, Brian stopped. What was that smell? He had a lousy nose, but he could taste strong odours in the air, an oddity because people who couldn't smell weren't supposed to taste. But this odour was strong enough for him to pick up. Oregano? Marjoram? It was coming from the crushed plant he was standing on. The field was scattered with herbs gone wild, and ringing the meadow were trees and shrubs he'd never seen before, though a few he recognized: eucalyptus, garry oaks, burning bush, ocean spray, rhododendrons, the exotics partially overwhelmed by the native plants. Near the crest was an orchard. Below was a vegetable garden rich with flowers, verdant and luxurious; surrounded by a tangle of old fish netting to keep out deer.

An outlandish treehouse, twenty feet above ground, built into three large firs with their lower branches stripped off, overlooked the garden.

A stand rose above its flat-topped roof, with a view in every direction, and on this improbable throne was an old man, grey-bearded, his eyes shut. He sat in the lotus position, his fingers splayed in the classic posture of the Buddha. A straw hat shrouded his cherubic, sun-reddened cheeks.

The treehouse was ringed by a shake-roofed verandah with a ramp that wound down to the garden. Behind this structure, on a south-facing slope, an assembly of solar panels were mounted above a pile of wooden boxes spider-webbed with wires — next to a large pond where a kingfisher screamed and dived.

Brian crossed the meadow and stood by the garden gate, waiting for the man to notice him. He was not noticed.

"Charlie?"

The silent figure continued ignoring him.

"Charlie Baker?"

With a disgusted expression, the old man opened his eyes and glared down at the intruder.

"I know you're Charlie Baker."

"I might have been called that yesterday, but as for today, I can't say. Depends what you want." He had a stagey, baritone voice.

"I want to talk to you."

"Nope. I'm not Charlie Baker."

"I know who you are, and what you've done."

"You do, do you?"

"Yes I do."

"Good for you."

"Charlie, if you don't come down here, I'll just come up there."

"If the mountain will not come to Mohammed . . . "

"What kind of answer is that?"

"My kind. I've got a gun around here, somewhere." Charlie grew thoughtful, as if trying to remember where he'd put his rifle. "Come on up and I just might find it."

"Are you threatening me, Charlie?"

"This is private property and you're trespassing — 'round here we shoot stray dogs. We also don't like city boys who leave farmers' gates unlatched, or light camp fires that burn down good forests, and we especially don't appreciate fat assholes who tell us they know who we are."

"But I do know who you are. I know you ruined pulp mills, released animals, and bombed buildings."

Charlie said nothing, eying him. When he spoke his voice was flat yet questioning. "Now boy, you arrive on my property, and the first thing you do is accuse me of committing illegalities. Do I seem the kind of man who'd run around bombing pulp mills and shooting animals, or whatever it is you're claiming?"

Still in the lotus position on his podium, he displayed such a benevolent expression that Brian was temporarily lost for words. "Come on down, Charlie, and talk to me. I bring news of a friend."

"Who?"

"Rita."

The hush of the meadow rolled over the two men. They remained motionless.

"Love; it constantly amazes me how love will bring a man to earth. What's your name, boy?"

"Brian. I've come to tell you Rita has disappeared. Almost a month ago."

"Disappeared? You were expecting maybe to find her sipping tea in the treehouse?"

"Either that or a pile of dirt behind the pond. No, I'm just joking . . . but it's not a subject to joke about. She disappeared mysteriously. I felt I had to come up here and talk to you — for a number of reasons . . . "

Charlie sighed deeply. "Okay, Brian. You can come inside."

From outside, the treehouse appeared tiny, yet as soon as he stepped through the door, Brian recognized it was larger than it pretended — one big room, sparsely furnished. A wood stove on a stone base stood in the middle of the room, its pipe disappearing through the ceiling, the chimney probably hidden behind the high seat where Charlie meditated above his acreage. There were two single beds at opposite walls, a table, and two wooden chairs which made Brian think of Thoreau. "I had three chairs in my house: one for solitude, two for friendship, and three for society."

The window was adorned with hanging prisms that cast ghostly rainbows in the breeze from the open door; red, white, yellow, green, blue bars floating across Brian's hands.

The extra bed meant the old man accepted guests on occasion. Either that, or he was hoping.

The far corner held a tacked-together kitchen counter made from driftwood and lumber scraps. There was a propane stove and oven under high shelves piled with an assortment of jars: herbs, dried vegetables, spices.

In contrast, the opposite corner of the room was dominated by a glass-doored stand containing an advanced stereo system, including a six-changer CD player that Brian had recently admired in an electronics shop. He hadn't seen any wires running from the High Road to the treehouse. That jumble of lines and solar panels must actually work.

The walls were lined with books. A lot of the books and the bookcases were chewed. Was an animal gnawing at them? That applied to the furniture as well, most of which was splintered and munched. Maybe the old man was eating his own home.

On the back wall, framed by the bookcases, was a poster of Bosch's *The Garden of Earthly Delights* — a common leftover from the sixties.

"A gift from a friend." Charlie peered through a hatch in the roof, above the ladder leaning against a bookshelf. "I never had the heart to throw it away."

"Sure." Brian smirked. There were several small pottery sculptures scattered about the room, including, on the table, a double bust of Charlie in a straw hat and a younger woman with long brown hair and crooked teeth. They were both smiling, their cheeks squeezed together, sharing an affectionate hug. Behind it, resting against the wall, was a ripped up grey board stamped: ACME MANUFACTURING INC.

Charlie descended the ladder, muttering. "Judgement. It's in your eyes, boy. Sniggering at my Bosch. Contempt. There's nothing but contempt these days. Well, I appreciate *The Garden of Earthly Delights*. That's all we ever know — paradise and pain. Don't you relish the guy getting bitten in half, the tortures next to the apple?"

"No."

"Neither do I." Charlie shrugged. "But I think about it some nights."

The cedar plank door was engraved with a poem.

> *Prince, gent comme esmerillon,*
> *Sachiez qu'il fist, au departir:*
> *Ung traict but de vin morillon,*
> *Quant de ce monde voult partir.*

"François Villon, in the original French? That's difficult material for an island farmer. Besides, I'd have thought you'd be more fond of *Where are the snows of yesteryear?*"

"I used to think I was an intellectual before I learned better. I can tell you consider yourself one. And who said I was a farmer? Do I look like a farmer?"

Brian doubted the door had been carved that long ago, but he let the issue drop. "Do you have anything to drink? I've worked up a thirst getting here."

"Demanding, aren't you. The water is in the bucket by the door and the cups are under the table."

"Water?"

"Sure, water. The best drink in the world. You don't mean alcohol? You didn't come here to beg for alcohol?"

"I could use a good shot of scotch. But I was thinking about coffee. That's fine." Brian rummaged around in the boxes beneath the stove, found a clean mug, and dipped the lukewarm liquid out of the bucket. "Water is better when it's cold."

"You go to the well for that."

Brian nodded. There was a clumsy silence, an inertia. "A lot of books. You're a reader."

"I was once. They make good insulation in the winter. Keep the bite away."

"The bite?"

"I'm getting old. Can't take the winter like I used to. Anything that keeps it from gnawing at my bones is good enough for me."

"I see somebody has been gnawing around here. Rats? You've got enough money for better than this."

"I don't have any money. You a robber?"

"Charlie, are you trying to accuse me of criminal intent? I didn't bomb clinics for women."

"Who said I did?"

"Rita."

Charlie's face caved in. Then he stamped through the door, slamming it behind him, shouting: "Get out of my house. Get out!"

Outside on the ramp, a few minutes later, Brian saw no sign of the old man. Finally, there was a flicker of movement among the waist-high flowers.

His straw hat slanted back on his head, Charlie resembled a sunflower, the way it'd look in autumn, with the seeds picked clean — as if birds had been at him.

The vegetable garden was so rich with green life it made Brian feel guilty. "I should go," he thought as he opened the gate and entered the maze of netted plants, past the flowers, the budding monkshoods, poppies, nicotiana, snapdragons, daisies — the whole blooming mess. He followed the plank walkways between the rows.

Charlie remained among the sunflowers, shadowed. Across the meadow, beyond the trees, the strait's blue water ringed the other gulf islands like a haunted Chinese landscape.

"You a cop? You gonna arrest me? Take me away from the garden?"

The tension ebbed from Brian's veins. He couldn't keep up the pressure any longer. Rita would never forgive him now. "No. I want to hear your story."

"I've got no story."

"Yes you do. She told me you did. I want to know what happened."

"She didn't tell you anything. She doesn't know anything. Nothing. And I've had nothing to do with her disappearing acts. I haven't seen her in years."

"She knows what it is to love an old man, one full of dreams nobody had before him. And she knows what it is to love a pig like me." Briefly, he flashed his best pig-like expression.

Charlie nudged a wilted head of broccoli with his foot. "The root maggots. They're bad this year." He sighed.

"I can walk away, Charlie. I can go to the cop shop and tell them what I know. I've already done a little research. They'd throw me enough scraps of your story for what I want. And what I don't get, I'll make up. That's how writers work. That's the way the world is."

"That's the way the world is. Yup!" Charlie stomped out of the garden. "Now you get off my property. Take your slanders, your extortions, your threats, your love, and your pig with you, because I don't want any of it."

Brian watched the old man go up the ramp and disappear inside. Charlie was beautiful. More than he'd hoped for, and yet he'd lost. It had to be the business about the pig.

In a few seconds, the amplified strings of a guitar concerto floated through the meadow.

Brian kicked over the wilted stalk of broccoli, white things wriggling out of the swollen roots. There really were root maggots!

Then he glanced back at the treehouse, wondering if his outburst had been witnessed. No movement. He stooped down and straightened the plant, clumping the humusy earth around its ruined stalk.

He slammed the gate behind him as he left, shuddering the web of nets. "Screw you, old man. Screw you all. I need a drink." But there was nowhere to go. The last ferry had gone. The thought of spending a night in a tacky resort with its stupid butterfly mythology and New Age cures was more than he could bear.

At the end of the meadow, facing the path, he stopped and wheeled around, and considered returning. But there was the gun. He didn't know Charlie's limits — this was America's first eco-terrorist, a man who'd practised a decade of terror and survived to retire peacefully for another decade.

The complications made him squat on his haunches, facing the music across the meadow. After a while he relaxed, sitting cross-legged in the pungent wild oregano, becoming a poor facsimile, he knew, of the old man on his perch. And he couldn't smell all the glory of this obviously redolent meadow. Another knock from the ugly world of nature.

The sun, a big red egg, fell towards the western shores, and the waters of the strait grew misty, mysterious. Then the music stopped, and silence assaulted him.

It was soon broken by the evensong of birds filling the woods, a cloud of odd hymns flowing over him. He'd forgotten dusk in the back country, the way the birds sang goodnight to a radiant afternoon.

A thunder of small wings drummed to his left, a flock of California Quail. They darted onto the trail as if they were on drugs, skittered and raced, cross-circling each other's path. It was a dizzying sight. "Chi-ca-go. Chi-ca-go," the big male called. The little thunder again, and they were gone.

A stellar's jay appeared, and hopped obnoxiously through the overhead branches of the arbutus. Brian feared ticks, carriers of Lyme's disease. The arbutus trees were notorious habitats. He lit a cigarette, and inhaled deeply before releasing a plume of smoke he hoped would be discouraging.

The sun ignited the horizon. The blue, jewel-like islands initially resisted its onslaught. Light and life. So much colour and brilliance, and so many shadows.

The crows arrived, arguing with each other, flying purposefully from tree to tree as if each flight was a statement.

He began to differentiate voices. Deep, chuckling ones, like old men laughing, enforcing a pecking order known only to crows. Frail coughing ones. Tuberculoid poets? Did crows have tuberculoid poets? And bitchy ones that complained about everything?

Then came the ravens. The squabbling of the crows ceased as the larger birds whistled into view, the *whup-whup* of their wings like a distant washing machine. They patrolled the meadow, occasionally issuing commands to unseen lieutenants. The ravens were the black-suited mafioso of the woods.

One made a husky cluck nearby, and Brian clucked back.

Startled, the bird told him a thing or two. He replied, and they conversed with an odd assortment of sounds. Then, distantly, he heard a deep booming raven speak — the real king of the woods, warning everyone to shut up.

Once their protectorate had settled down, the ravens flew off.

He became conscious of the deep colour of the gathering night. Blue like indigo. Blue like cobalt — a ruined roller in a pulp mill. Mills. Factories. Suns. Stars. A big wheel. What was he doing on this island? — following his instincts — the same way he'd always followed his mother righteously sniffing out sacrilegious objects in crowded department stores?

A deer browsed in the dry grass, not noticing him seated cross-legged where the trail entered the meadow. In front of Brian was a pile of cigarette butts, and he began to sing to himself, so softly the deer didn't notice. "Coyote, coyote, open your door, open your door. Mighty Grendel has arrived."

As if on cue, the door in the lamplit treehouse creaked, and the deer faded into the brush.

A figure appeared, shadowed in the doorway. "Brian?"

"Charlie?"

"Just checking." The door shut softly.

Brian was confident again, though he couldn't fight off sadness, and other thoughts. "I'm getting hungry."

The great bear pointed at the smaller bear — Polaris. The north. The arctic had often been home for his fantasies when he was a child, sitting on a scrubby hilltop near the subdivision, dreaming of the aurora borealis and polar bears — a wild and untouched life. Now it was definitely a dream. The arctic ozone layer was breaking down, which meant skin cancer. The north was pregnant with DDT and dioxins, gifts from the world's currents.

How we change. When he was young, Brian would admire photographs of fishboats, their exhausts billowing in the lonely inlets of northern bays, and he yearned for that freedom. Now, when he saw such pictures he thought of clouds of pollution scumming the air.

Yet this didn't stop him from filling his own lungs with smoke. He considered the fresh cigarette in his fingers. More than anything, he wanted to quit, and the more he wanted to quit, the more he wanted to smoke.

He shivered. It had grown cooler. His jacket was in the car, but he couldn't break the thread.

The crescent moon had hooked into the treetops when the door opened a second time. "You still out there?"

"Yup."

The shadowy figure, backlit at first by the open door, came down the ramp. Brian couldn't see if the man was carrying a rifle. He decided to remain under the arbutus.

Charlie slipped across the meadow, ghostlike; it was scary for a minute, the way he walked, so light and purposeful for his age. Like a soldier. Like a native warrior.

He stopped, planting his hands on his hips — the way a teacher would face a hopeless student. "Come inside, then."

"Does this mean you'll tell me your story?"

"I'll tell you a story. You can be sure about that."

Brian creaked to his feet, his knees stiff and aching. Yes, he was definitely growing older.

IF A STORY HAS MYSTERIES, AS ANY GOOD STORY SHOULD, we need to have them investigated, and for that we need investigators. Perhaps we're leaping into a deeper realm than a lad your age needs, but we're not going to worry about that now — not at the rate your disease is spreading.

Man-child, I look at your old eyes in your young face, and I want to tell you everything. Already, it's difficult for me to call you a child, because you're maturing so quickly. The world passes through us too fast; how unfair that your disease makes you age more rapidly.

You asked for a story, and a story you'll get. I'll present it to you on your twenty-first birthday, if you live that long. However, for now, let's introduce our investigators on a sunny afternoon. And times being what they are, we'll need an appropriate pair of cops for the age. Imagine this:

Inspector Janwar Singh paused at the shadowy entrance, as the manager stepped aside after unlocking the door. The hall of the apartment complex was so bland he wasn't expecting the exotic suite within.

The blinds were drawn. The front room, cluttered with the paraphernalia from at least five different religions, looked as if it had been ransacked by a giant searching for a troll in a deranged fantasy novel. Among the crystals, brass Buddhas, prayer rugs, dead incense sticks, zodiac star-charts, argillite whale carvings, and rainsticks, there was such an upheaval it took the inspector a few minutes before he realized this was not the result of violence, but a normal living pattern. Skewed garments were draped over the sofa and the dining table: brassieres, blouses, panties . . .

"It appears," Janwar offered, "she was in a period of transition."

Corporal Kirsten Crosby slid into the room, almost as impressed as Janwar by the confusion. "Maybe she likes it this way." There was an awkward silence. Both Kirsten and the inspector were attuned to social assumptions. It worried them that they might be making some themselves. "What are we looking for?" she asked.

Janwar shrugged. "Incriminating evidence."

"Well, there should be plenty of that here, Inspector." The corporal picked up a hash pipe sitting on the dinette table and sniffed at it.

"Of the right kind, Kirsten." Janwar said. He realized that was a rather witless statement, since a pair of black lace panties dangled from the tip of his index finger. "And please don't call me inspector. It's too formal." Dropping the panties back onto the sofa, he turned to the bemused manager. "Thank you. We'll lock up when we're finished."

The man shrugged, taking a last dismal glance at the room before he left.

"Shouldn't we be? Formal, I mean." Kirsten continued. "On our first case together?"

"This isn't a date."

"It sure sounded like that listening to the gang at headquarters. Did you hear the remark about the 'token twins'?"

"Chief Inspector Blake? He was a little rude. That's his nature. You'll get over it. What's this?" Janwar picked up a bra with flaps on it.

"A nursing bra."

"She had children?"

"None that I'm aware of."

"Perhaps we should check this out."

"Her sister said on the phone that she was single."

Janwar carefully put the bra back on the sofa.

"Hey Jan, look at this."

"Janwar, if you please. My name is Janwar."

"First, you tell me not to be formal; then you're correcting how I say your name."

"The name is Janwar," Inspector Singh said as politely as possible. "To shorten my name distorts it. I'm sorry if that offends you."

"Oh no, it doesn't offend me. I'm only trying to figure out the parameters. This is all new to me, and I want to make good in homicide."

"I'm sure you will. What have you found?"

"An address book. There are interesting names in here. I'd say she shagged just about everybody."

"Kirsten."

"Sorry. But it is odd, all these men. There are dozens. Famous ones, too. Michael Kuhr. He's an actor, and Cole Younger, a big-time painter. Oh Christ, she's written 'a long fat one' beside his phone number. This will be hot stuff for the newspapers." She looked up from the book, frozen in the striped light cast by the blinds. Her thin, pretty face temporarily lost its tension, and for the first time, the inspector got a glimpse of the person behind her uniform.

She'd been followed by a river of gossip from the patrol squad, where she'd proven herself over several years. She had an odd way of flitting from strict and formal, into being arch, close to loopy; then back to formal, as if she was constantly catching herself being different. And different she didn't want to be, despite those sharp eyebrows and the eerie black eyes beneath them.

"We're not interested in the newspapers." Janwar took the address book and leafed through it. He also recognized familiar names. "Oh dear," he said, "you might be right."

"What are we going to do with it?

"I don't know. Perhaps we should confer with Chief Inspector Blake."

"Once is enough for today."

"Kirsten. He's our superior."

"He's a wig."

Janwar glanced disapprovingly at her; then disliked himself for being so pompous.

"I'm sorry," she said. "We're having a bad start. This job is still awkward for me, and I guess being flip is my way of dealing with it."

"You'll be fine."

"So, what are we going to do with the book?"

"Take it," Janwar said. As he held it up the pages fell open to a double page spread at the back, one which held only a single name scrawled large, and no phone number:

CHARLIE — ARTEMIS. The pen had dug so deep into the page that it'd left creases on the inside of the back cover.

Corporal Crosby took the proffered book from his fingers and deposited it in the zip lock bag. They went back to their rummaging. "Artemis?" he said. "Isn't that one of the Gulf Islands?"

"One of the upper islands. You don't take the regular ferries to it. You have to catch a ferry from Sweet Water."

"Sweet Water?" Janwar paused in front of the desk stacked with books and papers. "Sweet Water? A town?"

"A town and a river." Kirsten opened the closet door, and frowned. There were more clothes dumped onto the floor than hung up.

"Two years ago, there was a student from the university who died mysteriously. She was from Sweet Water, if I remember correctly. It's such a pretty name it sticks in your head."

"How did she die?"

"Hanged herself."

"What's so mysterious about that."

"It was from a closet doorknob."

"She hung herself from a closet doorknob?"

"Don't be too shocked," Janwar said. "It's not an unknown method for suicide. There are illustrations of the technique in your *Criminal Investigations Manual.*"

"Why would she hang herself from a doorknob?

"That's the question I kept asking. Inspector Woodsun wasn't worried about it when he testified at the coroner's inquiry. After the ruling of suicide the family was very upset. They claimed she wasn't the type, had no history of depression, nor any reasons — apart from rumours of a relationship that went on the rocks — though we couldn't find the fellow, or learn who he was. She didn't leave a note, either. Inspector Woodsun was eager to have everything wrapped up for his retirement. But I keep the file in my desk. What do you know about Artemis?"

Kirsten peered wistfully through the blinds. "A lot, actually. A friend from my university days owns a New Age retreat there — The Last Resort. I was kind of wild then, too." She tilted her chin towards a pile of laundry. "I guess you've heard the gossip. One day I woke up and realized I was behaving like a fool. I fled that scene. So did she, but in a different way. She's a herbalist now, and sponsors workshops on everything from shamanism to crystals to aromatherapy to men's groups. The island is like a time warp. Hippies invaded it in the sixties, and gradually bought it up; they have a real stranglehold on development and who buys land. She fits right in. You would like her. She's a special person. Her name is Wren Dancing."

"Rendan Singh?"

"No," she laughed. And suddenly she was wantonly erotic, despite her uniform, or maybe because of her uniform — her thin figure posed jauntily amid the clutter of the room. Now it was Janwar's turn to feel embarrassed.

"It's Wren Dancing — used to be Veronica Dancing. We met in my first year at university, before she changed her name. The numerology didn't add up right, or something. She developed medical problems, cancer, and got involved with herbs and ancient Chinese healing stuff. One of her 'cures' worked. She's still alive and well, though the doctors said she should be dead."

Kirsten examined the covers of the three paperbacks on the desk. "I don't know what cures she was taking. Her skin turned this weird grey colour. It's almost creepy. Maybe I'm making her sound too cuckoo. That New Age stance is good for business on the islands. I went up there two years ago for a fast and a cleansing. It was fun, different."

"Is she a naturopath?"

"Highly regarded. She's written two books on herbs and healing, and I see her cited in the newspapers often."

"Maybe she could offer suggestions for my digestive problem."

"Stress?"

"It might be." Janwar picked up a calender from the other side of the desk, marked with class times and dates. "Our missing woman continues to be a student at the university, despite her age."

"She's also a sessional instructor in political science. That's how she makes her living, or so her sister said. She's collected a couple of Masters. One of those eternal students who never quite get the Ph.D and the permanent position. Still hanging in there at forty-four. Mutton dressed as lamb."

Janwar wandered over to the bedside table and pulled the drawer open. Empty, except for some creams, and a long, elegant, slightly-curved black rod. He lifted it out. A dildo. He'd never handled one before. It was so big and stiff it made him feel inadequate. Then it turned on, somehow, as he examined it. The thing began humming wildly. He couldn't find the switch.

"Janwar, put *that* back!"

Flustered, Janwar groped at the machine until Kirsten reached out and rotated the base, shutting it off. He stuffed it back into the drawer and slammed it shut. "My apologies."

"We shouldn't go messing with people's private stuff, at least until we've got better reasons."

Janwar was mortified. "Let's leave. I see nothing here that will assist us in understanding her disappearance. We'll talk to the staff at the university tomorrow, and her sister, when she returns from her business trip."

"I don't know about that sister. On the phone she said the place was ransacked. But this is lifestyle. It was probably cleaned up when she came for visits. Besides, the missing woman is supposed to be moving soon, isn't she?"

"She gave notice for the end of the month; maybe she fell into a torrid relationship, and is holidaying with this Charlie fellow on Artemis." Janwar gestured at the book in the baggie. "If anything develops from the interviews, we can send in forensics to sift everything. Right now, I feel intrusive. Let's leave the address book for the present. I'd rather not have anything as hot as that in our possession without good reason."

***

After trying the intercom buzzer which didn't sound as if it were functioning, Kirsten knocked politely on the door of the house. She was wearing her uniform again, unlike Janwar who, being an inspector with 14 years of service behind him, often preferred a suit. They were in an upscale suburb; monster pseudo-Tudor houses, brick fences, smart landscaping. A new Jeep Grand Cherokee was parked in the driveway.

The bright green, weedless lawn was divided by a curving cement walkway lined with dozens of magenta pansies and yellow primroses, a particularly gaudy combination which Janwar thought had charm, setting it off from the too-discreet, landscaped lots of the neighbours.

The sound of latches being pulled on the other side of the door. Kirsten put on her best official expression. More latches. The steel door, faux-painted to resemble wood, was heavily fortified. The door opened a crack, held fast by a chain. Seeing Kirsten's uniform, the woman on the other side unhooked the chain, and swung open the door. "Hello," she said. She was short and dumpy, with bright yellow hair and the purplest lipstick Janwar had ever seen. She looked like her flower bed. "Sorry about the intercom, but we've had another break-in. The vandals cut the power. Come inside. You're here about my sister, aren't you?"

"Yes, we are. Mrs. Kay Harwood? I am Inspector Singh." Janwar showed his badge."

"I'm Corporal Crosby."

"You aren't what I was expecting, sorry." The woman sounded oddly contemptuous.

The hackles rose on the necks of both officers. "Are we objectionable to you?"

"No, no, dear me. I'm sorry, Inspector. I didn't mean it that way. I was just expecting an officer to come about the vandals. You're from missing persons, aren't you? I can tell. Call me Kay."

"Actually, homicide," Janwar said.

"Homicide! She's dead?"

"No, no, not at all," Kirsten said. "Missing persons is understaffed right now, so we came down to interview you. But there have been several cases of women

disappearing recently, and you did say her apartment
was . . . " Her voice trailed off as she realized how this
sounded.

"You think she's dead?"

"Not in the least," Janwar interrupted. "There's no
evidence to suggest that. Our words were unfortunately
chosen. May we come inside?"

"Oh, of course." Still flustered, Mrs. Harwood ushered
the pair through the hallway to the living room. Facing
them, on the expansive white wall, a scrawl of red spray-
painted writing looped around a large painting of two
wolves without damaging it. HOW WOULD YOU LIKE IT IF SOMEONE
WORE YOUR SKIN? By the flight of stairs leading to the upper
floor, the same paint said: THE SONS OF COYOTE ARE ALIVE AND
WATCHING YOU.

"My husband is the leading furrier in Vancouver. We've
been vandalized. As you can imagine, I'm so upset and
confused by all this . . . everything going on at once. It's
just too much."

Her purple lips squeezed together into an impressive
pansy shape. "We have an alarm system, too, a very
expensive one. It only goes off at the wrong times. My
husband, he made sure it had every gadget and sensor
money could buy. A lot of good that did. They cut the
power and phone line. It's so scary."

Janwar looked up at the cold eyes of the wolves in the
painting. The canvas was by Robert Bateman. Very
meticulous. And very expensive.

"The animal rights people want to scare my husband
out of the business. It started about a year ago. This is the
third time they've defaced the house. They never steal
anything, only write these awful threats on the wall."

Janwar didn't know what to say, so he nodded officially. "I'm sure we'll catch up with them, Mrs. Harwood."

"Call me Kay. Would you like coffee? I have a fresh pot brewing in the kitchen."

"Where else did they deface?" Kirsten asked.

"The master bedroom. I don't want you to see the filth they wrote on the walls. How do you like your coffee?"

"With milk and very sweet, two teaspoons, please." Janwar said. "Corporal Crosby takes hers black." They followed Mrs. Harwood into the kitchen.

She poured their coffee and they sat at a large lacquered table, across from the latest blacktopped Jenn-Aire range which Kirsten had recently admired, until it struck her that it would be stupid to buy a toy like that for herself. A stove is only as good as who it cooks for, and one lonely woman doesn't count for much. Perhaps asking about its merits would be a good icebreaker — or maybe not, with this odd woman. She decided against that route. "We could come back another day if this is too trying for you."

"No, it's fine. My sister is more important than these hooligan environmentalists."

Janwar opened his notepad. "Corporal Crosby informed you on the phone that your sister's car was found Friday?"

"Yes, she did. I know something's happened to her."

"What makes you think that?" Kirsten asked.

Janwar took a sip of his coffee. He helped himself to another spoon of white sugar.

"My, you do like it sweet, don't you?"

"Yes, I do, Mrs. Harwood."

"Call me Kay. Maybe we should get one thing straight. I live a very different life than Rita. We don't see eye-to-eye on politics, on hardly anything. But we're sisters. That's why I know a tragedy has happened. She might be immature, hanging around at that stupid university all her life, yet she's reliable, too. When she makes an appointment, she keeps it. When she didn't show up for dinner with her new sweetheart . . . I mean, I was grateful, she'd finally given up on those deadbeats, and found herself a nice university professor, one with money. Then wham, she's gone." Mrs. Harwood threw her hands towards the ceiling, before fading back into her chair with a look of utter sorrow — her painted face collapsed, her silence disturbing. It didn't last long.

"And when I saw her place ransacked like that; well, the caretaker thought it was suspicious, too. And the apartment door was unlocked! I know that neighbourhood, and every intelligent person locks their doors. Now your officers have found her car with the keys still in the ignition! Damn her! She was always picking up hitchhikers, perfect strangers, despite my warnings, but she insisted she was the last holdout. She was only a teenager in the sixties, and everyone gave her rides; now she's paying it back. Can you figure? A mature woman, forty-four-years-old, carrying on like that?"

"We did check out the apartment, Mrs. Harwood," Kirsten said, "and despite the mess, it appeared to us that it was more an extreme case of dirty laundry than a ransacking; mind you, that was before the car was discovered."

"Maybe there's a stalker after the whole family? Look what we've been going through here."

"Is she involved with the fur business?"

"No, of course not, Inspector Crosby, but when I come home and see this — ?"

"It's Corporal Crosby. He's the Inspector."

"Sorry. So what have you found out so far?"

"Very little as yet, the Inspector and I were waiting for your return before we did any further investigating. We thought it might be more helpful to talk to you first."

"You haven't done anything? There's no fingerprints? No suspects . . . ?"

Janwar put his coffee cup down. "This isn't a murder mystery, Mrs. Harwood. Investigating a disappearance is a long, slow process. Ninety percent of disappearances are voluntary. The missing person usually shows up, often ashamed of the trouble he or she may have caused."

"We did check with the university," Kirsten said, "and they confirmed her attendance record and reliability, which I'm afraid is not the best, actually. When the car was found in its odd state we decided to have it finger-printed; there was nothing of any interest. What we could use from you are the names of personal contacts such as this professor, or other friends."

"How should I know? I never met him; though, now that I think about it, she told me his name once. It sounded Jewish, Albert something-or-other Jewish, and he drove a Mercedes. There was a friend, Kim Darwin, an anthropology professor she talked about a few times. They went back for years. And another professor, a Punjabi fellow I think. Or Hindu. Can't remember his name, either. I ran into her with him last year at a coffee shop downtown." As if this reminded her, she stood up and collected their only-just-emptied cups and set them in the sink.

"She said they were friends, but she was always falling for exotic guys. He shouldn't be hard to find. How many Punjabi professors do they have up there? And he wore a turbine, too, the same colour as yours."

"It's called a turban, Mrs. Harwood." He could feel another headache coming on.

Outside, as Janwar backed their car down the driveway, a police vehicle drew up. Constable Hartley on the B&E detail. He smirked when he recognized them. Janwar nodded politely as he put his own car into drive and left the cul-de-sac. He gave a loud, involuntary burp.

"What's the matter, Janwar, did she give you gas? With a sister like Kay Harwood, I'd disappear, too."

"I'm not feeling well, haven't for weeks . . . I think I should go for a checkup. Headaches, upset stomach, joint pain. I feel as if I have a continuous low-grade fever."

"Try cutting down the sugar. Considering all the coffee you drink, you're going to end up with diabetes."

"I fear," Janwar said, "we were too cursory in our inspection of the apartment."

"You're starting to worry our missing lady is another one for the list?"

"Yes." A bead of sweat worked its way down Janwar's cheek. He grew quiet, his expression distant.

3

Blue Day In Sweet Water

HIS NAME IS COYOTE, OR THAT'S WHAT HE CALLS HIMSELF. He's a killer.

It didn't start out that way, it never does. Murder was not in his thoughts in 1973 as the sun sank into the last mountain range floating on the western horizon, far out beyond the mouth of Sweet Water River.

Sweet Water? It might taste fine at the river's source, but not here — the mouth of the river oozing into the bay was a confluence of brown, foamy slime and the deep green sea. Sweet Water River — a dirty lie.

Now the lie was going to receive another tainting, one that would colour the bay and mark the extent of the chemical soup from the pulp mill for everyone to see. Once Coyote started thinking about it, he didn't have a choice. The scheme was brilliant in more ways than one.

His headlights found the abandoned logging road. The packsack was stuffed behind the seat.

It was dark and moony, beyond midnight, when he finally parked beside the trailhead. He dozed uncomfortably for a few hours: it was pointless to stumble around there in darkness.

At the first grey light, he climbed stiffly out of the jeep, shouldered his pack, and began plodding up the trail. He was tired; it had been a scary night-drive despite the moon that floated through the spidery trees. The rolling, lumpy road had floated like whale humps cruising a woodland sea.

The air was fresh and pungent, the silence broken only by his footsteps and the hammer of a pileated woodpecker driving its skull against a beetle-riddled trunk.

The footpath didn't take long. He had to navigate one last gully before the climb to the old picnic site above the canyon.

Here, the river was a clear lime-green, pristine. The thick moss muffled his steps. There were so many kinds of moss. Moss like star clusters. Moss that crawled over the rocks. Ferny moss. Dark moss. Moss dotted with mushrooms: destroying angels, perhaps. He pulled four plastic bags from the nylon pack and set them at his feet. Then, one-by-one, he scattered their contents. Brilliant clouds struck the water: cobalt blue, perhaps the most powerful colouring oxide in existence. Eighty pounds of it. A quantity only a rich man could afford. He grinned at that thought. Not only was it expensive, it'd taken a long time to collect, cruising pottery suppliers for months, buying a few pounds at a time.

After he'd emptied the last bag into the river, he took his lighter and ignited the bags on a rock — a whiff of black smoke before they transformed into tarry scum, which made him feel guilty. Carefully, making sure there were no fingerprints, he hung the note from a branch where they would find it when they followed the stain upriver. THE COYOTE WILL SHOW YOUR TRAIL FOR YOU. But not for too long. He was assuming the cobalt would dissipate in a couple of days, fool that he was, back then.

His hands were tinged with the oxide, so he wiped them clean on the moss; then dusted his clothes free from any residue.

He straddled the rock. Near his feet a green tree-frog basked in a ray of sunlight glancing off the cliff. A hundred feet below the overhang the river had turned a deep blue, surging towards the sea. The colour made him think of many things — a child — himself — taking gumdrops from a stranger; then running. A new car's fender, a woman's hand resting on the cool sheen when she said goodbye. The way a young boy's hair shone metallic as the moonlight reflected off the pocket knife in his hand, and the dark stream of blood on his forearm. The blue of his brother's eyes.

He turned and ran down the trail as if hell were following him.

***

As he opened the door of the jeep, something reflected in the mirror, a white clump on a dead maple. Oyster mushrooms — pounds of them! *Pleurotus ostreatus*. First identified and named by Fries. His pocket field guide listed its edibility with one word: 'Choice.'

He found himself standing by the maple, his arms filled with the pale flesh. Then he raced back, dumped them onto the passenger seat, and drove happily down the road.

***

Hours later, he arrivbared at the near-empty parking lot of the Shiftwork Cafe & Bar above the waterfront. It wasn't the most popular spot in Sweet Water, the locals had rechristened it the Shiftfood Cafe, but it had an excellent view. Inside, he found a window seat overlooking the government dock and ferry terminal, and ordered the full bacon-and-egg breakfast, craving a little grease and cholesterol.

He ate slowly, nursing his coffee, gazing at the smoke discharged into the sky from the mill's chimneys. Despite the rotten odour of sulphites hanging over the town, there was only one active stack. The smell was enough to make him abandon his eggs.

The fumes from the last smokestack ceased abruptly. A dark smudge began seeping into the bay. By the time he'd finished his second coffee, the shoreline was stained a deep cobalt blue.

He paid his bill and strolled down to the wharf where he could listen to the fishermen as they clustered about their boats, watching with horror the spreading contamination that might end their season.

It pleased Coyote that they blamed the mill, though he knew they'd change their tune soon enough.

He decided the view would be better from the windows of the bar adjoining the cafe, where he could eavesdrop on the usual batch of hardcore millwrights having a beer before the afternoon shift. There might be a few insomniacs arriving from a chaotic night at the mill.

The mushrooms suddenly made him nervous. If the police were smart enough to reach the cobalt's entry point and found the note before he caught the late afternoon ferry they might espy the broken mushroom clump on the stump.

Still, the local police didn't have a reputation for efficiency. He was reluctant to throw the mushrooms away

— that was too wasteful — so on the way to the bar he returned to the Jeep and tucked them into a folded-up grocery bag in the back. At least they weren't obvious now. Besides, the police would be expecting hot-headed young radicals, not a venerable, middle-aged islander going home after his bi-monthly shopping trip to Sweet Water.

Inside the bar he approached the counter and ordered a tomato juice, and since it was a special day, a beer to mix with the juice. Every man should celebrate once in a while, though he was dubious about why celebration meant confusing the mind with drugs.

He paid the bartender — a tall thin women with crooked teeth and long brown hair, a shank of which dangled into the foam on his beer. She observed him staring at his glass, and was abashed. "Sorry. Do you want another?"

He shook his head. "I've always thought the stuff needs a woman's touch." She nodded and turned away as a client ordered a beer. Behind her, his face in the mirror gazed back at him. His short grey beard was flecked with a few tiny spots of blue. Cradling his glasses, he forced himself to remain calm, backing away from the bar to a table beside the window and next to a clutch of millworkers — keeping his back to them.

After setting the glasses down he draped his jacket on the chair and wandered casually over to the washroom. As soon as the door shut he rushed to the mirror and stared at himself in the bright fluorescent light. He'd been walking around town half the morning! And nobody had noticed!

He turned on the water, and splashed his face. That made the blue darker. He stuck his head into the sink and scrubbed maniacally.

Finally, it was gone, but his face was flushed beet red. He dried himself off, stood there for a couple minutes, waiting, calming down . . . looking at his reflection. He thought of the mushrooms again. It was strange how, after almost a year of planning, he'd risk throwing them into his Jeep. Was this the desire to be caught the police claimed all criminals had?

At last he felt he could leave. He walked out of the restroom, a satisfied expression on his face, as if he'd just taken the ultimate crap.

Nothing much was being said at the next table. The men were too interested in the fight during last night's hockey playoffs.

The bar was decorated in the usual frontier chic, the fake log walls festooned with hunting and fishing instruments common to the raincoast. Stuffed heads of game animals were mounted in all the obvious spots. The proudest collection was lined up above and behind the bar, a row of deer trophies, each bearing a small brass marker proclaiming the kill date, beginning in 1937 and extending to 1971, with only three mounts missing.

For the years 1944 and 1945, instead of antlered animals there were two German helmets, each pierced by a single bullet hole. The last mount on the line, 1971, was a life-like sculpture of a grizzled-looking man's head, between his teeth a dried rose.

The young bartender watched Coyote studying the row, and she looked sheepishly up at them. She strayed over from the bar, pulled up a chair, and sat down with a disarming smile.

"It's quite the collection, isn't it?" she said.

"You're too young to have killed all those animals . . . or people?"

"My father. A skewed sense of humour. You're not German, are you?"

"Nope."

"We get the occasional German tourist who goes nuts when he sees them. You looked kind of German to me. They're not real, the holes in the helmets. My father, he was always pissed he lost two years of hunting when he was in the war . . . He was a cook in a commissary. Then he found those helmets at an auction about ten years ago — shot 'em up behind the house and had them mounted. They're a real conversation piece. I haven't the heart to take them down."

"Your father must be lots of fun at parties."

"He was. He died two years ago."

"I'm sorry to hear that."

"That's Dad at the end of the line."

This girl intrigued him. He wished he was younger. But the workers at the next table were talking. "What the hell's going on up there," one said, "that stack shouldn't have quit so early."

"And that blue stuff in the bay. Scary shit, eh?"

"Just what we need, on top of them starting the shutdown."

The girl half-turned her head, also listening. "The blue water's amazing," she said to Coyote.

"Sure is." His stomach was churning after the last man's remark. Shutdown?

"I made the sculpture," said the barkeep. Coyote saw her left eye was dark, bruised. "I'm a potter. He never got to see it finished, but I thought maybe he'd enjoy it at the end of the line, so I had it mounted for the wake. It was quite a funeral. We almost wrecked the place. People tell me I climbed up and put the rose in his teeth. I can't remember."

"You've inherited your father's sense of humour."

"I need it." She displayed that sad smile again, her hair falling over her face.

There was a long, mournful wail from the plant. He thought of sirens — the way police cars in films screeched to a halt, blocking the entrances and exits; then the dog sniffing at the mushrooms in the Jeep. He was getting obsessive again. Besides, if this hopeless lot of police got their act together today, they'd assume the culprit was long gone on the highway to Vancouver in a van painted with environmentalist slogans.

It was noon. The siren had announced the shift change at the mill. One of the men said: "It's official now, boys. Two weeks off for maintenance."

"You think they'll be taking us back, George, when that's over?"

"They always talk sweet and act mean. Bet it's a month. There's too much paper surplus. They don't need us. And now there's that blue junk in the water."

"I'm going to have me one hell of a long party."

"I'm going to fix my back porch."

"I'm going to need a loan to pay my mortgage."

"I told you not to buy that house."

"You live around here?" the barkeep asked, suddenly aware that they'd both been eavesdropping. "I think I've seen you in town before."

"I've got a summer cabin on Artemis Island, where I hide out when I can't take Vancouver. It's my retreat. I come over here a couple times a month to shop."

"Artemis? One of the great islands, isn't it? I want to buy land there, maybe five acres, sell this place and move on, just make pottery. If you hear of any acreage coming on the market, let me know about it. The good land is so hard to buy. The locals only sell to each other. But my husband doesn't want to leave; he likes the bar . . . Sometimes he samples it a bit much." She looked at him meaningfully.

Coyote debated with himself whether he should get up and leave — either that or he could stay and fall in love.

The door opened, and a man rushed in, carrying a cardboard box. He was tall, skinny, sporting a thin moustache, his eyes dark and sunken, yet not unattractive. He acknowledged no-one, put the box down behind the bar; then disappeared through the back door.

"That's my husband. I better get going. There might be guys dropping in from the mill for lunch and beer. It's been nice talking to you." She stood up and held out her hand. "Elvira's my name."

He touched her cool, long fingers. "Charles."

She flicked the hair from her face, exposing the bruise in the yellow light streaking through the window. "Let me know if anyone's selling."

"I'll do that."

He watched her return to the bar. He was about to leave when another man entered and joined the group next to him.

"Hey Brian, how's it shaking?" One of the millworkers made room for him at the table and he pulled up a chair, calling to Elvira for a scotch. He was young and thin, his lanky blonde hair falling over his eyes.

Yes, it's Brian, again — as he was twenty years ago. This is my story, I'm telling it, so why can't I make myself a character? But is he me and is this my history? Sure, he looks like me, or me the way I was, though he also resembles a lot of men. You asked me to give you a story, and I will.

I will take you down to the water.

You can call it a story.

Brian was ebullient. He was obviously a summer worker, a student cruising for money in the back country before he returned to university.

"Somebody tried to sabotage the mill," he stammered.

"You're feeding us a line."

"Naw, it's real."

"What happened?"

"I'm shift supervisor now . . . when we start up again. I just came from the foreman's office. That asshole, Jake, he's been suspended; they're going to put him on the floor, maybe terminate him. He nearly let the fourdrinier get totally ruined."

Baby-faced, skinny and high cheek-boned, Brian was out of place with the others. And he spoke strangely. It wasn't a real stammer, but close, an odd speech impediment, a man wanting to utter too many words at once, yet fearful to mispronounce them, every word like a plug at the end of a hose — popping out into the air, spoken almost too clearly. He didn't seem to care how odd he was, how alien — the stumble in his voice made him want to out-speak everyone. The effect had a curious charm.

Coyote pictured him twenty years into the future — going to fat, a writer, or more likely a professor at a university, seducing freshman girls with a combination of learning and lurid tales about his young life in the back country.

He would overcome his problem with his mouth, even if everyone had to listen to him practising for years. Coyote had been there himself. The many embarrassments of his own young manhood flowed through him as Brian began recounting the incident at the mill.

It was a strange, awkward performance, and the pulpworkers sat there, bemused, like cruel kids watching an injured frog slowly die in front of them. Brian was so thrilled with his story he didn't catch the mood.

Coyote waved to Elvira. "Another tomato juice."

She brought it over, grinning. "Not the most popular request in these parts."

"I ain't a drinking man."

"That's good."

Brian was now well into his story. "Jake was doing his usual, leaning back in his chair, feet up, as if the hardest part of the job was finding a magazine to read."

"Yup, he's an asshole, alright."

"We were skeleton crewing the last of the pulp in the beater tank. He wasn't too happy about the layoff, but he had his porno mag. I guess he was hoping for something new under the sun."

Brian leaned back in his seat, elbows on the armrests, hands up, flicking his fingers dismissively. It was a weird gesture. He was rolling.

"I was on the floor. I had this feeling, like a sixth sense. I looked down the line to the head box, and a strange, blue mash was coming out of the slicer onto the fourdrinier. Then the screen mottled."

"Oh man, the fourdrinier, that's expensive," said one of the men into his beer.

"The other guys were by the slicer, chatting with the new forklift driver. Gawd, is she stacked. Equal opportunity, eh? I was, like, paralysed, hypnotized by the junk sweeping towards the rollers — the pulp rolling past at three thousand feet a minute! It took me a second."

"Gee, you sure know a lot for a green, summer kid."

Brian ignored him. "'Hey,' I shouted, 'this ain't right!' I didn't know what to do. So I hit the safety release and shut down the fourdrinier, but the dandy roller and the couch roller were a solid blue. And the first two felts!"

"Two of the felts?"

Brian nodded importantly. Charlie was waiting for one of the workers to slap him. The boy had no clue how 'his story' was going down.

"Jake didn't wake up from his porno mag until he heard the siren as the jagenberg braked. He probably thought a man got his arm up a gear. Then he saw the tinted mash, the rollers, and I guess, the stunned expression on my face. He dropped the mag and it fluttered down to the floor just as the plant manager walked in — giving a tour to a stockholder type."

"Oh Christ, isn't that the way it works?"

"At least the stain hadn't reached the last two felts and the calender — not much consolation for Jake who took one look at the plant manager and said: 'I'm going to lose my job, ain't I.' It was kind of funny."

"Hey barkeep, a scotch for Brian," the guy by the window called out, making it sound like an act of charity.

An old Italian, balding, with chipped black teeth, stood up from the table and walked away.

"Congratulations on your promotion, kid," another said, picking up his jacket. "Tough for Jake, I guess, but he is a shit isn't he?" The last man to leave winked at Brian whose face was flushed pink. A rainbow of emotions passed across his face as he sat alone.

Coyote left also, now that the show was over. Brian was the only client remaining in the cavernous bar. He was practically weeping.

***

Coyote caught the late afternoon ferry to Artemis. He was standing on the deck when, as usual for Wednesdays, a van rushed up to the terminal — the reason why he'd planned the action for today. There was time in the morning for the local small newsrag to pick up the first reports, since it went to bed at noon, the first copies on the street by four P.M. Plus, there would be enough missed details to rate a headline the following week. There was no way of knowing how the major media would bite, but he figured it would go national. An act of aggression is only as good as its publicity.

The crew was unhooking the ferry when the driver tossed a bundle of *Sweet Water Herald*s over the rail, the copies bound for the lone, small store on Artemis. Since it was a free newspaper, Coyote slipped one out of the bundle, a few other people doing the same while a gull wheeled overhead as if considering the edible qualities of newsprint.

Coyote scanned the headline. He didn't read any further. This wasn't good. He folded the paper and stuffed it into his back pocket.

He'd gone off having mushrooms for dinner.

After they docked, he drove off the ferry, up the steep ramp, and home to the little cabin his parents had built years ago. The dog, a border collie, was crying against its chain, tangled up. He put down his groceries and unleashed it. The dog bounced around him as if it were a yo-yo on a string. He noted the knocked-over dish. How long had it gone without water?

After he'd fed and watered the dog, he fell into his favourite armchair and opened the newspaper again.

The headlines weren't about the permanently damaged felts on the fourdrinier, or the public shock at the now-mapped-in-blue radius of the pollution from the mill. There was mention of a shift supervisor being suspended for inattention while the dye rolled through the mash, and of an intrepid student-employee shouting out a warning before hitting the emergency stop, saving thousands of dollars worth of equipment further along the line. That was it for news about the mill.

The new hospital.

Erected at the edge of town, it also had an intake pipe on Sweet Water.

All the laundry in the washing machines was dyed cobalt blue.

An old lady in the extended care ward had a heart attack when she turned on a tap to wash her hands. He pictured the code light flashing in the hallway, the mechanical voice on the intercom calling out "Code 99," the surgeons and nurses rushing from the wards.

Worst of all was the cynical portrait of events in the kitchen — how the vegetables in the steamer trays turned blue. That was the headline: PRANKSTER MAKES BLUE CAULIFLOWER. The effect on the mill was incidental, as if everyone already understood the plant was cancering the town with its dioxins — that wasn't news.

Finally, there was discussion about how much it would cost the town and the pulp mill to develop systems that would protect their water intakes in order to prevent this sort of vandalism in the future.

The paper made him so angry he threw it onto the floor by his chair. The dog, thinking it was invited to a game, began to bark and leap around his feet. It shredded the paper in seconds.

Enraged, Coyote kicked the dog — and his guilt grew enormous.

4 The Dancing Zebras

SEVERAL MONTHS LATER, FAR FROM THE NORTH COAST, Coyote sat on a bluff in the interior, the rock seamed with a mineral that resembled zinc. The forest floor was coated with yellowed pine needles.

Below the hill, in the flats, walking between the barred shadows of the pine trees, a family straggled out of the Kootenay Game Farm towards their car. The girl at the ticket booth turned on the security lights, closed the window, locked the gates, and drove away. The truck disappeared over the crest, towards the town of Radium, trailing blue smoke. The piston rings must be gone. There weren't too many miles left in that machine.

A single vehicle remained on the lot, the night watchman's van. The old fellow lived in a trailer inside the compound with his Doberman, near the ticket booth.

A sparse clump of mushrooms had erupted among the dead needles beneath a pine. Their curious productive drive had caused them to fruit beyond the autumn flush — tricked by this week's chinook, a respite from the cold that would soon return to kill them. Pine mushrooms. *Armillaria ponderosa*, as classified by Saccardo — worth a lot of money in Japan. *Matsutake*. Twenty-seven dollars a pound. A great delicacy. "I'm not going there again," he muttered. Besides, he didn't particularly like *matsutake.*

He pulled the nylon stocking over his head, his frosty breath smouldering out of the distorted skull. He checked the Browning .308 again, needing to convince himself a bullet was in the chamber before he scrambled down the hill.

He'd changed his method this time, bringing his 'mooncalf' brother, Tom, to drop him off and pick him up three hours later. Coyote didn't relish parking in front of the site, though it was on a side road seldom used when the game farm closed.

Tom would never question his brother. Told he was going to drive the Jeep, he was proud to be chosen, beaming and jumpy like a pup offered a morning walk.

By the time Coyote reached the gate, it was twilight. He snapped the chain with his cutter, opened the gate, and ambled casually inside.

Last week, when he'd first come here to the zoo, checking out the pens, he decided the Doberman was as ancient and useless as the watchman.

He was right. The dog was asleep on the makeshift verandah of the trailer. It opened its eyes to the plop of a chunk of raw beef liver in front of its greying muzzle. After a brief, suspicious glare, the dog gulped the meat down; then directed its attention to him, growling low. He threw it another piece.

There was enough fast-acting liquid morphine in the beef to knock out a horse. By the time it wolfed down the fourth chunk the dog was wobbling. It gave him a puzzled look as it keeled over. That was easy. He didn't have to use the rifle, which was good, because he didn't know if he could shoot a dog. He didn't know if he could shoot anything.

He started to worry there was too much morphine, that the dog's lungs would shut down.

The trailer was overgrown with a dead vine, cold-struck, but still displaying its bright berries. Climbing nightshade. Not good for a public park where little children might be tempted. That wouldn't matter soon.

Coyote stepped over the dog. 'You will wake up again, won't you?'

He rapped politely on the door. After a few minutes of shuffling noises, it opened a crack. The old man blinked at the barrel of the Browning. Coyote pushed open the door and stepped inside, backing him up. "You're the night watchman?"

"Mister, mister — I don't know what you want. There's no money here. I'm an old man. Don't point that gun at me."

"Sit."

"I'm sitting." He crashed backwards into a raggy armchair.

"I want the keys."

"What keys?"

"The cages."

"Look mister, I don't guard against people here. They let me stay so I can keep the varmints away from the animals. You aren't going to hurt them, are you? You won't hurt the animals?"

"Where's the keys?"

The watchman was thoughtful for a moment. His gaze shifted briefly towards a hook by the door holding a large ring of keys.

Coyote nodded. "Now take this rope, knot it tight around one hand, lie on the floor on your stomach, and hold your hands behind your back."

Coyote had already decided he'd start with the ungulates and the birds, and work his way up to the carnivores. 'A zoo on the run.' It would take hours, since the game farm encompassed several acres. Still, everyone would be free around midnight, and the watchman wasn't going anywhere.

The birds were easy. Quick. He loved the stupid peacock strutting from its cage until it reached a patch of snow remaining after the surprise thaw. Defiantly, it fanned its tail in the twilight, outlined by the rising moon behind the hill.

The giraffe was difficult, hiding behind the hay loft after Coyote swung the gate open. It refused freedom, unwilling to leave the rich alfalfa in the rack.

The antelopes almost knocked him over in their run for freedom. The mountain goats took their own sweet time, munching towards the perimeter fence.

Here was a detail he hadn't considered. That perimeter fence! Most of the animals would take too long to find the open gate. He returned to the trailer and confiscated the watchman's keys to his van.

He drove the vehicle to the gateway, backed up, drew a bead on the steel posts, and punched his foot onto the gas pedal. The windshield shattered at the first post, showering him with glimmering chunks of glass, but the van covered almost a hundred feet before hanging up in a mess of wire and posts, and the path he'd cleared was hardly visible from the road.

The antelopes, who'd been running ever since released from their pen, discovered the hole first, and were gone, followed by a few stragglers — reindeer and buffalo. He returned to the enclosures.

The three moose studied him with suspicion, ready for any surprises, before exiting.

The lone camel thought this affair was interesting, and ambled up to him, chewing its cud as it examined his face with an air of profundity that reminded Coyote of a yoga instructor he once knew. Then its attention was diverted by the sudden re-appearance of a bull moose which eyed the female camel with unconcealed lust. It was rutting season. The camel, sensing this, trotted off, the moose in slow but unrelenting pursuit.

Kicking the dog. That's right, boy-man, kicking the collie back at his cabin had caused this. As soon as his foot lashed out and the dog ran whimpering to the corner, its tail curled between its legs, he was overwhelmed with guilt, the guilt that told him he had broken an unspoken agreement with the animal. He'd had no right to inflict pain on it. The dog had its own life. It was colonialism. Speciesism. It was madness, the awful authority of power. After several months of intense research, he set off for the Kootenies.

I've watched you with our neighbour, Old Jake, and his ancient collie, Samantha, rounding up the sheep, the way you work with her, command her so patiently, gracefully. You know what I'm talking about. Think of her as the great great granddaughter of the dog Charlie once gave to the farmer.

Yes, that's what we're doing, if you hadn't guessed it by now — taking your friends and neighbours and re-assembling them into a different world. You asked for a story. Here it is.

Now, the hippopotamus. It lowered its head suspiciously as he opened the gate. Then it saw the half-frozen lake across the compound — a swim, a little winter dip. The hippo waddled towards the lake.

The foxes disappeared as if lightning were chasing their tails.

He spent several minutes studying the coyotes. They were sad and mangy, pacing their too-small cage, manic, lost, probably injured permanently by their confinement. He opened the gate and they were gone.

The rhino ignored him and the swinging gate. It would take its own disdainful time.

The elephants thought they were being offered a new and exciting experience. They followed him to the ostriches, begging for peanuts or whatever it was they wanted. The ostriches performed a fan dance in front of the yaks, under the light of the moon that had now risen high above, and then they were gone. Coyote couldn't get rid of the elephants; they trailed him everywhere.

Next, the lions. He was lucky. The half-asleep pride gazed at him and the elephants beyond, and decided this was ridiculous. They refused to leave their cage.

The wolves were scared, proud, jumpy. They saw the gate, him, the elephants, and ran frantically back and forth before they suddenly lunged for freedom, past him and his gun and the startled elephants, into the dark.

Despite the moon and the security lamps, there were many pockets of darkness, and he kept his flashlight lit.

The wilful tigers ignored him. They were a pair, long-confined, mates, too contemptuous to lift their heads. This would all clear up tomorrow; they had serious sleeping to do. Coyote was distrustful. Of all the animals, they scared him most. It was an act. The elephants were also nervous, keeping their distance. There was a limit to excess.

As he retreated, he grew aware of the trailer, its lights, windows — access for the predators . . . He couldn't leave the watchman vulnerable to this carnival.

Inside, he picked up the man's feet and dragged him into the bathroom. "You'll be safe here."

"You didn't hurt the animals, did you?"

Coyote studied the ignominious bundle of man and rope. "No. They're free. Whatever damage comes, will come out of their free will."

"The lions? The tigers? The bears?"

"Yes, them too."

"This is crazy. You're mad."

"Aren't we all?"

He took the note from his pocket and placed it on the toilet seat. COYOTE WANTS EVERYONE TO BE FREE. An embarrassing statement next to the trussed-up watchman in the shower stall.

After he locked him in, he shoved the frontroom couch against the door, and piled on top of that what furniture he could fit in the hall until he'd made an inaccessible barrier. "Sleep well, old man. You're safe. Better off than most of us."

When he stepped outside a blur of yellow stripes rushed past, snatching up the unconscious Doberman. His heart flew into his mouth. The tiger disappeared into the shadows with its prey.

Further on, across from the picnic area, a large shape glittered grey in the moonlight: the hippo waddled across the ice towards the open center of the lake, determined on a midnight swim. Halfway out, the ice collapsed under its weight and down it went, snorting and huffing in the frigid water.

Sadness fell upon Coyote. The weirdness of the world.

Less than a block away, in the parking lot, five elephants clustered together, nervous, waiting. A zebra stood nearby, frightened, recognizing their size and tenderness were its best protection.

Coyote crossed the parking lot and returned to the hill. The pine forest had become different, alive, full of threatening shadows. There were tigers here, lions, polar bears. Polar bears? The thought of polar bears in the Kootenies amused him, until a giant shape rose from the shadows, approaching.

An elephant's trunk nuzzled his arm. He patted it affectionately and resumed hiking while the zebra skittered about in the distance. "Now go away," he said to the elephants. "Go home. Go somewhere. Get out of here." They refused to listen. He was their meal ticket, their friend, their safety. They stuck by him, no matter how far he went, while the zebra danced through the yellow pines. It was madness. Gorgeous. Sad. He stopped to catch his breath beneath a giant ponderosa. "You animals. You beautiful animals."

He could hear, not far away, the idling motor of the Jeep. He was late. Tom was waiting.

A noise rushed through the trees. For a moment he saw a vision of colliding stripes in the moonlight, black and white. The rest of the zebra herd. Then they were all gone, and the elephants were close again. He reached the bluff.

Slinging the rifle over his shoulder, he crawled up like a quick spider, and was over the top in seconds. Beneath him, trunks raised, the elephants bellowed, betrayed, as he turned towards the highway, the jeep, his brother.

"Elephants!" Tom shouted. "Did I hear an elephant?"

"Let's go; it's a jungle out there."

***

The venture was almost successful. For years, the residents recalled the tales. Three of the wolves raided a chicken coop not far away and were shot by a crusty farmer who became a local hero. The hippo swam beneath the early winter moon, basking in the silver light, until it dived and swam towards land, coming up under the thicker ice. It drowned, thrashing, twenty feet from shore.

The tigers were found in their cage, asleep, having feasted on nap-inducing dog meat. The lone polar bear was never captured. It became a near-mythical creature . . . roaming the pine forests, scaring the occasional camper and fading back into the trees.

The elephants returned to their pen, desiring nothing but peanuts and hay.

Many of the animals were never seen again — the remaining wolves, the coyotes, the foxes, the mountain goats . . . There were rumours of baby zebras prancing through the pines for years to come.

A couple of tourists from Montana became temporarily famous when they had to swerve off the road in the dawn, dodging a sleeping lion on the asphalt. The lion was hunted down later, paralysed by a narcotic dart and collected, while the tourists returned home with their tall tale.

This was the first political 'eco-action' against a zoo, and the media immediately hurled the question of animal confinement into public debate. If you're lucky enough to live into old age, man-child, despite the doctors' predictions, I'm sure you'll hear the debate grow louder still.

The game farm soon went bankrupt. The remaining beasts were sold, the acreage converted to a subdivision by a group of dentists seeking a tax write-off. They got one — it was too far from Radium to survive. The dentists, also, eventually, went bankrupt.

5

Adventures in the Academy

INSPECTOR SINGH FOUND THE DOOR, NO. 233, halfway down the antiseptic corridor of the anthropology department. Every room with a light on also had an open door — the professors always visible — especially when there was a student in an office. Privacy was too dangerous. In fact, it was against the university's much publicized and controversial moral code to meet a student behind a closed door, which had done little to stem the flood of harassment complaints. Professors had taken to refusing interviews with students unless witnesses were present. Janwar found the change from his student days frightening, yet he'd also disliked watching instructors regularly cruise their students for fresh game, male or female.

This door was different. There was a light on though it was shut.

It irritated him that the campus architecture was so badly conceived that all the offices needed artificial illumination during the daylight hours. Another victory of design over function.

He was irritated by several things this morning, including a sudden brief spasm of diarrhea he'd had after breakfast — as if he'd been poisoned — and worse, there was the uniform. He always felt awkward in uniform. It had a presumptuousness he'd never learned to accept.

So why was he wearing it? Returning to his old university, parading his success? And the RCMP uniform under a turban, that always got stares. Or was it because he was going to interview a fellow Sikh he could impress? This morning was full of self-doubt.

Sometimes, he imagined resigning from the force and retreating into faith. That would horrify his mother, especially since they both knew he was on the fast track to promotion, the force eager to use him as an example of its racial tolerance. He knocked on the frosted window.

"The door's open."

Janwar stepped inside.

Professor Variander Singh glanced up from a pile of essays and acknowledged him pleasantly. *"Sat Sri Akal."*

"God is indeed truth. I am Inspector Janwar Singh. Your secretary said this would be a good time to find you. Is it possible to speak privately for a few minutes?"

The professor waved towards an expensive leather chair facing the desk. "Yes, she told me you were coming. What great joy it gives me to see a man of our faith wearing a RCMP uniform. And an inspector, as well. The world is improving."

"Thank you. I do my best to live up to my responsibilities."

"Sit down. Heavy responsibilities they must be, not only wearing the uniform but the five Ks."

Janwar sat down stiffly. "I am here, unfortunately, on a troubling business, the disappearance of a university student, a Miss Rita Norman."

"Disappeared? That's terrible. I know her well. I saw her a few weeks ago." The professor looked more smug than worried.

"Good; then perhaps you could supply us with background knowledge of her, and her acquaintances, or any incident that concerned you."

"Surely you do not suspect foul play."

"Not at present, but we are trying to gather information that will give us a clue to her disappearance."

"I'm curious why the temporary disappearance of a woman would come to the attention of a busy RCMP inspector." He was a profoundly ugly man with dark cold eyes and ruby red lips peeking out from his black beard, or was it only the pompous way he spoke that made Janwar dislike him immediately?

"There have been other disappearances. And she vanished rather oddly."

"You are after a madman?"

"No, I didn't say that. I am looking for Rita Norman. What can you tell me about her?"

"A classic case of infantilism. A perpetual campus hanger-on with a loose reputation. Fun, but a real headhunter, and I mean that literally, considering the erotic stories she's regaled me with."

"She got around?"

"To say the least. Between you and me, Inspector, and off the record, she's a real slut."

"Truly?"

"Truly. Mind you, she has one hell of a set of knockers on her. Although middle-aged, that woman has a body that would make you stand up." The professor lifted his eyebrows, emphasizing his buggy eyes. The gesture was so disarming that Janwar started coughing in order to restrain a smile. The professor's heavy accent and campus slang were a poor combination. "Well, we only have pictures of her face."

"She's been through half the department. She attempted to seduce me — add a little brown skin to her C.V. But I rebuffed her. I am a married man. And you?"

Janwar shuffled with embarrassment. "No, not yet. My official duties haven't allowed me the time, so far, needed for such a task as marriage." There had to be a motive behind the professor's wildly indiscreet revelations.

"Married life removes many of the rough edges of living in this world."

"I'm sure it does. You were saying that Miss Norman had a few affairs."

"She is seeking an affluent professor to provide her with the comforts she desires." Professor Singh leaned forward conspiratorially. "One of my colleagues. Albert Sowinki, he's the most recent to fall into her clutches."

"Albert Sowinki?"

"Yes, a senior professor. You would have thought he'd be more intelligent. Their affiliation darkens his reputation. On the other hand, his history in this department hasn't been sterling silver."

"No other serious relationship in the recent past?"

"Serious relationship is an oxymoron with that woman. Though there was another, she told me once, an eccentric older fellow she'd lived with for several years. That was long ago. She's definitely targeted Sowinki during the last few months."

"Did they have any plans to marry or live together?"

"I believe so. Yet a while ago he did speak strangely to me."

"What did he say?"

Professor Singh grew contemplative, and Janwar couldn't escape the unhappy feeling he was being dragged into departmental politics. The professor carefully interwove his fingers on his desk. "That he thinks as much about killing her as loving her."

"Truly?"

"Said personally to my face."

***

Kirsten found Jay Hillhurst's classroom with difficulty, and getting lost in the quadrangle made her late. The discussion seemed animated, so she slid into one of the seats at the rear of the small auditorium.

Hillhurst, a young and bony woman in her early thirties was a sessional instructor like Rita, the most popular on campus, according to the secretary at administration. The room was crowded with nearly fifty students, most of them female. Their subject was, apparently, early feminism and the film noir genre.

It was evident that the key to Hillhurst's lecturing success was in letting the students speak. They spent more time raising questions and engaging in discussion than their instructor.

Kirsten thought this was cheating, a lazy way of teaching, and the students were too flakey for her taste. Did they really believe that using a right-handed camera angle was more positive to a male presentation than a female one? That the nature of black and white film conceptualised the curves of a female body more than a male's? Or that the male body was never portrayed sensually, except in a latent gay sense — the reason why Steve Reeves became such a gay cult figure?

The debate veered in several directions, and Kirsten realized it was slamming back and forth between irony and idiocy. Several wise comments made her recall the hunger for knowledge she'd had as a young woman, but they were interrupted by silliness. She grew sad, remembering her own long-gone desperate innocence, and her greed for love, her idiot greed.

"That's right. That's why it was so important to hush up the competition between Rock Hudson and James Dean in *Giant.* Same sex desires were taboo then."

"Uh, Janice," Hillhurst spoke up, "as much as we're approaching one of my favourite topics, we have to keep the subject of discussion in mind. Many of the actors being cited don't fit our parameters. Rock Hudson and Steve Reeves and James Dean have little relationship with American film noir."

Kirsten must have dozed off despite the lively discussion. It had been another sleepless, lonely night. She lifted her head with a start, aware of moving bodies. The class was leaving, many with their heads high, proud, as if they were going to change the world. This made her feel old. Worse still, Hillhurst bore a striking resemblance to the only picture of her mother that she had, a mother she could barely remember. A few hanger-ons gathered around the teaching assistant, scoring last points.

Soon, there were only two women left with Hillhurst, and Kirsten realized they were going to follow her outside. Kirsten stood up, grateful she'd decided not to wear her uniform. She would have stuck out like the plague. Though it had made for an awkward moment this morning, when Singh, who never wore his uniform, showed up wearing it, and they had to smirk at each other.

"Miss Hillhurst, would it be possible to speak with you on a private matter?"

Jay Hillhurst turned towards her, distracted. "Maybe you could make an appointment with the office secretary. I have another class."

"I'll only take a few minutes of your time."

There was a note in Kirsten's voice that stopped the instructor. This wasn't a student. Hillhurst said to her groupies: "I'll catch up with you in a few minutes, in the coffee shop."

The students gave meaningful, interrupted looks to Kirsten. She flashed an icy glare at the two as they trundled up the aisle and out of the auditorium, looking back over their shoulders.

"I'm sorry to interrupt. I'm Corporal Crosby with the RCMP."

"RCMP?" Jay Hillhurst shrivelled, becoming bonier than she already was.

"Yes, I'm investigating the disappearance of Rita Norman, and I understand she's an acquaintance of yours."

"It's a whacko, isn't it? There's a whacko running around!"

"I've not heard that. We are just trying to find Rita. I expect it's a false alarm."

"Not Rita, no, it couldn't happen to her. She's a beautiful person."

"Most incidents like this amount to nothing. But we do have to check the information we receive — in case people have observed anything disturbing or suspicious. You were good friends with her?"

"I'd say so. We've both been run through the mill, by the system, you know. But she's one smart lady. I can't see her getting into any trouble that she didn't invite."

"What kind of trouble would she invite?"

"That's just an expression. She's real solid, working through the politics, the sexism; she has a head on her shoulders."

"Did she have many friends?"

"Lots."

"Any close relationships?"

"She's been seeing a professor in anthropology. Sowinki, I think. And Angie."

"Angie?"

"She's delivering the new course on nineteenth century lesbian literature. Angie Gorgioni. She's hot; she's got great original angles on Radclyffe Hall and the influence of underground women's literature on Woolf."

"Did they have a relationship?"

"Well, Rita likes guys, but I guess so. I don't ask for the details, but I did see them get real drunk together one night and put their tongues in each other's mouths at a party. Any objections?

Hillhurst stopped and stared at her in the fluorescent light of the sterile hallway. Kirsten's milky white skin had just gone a shade paler. "What's the matter. Don't like lesbians? I'm sorry, this is upsetting news, and I know I sound catty. They're friends of mine. They had a fling. We have that right . . . to like each other. I shouldn't be talking about this to the police."

"Is there anyone else?'

"What, am I making her sound like a slut? Rita's not like that. She's been around, sure, but so have we all, haven't we?" Hillhurst paused momentously, waiting for a reply.

Seeing there was none forthcoming, she continued: "Sorry. I know. It's a new age now. AIDS and everything. There was someone else, a wild guy named Charlie she lived with for several years. That was long before I met her. She often talked about him — said he ruined her youth, and then ran off to an island. Otherwise, she works hard. She's a feminist. You know what it's like. How many women are in your department?"

"I'm it."

"That's what I thought. Why do you think she and I are still sessional instructors?"

"I don't devote my life to those kind of questions. There's lot of problems in this world, and that's just one of them."

"Right. So what's happened to Rita?"

"We don't know. We're trying to find out. Do you remember the last name of this Charlie?"

"Nope. Cops. All you want is more information and more guns."

"Really, I don't think that's fair."

"Sure, honey. There's a lot that's not fair out there, and you're telling me you don't know about it?"

***

"So what did you get?" Kirsten asked as soon as Janwar climbed into the car. He was still putting his seat belt on when she shifted into drive, pulling out onto the ramp for the road off the mountain.

"A little. The man she was dating is Albert Sowinki, but he's not on campus for the summer session. We'll have to speak to him at his home. I'm told she was promiscuous."

"That's not quite what I got. Hillhurst claims she was a righteous, hardworking feminist. Besides Sowinki, though, she might have had a close relationship with one of the lesbian instructors. These people are in nevernev-erland here. I'd forgotten what it was like. Hell, I'd almost forgotten what *I* was like. I was just as nutty then." She scowled wistfully.

Her expression was so ludicrous it made Janwar chuckle. "Universities are hothouses for the mind. Strange blooms will develop."

"Hillhurst also told me Rita had a long-term relationship that went wildly wrong."

"Recently?"

"It must be that Charlie in the address book. But it sounds like the relationship folded years ago."

"We can check him out later. We should contact Mr. Sowinki soon. I was told he's made threats against her. Would you mind stopping at the pharmacy near the bottom of the hill? I need a bottle of Tylenol."

"This business — these poor women disappearing — is it giving you headaches? I'm having trouble sleeping at night."

The way she spoke, so tenderly, made Janwar turn his head and look at her as she drove. She kept her eyes on the road. The throbbing in his temples grew worse. "My body is giving me headaches."

6

NOW WE GO BACK AGAIN, THE WAY ALL MEMORY GOES BACK, the body walking in the present, the thoughts hooked on their own odd version of the past while hoping for the future, until time becomes a tug of war, both tightening and loosening the rope it has slung about our necks, dragging our stories into the life around us.

A luminous centipede humped across his boot, intent on important business beyond.

The mosquitoes were eating Coyote alive in a carnival of blood: "Hey gang, we've got a northerner here. Let's throw a party, suck back a few pints of blood, and paint the bayou red."

Swollen and satiated, one was unable to fly, dropping to the marsh floor like a confused leech.

At least they didn't put his blood in a bank

Then he was out of the Gomden swamp, facing the lawn and the modernist facade of the factory. Time to do a little scouting.

***

He spent the next two weeks in New Orleans, reading, researching, blending into the exotic streets like a tourist, dutifully admiring the portes cochères and the banquettes and the other pleasant claptrap the brochures told him he shouldn't miss. Finally, he pointed his rental car down the lonely highway to Gomden again.

Gomden was a suburb south and east of New Orleans. Bayou country, it didn't have much reason to exist except for an enterprising town council that had created one of the largest industrial parks in Louisiana, using minimal taxes to attract multinational corporations.

Over the years, levees had diverted much of the lowland water, and the development had expanded massively, with the swamp constantly at its door — yet retreating.

Town councils. You've heard me ranting about them before. They're the ignoble cheerleaders, the driving heart of the consumption syndrome overtaking our continent — the plague of money worshippers — pushing the zoning envelope, the development potential, the profit line that cultivates the tumours in our communities.

History may look back upon them as war criminals. One day, there might be trials. If you live that long you could end up a judge! What a wonderful chance for retribution, but I doubt that's your style.

We should make all former mayors drive every day in the rush hour traffic they created with their suburban sprawl, imprison town planners in the shopping malls they designed.

Maybe not. Most of these people have become so victimized by their own propaganda they might relish such punishment.

They think if you can't change it, you might as well enjoy the globalized commerce swamping our communities and environment. This is also the logic of the 'realist' who meets the rapist. Yes! In the modern lexicon of the entrepreneur, rape can become elevated to prostitution — a genuine commercial transaction — and commerce is the god whose altar we wash daily.

But this is just common sense. Everybody secretly knows what's going on. You already understand what's happening at your young age, so why do we continue destroying the world around us? Well, that's a story, isn't it?

The drive took a few hours, giving him time to think, though he didn't want to think. He had to act, get this over with, fuelled oddly by the dead bird beside him on the front seat — a red cardinal.

Earlier in the morning, he'd gone wandering again, past those 'picturesque *banquettes*' whose quaintness irritated him in a way he couldn't define, yet the sidewalks, the bazaar of human life was so alluring with its endless games. He ended up in a seedier district, an alley trapped between the stone walls of backyards. There was an iron gate. Because it was a gate he had to open it.

It was a vegetable garden thick with the scent of rotting fruit and jasmine. More walls. There were a few gaudy articles of underwear on the line; slips, a brassiere, panties. Who was this woman? It was so easy to make assumptions. He was sure she was black. He wanted to be wrong. He didn't want to live the way everybody did, nourished on the easy judgements dispensed by the media.

"We live on what we are fed, and all of us become what we have eaten."

There was a bird feeder in the tallowtree. A miniature, plastic gazebo beckoning the last strays that survived in the city.

Something whistled past his head, and he instinctively ducked. It was a cardinal, diving for the rim of the feeder from the camphor tree in the neighbour's yard. A flash of brilliance; then the vermilion bird somersaulted in the air, as if at a circus, a trapeze artist of the backyard.

The cardinal had hit the clothesline. It flopped to the grass, dead at his feet. Neck broken. How did this happen? Is that all we get?

Is death a gift?

One minute, it was a joyful bird zooming in on a feeder, another survivor in this human wasteland; then it had suddenly made a circle of its life on an unseen wire.

Some would say everything has a purpose.

He parked the car in the shrouded water oaks near the industrial park and waited for dark, cradling the dead, stiff cardinal in his lap.

What we have to remember, man-child, is that Coyote, although defiant and rebelling, still believed in human progress back then — he was a bitter optimist. Perhaps, that's why human society confused him. He assumed the purpose of 'business' was to enrich the life of people, rather than the other way around.

There was a piece of the waxing moon, a silver nugget that betrayed light. The approaching clouds in this foreign landscape were malevolent. Is there a quality about Louisiana clouds? Are they more terrifying than northern clouds? They promised wolves and vampires. It was time to get out of the car.

Wading through the purple water hyacinths beneath the cypress was magic, the same magic he had known in the north, only now it was alligators and water moccasins instead of bears and rattlesnakes, and because it was foreign, the fear was more intense.

The bird was a lump in his shirt pocket.

Coyote clambered onto the final levee. He'd reached the ground behind the loading ramp of the LaCoeur laboratory. The long way around. 'Those are best,' he thought.

The entrance, as he'd learned from his first scouting expedition, was very modern, very glass, impressive to the impressionable. The back was functional, cement-block construction. A door with a bell and a loading ramp joined the complex with the paved web of roads leading to the world. There was a row of mirrored windows which, up close, he could peer through. How interesting that horror laboratories like this still demanded windows overlooking the bayou, despite their desire to conceal what existed inside.

He slipped around to the front. The parking lot at the entrance held only a single car. In the austere lobby, beyond a wall of glass, the lone guard was reading at a desk of black arborite.

Coyote wedged himself into the patch of wild cane behind the lawn. Near where he sat there were several odd plants. Belladonna? They must have escaped cultivation and naturalized. 'Oh, what beauty could you deliver? Let me squint and dream.' He settled down and waited.

He waited all night.

The guard resembled an aging southern colonel, the man in the fried chicken ads, sitting motionless like a discarded puppet behind his desk, except that every hour he stood up and disappeared. Coyote guessed he had a round of punch clocks to visit, proof he was touring the entire plant. That left a maximum of forty-five minutes. Enough time. The guard moved only when the clock struck the hour and never varied his return. A seven minute round. Add seven or eight for safety's sake, and this ensured a lot of rabbits would be running for their lives.

"So let's test the alarm, if there is an alarm."

Coyote returned to the rear of the factory. He waited until the middle of the hour before he raced, crouching, across the lawn, to the row of lab windows. Nothing. He rapped the back of his knuckles against the glass. Nothing. He pulled the small rock hammer out of his back pocket and tapped on the window, breaking it. Nothing. Silence. A few shards. They weren't expecting trouble here, and why should they? Coyote wasn't exactly famous yet, and they were merely doing business. He dropped the cardinal on the ledge. Now they would have a reason for the broken window. One poor, sad, cardinal that flew at high speed and died against the glass.

By morning he was back in New Orleans.

Tom stirred in his hotel room bed.

"Where'd you go?"

"It's okay, Tom. I needed air. It's too hot for me here. But I've got a treat. You'll love it. Rabbits. Lots of rabbits."

"Rabbits?" Tom's face registered several confused emotions before it went still. The last switch didn't ignite as he fell quietly back to sleep, reassured by his brother's presence.

It was a week before Coyote approached LaCoeur laboratory again. Money wasn't the question, courtesy of his parent's diligent industry, and their sailboat encountering the wrong wind at Riphead Rock Narrows. They'd certainly be horrified if they knew their inheritance was being used to ruin stock prices.

LaCoeur was a choice target. One of his father's old investments. He remembered the lectures during his childhood, daddy, arrogant and jowly, announcing that cosmetics were smart for the speculative side of the portfolio — a generally stable market with the opportunity for big paybacks if the buyer chose a company wisely.

"Women always want to get their man, and will pay for any weapon they can use."

The car was rented with the identification he'd bought in Cleveland — untraceable. Coyote's companions in the EarthHouse cell had done their part. Everything was ready.

His brother loved New Orleans, but he'd get used to the next place. Tom loved every town; it was the freshness, the virgin sights that gorged his spirits. As long as there was a local gym where he could practice his karate, he was happy.

Despite the gap that had been born into his brain, Tom had a magnificent facility with his body. Half the time he couldn't find where he'd left his pants the night before, yet he could repeat hundreds of complicated moves in a kata.

***

The swamp again — the oaks draped with Spanish moss, the little clump of native lotus at his feet.

Not far away, a snapping turtle rested on a log. Coyote's wet clothes squeaked when he walked. It was another muggy night, so he didn't feel chilled.

LaCoeur was a star in the constellation of the industry — where they made women into dreams — creating success out of the chemical necessity for love, a few hundred dollars worth of colour film, a pretty but scrawny model hungry for fame, and an expensive photographer. Afterwards, there might be a dab of coke sniffed off the hollow of her throat, an interlude of casual sex, perhaps including a few choice guys in the crew, depending on how stoned she got.

Nobody thought about the rabbits.

Nor the cardinal. Security had believed its body beside the broken window. The laboratory was the same as last week.

The glass had been repaired beside the loading bay but nothing else had changed. There was no silver tape or thin wires betraying an alarm system. Naivety remained in fashion.

Around the front, the guard sat like a vegetable behind his arborite desk. His capacity for immobility was impressive.

Coyote pulled on his gloves as he returned to the loading bay.

He used a good glass cutter, one with a carbide blade and kerosene lubrication. His circle was embarrassingly irregular. Coyote definitely wasn't Giotto who, centuries ago, showing off for a prince, drew a perfect freehand circle with a long brush. Pressing the suction cup against the glass, Coyote tapped the window. The egg-shaped knock-out clinked free, held fast by the suction cup. He waited. Silence. Nothing. He realized he should have used the suction cup first, and then cut the glass. Oh well, it worked.

He reached through the hole, lifted the latch, opened the window and crawled inside. He could lean a book or a file against the small hole and it wouldn't show. There was still lots of time. The room was dark, filled with the muffled scratching of tiny feet.

He slithered down the aisle, found the door, opened it, encountered the further darkness of the windowless loading bay, and groped around until he touched the lock on the small entrance door beside the bay. Then he was outside again. Those same, cryptic, primeval clouds from his first visit floated about the now full moon.

Bring on the vampires, he thought.

He checked his watch. The guard would make his rounds in a few minutes. If there was no light in the lab, it meant he didn't have a punch clock in the loading bay either, because Coyote had left the inside door to the loading bay open and any light would show dimly on the outside.

As soon as the man finished his round, Coyote would have another forty-five minutes.

Since he was waiting there was time to reconsider his approach. While inside, he'd studied the layout of the cages. The majority of rabbits were in holding cells; about fifty pens against one wall. Then there was another cluster of individual rabbits sequestered from their fellows on the left side of the room.

Against the opposite wall, near the door to the loading bay, were the current crop of experiments. He'd deal with those last.

One A.M.

Ten past one. And no lights flicked on. Time to move. He casually opened the door beside the loading bay as if he were coming on shift, and crossed the corridor. Inside the lab, he turned on the lights. They wouldn't show out front and he didn't want to miss anyone. This was going to be a clean sweep.

He wheeled around and faced the first rabbit in the current experiment section. "What's up, Doc?"

The rabbit didn't reply. It was bound by leather harnesses. It trembled as much as possible, considering its circumstances. As well as the leather braces, there was a steel clamp that locked its head into position. Its eyes were held open by two metal clamps. Above them was a drip apparatus, allowing so many drops of chemicals to fall upon the exposed corneas per minute. The advances of science and technology had caught up with medieval torture.

"I'll never wear eyeshadow again."

The holding pens. The latches had no locks. Rabbits weren't smart enough. He opened the doors. Within a few minutes he had several hundred rabbits milling about his feet.

They were all the same; white, fluffy, long-eared. They'd been bred for this, orchestrated from copulation to death. "I get the same feeling."

"Seven hundred thousand rabbits." These ones were a small percentage of the total. Seven hundred thousand rabbits in 1971 died this way, and that was before the escalation, before the experiments in the cosmetics industry really began. He pulled the note from his pocket, and laid it on a dissecting table. THE COYOTE AND ITS KIN MUST LIVE AND DIE IN FREEDOM. Handled only with surgical gloves, it carried no fingerprints.

Unlatching the cages of the sequestered rabbits took longer. There were a few hundred of them. They hesitated, preferring what they knew over what they didn't. They reminded him of too many people he'd met

— he had to scoop them roughly onto the floor of the lab.

Then he arrived at the current crop of experiments. They were motionless circus performers, wired up for the Draize test, the standard testing method of the U.S. Food and Drug Administration.

He stood before the rows of immobilized rabbits while their freed comrades milled around his feet, confused.

Maybe it wasn't the Draize test, maybe it was L.D. 50. Maybe it was both.

He tried to imagine the sadists who worked here, considering it a job, or perhaps a new world they were exploring at the frontiers of experience. They might, one day, develop a revolutionary eyeshadow that makes women attractive to men, and retire with glory and money to the suburbs.

L.D. 50. Lethal Dosage 50. The purpose of the test is to see what amount of a chemical kills 50 percent of its victims. Eventually, in enough quantity, even spinach or rhubarb could kill 50 percent of their consumers. But that's another story. The safety of edible products isn't all that L.D. 50 is used for . . . the new lotion, the new pesticide, the new hair-colour . . . This, after all, is scientific research, most of it funded and approved by our governments, universities, and corporations.

Nor is it correct to put the animal out of its misery when it is obviously dying. That would interfere with in the scientific method. It is more accurate, scientifically, if the rabbit dies slowly. The numbers of those who convulse, who haemorrhage, who salivate too much and choke to death, can then be recorded. And when that number of tortured animals reaches the magic 50 percent mark; then the rest can be killed quickly, allowing the researchers to declare the process has been handled humanely. I love the freight we pack into the word 'humane,' don't you, man-child? Sorry. I know you keep a pet white rabbit. But you wanted a story, a reason for your mutant body, didn't you? This is that story.

So let's complicate it further — animal testing might lead to a medication that could save you. Are you worth 500 rabbits? 5000 rats? 50 autopsied cats? How do we value life? Are 10,000 deaths worthwhile in a war that leads to democracy?

"What am I to do with you, friend?" Coyote faced the blind rabbit in the cage, its eyeballs swollen and weeping. He could release it, watch it flounder in the aisles among the others, but it wouldn't escape, and if it did, would be even more helpless among the predators in the bayou.

"If I truly believed in what I believe, I wouldn't do this." He swallowed. The humidity of the southern night had just become uncomfortable.

There was a metal bar among the torture instruments on one of the tables. He picked it up and brought it down on the mutilated rabbit. Blood squirted onto his shirt.

He ran down the rows, hammering in the skull of every rabbit until the bar was bent and none was left alive. His shirt was saturated with blood and there was a spray of vomit on the counter. It was his.

The survivors on the floor were terrified, scuttling into corners where crowds of them milled together, sniffing at the blood-tainted air. A few brave or eccentric individuals kicked and cavorted their way down the aisles.

Twenty minutes left.

He fled the lab, groped with his sweaty, blood-stained gloves for the lock. He found it, and raised the door. It made a noise, but the watchman wouldn't hear it on the other side of the building. A couple of the more intrepid rabbits leapt past him to the grass, and began a crazy, skittering dance across the back lawn towards the swamp.

Coyote returned to the lab, and directed, with much hand waving and foot shuffling, the main herd into the corridor where they discovered the door. For a moment, the leaders paused, terrified by the vast dark world beyond. Then they saw their cousins on the lawn, and leaped. The others followed in a boiling, snowy mass.

A few remained, huddled in the corners, shivering. Without sufficient time to catch them, he turned out the lights, hoping more would escape before they were discovered.

Then he was running across the grass, his wet jeans chaffing his thighs. Ghost rabbits everywhere, hundreds milling on the treasure chest of the green lawn — so much food. "Let's do the bunny hop!" Others were already bounding into the swamp. He felt like the pied piper.

Rabbits, of course, are not the only animals used by industries involved in animal research. Let me quote, Peter Singer from his book, Animal Liberation, on skin testing with cats. I know you will read it if you are still alive when this story is finished, but if you decide to pass it along to any squeamish friends, they can skip this section:

"Skin testing on animals requires that hair be removed first. This can be done by applying a strong adhesive tape and then rapidly removing it. Repeated applications of the tape on the bare skin may be used to removed additional layers of skin. After the skin has been prepared the irritants are applied and covered with a patch of adhesive plaster. After one or two days the patch is removed, and the skin examined. If a test of repeated applications of the substance is wanted, however, the patch is not used. Instead

the animal is restrained in a device that prevents it from scratching or licking off the irritant. In this way applications can be repeated at frequent intervals for a year or so."

Nor are animals abused only by private businesses. Various government institutions do their share. Here, again from one of the best books written on the mistreatment of animals, are a few samples given by Singer:

*Strontium-9 poisoning; beagles. *X-ray irradiation; beagles. *Variable current electric shock; rats. *Electric shock with warning; rats. *Electric shock, delayed response required; dogs. *Electric shock, inescapable; dogs. *Electric shock; ducklings. *Terminal deprivation of food and water; rats. *Maternal deprivation, designing of "well of despair" and "tunnel of terror," isolation in well of despair, inducing of psychological death; monkeys. *Malnutrition; kittens. *Pain in testes; cats.

And so on. A real catalogue of horrors. Needless to say, I've barely touched the varieties of torture we inflict on animals because of our belief that we are more important. Certain scientific tests are almost exotic, such as the researcher who microwaved dogs to find out what temperature they explode at, or the man who shot cats in the head to see how a bullet wound to the skull would benefit the U.S. military effort.

"Give me your rabbits and I will lead them to paradise and death." Coyote had no fantasies about this escapade. The rabbits would discover real fear in the swamp with its alligators, snapping turtles, and snakes. Most would die. Others would interbreed with the endangered local water hares, and no doubt, in a few years, there'd be swamp rabbits with a corrupted genetic pool.

But these few were free. "Seven hundred thousand rabbits" he said to the night. The night didn't reply.

He was breathing heavily, panicking, as he whipped through the second-growth tupelos and into the first bog, clambering over the leggy knees of the cypress. It wasn't snakes or any dangers in this benign bog that frightened him now, or the weird vampire clouds — it was the fear of being caught.

A tangle of water hyacinth held him up. A creature slithered past, an animal, a river rat. There was a crashing sound, a startled egret winged towards the clouds, ghost white against the black sky.

He reached the wild cane, and beyond, the road, the waiting car, Tom eager at the wheel.

Coyote opened the door, pulled off his slimey blood-stained shirt, pants, shoes, and socks, and stuck them in a garbage bag with a rock in it. He slipped into the spare clothing he'd brought, and sat down with a thump on the passenger seat, slamming the door, aware that Tom had seen the blood-soaked shirt. "Let's get the hell out of here."

"Look," Tom said, forgetting the shirt, "a white rabbit." There in the headlights, one had already reached the road.

"Hit the gas, and let's go!"

Tom just sat behind the wheel, watching the rabbit, until Coyote hammered his foot onto Tom's and the gas pedal, and they sped away, barely missing the petrified creature.

A few miles down the road, on a bridge between levees, they stopped. Coyote threw the rock-heavy bag into the sluggish, muddy water. He knew he was being paranoid; still, he intended on remaining in business for a while yet.

They were off again. Another hundred yards down the road, Coyote felt something in his hair. It was moving. It fell from his head onto his chest, and walked down to his crotch, an enormous spider, perhaps a tarantula. Do they live here? He watched it, partially afraid, and partially curious. "Stop the car."

Tom dutifully pulled the car over. "What's the matter?" Coyote withdrew the rental form from the glove box, gingerly poking it at the spider, which, annoyed at first, grabbed it before climbing aboard. Then he opened the door and shook it onto the road. "Okay, let's go." He shoved the rental form, now speckled with spider shit, back into the glove box, while Tom leered beside his shoulder, trying to see it through the window.

Once they were driving again, Coyote settled back, shutting his eyes, exhausted, as much from tension as the loss of sleep. "What a production for a bunch of crazy rabbits."

He awoke between two walls of oak. One of the walls broke up and he faced a maze of winking lights and bursts of flame shooting into the air. New Orleans? No, the show was beyond the swamps, out to sea, a cluster of oil rigs, an entire city of wells drilling through the night. Up ahead, inland from the bay, lay a disorderly mass of buildings, smokestacks belching multi-shaded fumes in the hazy light before dawn. No wonder the locals called this Cancer Road.

7

Tell Your Story

WE'RE BACK AT THE TREEHOUSE. We've done some travelling, but we're back. Now it's time to start asking questions. Go to sleep, and wake up . . . like this . . .

There was a flutter, a wind on his face. Brian was coming home from the sea, the spinnaker full, the sun glinting on the water. The circle of light grew, advancing. It developed a black hole in its centre — a planet bathed in yellow light approaching his head. It became an eye. He awoke.

Only inches away the amber eye surrounded by tiny grey feathers meshed into a downy armour glared at him with baleful intensity. Was it going to attack? There was a lizard-like creepiness about the bird. It made him think of dinosaurs.

"Get up and roll that rock," the parrot said. "Get up. Good morning. Roll that rock."

"What rock?" He couldn't remember where he was. The cabin? He was inside Charlie's treehouse, and the parrot had him pinned down on a cot. Brian jerked upright, wrenching his exposed face away from the hooked beak with a speed that unsettled the creature. It fluffed its feathers and retreated. Then, satisfied that it had accomplished its duty, it strutted to the end of the table and fanned a slow wing until it resembled a ballet dancer stretching. It lifted a claw and pointed it at him like a hook. "Roll that rock."

"Where'd you come from?" Brian asked, still confused. "I didn't see you here yesterday."

The bird stood silent, grumpy.

"What's your name?"

The black planet inside the bird's eye scrutinized Brian. The creature had him figured out, and wasn't impressed, brandishing its claw again. "Roll that rock. Roll that rock."

Growing bored with its refrain, Brian inspected the treehouse. He was hungry.

Most of the foodstuffs on the shelves framing the stone hearth behind the stove looked unappetizing. There was a loaf of homemade black bread. He found a container of margarine and honey and slathered them on a few slices. There wasn't a sign of coffee anywhere. Annoyed, he recognized it was soy margarine. It tasted good despite being made out of beans.

The parrot discovered a large, black-and-white striped, beetle crawling across the table beside Brian's bed. It snapped the beetle in half, and tossed the pieces onto the table, as if informing him he was next.

Disturbed, Brian stepped outside. Behind him the parrot shouted: "Watch that hawk. Roll that rock."

"Get lost, bird."

The vegetable garden below shimmered in the morning heat — a vibrant green meant to be eaten. Rita would have loved it here. He could see her down by the gate, wearing one of her embroidered Guatemalan nightgowns, barefoot, the dawn exciting her so much she had to leap through its inviting light, collecting food and dreams for the day.

"Come on down and play!" she called up, a cauliflower in one hand, a sunflower stalk in the other — clutched like the exploded head of a lance. Her smile was as wide as her face while she leaned on the gate post, backlit by the rising sun, so that her large breasts and stocky figure were revealed through her flimsy gown. "Come on down and play," she dared him.

"When I look at a garden, I only see work . . . not play."

"But they're the same thing." Then she began to fade, leaving behind an old sunflower head, picked clean, leaning like ancient embroidery into the netting.

There was a flurry of movement among the trees beyond. The old man. He was running. He crouched and did twenty push-ups before he bounced to his feet and approached a tall fir, which he climbed nearly to the crown before he charged back down. Then he went up again. After the third climb he performed five chin-ups on the lowest branch. It was exhausting just to watch him.

He was shirtless, his skin tanned, the hairs on his chest white and curling. Although built like a barrel that could go to fat at any moment, he was more than healthy . . . excessively healthy for a man in his mid sixties, maybe older.

It was an odd but organic exercise course. The old man leaped back and forth several times across the stream dividing the meadow. His grace was surprising, a sturdy agility and surliness both amusing and inscrutable.

Charlie reached the foot of the treehouse, gasping, yet his posture suggested further strength, a billy goat's enthusiasm for life. "So you're awake?" He dried himself off with a towel, and pulled on a dirty, old T-shirt.

"More or less. Your parrot informed me it was time to roll some bloody rock. Then it murdered a beetle."

Charlie glanced at the sun. "It is that time, but that's not my parrot. He belongs to himself. Are you hungry?"

"I found bread and honey."

Charlie cocked his head. "What more could you ask for?"

"I can think of lots. But what I really want is you, Charlie. I want your story."

"I don't have one. And I just gave you a bed because I felt sorry for you last night out in the cold. Now you can toodle off and catch the ferry."

Brian walked down the ramp. "Everyone has a story. Besides, I thought we made a deal last night. And I suppose you've got no coffee in your organic household, either?"

"That's right, Mister Twisted. There's no coffee and there's no deal."

"I know you're Coyote."

Charlie scanned the wild meadow beyond the garden. "I don't know what you're talking about."

"Yes you do. Rita told me."

"She did?"

"I was on top of her, and she had her legs up, and she told me."

"You're an evil son-of-a-bitch."

"You confused a generation."

"I'm no coyote. I'm a man."

"Okay. I'm prepared to let you imagine him. But I have to know the story. Everything."

"There ain't no story. And I haven't got anything to tell. I thought you were looking for Rita? You're abusing my hospitality."

"You're so pure, aren't you? How come you caused so much destruction?"

"I didn't cause any destruction."

"Is this what you're about? Is it all games? Let's run for what's real."

"You start running, boy, and tell me what's real."

"We're going to make an agreement."

"What kind of agreement?"

"I have two choices. Like I said yesterday, I can call this a loss and take the ferry back to the police station in Sweet Water and tell them what I know, and then I can glean what I need from their reports. I'm sure they'll help me for such a gift. Or else I can make a pact with you."

"What kind of a pact? No wonder the woman took off. You're a creep."

"It's simple. You tell me everything you know and I write a novel, a fictional work that describes the location of this scene on a godforsaken island never discovered, the history so warped that no-one will know if it's real or imagination. I walk away with my story and you grow your garden and talk to your parrot. How's that?"

"Are you an artist?"

"Yes, I am."

"Is art blackmail?"

"Depends on the situation."

"I enjoy you, kid. You remind me of me when I was a real jerk . . . just like my father . . . before I got wise."

"I doubt you've changed much since the day you were born. I'll bet you came out wearing that straw hat and beard."

The image was so incongruous it made Charlie feel warm in spite of himself. "No, I haven't changed much, boy. I just got smarter. What's your guarantees?"

"There aren't any guarantees."

"You telling me there's no safety?"

"I've always said that if we valued safety more than freedom we'd end up with neither."

Charlie flashed an evil grin. "I might kill you when you sleep."

That's what Brian had always known, the terror so mundane, waking up as the knife came down, or the frying pan on his skull, the foolish uselessness of it all. It sent a thrill under his skin. "Yes, you could."

He'd known a woman like that once, full of violence as well as love. Every night together was a contest. Can I sleep? Will I die? Does it matter? Does she love me?

"You could kill me, but you won't," Brian's mind began to run with a host of thoughts. "It's hard to explain. Your escapades fascinated me since your first action. I witnessed it. But it's more than that, I had to meet you in order to understand Rita — why she loved you, and not me."

Charlie, registering the import of what Brian had blurted out, stiffened, his face sad. Then he walked past him, towards the meadow. "I got work to do," he said, standing in front of a boulder as tall as himself, and several hundred pounds heavier.

"You can't dodge me."

"I'm not dodging anybody. You can tell me your story while I work."

"It's you that's got the story."

"We'll see about that."

Charlie crouched and examined the freshly dug hole under the rock. There was a cluster of tools strewn nearby. Like a doctor contemplating his instruments before an operation, he considered the various peevees and shovels before finally settling on a smaller boulder which he rolled into the hole next to the big rock. Then he took a long, steel peevee and wedged it between, and began to pry at the rock.

"Do you want a hand?" Brian asked, alarmed by the popping veins on the old man's forehead as he struggled with his leverage.

"Get your own rock."

The rock toppled over.

"What are you going to do with it?"

"I'm trying to push it up the bloody hill. Whaddya think I'm doing?"

Brian shrugged. "Why do you have to push it up the hill?"

"So I can roll it back down again."

"That's what I was afraid you'd say." Brian lit a cigarette and watched as Charlie began jamming bars along the rock's side, cranking it up a few inches at a time before bracing it and moving along to the next bar.

The teardrop shaped chunk of granite proved to be more reluctant on this roll. While the old man grunted and fiddled with his bars, Brian considered the distance to the top of the meadow. This was one hell of an undertaking.

There was a whisper of knocking wings and the parrot swooped past Brian's head, landing on the rock, strutting like a juvenile delinquent showing off for the girls.

Charlie jerked upright. "Watch that hawk!"

The parrot broke into a tremble, its eyes scanning the horizon; then it scurried closer to where the old man worked, perching on the edge, keeping sentry to the sky.

Brian, for a moment, saw nothing but the blue atmosphere and thick cumulous clouds; finally, he noticed a black speck circling.

The parrot chuckled. "Watch that hawk. Roll that rock."

"What's his name?"

"Ask him."

"What's your name?"

"Drop dead," the parrot said.

Brian stubbed his cigarette butt on the ground, quenching it with the heel of his boot while the parrot observed. The meadow was a firetrap, the dried grass crackling underfoot. "I assume his name is not Drop Dead."

"No idea what it is. He gives me a different answer every time I ask him. Only he knows what his name is, and he ain't telling."

This slip-sliding around was beginning to annoy Brian. "Where'd you get him?"

"I didn't get him. He got me, came wandering up the ramp one day, half-pulling himself with his beak, a bloody mess, most of his flight feathers ripped out. A runaway, I suppose. Though no-one ever answered my notice at the store. The crows had mobbed him. They do that, the crows; they'll kill any bird that doesn't belong — some who do belong, for that matter. They're like starlings. Between the two of them they'd kill every songbird in the neighbourhood if they could. I gave him my breakfast grain. He let me wipe the blood off his feathers. One of his eyes was sealed. It's fine now, except I don't think he sees well to one side. That was maybe four years ago. He sticks around, but he's a free bird. He can leave whenever he wants."

"To die? You'd let him run free to die in the winter or be killed by hawks or crows?"

"I wouldn't prevent it, if that's what he wanted, but I share what I've got with him, and I suppose he's satisfied. Doesn't show any inclination to leave for more than a day or so. Parrots are real dumb about directions, yet this one knows his way back to the treehouse if he gets out of sight."

The bird bobbed in agreement, momentarily, before returning its attention to Brian with a melancholy tilt of its head. Then it launched into a grumbling monologue punctuated by whistles and clicks that verged towards meaning, but were senseless in the end.

A recalcitrant steel bar flew out of Charlie's hand and rang against the rock, startling the bird into flight while Charlie hop-danced around the stone, nursing his hurt finger in his mouth. The parrot fluttered to the ground and repeated its grotesque monologue, this time more vociferously. Charlie sat on the small leverage-boulder beside the rock while the parrot crawled onto his lap, slowly tugging its way up with beak and claws, like a man shimmying up a rope, until it reached Charlie's shoulder where it perched triumphant, waving a defiant raised claw at the meadow.

"The rock," Brian said, "it reminds me of the Greek legend."

Charlie raised an eyebrow. "*Sisyphus*?"

"Yes."

"It's got nothing to do with him."

"Didn't he have to roll a rock up a hill only to watch it roll back down, forever in . . . "

"I know my myths too, boy. That was his rock. This is my rock. They're different."

Brian fell silent. The old man ignored him. Recognizing there was nothing more forthcoming, Brian said: "You're going to roll it back down once you get it up there?"

"Originally, when I dug it out of the garden, I was going to plant herbs around it. But it rankled me, so I heaved it onto the meadow; took a few weeks, working at it a half-hour a day, and you know, I enjoyed it so much I kept on going. Honest and interesting work, it was. Took me almost a year to make it to the top of the hill."

"You mean . . . you've already had it up the hill and down again?"

"Sure. Done it three times. Right back to the garden and then to the crest."

"That's insane."

"Naw. Everyone's rolling a rock. Their rocks merely look different. We're all doing the same thing. Mine's simple. It isn't your way or the Greek way. This is physical delight. Different. Sisyphus; his rock was punishment for telling on the gods, naming the evil he'd seen. My rock is pleasure, a real task that beats weightlifting." Charlie lifted his arms and flexed his biceps. They were impressive.

"In fact, it works on the muscles in a better way. Weightlifting is too specialized. I once knew a guy, a Mr. Canada. Built like a god, he could rip a muscle bending over to pick up a pencil. This work always makes me move at odd angles, tones the muscles. It's healthy. It allows for perspective.

"The other question, of course, is damage. Everything we do causes damage. When a rock is moved, when soil is turned, when an animal is killed, we interfere with the ecosystems around us." Charlie lifted his open hands gracefully, as if offering Brian the world.

"But this rock rolling is at a fairly minor level, and the soil, the insects, the weeds will replenish themselves. Consider it an act of mercy to the planet. I'm restricting my area of damage and living a satisfying life at the same time. What more can I ask for? You think I'm doing a Sisyphus? Cripes, you might as well accuse me of being a penguin. They roll rocks, too."

"Why do penguins roll rocks?"

"To attract a lover. They make their nests out of rocks, so if the male can roll a lot of rocks up to a female, she gets impressed, and he's won himself a lady."

"Is that what you're trying to do, attract a lady?" Brian was beginning to feel like an inquisitor on LSD.

"Do I look like a penguin?"

"This is nuts!" Brian said. "It has nothing to do with anything!"

"It has everything to do with everything."

"It's crazy."

"Not as crazy as writing a pappy book that'll entertain people for a few hours, destroying several acres of forest in the process, occupying the time of loggers, truckers, pulp workers, editors, typesetters, lithopreppers, photographers, pressmen with all their carcinogenic chemicals and inks, newspaper and magazine reviewers, sales people, mail carriers, book distributors flying and driving it all around the country, and then for the grand finale, the thing throws ugly gasses into the air when it's tossed aside and burned."

"Maybe it'll contribute to people's knowledge."

Charlie lifted a bushy white eyebrow. "Join the thousands on the walls in my house, eh? Look at where our knowledge has taken us. Books? Take them to a second hand bookstore and try and sell them. Then you'll get an idea of their value."

"You read all your books, and then you tell me you're not interested in knowledge?"

"I didn't say that. I was just warning you that knowledge hasn't done us much good so far. It's like technology. It limits us. The more tools, the more machines, the more ideas we have the more we need to restrict ourselves with laws and limits, so we don't cause further damage to each other or the ecology. Our tools — so-called labour-saving devices, and books, too, restrict our lives. Look at the enormous, mind-numbing bureaucracy and rules we labour under."

"Aren't you restricting yourself with that bloody rock?"

Charlie wrenched at his peevee. The rock still wasn't moving. "Not legally, boy. I don't have any bureaucrats and policemen running around the thing and measuring her up, and organizing their processes and their restrictions and their permits and licences. Gawd, this blathering has given me a headache, and I've done my half-hour for today. Why don't we go inside and I'll make my famous barley and bean soup."

"I hate barley soup. And beans, too."

"Tough. You'll learn to enjoy it if you stick around here. Why'd you decide to become a writer, anyway?"

"I don't know. I had a problem when I was a kid. I couldn't talk well, so I started writing, writing everything, pouring it all out. I had what they called electrical aphasia then. I've gotten past it. But I've spent most of my adult life hovering around universities, learning philosophy, everything, though I'm no good in the sciences. I tried them a few times. Never could remember past the 33rd element in the periodic table. At least as a writer I can express myself — "

"Express yourself! You think that's what writing is? Self-expression? Luring people into admiring your talent? That's scrawling your shit onto paper. You can do that in the outhouse, and save the world a lot of trouble. Come on, let's go make that soup before you ruin my lunch." Charlie thumped across the meadow towards the treehouse, the parrot clinging to his shoulder, bobbing its head as if it were dunking for apples. They made a good pair.

Brian regarded the rock with no little disgust. 'What have I got myself into this time?' Though everything was working so far. Besides, there was nothing else to do, nowhere to go. The lonely anger of the old man as he walked away weighed heavily on him.

There was a tree not far from the rock, loaded with tiny seed pods. They weren't ripe yet, but recognizable. Brian had never heard of almond trees growing this far north. 'Cyanide, beautiful cyanide,' he whispered to himself.

"Wait a second, Charlie." He ran after him. "When are you going to start telling me your story."

"I already have."

Brian reached his side. "This is going to be a long story?"

"You want the truth, don't you? Everything?"

"Sure, everything. Including the history of the peacock on the path."

"I suppose you've got a little time?"

Brian was thoughtful, following Charlie and the parrot up the ramp to the treehouse. He had nothing but time . . . restless time without peace from the questions in his head. Forever. The idea of forever scared him. "How long will it take?"

"You'll know when I'm finished."

8

DINNER HAD LEFT A BAD TASTE IN JANWAR'S MOUTH, like licorice saturating his gums. His stomach was bothering him again, and he worried that he'd contracted an exotic disease.

He moved the mouse, stalling the screen saver, and brought Newcomm to the foreground window. Then he double-clicked Kirsten's number.

As soon as her computer answered he clicked into chat mode, and started typing.

Janwar: Are you online?

There was a pause. He sat stonily at his desk, staring out the window at the darkening park across the street from his apartment, as letters began filling the screen.

Kirsten: Yes. This is neat. I've never used a chat mode before. It rang me while I was working on an essay for my night school course on computing. I'm tired of being such a Luddite, and I'm upgrading myself on this thing.

Janwar: I didn't do much. I dropped Newcomm into the startup folder, running as an icon at the bottom of the screen. In five years this will be laughably primitive.

Kirsten: Why don't you like to use the phone?

Janwar: I prefer typing rather than talking. It forces me to think more when I am conversing. I receive many ideas while typing. How are you feeling?

Kirsten: Not bad, considering. Do you think I'll be transferred out?

Janwar: That's the easiest way of dealing with problems like this, though times are changing. It wasn't very tactful calling Chief Inspector Blake a "sexist goof."

Kirsten: You were told everything?

Janwar: In graphic detail.

Kirsten: I know it was dumb, but I couldn't put up with it any more; not only is he a sexist prick, he's a racist, too. You should have heard what he said about you. Unfortunately, no-one else heard him. They sure heard me. My voice carries better, especially when I'm upset. I filed a complaint to counter his suspension.

Janwar: He'll probably survive it; still, you stood up for your principles, which has unfortunately led to a new partner for me, Corporal Kookoff. I'm not overly impressed so far. He's good-hearted but clumsy, and he has the ear of Chief Inspector Blake. Perhaps that's why he was assigned to replace you.

Kirsten: I'm afraid the 'token twins' have no future.

Janwar: My opinion is the same.

Kirsten: I did interview Rita's 'friend' before I was yanked — Angie. According to her there were no suspicious incidents or people around Rita before she disappeared. She's even more righteous than Hillhurst, insisted Rita was a proud feminist and that her relationship with Sowinki was merely a case of a polite student having to deal with unwanted advances from a cruising professor. But Angie is uniting with the dean in bringing academic charges against Sowinki, so I don't know how seriously to take her. What a Peyton Place that university's become. How was your interview?

Janwar: Strangely, he behaved in an incriminating manner, yet he was guileless. I believe I was dealing with naive arrogance rather than guilt. Blake, on the other hand, after reading my report, is ready to nail Sowinki to the cross. I fear the Chief Inspector is not fond of Jews either, along with his many other public dislikes. By the way, are you recording this?

Kirsten: Of course not. I also learned more about this other relationship. Charlie. They were together nearly ten years. They had a bitter split up, and he moved to Artemis. But Angie doesn't know how long ago that occurred. Are you going to check him out?

Janwar: Not yet. I'll respect Blake's wishes (he is my boss, after all) and give Kookoff a turn with Sowinki. I never revealed to Sowinki I'd heard about his alleged threat against Rita. I wanted to watch him speak without pressure. Kookoff has a different strategy. I consider it premature.

Kirsten: How are your ailments?

Janwar: Worsening. I don't know what is happening. My doctor says I have a nervous disposition, but how does that give me headaches, bowel problems, and joint pain? And this constant tiredness? Yet my blood tests claim I am healthy.

Kirsten: Why don't you book your holidays earlier, and go to Artemis? You can check out Charlie, and take the cure at Wren's resort and healing centre. A few of her therapies appear crazy, others are smart and ahead of the medical literature. You'll know what I'm talking about when you meet her. If Blake won't let you change your time off, you can try a sick leave. It's a great spa, and you might build a better picture of this Rita woman. I know you're right; terrible things are happening. Too many women have gone missing . . . or have been found in the bush. There's a maniac out there.

Janwar: Yes, I'm sure there is. Rita Norman's phonebook has also disappeared from her bedside table. Forensics couldn't find it when they dusted. They searched the whole place.

Kirsten: There's a killer in that book, then?

Janwar: Its theft would suggest that. I could kick myself for being too discreet on our visit, and not seizing it.

Kirsten: What did the dusters pick up?

Janwar: A few hours overtime in the lab. At least seventy-five different prints. The dusters said the apartment manager told them she had an 'epic' party the week before she disappeared. The prints wouldn't mean much in court, except confirming an acquaintance with Miss Norman.

Kirsten: We must be grateful for small favours.

Janwar: I've booked access to an interesting Internet police link, and I'm going to speak with officers more experienced at this kind of case. I certainly can't make anyone around here believe we have a serial killer on our hands. I will keep you informed, for your own interest. I enjoyed working with you. Meanwhile, I will consider your suggestion about Artemis. Bye.

Kirsten: We might not be finished working together yet. Bye.

He clicked out of Newcomm and leaned back in his chair. His gut began boiling — a wave of gas. He was tired, so tired — he felt like a middle-aged man contemplating his life and collapsing body. Is this it? Is the run over? Did I reach as far as I could? But Janwar had only recently turned thirty-six. He was too young for such speculation. It was the pain in his joints causing this, the tiredness, the belly, the terrible belly of a man losing his grip on the life he'd fought for since he was a child.

He had no guilt about chatting with the boys on the beat. After all, Kirsten's encounter with Blake was a source of much gossip. It gave him an opportunity to learn more about her. She was an interesting creature, the most intelligent officer he'd ever encountered. He saw it in those cold dark eyes the first time he met her. Yet sporadic incidents of eccentric behaviour often betrayed her intelligence. Well, with a past like that . . .

The daughter of a junkie prostitute who overdosed, she'd been adopted at seven by a Mormon family. Enjoying the stability at first, she eventually rebelled in university. She hadn't told the boys on the beat much about those days, though enough to generate gossip that was further inflamed by the fact she had a healthy sex drive and had enjoyed a few relationships with other officers, though all were temporary. She was a loner, living in her small house, its walls lined with books.

During her ten years on the force, despite her occasionally quirky behaviour, she'd been steadily promoted. So why had she suddenly exploded at Blake?

Janwar worried that his speculations about the missing and dead women had agitated her, especially since Blake had been stonewalling an expanded investigation. The majority of the missing women were prostitutes, and

Blake's lack of sympathy for those trapped in the criminal underworld was notorious.

Janwar clicked off his laptop and shut the case. He couldn't handle any more mail tonight. No, that was an uncourageous course. He reloaded it and then stood up. He'd just have to hope there'd be no mail. Maybe he would have a nice warm shower.

***

Across town, Kirsten closed her laptop, took the sheets of screen dump printout and slipped them into a brown envelope on which she wrote the date and time. Then she put the computer and the envelope in her gun safe.

***

The computer was ringing softly as Janwar entered his apartment. One of his perks as an Inspector was a permanent Internet connection. It must be her. He opened up Newcomm.

Kirsten: Are you there?

Janwar: Yes.

Kirsten: How are you?

Janwar: Reasonably well.

Kirsten: That's good. I've been transferred to Vice. The hooker trade. I guess Blake knows about my mother, along with everyone else. He must have pulled strings. What an outfit!

Janwar: Your mother?

Kirsten: Oh come now, Janwar, show me a little more respect than that. My past has been all around this department since a weak moment on a date with a beat cop a few years back. But this is going to backfire on Blake. I'm going to grieve this, too. I'll take his cronies down with him. I don't want to talk about my problems. I've got other news. Vice squad might be no fun, but my current partner introduced me to a few people I should know. One was a working girl who talked a blue streak, the founder of a hookers' rights organization. She insists there's a serial killer stalking hookers. She knew Rita via her work with Angie, knows she's gone, too. The hooker claims they were all 'acquaintances' but she was crowing too much, self-important, slightly crackers. I know this is forward — I took the liberty of interviewing Angie again, though I'm off the case. She's friends with a lot of the girls. They're her Ph.D thesis, (a little more thrilling than nineteenth century lesbian literature, I guess) and she said an American accountant is creeping the streets. Nobody knows his name. He made a strange move on one woman who got away, and was the last guy seen talking to another who disappeared. She says no one on the force cares about her story because she's a hooker.

Janwar: I'll take this into consideration. Impressive work!

Kirsten: Thanks. I get little enough of that (praise) around here. How's your health, or did I already ask that?

Janwar: Reasonable, but I must sign off. Rushed. Bye for now. This is valuable news.

Kirsten: Bye.

Janwar sat back in his chair. Was he growing too close to Kirsten? Why was he imagining her dressed up to lure johns on a midnight street corner — red heels and a leather miniskirt? This was becoming too uncomfortable. Perhaps he should withdraw from discussing this case with her, yet she was so good at digging up information, and besides, she needed a friend these days.

He closed her window on his screen and double-clicked his navigator. Then he bookmarked to Lawtalk, webmastered from Illinois, the site he'd found last week.

WELCOME TO LAWTALK. 19 DISCUSSION GROUPS (DONUT SHOPS) RUNNING SIMULTANEOUSLY, CHECK THE MENU. 1733 FILES AVAILABLE FOR DOWNLOADING. UPLOADED FILES WILL BE SCREENED BEFORE THEY ARE MADE AVAILABLE. THIS SITE, ITS FILES AND DISCUSSION GROUPS, OPEN ONLY TO LAW ENFORCEMENT OFFICERS. PUNCH IN YOUR CLEARANCE CODE NOW. IF YOU ARE NOT AN OFFICER OF THE LAW, THIS SITE ISN'T FOR YOU. NO ENTRY PAST THIS GATE IF YOUR CODE IS NOT VERIFIED. THANK YOU. MAY THE FORCE BE WITH YOU.

Janwar had received clearance after the site-master confirmed him via Blake, so he punched in his code, and drifted down the menu. There weren't as many DONUT SHOPS as advertised. He assumed there must be sub-groups. He clicked onto MURDER, and scrolled into a chatroom discussing a much-publicized killing in Los Angeles. For Janwar, these popular media cases were boring. He decided to break in, wondering if cops flamed other cops for rudeness.

JS: Hello. JS here from Vancouver, Canada. Sorry to interrupt. Is there a chat room for multiple murders?

Opcop: Hello JS up there in frozen Canada. What are you looking for, mass or serial? Double click the header icon for sub-categories. Mass is MASMUR and serial is SERMUR. Do you have grim action?

JS: I fear so. Thanks for your help. Bye.

He clicked himself into the sub menu SERMUR. The screen scrolled into the new group and another dialogue.

Tracer: He claimed he got to like the "gentle pop" of the head separating from the body.

Max: How many victims?

Tracer: At least a half dozen. You can find more in the book *Hunting Humans* by Leyton.

Follows: A good text, that one. He explores the psychology in several classic cases.

Max: Is it still in print?

Tracer: I think so.

JS: Hello. This is JS, RCMP inspector. Canada. Sorry to interrupt your interesting conversation but I'm in need of advice.

Tracer: Hello JS. Hey, what's dogsledding like? And how do you guys get around in the summer up there, anyway? Or do you get summer?

JS: Sure, we have summer, for about three weeks. Then we can travel by canoe or horse.

Max: Really? I'm in Georgia. Man, this is wild stuff. You have moose up there, too, don't you?

JS: Sure. We all wear mooseskin coats in the winter, but the animal rights people are kicking up a fuss, so everyone is switching over to artificial furs.

Max: You still use dog sleds? Gawd o'mighty, that sounds great. What about ski-doos? I thought you guys invented them.

JS: It's true some have switched to ski-doos, but it's hard to eat your carburetor when you're trapped out in the wilderness.

Max: Aww, your pulling our legs.

JS: Why would I do that?

Tracer: How can we help you?

JS: I have a fearful situation here, I'm afraid. Seven women have disappeared (hard disappearances) in the last three years. Four now confirmed as prostitutes. A hitchhiking runaway's body was found. Two women were of good reputation — one working with a friend on a study of prostitutes, a university instructor. Only five bodies discovered. Two buried by the Chilliwack River, near Vancouver, close together, though buried at different times. One found by the Goose River, on the far side of Sweet Water town. One discovered hanging from a door knob in her closet. A purse discovered at Sweet Water River, belonging to the disappeared student/teacher. The woman found hanging from the closet door was also a student at the same university, SFU. She originated from the Sweet Water area. Several other women, mostly prostitutes, have also been reported missing, but with no hard leads.

Max: Sounds grim, surely. How close are you to Alberta? Isn't that up there in Canada, too?

JS: It is the neighbouring province.

Max: We had a guy online named Hageldorf from Alberta, a little town called Edmonton. They've got a fancy shopping mall up there, or is it a theme park?. His people found two prostitutes by a river as well. You were online, Tracer, do you remember more?

Tracer: We directed him to the detective in Portland. I can't recall his name. Cheechers? Cheevers? Sounded like that. He was following similar material known as the Wild River murders. Claimed he was getting close to the psycho; that was the last we heard. Phone up Portland, they'll know who he is.

Max: Either that or the sysop, or Hageldorf should have an address.

JS: This is invaluable information. I'm very grateful.

Max: Any time.

JS: Signing off. Thanks.

***

Janwar: Are you home?

He waited a few minutes to see if she would answer. He was about to sign off when her connection flashed.

Kirsten: Yes.

Janwar: Are you well? I heard distressing rumours.

Kirsten: I'm afraid I really am a 'pain in the ass' now. We might have to use the phone if it gets 'discomforting,' as you would politely put it. You're still keen on computer conversations?

Janwar: Sorry, if it's too inconvenient we can switch, but the slowness of the computer helps me think. You were hurt while on duty? What would you like to do, phone?

Kirsten: Naw, we can stay online. It's not that uncomfortable. I don't know if I can bear working in Vice. I'll reconsider my life when sick leave ends. No, that's not true. I visit headquarters almost every day, and chat with the gang. I should be over this soon. They gave me a few days leave. I was posing as a hooker, trying to scoop a john, and he got rough. Knocked me on my ass. Cracked my tailbone a good one. He'll be going upriver for a while. My partner nabbed him, and Robert's nearly as artistic as Write-em-all-up O'Rourke at figuring out additional charges to lay. He's already come up with seven.

Janwar: I was worried when I heard the news.

Kirsten: I'm fine. Everyone's making a big deal, so they can crank up the sentence request for the prosecutor.

Janwar: They usually do in circumstances like that.

Kirsten: Strangely, I feel sorry for him. It was kind of an accident, but the guys at the station took the bag of oranges to him — the usual for messing up a cop — thumped him hard. He was just a panicked john. How are you making out with the murders?

Janwar: I talked to a man named Hageldorf in Edmonton who had two similar cases to the prostitute killings, and he put me in touch with an Officer Cheevers in Portland. Cheevers couriered me a box full of files. He's chasing a prostitute stalker, very grotesque. Unfortunately, the shipment might have been misplaced by the courier and hasn't arrived. If it shows up, I've instructed that it be redirected to me at the resort.

Kirsten: So you're going for the 'cure?'

Janwar: I managed to switch my holidays around so that I can leave immediately.

Kirsten: Are you going to check out this Charlie fellow?

Janwar: Of course. That is the secondary purpose of my visit.

Kirsten: I heard about the purse getting found. Sweet Water River, eh?

Janwar: My, you do have good ears. I didn't realize this case was so interesting to staff.

Kirsten: I ran into Kookoff this morning, we had coffee. I gather there was nothing in the purse.

Janwar: Nothing interesting, except for its location. Aside from the other woman originating from that area, I've heard something else about this place. Why does the name sound familiar?

Kirsten: Sweet Water? I speculateed about that, too, and checked. It's the first site the famous eco-terrorist, Coyote, sabotaged . . . contaminated the pulp mill and the hospital water supply, if I remember correct, with a blue dye that later proved to be mildly carcinogenic. It sort of backfired on him. That was twenty years ago.

Janwar: The vandalized wall at Rita's sister's home?

Kirsten: That might be stretching it. I think he died several years later. Activist copycats have taken to calling themselves "Sons of Coyote," like those spray-painters. I wouldn't get overly excited about the coincidence. It's a common term among the eco-crowd.

Janwar: This friend of yours, Wren Dancing, she is good? She sounded rather 'unusual' when I phoned to book my stay. I'm not going to get poisoned with New Age cures, am I?

Kirsten: She's unusual, but she is good. You'll like her.

9

IMAGINE THE DEAD OF THE WORLD. The monstrous pile of corpses over millions of years, dinosaurs, meerkats, insects, mothers, bullheads, children, lab mice. Oh, there is not enough room for all the dead, so we eat them. Everything in our ecology is designed to eat the dead in order to make room for the living.

We are all eaters of the dead. And then we go on.

Long after Coyote had ceased his activities, Eileen Chavez, who'd written a popular ecological book about the river behind her house, was found mutilated beside its rushing water by a fisherman. It was the summer of 1990. She believed to the day of her death that no one knew she had a secret history.

With three words, "I am Coyote," the Earthouse cell became one creature, though most were half-hearted and took few chances. Undoubtedly, they'd guessed who among them the real Coyote was, but nothing was ever said, and the fiction they'd created opened up ideas, avenues of research, techniques for stealing and using explosives, identification forging methods . . . This gave Coyote a greater range. He was always uneasy about his position, but there was no choice except to trust them, and as far as he ever knew, they repaid his trust. No-one betrayed him.

But one old lady was found naked near a creek that she had gloriously identified as a river and lovingly documented in a book

that sold tens of thousands of copies. Beside her was a propane
bottle with a torch attachment. Her fingers were burnt into black
claws.

The police unearthed a sex molester with a violent history who
lived nearby, but they lost him in a mistrial due to an incompetent
prosecutor. The lucky man went free, unpunished for a crime he
claimed he'd never committed.

And if you followed all the rivers of the continent you would
find more women and men, buried under leaves, skulls surfacing,
bits of jewellery, carrion. Treasures for flies. What we lose every
day. How we feed our planet with ourselves.

The media soon recognized the diversity of sabotages
that included mailed death-threats to the presidents of
arms manufacturing companies, an anonymous offer of
a $10,000 bounty for the sexual organs of polluters that
was mysteriously inserted in the classified section of a
newspaper, the liberation of a mink farm on the Isle of
Man which proved to have disastrous ecological
consequences due to the mink devastating the nesting
shorebird population, and a kidnapping raid on a
chimpanzee research centre in Washington.

The obvious copycats were eventually dubbed Sons of
Coyote, a name gratefully confiscated by various saboteurs
beyond the original EarthHouse cell. Sons of Coyote
continued to be used as a homage after Coyote's reported
death during the infamous ChemCity raid in Chicago.

And this story? It's not only for you to read when you become
a man, if you become a man, or for anyone else who wants to read
it. It's for me. It's my story, too. You broke my heart. You break
my heart every time I look at you. A world that slaughters old
ladies and threatens innocent boys with toxic diseases demands
answers. The truth, at least.

"What is truth?" Pontius Pilate said in the shortest character study in the New Testament. You might have to wander between Matthew (27:24) and John (18:38) for it, but the story is there. When the put-up crowd shouted out the fate of Christ and the Roman procurator was trapped into murder, he called for water, precious water, and washed his hands clean of the matter. He might not have known the truth, but he sure knew a story when he heard one.

***

That terrible feeling wouldn't go away. He was going to be caught, or hurt somebody. His bad luck would kill him.

Coyote sat with his back against a tamarack on the ridge. Below him, the bridge across the gorge was empty, silent — an impressive network of wood and steel and cables. It resembled a living, mechanical insect resting for a while before moving on.

The sun had risen an hour earlier. From where he sat in the stand of butter-yellow tamaracks, he could see for miles. Beyond the gorge the bridge straddled was a series of rolling hills — a lush, profound green — one of the largest stands of the deep black spruce taiga, most of the timber vulnerable now that the bridge was completed. There was a tainted patch in the hills to the west, a clump of dead and dying trees, assaulted by an outbreak of budworm. On the outskirts of the patch flew the speck which was the source of Coyote's problem — a plane spraying pesticide.

He wasn't inclined to detonate his blast until the plane disappeared, and since he knew nothing about the spraying program he had no idea how long the plane would remain. This wasn't going well. It'd taken longer than he'd planned to wade through the muskeg alongside the gorge and set the submagel charges. Now he was cold and paranoid.

The dawn breeze ebbed and the blackflies found him once more. They swarmed around his head, falling into his eyes, crawling up his nose. He was already bloody from last night when he'd first encountered the muskeg and the flies, and he'd almost gone mad, stomping through the moss between the scraggly, stunted conifers, only to find the moss lay on nothing but bog. He was in slime to his knees, sometimes to his waist, before finding islands of dry land; then back to the muskeg. In the mud and scum of things the flies exulted. The flies. At first he swatted them, tried to brush them away, yet that merely excited them. Why were there so many in September? This wasn't the Ontario he remembered; the rush of bugs in the spring, peaking at June, before ebbing until the placid woods became nearly habitable in the late summer and the fall.

Whoa, I'm back again, man-child. I'm difficult to lose once I get started.

A while ago, in a funky and correctly designed Vancouver bar, I met a man who told me there weren't enough people in Canada, that there's too much unused space, like northern Ontario — nothing but blackflies and muskeg and scrubby trees. A landscape that empty (he didn't mention the Native communities) needed people, though I'm sure the blackflies consider it a crowded slum. Fifty thousand blackflies per square inch can hatch along those creek beds. Talk about over-population.

Empty? Tell the deer, the bears, the trees, and the bugs that their homeland is empty, that a world without people is uninhabited. We mouth philosophies declaring the sanctity of life while assuming anything non-human isn't as important as human.

Once we begin with that premise we can justify factory farms and using rabbits to test cosmetics, and then leap to medical research and finally further, the eradication of diseases. Yet, aren't diseases and parasites ecological functions?

Is your disease part of the ecology? Should I be celebrating your potential death? That you will make good food for the worms? Is a virus as important as a young mother who catches it in her lung? Are you an old woman beside a creek bed that she called a river? Does a broken gene have the same right to existence as a truck driver? These are questions we will have to discuss more, later. Right; you're part of the story, too.

For centuries, many of us believed the sun revolved around the earth. Now we have scaled down our pride to merely having the earth and its inhabitants revolve around us. What will the paradigm be in the next century, if there is a next century?

The bugs and rocks might yet have their day.

On the other hand, if you were sitting around the table in the treehouse and asked my twisted alter ego, Brian, his opinion, I know how he'd reply, despite his ecological pretensions, or maybe because of his ecological pretensions: "Nuke the blackflies!"

Coyote might have agreed, too. Why did he always pick mudholes to sabotage? The flies preferred the skin behind his ears, and the blood from their bites circled his neck, soaking into his collar, until he resembled a man with a slashed throat.

And none of this would have been necessary if it wasn't for the logging of the valley beyond the bridge. The clearcutting had been stymied for years, the bridge's construction made impossible by a land claim from the tribe downriver who'd allied themselves with a few environmentalists demanding a wilderness preservation area. But the tree huggers were stonewalled by the government and the ecological sympathies of the tribe dissipated after their claim

*was settled, and the people who had pronounced themselves
guardians of the resource, reconsidered, and decided that a little
clearcutting wasn't so bad after all. After all, the site was hidden
away, twenty miles from their village, and nothing but a bunch
of scrubby spruce. Though they lost the logging claim in the final
negotiations, they owned the access route and a percentage for
the use of their territory to remove the timber. Besides, most of the
old trappers had died off during the twenty years of conflict, and
a lot of Natives don't appreciate blackflies either. Sounds ugly
doesn't it? Nobody's clean, including those who believe in
cleanliness. The bridge was built. The poor tribe sold its backbone.
A few have done that before them.*

The pilot made a farewell gesture to the unwatching
forest, performing a last, playful loop with the plane,
engulfing himself in the vestiges of spray before he set a
new course for the horizon. "How twisted," Coyote said,
watching the plane fly out of its own excretion, and
disappear.

Then he pushed the Play button on the tape deck
beside him. The haunting song blasted out of the
machine into the serene, primeval forest.

> *"To everything there is a season,
> and a time to every purpose under heaven:
> a time to be born and a time to die,
> a time to weep, a time to laugh,
> a time to get, a time to lose . . . "*

And behind the song, inaudible, the microwaves surged
from the tape deck. A spray of water erupted at the base
of the columns supporting the bridge's web. A deep
booming fluttered against his chest. Then nothing.

The bridge remained standing.

"Well . . . " There wasn't much else to say. The monster was upright and laughing at him. He leaped to his feet and kicked the tape deck into the trees.

A June bug, perhaps distracted by his sudden spasm, collided with a branch above his head, before it fell stunned to the ground, its antennae and legs jerking as it reorganized itself. The sunlight reflected on its metallic shell, an odd green-blue among the yellowed needles beneath the tamaracks.

His thoughts went in too many directions, but there was a core behind them — one thought that was, at this moment, too important for anything else. The bridge . . . the bridge . . .

Then there was a last burp in the river, a small spray near the shore as a girder snapped, and the world began to change.

It looked at him. The bridge looked at him — it folded into an awkward bow, and shuddered at the edges before it reached equilibrium. It grew still again. Mute.

It walked away, literally. It lifted itself off its pilings and began to totter towards the spruce forest like a cripple blessed by a crank evangelist. It arose unsteadily from its cement pylons, pieces flying off as it walked, an arm shattering with an explosiveness that was awesome, and another limb. Rotating on its last leg it folded into the river with a low thunder more terrifying than loud.

"Shiiiite," Coyote muttered at the foaming river, "that was impressive."

The note. The sheet in his pocket that he'd forgotten to leave by the riverbank. It felt insignificant now.

Coyote surveyed the empty sky, the vacancy at the end of the road; then he ran towards the smoking chasm.

The blood from the blackfly bites had run and created an arrow line down the front of his shirt, as if he were a target. He stopped, tiny, beside the rubble of pipes and cement and wire.

An iron rod. He picked it up and began to scratch out his name. He was sweating in the early heat of the sun as a new crop of flies found him. They were no longer important. He carved his words into the gravel on his side of the river. COYOTE WILL NOT BRIDGE WITH YOUR FUTURE BECAUSE YOU HAVE ABANDONED HIM . . .

Ahh, how his corny aphorisms made him feel warm at night before he went to sleep.

This is where we begin the sea change; the crisis that overwhelmed him. The other excursions might have been complicated, near-failures; yet they didn't confront him so much with the awful edges where reality works. Now he discovered himself fighting the ostensible defenders of the forest (the tribe who had a financial interest in this clearcutting operation) and being saved by the loggers. And that's what he got. The awful truth. The world is not as simple as a corny slogan.

When he glanced up, there were three young loggers, hardhatted, leaning against a krummy on the other side of the river, smoking cigarettes.

The handsome young logger smiled at him. We don't know the reasons, and we don't have to. The incidents that hook us don't need reasons.

He froze, neck twisted, and realized how crazy he must look, middle-aged, white-bearded, sweating, streaked with blackfly-drawn blood, dragging a bent rod across the dirt. He hurled the rod into the river, and glared back at them — trapped on the other side of the gorge. The pretty one seated on the truck's bumper, soon to be unemployed due to the destruction of the bridge, smiled and flashed him a peace sign; whether it was out of respect for craziness or courage, or a gesture of solidarity, Coyote would never know, because he was gone, running into the trees.

Dead insects in his eyes. The flies. He ran harder, choking, feeling them inside his shirt. He stooped and grabbed the broken radio/transmitter without a misstep. And he was running again. The branches whapping against his head gave him moments of relief before the flies came back, chewing on his skin as he ran, swooping into his lungs. He kept thinking about June bugs — big and metallic.

The site and its escape route, like those of his other forays, had been mapped out; however, there was still the run through the bush to the highway.

The branches. The flies. More branches. More flies. Then he was clawing at the Jeep door, tossing the dead transmitter onto the seat, and leaping in after it, Tom, behind the wheel, gaping blankly at him.

Coyote, angered by the stupid expression on Tom's face — and annoyed that he held such anger — discovered his thoughs had fixed on two lines by Emerson:

> *But in the mud and scum of things*
> *There always, always something sings.*

It was Coyote's most successful ecotage. He'd accidentally stumbled onto a political battle that was taking place in the Native village downriver. It was soon discovered that the chief and several members of the band council had received kickbacks from the logging contractor, a surprising detail unearthed during the arguments over who should pay for rebuilding the bridge. The battered but now reorganized environmentalists returned to the melee, and with the help of villagers who'd always regarded the logging site as sacred, managed to create a legal mess that led to the development of a tourism and nature centre, and the stranding of the multinational contractor with a valid provincial timber lease but no road access, making logging unviable.

Like every victory, though, it had its repercussions, five loggers, including the three in the truck at the bridge — two of them natives from the village — died in a small plane crash following the closure of the camp. Flying up to their next show, they never made it through a foggy night.

The village, after the arrests of the crooked council members, held a new election, and a sacred dance to celebrate the protection of its homeland, which gave the national television crews good film footage — a pair of gawky, redheaded environmentalist twins clumsily dancing out the new names bestowed on them by the tribe, Frog Catcher and Bear Boy, and although they had nothing to do with the ecotage, they were the first ones to be dubbed Sons of Coyote by the national press.

Unfortunately, the village's jinx wasn't over. The celebration was marred by the death of one teenage partier and the permanent brain damage of another after they overdosed on an lethal combination of glue and ethyl alcohol.

The blackflies? Unaware of the tumult around them, they continued building their over-crowded slums, blissfully laying eggs along the riverbanks of the wilderness.

10 Sweet Dreams, Dead Dogs

A THING ON THE RAMP — INANIMATE, BUT MOVING, limbless, ascending heavily — a dream, an idea, a lumpy mass that floated, yet bent the wooden incline with its weight. It was the rock, or was it his death? God and judgement. Brian lay frozen in the bunk, pinned by the enormity of the world, and he knew if he didn't move he'd die.

The thing was real, unbreathing, alive, approaching, while the invisible pressure on his chest held him down. I'm going to die if it touches me. He was thinking like a neglected child inventing superstitions: if I step on the third crack in the sidewalk I will disappear down it — or the time he'd forced himself to remember a red sunset, fearing he'd die as soon as he forgot that sunset, and worse, never know that was why his heart ceased beating.

The door creaked and the presence entered the treehouse, the floor sagging. Think of something. Wake up; if you don't, you'll die in your sleep. Try oceans. A sailboat silhouetted on the glinting water at the river mouth, a torrent of lime-coloured river boiling under a bridge, a wet shoe wedged in the riprap, and a piece of blue cloth unwinding in the water like an eel. No, don't go there . . .

The figure swelled before him, rising above the cot. It had a wide-brimmed straw hat and was a lot skinnier now. Yesterday's paranoia overwhelmed him. The crazy old man would shoot him while he slept! He struggled to move, despite the heaviness on his chest.

"Wake up, boy; how am I supposed to sleep with you carrying on?"

He focused on Charlie. There wasn't a gun. "I had a nightmare."

"Think I was going to shoot you in your bed?"

Brian jerked upright. The weight had gone. It was still dark. Beyond the window the last of the stars shone above the silhouetted trees. "Your rock was alive, coming to kill me — my death was on the ramp."

"The rock?"

"No, maybe not. It was big. I don't know."

The old man lit a stubby candle. The glow illuminated his face as the cabin filled with shadows. Charlie sat down. When he spoke, his voice was pensive. "I'm a crazy old man. Too much history. There's a spirit in this place."

"A spirit?"

"It comes differently. The first time, I awoke and there was a pressure on my chest; invisible bricks were being piled on me, one after the other. It was near dawn. I managed to get up, and staggered to the door. There was a thing in the garden, I don't know what, and the clearing was full of dead dogs, thousands of them, everywhere, in the garden, the meadow, all the way to the almond trees. Only one was alive, my dog, the one I'd owned before I realized no-one can own living animals.

Yes, the yard was full of dead dogs, his border collie among them, only alive, wounded. Charlie, like most of us, immediately placed himself there. It's one of the graces of our minds, this ability to see ourselves among the wounded.

"It was pitiful — the expression on the dog's face. And there was a creature on the ramp; big and dark, coming for me. I couldn't keep my eyes from the dogs, and my dog among them, but I knew if I didn't break away the thing on the ramp would reach me, and I'd die. I was paralysed. It advanced closer. Then I fell back from the rail, through the door, and woke up in the daylight; there was nothing around. Everything was the way it always is."

"It sounds closer to guilt than spirits," Brian said.

"Aren't they the same?"

"No."

"We'll see about that."

As dawn approached the sky grew radiant beyond the trees, a saffron halo blending into the lavender stratosphere. The hues were too intense to be real — a fake, hallucinatory sunrise. The men grew silent, witnessing the spectacular arrival of daylight while the candle guttered. Brian's attention shifted to Charlie's hat. Did he sleep with it on his head, or had he been up already?

Charlie nodded as the last of the stars faded. "Time for breakfast, I'd say."

"What are we eating, or dare I ask? Arsenic muffins and carrot juice?" Brian felt better, ready for the game again.

"Granola with milk."

"I should have guessed. Milk? Animal fluids?"

"I have my weaknesses."

"I thought you were a vegan. Wearing no animal products, or eating them. But you use honey, too, now that I think about it." There were also cast-iron frying pans, one large and two small matched pans, hanging on the wall near the stove. Did that mean the occasional fried egg? "If you really believed in leaving animals alone, you wouldn't use them — only vegetables."

Exasperated, Charlie marched down the ramp, Brian following him to the shed beneath the treehouse. "Vegetables?" Charlie said. "That's discrimination, too — why should we only eat vegetables — because they can't think? Vegans are also swine, righteously abusing beautiful, growing things. Me, every time I sink my teeth into a lettuce leaf, I can hear it scream." He opened the door to the shed under the treehouse. It was impossible to tell if he was joking or not.

Despite the dirt floor and only one window, the shed was cosy and cool. "I hide out here in the summer when it's too hot upstairs." The room was adorned with a few psychedelic posters from the sixties, the window sill arranged according to the Island Rococo school of ornament — old bottles, seashells, prisms, and a cymbidium orchid in perfect bloom, as if it had been bought at a florist. There was a rickety table in front of the window and the overgrown salmonberry bushes outside — a chair, a cot — an old fridge against the wall, humming intrusively, its noise irritating and out of place.

Beside the fridge was a workshop, packed with enough hand tools to rebuild the island. When Charlie saw Brian studying them, he said: "I used to love the mechanical world, still do a little. I'm teaching the neighbour's boy, Festus, a few things, basic car repair, but my heart ain't in it any more." Charlie opened the nearly empty fridge. "I get the milk from a local farm, not a factory farm. They treat their animals well, I suppose, but I know what you're thinking."

"Chlorofluorocarbons." Brian nodded at the fridge. "Doing our bit for the ozone layer, are we?"

"Keep talking like that and you'll be sleeping down at the ferry terminal. Someone threw it away. Must have bought a new fridge. There's enough stuff in this island's garbage dump to keep an entire village going in India for a year. Now you'll tell me that's a racist statement. Right?"

"Actually, I was wondering where you get your electricity. I didn't see any lines along the driveway."

"I got my own system." Charlie opened the back door of the shed and walked out to the solar collector array, the milk jug in his hand. He lifted one of the lids, and Brian peered inside — rows of ceramic batteries were inter-wired together.

"I've been working on this forever, improving the array, trying different electrolytes. It kept Elvira, she's a local potter, busy for a year creating the cases; she needs the money, though she got bored making them. They're more efficient than your standard battery. Bulk produced, they could make solar power competitive with oil, especially combined with the new inverters being built these days."

"I don't understand. People have been working on this for years. If these batteries are that good why haven't you told anyone about them? You could make millions."

Charlie put down the lid and sat on it, balancing the milk bottle on his thigh, running a finger slowly up and down the condensation. "I don't need money. Cripes, I spend too much time figuring out how to get rid of what I've got."

"If not for the money; then what about the environment? They could do more than Coyote did in ten years of sabotage. I thought you were an environmentalist?"

"All in good time. Besides, I distrust the gadgets we invent. The more we make, the more we wreck things. We're a consumer society being consumed by its need to consume. I want to think about these a while longer before I release them."

"But you might die, and them with you."

"I've got no intention on dying yet, or do you want to hurry that along?"

"You're a strange one, Charlie. You've got power, a fridge, a top-of-the-line stereo, yet you use candles and kerosene for light?"

"I have an aesthetic argument with light bulbs. I enjoy music and milk."

"How do these batteries work?"

"I'll explain that later, maybe; if you can learn to keep your mouth shut. Artists sure are nosy."

"You have to know everything in order to understand everything."

"I'd say you've got your work ahead of you." Charlie gently wagged the milk bottle at him, and got up and walked back to the treehouse.

As they ate breakfast, the parrot winged through the open window, landing on the table beside Charlie. Imperiously, it stamped up to his bowl of granola and began to drag it away as if the cereal were its deserved booty. Charlie raised an eyebrow, the bird ignored him. There was a brief tug-of-war. Finally, the old man stood up and took another ceramic bowl from the shelf behind the stove, into which he dumped a sprinkle of granola before placing it, dry, in front of the bird. The parrot cackled ungraciously and began gulping down its breakfast.

"None of us, including him," Charlie said between spoonfuls of cereal, "have all our switches operating. Makes for variety I suppose, though it's irritating. We think we're important — people — because we've got a few switches animals don't have. Speech. Logic. We use them to create empires and slave-built pyramids and atom bombs. Our extra functions cause us more trouble than they're worth. I'm jealous of this bird, you know. And the rock, too. Sometimes, I want to be like the rock. No switches at all, alive, a real yet non-sentient being, filled with what rockness is.

Hey, let's have some fun! I agree with Charlie. Completely! I intend to be the first (human) leader of the Rock Liberation Movement. Rockism will become a thing of the past. Already, I am planning my campaign and gathering supporters. First, we will attempt to instill rock consciousness in people. We will make rock posters and postcards, take over podiums at public events so that we can announce our program. If people disagree with us, we will throw rocks at them. We will create funds for retired (the oldest ones in the world) rocks. Eventually, we might convince governments to set aside rock sanctuaries, where rocks can live undisturbed by people. And man-child, I could be serious. After all, this is my story, not yours.

"Now you, you're an artist, or so you say, trying to write and understand everything, but your world is so limited. You have to make it suitable to people, you have to control point-of-view and authorial voice and all the other claptrap everyone demands in a novel."

Charlie's blue eyes fixed on Brian's forehead. "But can you write a story where a rock is one of the main characters? Bore the audience, it would. Who's interested in a novel about a rock? Everybody wants gossip; they want to be told what they already know so they can feel better or worse off, only in a new way. That's the single thrill of great literature. Everything has to be from a human point of view. As smart as we are we can't understand anything else. We've all got switches missing."

Abruptly, Brian jabbed at the parrot with his spoon, as if trying to change the subject. The startled bird stood back, head erect, hissing. It grabbed the spoon with a speed that surprised Brian, and he jerked it back. "Well, his self-defence switch sure is working."

"My brother had a switch missing, a big one. It got forgotten when he was born. The lights were on but nobody was home. Still, there was brilliance in his body. He knew karate, studied it from childhood, moved like a dream, yet a beautiful body alone is useless against guns and computers — against intelligence."

Brian flashed the spoon at the parrot again. Although its head was in the bowl, it was wary. It jerked upright, pretending it was six-foot tall, wings slightly spread, ready for battle.

Charlie ignored their game. "You might say he was a dinosaur. Actually, we're all dinosaurs, and we think this beautiful, spinning planet was made solely for us, our little oyster; so we murder the animals, the trees, the fish, and call it harvesting — a farm — where we judge the vigour of our society not by our physical and mental health or by our ability to live without damage, but by our gross national product — the growth of the tumour called the human race spreading across the planet's skin."

I have a special fondness for that term — gross national product. My Oxford dictionary has several definitions for the word gross. This is one of them: "Big-bodied, corpulent, burly. Hence, overfed, unwholesomely fat and corpulent . . ."

"We're going to receive a surprise, one day soon. We're defying the laws of thermodynamics — we can't expand forever. What's the matter, did I turn you off your granola?"

So what's new about this story? Nothing. The news is that there's nothing new. We just keep committing the same crimes again and again.

Brian stirred the cereal thoughtfully. "I'm waiting for you to tell me it's full of pesticides." As soon as he said pesticides, he realized he'd made a fatal error. 'Oh no, I've set him off again!'

The old man can complain all he wants. We will continue to eat our plastic cereal in the morning, won't we?

"Naw, it's organic, certified, even though that doesn't mean much any more. The organic farms have to contend with residues and float-downs, dioxins and PCBs in the water, acid rain, and so on. We consume about four billion pounds of pesticides a year — it goes into the land and us. We're so full of poison your mother's milk should be illegal.

"And do you want to know something else? Eighty percent of our pesticides are made out of oil products. We're farming with oil now, eating it, living amid it, burying ourselves in the rubbish heap of oil packaging. It's the devil's excrement, and we're the oil people, converting petroleum to food and shelter and transportation."

An aging, bitter Robinson Jeffers, one of America's great poets was ready for Armageddon by the end of his life. In a poem he said the only permanent values on earth are the moon and the rocks and the tide. He was willing to accept the rest being nuked, and life having to start over again.

"We want to manufacture everything, including plants and animals — make pigs that don't crap, put frog genes in potatoes, pesticides inside canola. Imagine that — your food a pesticide. A variety of rice becomes extinct every three hours? Why? Because we only cultivate the latest hybrids. That leaves the new, improved strains open to every odd virus and bug that comes by; the devastation can be far worse than in the old days of genetic diversity. The factory farming of our so-called green revolution creates nothing but plagues of locusts and viruses."

We're like horses. The grass is greener beyond the fence. Only we burn our fields behind us in our desperation to improve on the natural world. And Charlie is like a great old horse, refusing to accept our destructive nature. He's bitter because he still believes. He still believes. And so do I.

Brian suddenly lunged at the parrot, but the bird moved so fast it yanked the spoon out of his fingers. It performed a little mock victory dance while twirling the spoon before flinging it across the table. Then it glared defiantly at him and said: "Bad bird."

Charlie refused to be stopped by their antics. "We put lye on our carrot crops because it kills weeds but not carrots. Some farmers use diesel fuel. Then we eat the carrots. Next, we're going to nuke our foods with low level radiation. I knew a guy who got sores on his hands picking apples in a commercial orchard. There was so much pesticide coating their skins. Our food is packed with artificial flavours, preservatives, pesticides, fungicides, residues, colour enhancers, additives, shape-keeping junk, vitamin enrichers, shelf-life prolongers — crap! And meat, who'd want to eat that nowadays? The chickens are fed pellets made with animal bones and rancid fat, their own chicken shit, poisoned grains, and occasionally, mercury-contaminated fish, Do you know how many growth hormones and steroids and antibiotics have been put in chicken pellets over the years?"

This made Brian recall the time a friend talked him into eating horse feed. Years ago. The stuff was supposed to be better than anything in the supermarket. It had every vitamin and hormone and antibiotic in existence. That was when those items were assumed to be good for you. He'd eaten only a handful of the mare-stud-plus, but he soon developed a fever, and spent the night in his room, dreaming of giant erections.

"Those poor chickens, the layers," Charlie continued, almost breathless now, "they must be permanently stoned eating that stuff. Then they're kept in cages so small they can't turn around, their beaks cut off so they won't psychotically peck each other to death, their trapped feet growing right into the metal cage wire."

Charlie's rant makes me remember a friend who once said to me "Every city is full of the cry of dying animals." It's a background noise to our lives. Just think, when you wake in the morning, of the despair, the torture. Hundreds of thousands of chickens, alive, hanging by their feet, waiting to have their throats cut.

"You *are* trying to put me off my feed, aren't you?" Brian asked, examining a spoonful of cereal. "I don't enjoy granola in the first place!" Something darted across the window sill, catching the attention of Brian and the parrot. Was that a mouse?

Charlie sighed. His face was red, and he sagged into his chair. His voice grew slower, almost morose. "A few years ago, I wandered into one of those fancy supermarkets — miles of foodstuffs under fluorescent lights."

His eyes seemed to fade into his head, shrinking. "I thought I'd check for bugs. It occurred to me that I hadn't seen a bug in food for years. So I wandered down the rows, examining the broccoli, the lettuce, the radishes — everything. I couldn't find an insect. There wasn't a living animal in the store, not counting the ones pushing their shopping carts around, and I wouldn't eat them. They looked so unhealthy, fat, their pasty skin full of pimples.

"Finally, two clerks showed up, and ushered me out of the building, threatened to phone the police because I was fondling the cantaloupes, or whatever . . . I tried to explain why there were no bugs in the store. I asked them to imagine the magnitude of the poisons that were being used to kill every single insect. They weren't interested. I'm just a crazy old man."

The parrot, still-excited after its mock battle with Brian and then the sudden appearance of the mouse, decided it needed more attention. It hooked the rim of its now-empty bowl with its beak, jerked sideways and heaved it off the table. It shattered on the floor with a finality that made everyone pay attention. The parrot, Charlie, and Brian gazed over the table's rim at the fragments. "Aw no," the parrot said, and began to cackle.

"I don't think the parrot appreciates your speeches."

"Old Congo has his opinions." Charlie bent down and picked up the remnants. The parrot laughed.

"I thought he had no name."

"I have no idea if he thinks he's got a name or not. I call him Congo, because that's how we label his variety. He's an African Grey Congo."

"So when are you going to tell me about the sabotages? The things you did. I'd like to start with the first one. The mill and the cobalt."

"Don't worry, you'll get your story."

"Roll that rock!" the parrot screamed. It was that time again.

* * *

While Charlie wrestled with the rock, Brian wandered about the meadow, frustrated. This morning had been hopeless. The old guy was fooling with him, trying to drive him away with his stupid lectures. And he wanted to strangle that insane parrot. Brian had pulled a thin book down from the shelves, in case he wanted to read, but his heart wasn't there, so the book remained scrunched up in his pocket. It was a limited edition; he'd have to sneak it back onto the shelf later. The bird had also wandered off into the nearby bushes.

Pulling out his cigarettes, Brian realized he was smoking his last pack. Sixteen cigarettes. It was important that he not break the spell and leave to buy stupid cigarettes. If he limited himself to five a day, he could last for three days; but, at the rate Charlie was twisting him around, he'd never get to the story. This could take a month. Then again, Brian hadn't really come for a story. He wanted more than that.

He had no guilt over deceiving Coyote. He was more mortified by the cigarettes — the sad expression on Charlie's face when he'd pulled out the pack yesterday. "What you do to your body is your business, but I won't have it in my house."

How strange to be talking with an ecological terrorist, demanding purity, while concealing his own life. What would Charlie say when he told him the truth? "The horror." The phrase had haunted him since he read *Heart of Darkness.* "The horror." I'm a liar. I'm a monster. *Monster.* that was the title of the book in his pocket, an earnest tract by an unknown poet attempting to understand what made people go sick — probably got a grant to write it. Then it sold a few hundred copies and was never seen again. Brian had wanted to write like that years ago.

There was no reason to be here except for cellular necessity — his body brought him. Thinking about it was too confusing. He'd always followed his body's commands before, so why should he stop now? He pulled out the slim edition and it fell open at a prose poem:

"God must be a frog, must be little things inside the eye and outside the needle. God must be flies. He must relish the carnivores, love diving beetles, and praise the snake. God must be evil to love decaying teeth and rotting kidneys, the grotesque scream of a snow rabbit just before it dies . . . "

"Hell." Brian stuffed the book back in his pocket. In the garden, he noticed several rough, home-made chairs. The old man must sit here a lot, overlooking the vegetables and the ocean beyond. The rustic simplicity was as idyllic as Brian could imagine, outside of a reclining chair on a Caribbean beach with a Pina Colada on a side table.

"So what kind of book are you planning to write?" Charlie's voice startled him. The old man walked softly.

A lost earthworm wandered across the surface of the path before disappearing beneath a leaf stalk. "A simple story, I suppose — narratives of the more notorious sabotages, maybe interspersed with our conversations in a weird house on a fictional island — leading up to where you died near Chicago, in ChemCity."

"Where I died?"

"The body in the cement — the one they said was the dead Coyote. Who was it?"

"You won't learn anything until you learn how to listen, and your story doesn't sound like it has much of a plot."

"Don't worry, there'll be a plot."

Charlie bent over, flicking a dead alder-leaf off an endive, and hesitated for a moment; then he began:

"My name is Coyote, and I'm a killer. It didn't start out that way, it never does. And murder was not in my thoughts nearly twenty years ago . . . "

***

After a while, Charlie became silent. He'd ended up sitting with Brian on the bench in the garden for so long that his knees crackled as he dragged himself to his feet. "That's enough history. I'll tell you more later. Let's go for a walk. You look like you could use a little exercise, and my legs need to keep working, otherwise they freeze up." He surveyed the horizon, the low sun. "Dusk is best for walking. That's when the forest really begins to breathe."

They went down a narrow path into the darkening trees, following a marshy, creek bed. Decaying skunk cabbages. Old man's beard dangling from the big leaf maples, overwhelming silence. A lone western tanager called hauntingly before fading away. The silence grew like a mould. "The only thing I can hear breathing is me," Brian said as he stepped over a rotting log across the path.

"City boys!" Charlie hopped back and forth across the log like a gymnast playing with a sawhorse at a track meet. His knees had obviously loosened up.

"How does a forest breathe?" Brian asked

"Why don't you ask it."

"It wouldn't answer."

"That's because you're a city boy. You have to listen."

They continued down the trail, the cedar growing taller, the forest darker. "What will it say to me when I learn to listen?"

"You've got millions of questions." Charlie stopped again, inhaling the sweet, cedar fragrance. "And no answers."

"What will it say?" Brian insisted.

"To you, nothing. An absolutely perfect rock-like nothing."

"Where are we going?"

"Christ, all these questions. Shut up and quit boring me. We aren't going anywhere." They reached the foot of an octopus cedar, its enormous roots almost surrounding them. It was creepy. They sat down and Charlie pulled a wadded up paper bag of trail mix out of his back pocket, offering it to Brian who peered inside before he refused. Charlie shrugged and munched away on the mixed nuts and dried fruits.

The roots of the monster tree were like prison bars. Brian thought the forest was unnaturally quiet, but that was a stupid thought. 'How can a forest be unnatural?' The tranquillity was broken only by Charlie's occasional rummage through the paper bag as he searched for choice bits. Brian relaxed, in a sheltered mood. There was a sudden flapping by his head. The parrot, out of nowhere, landed beside them and glared. "Okay, where's my cookie?" Sticking out its neck defiantly it studied the pair, daring them to make a dangerous gesture. "Where's my cookie?"

Charlie tossed him the paper bag. "I think he's clairvoyant. He always knows when I'm eating." The parrot harummphed; then peered inside. Before long, its entire body was engulfed by the bag as it ate and scratched and fidgeted within.

Charlie couldn't resist giving the bag a nudge with the toe of his boot. The bag went still; then, like a snake, its head curving out of the bag, the parrot peered at them. "Fuck off," it said.

Brian watched the bird disappear back into the bag. "It can think, can't it? It can think."

"Sure, everything can think, but how, or in what way, or why, now there's a question. It's smart. It even knows grammar. If you ask it 'Do you want a cookie?' it'll say 'I want a cookie.' It's done some saucy stunts on me — so wise they're hard to describe. That little pea-brain might be small, yet most of the switches are working." He climbed to his feet and picked up the paper bag, parrot and all. The parrot squawked and flew out like a partridge flushed from cover, perching on a nearby cedar limb.

"Where's my cookie?" it asked.

Charlie ignored it, stuffing the bag into his pocket and walking down the trail. "You better not have shit on my trail mix, bird."

Brian took one last glance back at Congo, who studied him plaintively. "Cookie?" Its voice was polite and sad.

"Don't worry," Charlie said, "he ain't hungry. He's just a natural beggar."

They reached a ravine beside a clearing and followed its fern-spotted bank, their trail marked for several minutes by the lonesome cries of "Cookie?" echoing through the forest. After a while, as if out of boredom, the cries developed variety. "Cookie nookie?" "Cookie . . . honey?" "I want a cookie!" "Yoooohhhhoooo, coooooookieeee?" Gradually, they faded as the men left the bird behind.

The crest of the ravine was thick with foxgloves: pastel, red, white, purple, the multitude of spires reflecting the sunlight falling through the gap in the deep forest. "Ah," Charlie said, "what a sight. Doesn't it make your heart stop?"

They soon found themselves winding through a nasty patch of devil's club. There was one last, distant cry that sounded like: "You asshole." They didn't hear from the parrot again.

Brian was having trouble keeping up with the old man, and he resented it. There was a mushroom beside the path, red, with nutlike extrusions on its surface. The shaman's mushroom. He stopped. Its potential for hallucination and coma threw him into a different world, a trance. 'Take me down,' he wanted to say.

The old man was behind him abruptly, like a ghost, and his arms were pinned to his side. He wasn't surprised by the strength of the grip. Charlie whispered in his ears. "Now, listen! What can you hear?"

Brian shivered, and hated himself, his fright, his fear of being murdered — of having his back broken by the robust grip of an old man. He listened. Silence. He knew he had to speak. "The wind, I can hear the wind." The crushing pressure and the fear made him wonder if this is what strychnine was like. There was a snort behind his ear, and his arms were released. The old man strode past him, down the trail. Brian followed, humiliated.

And then they were standing in the meadow, the setting sun glazing the branches around the treehouse with gold. They'd travelled in a circle.

11

Cops and Islanders

FIRST ON AND LAST OFF THE FERRY, Janwar drove up to the store beside the terminal. He parked among an assortment of beat-up Volvos, a Mercedes, several SUVs displaying American plates, and pickups decorated with cedar panelling and psychedelic paintings of angels and aliens. A crowd of tourists and locals were clustered about a hamlet of driftwood-garnished huts and craft tables dwindling into the arbutus grove overlooking the harbour.

In time he would learn that this area contained the only hot food vendors, grocery store, and source of newspapers on the island, and was affectionately nicknamed 'Mecca' by the locals.

A white peacock draped itself lazily over a dock piling, its tail feathers dangling out of reach of two children who leaped for them. The peacock, safe on its perch, gazed curiously down at their antics, reminding Janwar of his dead father — the icy distance of his regal gaze — a poor but proud man with a rich faith.

He entered the grocery store. Perhaps there would be coffee inside. He'd left at 3 A.M. so he could make the long drive to Sweet Water and catch the morning ferry. The only other one was late in the afternoon.

"Hello," he said to the tall gray-haired woman fussing with a clump of everlasting flowers beside the cash register. "Can you tell me how to reach The Last Resort. I have a reservation there. The owner informed me it wasn't difficult to find." He glanced around. No coffee.

"Sure isn't. Drive down the Low Road until you see the sign — a big, carved log with an eagle rising above it. If you come to road construction, you've passed it. They're ripping up the asphalt again. It keeps sliding into the ocean. Maybe after that we can talk them into fixing this chute off the High Road leading down to here. It's a death trap. Would you like to sign our petition?"

"Certainly." Janwar believed in safe roads. He'd spent two years on highway detail before he was transferred to homicide. He'd seen enough tragedy caused by bad road construction.

The raggy bundle of papers she pushed towards him contained hundreds of names and addresses. Briefly, he scanned the heading, which made sense, filled in the line near the bottom of the last page, and passed it back.

Janwar thought her a singularly striking woman, long-faced with gentle eyes. Despite the fact she appeared barely forty, a thick braid of grey hair fell down her back, reaching to her thigh. In the braid hung a few exotic feathers, peacock and ostrich, and a white one. An eagle feather? The rare bald eagles were said to be common on the gulf islands. The woman, however, wore a too-tight black sweater. She had large, astonishingly round and erect breasts. It was difficult not to stare at them.

"You wouldn't know if there's an older man named Charlie, living on the island . . . ?"

She studied him bemusedly. "You have any reason to be looking for this Charlie Whatever? We've certainly got a Charlie or two, though most aren't old."

"I only need to ask him a few questions. I'm a RCMP officer."

Her eyes narrowed. Janwar instantly regretted volunteering that information.

The doorbell jangled. A grizzled old man wandered over to the near-empty bread counter. His clothes were filthy, stained with what looked like blood. He sported an odd Fu Manchu moustache that gave him the air of a geriatric biker, and he stank. "No delivery from that inept bakery again, June?" He gave a hopeless grin.

"I guess they missed the morning ferry. Try tomorrow. Jake, I wish you'd change when you come in here after you've been slaughtering lambs. You stink like an abattoir. You'll scare my vegetarian customers away."

"Damn, I had a craving for cinnamon buns. No time to change. Gotta go back and do three more lambs. Big delivery coming up. Been at it since 5 A.M. I need a sugar hit."

"I thought I saw Ruth arrive with fresh baking an hour ago. Try her stand."

"Oh great. Maybe she made that cinnamon raisin bread." He started towards the door and June returned her attention to Janwar.

"So, you're a cop. First one on the island for months."

The old man's head swivelled.

"Well, I'm mostly a researcher. Where could I find this Charlie fellow?'

"Actually, now that I think about it I can't actually recall any older Charlie. I'm sure there must be one on the island. We got Jims and Georges and Alberts, all kinds of men. Too many, if you asked me. At least the younger ones have better names. Torah . . . Laxton . . . Alias . . . Festus . . . Crispin . . . more modern; they suit the island. Peacock Jim has a cousin living with him, on second thought, Charlie Lever — he's in his early twenties. Hey Jake, you know any Charlie?"

Jake had froze with his hand on the door. "Nope. And if I did, I wouldn't give the address to any goddamned, fucking cop."

Janwar interrupted. "I thought you said there were lots . . . "

"That was before you told me you were a cop. Now Jake, don't start on your swearing in here."

"What's with that towel on your head, eh? Is that part of a fancy new uniform? Hell, the cunts are taking over the world."

"Jake!"

"Sorry, June. But we don't need any cops on this island, especially darkies." The old man wrenched the door open and stomped outside in his gumboots.

"I'm dreadfully sorry," June said, aghast. Her mouth hung open for a moment, making her face even longer, horsey. "This is awful. Oh, I'm so sorry. I . . . I . . . I . . . He's an old man. I didn't mean it to go this far. I didn't think. A police officer shot his son after a drunken brawl at his farm several years ago. And I guess he's never forgiven. How terrible; such filth out of his mouth."

"I've encountered this before. I'm used to it. It doesn't bother me." He wanted to get out of the shop as gracefully as possible. He noticed, through the window, Jake speaking to a younger man who was staring inside at them. Then the younger man walked back to the cluster of food stands. That's it, Janwar thought, everyone will know. The old man climbed into his beat-up truck and drove off.

"You can be sure I'll speak to him about his behaviour."

"Thank you very much. It's really not necessary."

"I think it is."

"No, it's nothing. Don't worry about it." Janwar slid out of the store, smiling inanely.

He swung open his car door angrily, and found himself slipping on a mushy plum on the road as he fell against the door, slamming it, his thumb slipping off the old-fashioned button handle. He jerked it open and climbed in and sat simmering behind the wheel, slamming the door shut again. His thumb hurt like hell. Had he caught it in the door? He started the ignition, watching the blood ooze out from under the thumbnail.

***

June sat with a thump on the stool behind her cash register, catching her hair under her bottom and accidentally yanking her head back so hard it hurt her neck. The final straw. She almost cursed.

She picked up the phone and dialled The Last Resort. "Hello Wren? Is that you?"

Wren was confused by the question. "Of course it's me. How nice of you to call."

"It's nice talking to you as well. Do you know you have a plainclothes cop staying at your place?

"A cop? I had no idea, but if it's the man who booked for today, he's a friend of an old university buddy who joined the RCMP. He didn't tell me he was a cop when he made the booking."

"That's not the worst of it. He's looking for Charlie Baker. I don't know what's going on up there. First Charlie has that writer fellow arriving and staying on; then he's got a cop looking for him."

"You should phone Elvira and she'll send Festus over to tell Charlie right away."

"You're right. It was just terrible. Jake came in when he was here and insulted him. Not only for being a cop, you know how Jake hates the police, but for being dark-skinned. I never heard such filth come out of Jake's mouth. And I feel so guilty because I started it, blurting out he was a cop. I was humiliated. The fellow's wearing a turban. I suppose he's a Hindu."

"Or a Sikh?"

"Whatever. This was just awful. I feel so stressed out. Janwar Singh is his name. Nice man, actually. He signed my petition."

"Yes, that's my guest. Singh is a Sikh name. Now June, don't get upset over this incident. You know how stress disturbs your yin-yang balance, and your stomach goes sour. Perhaps you should meditate."

"You're right. I'll close up the shop for a break, and go recite my mantra in the arbutus grove."

"That's a wonderful idea. I'll come down later in the afternoon and smudge the store for you, to clear the vibrations."

"Thanks a lot. I saw Jake talking to young Laxton outside the door, so I'm sure all Mecca knows about this by now."

"We'll deal with Jake later. Before you do your mantra, you should phone Boomer, too."

Pearl Baginski, known affectionately by the locals as Boomer Baggins, The Lady Of The Rings — a three-foot-wide, older Polish woman lived up at North Point. She had a cheap, loud, and tinny-sounding phone, plus her voice automatically went into ear-bending pitch whenever she picked up the receiver. The gossip that a cop had arrived would allow her to deafen half the island with great moral purpose. She could be very useful in times of emergency.

"Okay, I'll call her up. He should be at your place in a few minutes. Talk to you later."

"I'll be expecting him, and I'll see you in the afternoon."

* * *

By the time Janwar arrived at the carved cedar sign with the elegant eagle taking flight above the words THE LAST RESORT, he felt calmer, though his throbbing thumb, wrapped in his once-white handkerchief was trickling blood onto the steering wheel.

He drove down the winding, salal-lined driveway, unaware that the phones were going wild across the island. All the unlicensed and unroadworthy vehicles were tucked behind houses. The casual marijuana growers packed their potted plants to hidden locations, or screened them from driveways and entrances (The professional growers had mostly made the switch to indoor grow rooms). The few gun fanatics on the island pulled down their 3-D targets so no cop would think about checking for exotic, unregistered firearms.

A neighbour sauntered down to the nude beach, only fifty feet from the road, and let the sunbathers know. It was still early in the day so few were about. A family, grumbling, went home for their bathing suits, but the others just dusted off their blankets and shut their eyes, absorbing the sun. One man defiantly cracked a beer, and insisted on his right to nakedness. "Screw the cops." The nude beach had long been notorious for its ability to generate radical political action on any issue.

Three miles from The Last Resort the local moonshine maker turned off his still. That way the odour wouldn't carry, much to the joy of his neighbour who was getting fed up with the stink. Within a few hours, the island had become an upstanding and semi-legal community.

The driveway ended at a knoll of sparsely treed meadowland where eccentric shacks and cabins nestled among scattered arbutus trees bent back from the sea by years of winter storms. The meadow was alive with butterflies. There were flowers everywhere — cosmos, nasturtiums climbing up the walls of the cabins, and a large, formal herb bed — a knot garden — an incongruous nucleus for the rustic buildings. As soon as Janwar opened his car door the thick scent of the flowers and herbs made him think of Punjab, that foreign and often dreamed country where he was born, yet could not remember. Would it smell like this?

There was an ornate sign pointing to a door in a small adobe-style building: CENTER OF THE UNIVERSE. He didn't know what to do about his still-bleeding thumb so he held it behind his back. He had to get to his cottage as soon as possible and tend to it. This must be the office. He opened the Javanese screen door and stepped inside.

A thin woman with short and curly black hair sat on an Oriental cushion like a pasha, reading a book. She had the greyest skin that Janwar had ever seen, and was beautiful in that chiselled, almost elfin look Irish women can have — the ashy skin fascinated yet unnerved him, contrasting so strangely with her dark eyes and lips.

"Hi. You must be our guest, Janwar," she said, setting her book down and uncoiling from the cushion, "I'm Wren."

"Janwar Singh," he mumbled, so enchanted he was at a loss for words. Instinctively, he stuck out his hand for her to shake, only it was wrapped in the bloody handkerchief.

"You've hurt yourself?"

Janwar was aghast, confused. "Yes, I'm sorry. I don't understand how I did it. I caught my thumb in my car door."

"Let me see." She took his hand in hers, the cool dryness of her fingers touching the inside of his wrist. She unwrapped the handkerchief, and blood dripped onto the floor, oozing out from the thumbnail. His knees buckled.

When Janwar woke up, he was on the cushion. She was holding his hand, painting a dark, medicinal smelling liquid onto his thumb. He looked at her, confused.

"You fainted."

"Oh no." This was truly awful.

"Don't worry, I won't tell." She winked. The tincture stained his skin, and stung as she continued painting. "It's a disinfectant, and a clotter, too. My own special blend. Your thumb will throb for a few days though — you might lose the nail. You caught it hard."

"Yes, I did. I'm so humiliated." If the staff at homicide heard about this, he'd never live it down.

"No one should be humiliated, not ever. All things happen naturally. Besides, June, the owner of the store at the terminal, let me know you were on your way. She told me how terribly Jake behaved. I can sense you've been under stress lately, and an episode like that . . . well, this is understandable."

"Did she inform you I was a police officer as well?"

"Of course. We don't have many police come here."

"I suppose half the island knows by now."

"At least half, I'd expect, if not more," she chirped brightly.

"I'm not really here on business. Kirsten said I should come; that you were an excellent herbalist. The doctors have been useless so far. They just want to give me prescription drugs that don't work."

"I know. You told me when you made your reservation, remember? I'll guide you to your private cabin and we'll talk later when you're feeling better. It might take a day or more to make my diagnosis, but don't worry, in two weeks I'll have you singing under the moon."

"Singing under the moon?"

"It's an expression of mine. Would you like tea? I was having a pot of fine Jasmine Pearly Down when you arrived."

Later, in his cabin, Janwar needed to sit quietly and think for a long time.

His window was facing the knot garden. He was in one of the earliest buildings, which is probably why it had electricity and a phone jack — two items Wren was not keen about, as she explained while discussing the resort layout. Nevertheless, a few of her guests were bound to these umbilical cords, so she'd allowed them to remain, though all the new cabins were woodstove heated, with kerosene lamps for light, even in the winter months.

Janwar's cabin had a sign on it, KWANNON. A calligraphic note on the back of the cedar door explained that Kwannon was the Japanese bodhisattva of compassion, one of those who refused nirvana until everyone else came with her. Sitting on his bed, he watched through the big window as Wren returned to her office. Her blue-jean cutoffs had a big rip over one bare buttock.

Conscious that he'd been staring, he looked away, towards the grassy dunes above the beach where two enormous and naked women stood, intent on creating a sandcastle, their Rubenesque bodies glowing in the sunlight. They'd stop occasionally to peck each other on the mouth or fondle a breast or thigh. He watched them for several minutes. He couldn't take his gaze away. Their innocence intrigued him. It was tender and erotic and childlike.

In the resort's central courtyard, ringed by the odd, architecturally-unique cabins, was an array of twig benches, where a gawky man sat wearing a foil-like futuristic uniform with an exceptionally tall collar, higher than his head — the kind obsessive sun tanners wear to radiate light onto their faces. His skin was dark brown. Janwar asked about him, when Wren appeared at his door again with her smudging paraphernalia.

"That's Bukwa. He's an alien. He was switched with an earthling as a child, and he's been waiting to go back ever since. There's not enough light on this planet, so he finds it necessary to enhance it during the summer months, you know, build up his reservoirs for the winter."

"How amazing."

"He's been coming to the resort for a few years. Unfortunately — I suppose I shouldn't be telling you this, but I just don't believe in secrets, and besides, you being a police officer, I'm sure I can rely on your discretion — he also is having difficulty with the poisons and additives and pesticides levels he's built up from his stay on our planet. He uses my healing room, that's the dome behind the herb garden, for colonic therapy."

"Colonic therapy . . . ?" Janwar began; then went mute. She wasn't fooling around about not believing in secrets.

"Enemas, you know, colon cleansing. He has to keep flushing out the toxins. There's a meter for water in that room. I use it to figure out my costs when an instructor gives workshops on the various techniques and formulas. Well, I'm afraid no one else is using it right now and it's going through forty-seven gallons a day."

"Forty-seven gallons a day! Up his . . . ?"

"Yes. Only him and his companion, Goan Cha, use it. I don't interfere when people develop successful paths for survival. But this is too unhealthy, and I'll have to discuss it with him; but first I thought I'd seek advice from a few, sensible people I can trust, like yourself. I guess I need perspective. You see, it's very hard for me to be judgemental."

"Forty-seven gallons a day of water injected up the buttocks?" Janwar was truly shocked. His policeman's training made him attempt to hide it, but his incredulity leaked out.

"Yes, that's a lot of water, and being an islander . . . water is such a precious commodity in our community . . . I have difficulties with that issue alone."

"I can believe that."

The freeness of her speech, her casual way of studying him, her eyelashes . . . her eyelashes against the grey skin that signified her escape from cancer. He had never known such grace. He was in big trouble.

Janwar had discovered love — as soon as he walked into the office and saw her on that Oriental pillow with her book and tiny jade tea bowl, and now he was trying to sort it out. He knew it was love, immediately. Everything the poets said was true. How strange. Perhaps he should begin reading poetry again.

Wren crushed some herbs, mingling them with dried sweetgrass in a large abalone shell. Then she put fire to it. She held it north. She held it south. She held it east. She held it west. He could see her small breasts through the gauzy, hemp, peasant-style shirt she wore. The lure of her skin was like an addiction. "I know this must seem odd to you, the smudging . . . ," she said. "My guests learn to enjoy it. It retunes the space, sets up a better vibration, it's a cleansing. Really, it means nothing; yet a lot. I smudge many buildings on the island. Healthy thinking can be difficult to achieve, and smudging provides a stimulus."

When she left, the gentle fumes hung behind her, like a suggestion, a lure. He caught himself unconsciously holding his breath. He needed protection. He needed safety. He needed to get out of here. This was beyond awful, it was catastrophic.

She was gone, yet the room, the whole resort was permeated with her. What happened? It had begun two years ago, at least; his stomach, then the headaches. It was almost a whim that brought him to the resort, and now he felt doomed, sitting alone in the cabin, watching the sandcastle builders through the window. Doomed. Absolutely doomed. Here he was on a crazy island, in love with a crazy women he'd only met an hour ago — a woman of another faith, who befriended sad people and tried to heal them.

He wanted to worship her, treat her like a god. At the same time, he wanted to go back to his office. He was a cop. He had his mother and his boss to worry about, and missing women — probably murdered. He should check out of this place immediately. He also thought: "I should like to live beside you until you grow old, or until your cancer takes you from this world."

He thought about Kirsten. Another beautiful women, even more attractive, her catlike awkwardness, the sharp, dark grace of her face, a classic beauty. Wren was harder to define. Spiritual. Why had he been confronted by two desirable women? Why was he so full of aching desire? What was happening to him?

Later, she brought a bowl of fifteen-bean soup from the cookhouse, and it was heavenly, meatless, but full of power. "A soup with power?" That was a thought he wouldn't have had yesterday. Is this how what they called *victimization* occurred? She hadn't made him eat with the others. He knew he'd instantly become a special case, being a police officer. There was so much politics behind his arrival, and within a mere few hours. He ate alone in his cabin, unhappy . . . or maybe not . . .

He savoured his privacy, dwelling on his new memories: the women on the beach, the alien, the soup, the smudging, the colour of his skin next to hers.

Then he plugged his laptop into the phone jack, mousing himself online to where he found SERMUR under the donut shop icon. There was nothing.

He typed: Hello, is anybody there?. Nobody was there. His typing didn't even appear. Where is everybody?

Nothing. Had the server crashed?

The next few days were tranquil, island tranquil. He spent them mostly in his cabin. Intermittently, he walked around. Wren came to visit him often, informing him when mealtimes occurred, that there was no meat served here, no sugar, no alcohol, and no coffee (if he was that desperate, he'd have to drive to Mecca where there was a cappuccino stand among the stalls), that her personal program for his health would become apparent in a few days. For now, he should drink his tea, eat the nutritious healing and cleansing food of the resort, and observe her community in action before developing opinions. He agreed to her rules without complaint.

Once, on Friday night, he heard drumming, screaming. There was a group of men. Most were naked. They were pounding on decorated, handmade drums, and yelling, chanting. He didn't understand much of it. What he did understand made him feel sorry for them, though he couldn't help admiring their candour. He stayed inside his cabin, peeking through the drapes.

He went online again. He soon discovered why the website had been silent. It was closed in memory of one of the founders of the online service, John Kilpatrick. He'd been murdered during a routine investigation, when an informant gave him a wrong address in an apartment complex. He'd surprised a drug deal. The dealer opened the door holding a sawed-off shotgun, saw his uniform and shot him on the spot. Then he also shot the well-known rap star who was buying the drugs — because he thought he was a fink.

Arizona Floyd: There was a notice on the main menu, JS. You must have missed it.

JS: I'm afraid I did.

Abruptly, a man named Arsenal came online, and a terrible fight broke out, as he denounced the other officers for being weaklings and traitors to their skin. It dismayed Janwar to see that sort of junk on a police server and he almost logged off. Then another officer, Tracer, came online and revealed Arsenal was a white supremacist who'd hacked the police network. That amused Janwar. Ah computers . . . Arsenal was disconnected in mid-reply.

Tracer: I logged in with the sysop, and we cut him off. He must have a closet full of phony cop ids. I'll have our people in Minnesota visit him. The sysop said he tracked the guy's new server. This is the second time he cracked us, but it's going to be his last. This line is clean now. Janwar Singh are you still there?

JS: How do you know my full name?

Tracer: Cheevers told us. You sent good information to him. Sorry you had to see that guff from Arsenal. We like a good cop here, whatever his colour.

JS: Thanks. I appreciate hearing that. What's this about Cheevers? I sent him a folder of material not quite two weeks ago, and he was supposed to send me a box of copies of his own files back, but it has never appeared.

Arizona Floyd: I was online when he was on, too. He said you gave him a piece of hot material in that stuff you couriered. He'll have a search warrant imminently.

JS: That's terrific news, though I don't understand it. The stuff I sent was pedestrian. Very minor.

Toad Hollow: He'll probably be faxing you once he has a judge nailed down. Cheevers said he thinks this creep gave his motel room phone number to a hooker. Can you believe that? He must have been desperate for her. She'd written it on her wrist. Enough of it showed faintly in one of the infrared closeups your forensic people made. There was that and a couple matched dates that justified a search warrant.

JS: I am gratified. Cheevers must have exceptionally sharp eyesight. We never noted anything as obvious as a phone number. I await whatever material he has. Thank you for this information. Signing off now.

He was still seated at his desk, focused on the blank screen of the laptop when he became aware of a tapping at the door. "Come in." It was Wren, with another of her infusions.

She placed a tea pot and a raku tea bowl on the table beside the window. "Here's tea for you. Would you like to eat lunch in the common room today?

"No, I don't mean to be rude to your other guests, but this time alone has become invaluable to me."

"That's fine. Don't worry about it. Your state of mind is crucial to wellness, so if you need solitude, you should take it. June phoned from the store at the terminal and told me a parcel addressed to you arrived on the ferry."

"Wonderful. I've been waiting for it. I thought it was lost. Your island is indeed a magical place."

"Not that magical. June said the parcel looks like someone drove a forklift through it. That doesn't mean anything, though. A lot of our stuff comes off the ferry like that. Even old Jake's cinnamon buns on occasion."

"Oh dear."

She sat at the table, pouring him the infusion. "After today, we're changing your program. Sweat baths will help cleanse your system. Have you ever had one?"

"No."

"You'll like it. I'll come for you tomorrow, after I give my Tai Chi workshop. A sweat in the morning and one at night will be sufficient."

For the first bath she arrived sharply at nine in the morning, displaying an almost unnatural cheerfulness which made Janwar sad. He knew how much sorrow can hide behind a smile. It was obvious in her.

They walked through the geometric herb garden. Near the forest's edge he glimpsed several marijuana plants half-hidden behind a flourish of echinaceas.

She saw him become aware of the plants. "Yes, they're what you think they are. It's helpful for nausea, especially for those who've been through chemotherapy. You won't bust me, will you?"

Janwar shook his head, embarrassed. "I don't know what you're talking about. Perhaps I could use instruction in plant identification. I have always felt lacking in the subject."

She nodded shyly and touched his elbow, guiding him into the forest.

They followed a mossy trail beneath evergreens to a pool below a trickling waterfall. Everything was so pristine he was entranced, even more silent than usual.

Perched on a low rock knoll beside the pool was a modest, cedar-shaked structure with smoke uncoiling from its chimney.

"I lit the fire before my Tai Chi class, so it should be ready." She opened the cedar door and a burst of hot air rushed at Janwar as she quickly slammed it shut. "Yup, feels fine."

Casually, she lifted off the print dress and was naked in front of him. Janwar was stunned. He gaped at the darkness of her bush, the thick nipples, the smooth grey stoniness of her skin.

She laughed. "Close your mouth and take off your clothes."

"Take off my clothes?"

"Silly. You can't have a sweatbath with your clothes on."

"Oh." Mortified, he began stripping, looking away from her, gazing at the pool until he was finished.

"Your shorts and turban?" she asked.

"I'm sorry. My turban, it is my religion."

"Even in a bath?"

"No," he laughed, "but in a bath with another . . . "

"Fine." She stepped inside.

There were towels hanging on nails in the exterior wall. As soon as she was inside, Janwar quickly unwrapped his turban, and replaced it with a towel draped over his head. He put his *kirpan* and comb in the orange folds on the twig bench by the door, and stepped inside.

Settling himself in the dim interior, he brushed his hand accidentally against her buttocks. It was difficult not to touch her in the tiny sweathouse. They sat awkwardly, mute, on the bench for several moments, his eyes adjusting to the shadowy light from the small window, grimy with soot and dirt. She leaned over and stuffed several sticks in the stove, clanged the door shut, and picked up a brass ladle which glinting briefly as it caught a shaft of light from the one tiny clear patch in the window. She ladled water from a bucket onto the pile of rocks cradled atop the wood burner.

The steam was choking, and he felt an urge to flee to the cool morning air beyond the door. Fearful of appearing weak, he remained perched stiffly on the bench, listening to the crackle of burning wood.

Soon, he could tolerate the heat, the soggy towel and shorts, the difficulty in breathing.

"You know what's wrong with me, don't you?" he said.

"I believe I do. You have *Candida Albicans*. Stomach yeast. Your intestinal floral has gone violently out of whack. Judging from your symptoms, I'd say it's the worst case I've encountered. You had intensive doses of antibiotics two years ago, didn't you, shortly before your symptoms began?" Her face was so close he could feel her breath when she talked. He wanted to relax and let his thigh touch hers, but couldn't.

"I did. I got pneumonia. I was in the hospital for three weeks."

"And no one suggested you take acidophilus or yogurt, right? Sometimes I can't believe modern medicine. It's a simple problem. Recovery from a case like yours takes a while, but you'll be fine. I'll give you my literature on candida later. That's enough talking for now. Let the steam cleanse you." They sat in silence, until finally she stood up and said: "That's enough for a first sweat. Let's get out of here and jump in the pool. It'll be a shock.

The water's cold but you'll learn to like it." She was gone, the door open behind her.

Her legs kicked up, flashing the split in her bush as she dived into the pool.

After a few seconds, he followed her to the ledge and slid gingerly into the water, the sopping towel still draped over his head.

12

Conversation is a Code

"TREES HAVE AS MANY ABILITIES AS US, only they're different abilities. But we can move and think and use tools, so we 'farm' them. We assume we know more about forests than forests know about being forests . . . what arrogance." Charlie, seated on a bench in the vegetable garden, had just given Brian another account of Coyote, talking himself into a sullen mood as he considered the fate of "wild rocks and trees".

Brian shrugged, admiring the black and yellow caterpillar crawling across his sneaker. On his other foot was a housefly with a tattered wing. Two oddly matched ornaments, like him and Charlie. He wished he could argue with Charlie better. Although he'd overcome his youthful aphasia, he still talked awkwardly, and he hated himself for that.

"That's why I only use deadfalls for firewood," Charlie continued. "It's more work, and no fun burning punky stuff in cold weather, but I haven't the heart to rip more holes than I have to in the web. Do you know how much wood North Americans consume? More than 600 pounds per person per year — 180 billion pounds of wood. Imagine how many trees that is! Hell, an entire island in the South Seas, half as large as Britain, was deforested in one year, just for toilet paper."

"Is that why you use glossy magazines in the outhouse?" Brian's ass was practically bleeding, but he'd taken revenge on Charlie's uncomfortable, spidery shed by urinating off the treehouse's verandah onto the monkshoods and kalmias below, whenever the old man wasn't looking. Charlie beamed. "I only use what I'm given."

Then Charlie launched into a harangue about people using their cute little blue boxes while driving millions of cars which foul the atmosphere.

"It's a start," Brian said, wondering why he was defending blue boxes.

"It's a lie, but it makes them rest easy."

Yes, rest easy as the tons of contamination spreads like an amoeba across the planet. But at least you're doing your part for the advancement of civilization. I've seen you take your mother's blue box down to the recycling depot. Rest easy tonight, boy-man, you've done your best . . . pork chop eater and package ripper . . .

"Everything," Charlie said, "is part of a universe which is one big organism. The trees are a variety of mitochondria; the rocks, they're organelles, and so on. Only, we're like a perverted enzyme, or maybe a virus. The animal is alive, but we've contaminated it. Though sometimes, I don't feel right complaining about that. Death is also a natural function."

Many years ago I knew this old poet, dying, near the end of his life. One night we were sitting on his verandah, the house almost engulfed by a massive flowering bougainvillea. We were both depressed, for different reasons. I was mooning over a lost woman in Mexico. He was counting his successes and failures, knowing he didn't have many years to live. He liked me because I was an unabashedly grunty kid, and I liked him because he believed in the beauty of the world, and the power of belief itself can be beautiful.

He told me about slime moulds. If you grow them in a culture dish, they stick to themselves, propagate, grow inwards while building tiny, nearly invisible, cities at first. When the miniature cities become unwieldy, when the food is gone, and there are too many cells, they explode, sending out spore explorers in every direction, creating new cities, until ultimately, they fill the culture dish, turning it into one heroic metropolis, having consumed everything, including themselves, as they fold up and collapse inwards. "That's us," he said.

I believed him. I still do.

Shortly after that night, I found a book by Loren Eisely in his library. One of its essays made the same argument about slime moulds. He'd obviously read the book and pretending it was his theory, enthralled me, a receptive kid. That was like him. In a way, I love him for it. He was a trickster. Besides, it fits right into the slime mould theory of the human species. Despite his protest, Brian's thinking is similar:

"Death is a natural function? The destruction of the human race?"

"You say that as if we're special. Maybe every disease thinks it's special."

Brian blinked. This was so close to his own ideas. "What's wrong with disease?"

Charlie's paused with his mouth open, surprised by the detour. "Disease is not healthy."

"But it is natural."

"Of course, it's natural."

Then if it's natural, it's good. The maggot and the cancer? Pneumonia and streptococci?"

"I suppose so, but I have my quarrels with them."

"And the developer . . . the rapist . . . the woman beating her child to death . . . the corrupt politician selling a river?"

Charlie snorted. "They have a choice!"

"What if they don't, what if they're fulfilling their natural function — destroying the planet? Doesn't that make us good, then? Natural? Maybe the only true ecologist believes in the inevitable course of life — the destruction of everything."

"Dimestore philosophy, writer boy! Is that why you're here? Promoting horror?"

"No. But why not? Or what if we go in another direction? Since we've evolved to a degree where we can control the world, make moral decisions about what's good and bad, and then implement them — haven't we reached the historic point where we have gone beyond nature, your god?"

"You can't control nature."

"Why not?"

"Because it is what it is."

"Shitty argument, Charlie. Nature is not God, not some all-powerful benevolent being. God is god. God is not flies and shit and still-born babies. That's nature."

"Cripes, here comes the religion. Don't bore me with that garbage. You know, I'm old enough to be your father, but it's you that reminds me of my father. He talked the same way. Maybe, that's why I let you hang around. I can't think of another reason." Charlie sat back with a humph, signifying the end of the argument, or maybe that he knew he'd lost it, which was what Brian thought, smirking. The caterpillar had left his boot, no doubt deciding the broccoli were more interesting. The fly remained, polishing its legs.

Halfway up the clearing, the rock's granite surface shimmered in the heat. Charlie was right about that, at least. The rock was alive.

As Brian stared, the stone seemed to vibrate and grow blurry in the haze. He returned his attention to the vegetable garden, aware that Charlie was inspecting him. He knew he should say something, but he was trying to figure out how a rock lived, what its spirit was. It had a spirit — a very stony spirit, heavy, solid, like the thing in his dream. "I want to talk to that rock before I leave."

"Oh, you can talk to the rock, but will it talk to you?" said the boy at the gate.

Brian started. The boy had appeared like a ghost, and he was as graceful as one, perhaps thirteen years of age, oddly pretty despite his birdlike face, and receding chin, thin black hair pushed back from his forehead. He was wearing a dirty T-shirt cut off at the shoulders, tattered shorts, and a bright red pair of sneakers. Brian felt the ulcer boiling up in his stomach. Almost as a reflex, he pulled out one of his remaining cigarettes and lit it while the boy set a small box of groceries onto the grass by the gate. "I've talked to the rock."

"And has it talked to you?" Brian hissed through a cloud of smoke, glancing again at the boy's feet. 'They're making red sneakers now?'

The boy lifted his chin. "Sure, but it only said what a rock would understand." He turned to Charlie. "Should I put your groceries in the treehouse?"

Charlie nodded; the boy snatched the box, and ran with it, agile and angelic, up the ramp and inside.

"Who's he?" Brian asked. Intruders didn't fit into his plans.

"A wild kid; had a rough start in life. He's Elvira Denison's boy. She lives next door — I subdivided, and sold her a five acre parcel a dozen years back. The boy comes here to talk to the parrot and the rock, and sometimes me."

The boy danced down from the treehouse and reached the gate again. He stuck out a small hand for Brian. "My name's Festus. I know it's weird, but I got a weird mother. She liked old westerns on television and Roman mythology. I'm sort of a festival with cowboys."

Brian shook the hand. It was limp and hot. There was a scariness about the way the boy quickly withdrew it, as if he were suspicious.

So there you are. Surprised? But hey, since you asked me for a story it's only right that you get included. Do you recognize yourself? This is the way I see you. Different name, sure, to protect your privacy, but it's my story and I can do what I want. You will be ten years older when you encounter this. That's one of the reasons why you are included — if you live you will have the opportunity to see yourself as I once saw you. Many people you know are here, only different, re-invented. Does that seem weird? Scary? This is a story about how dangerous stories are. You asked for it. Actually, I should tell you everything. I've been doing a lot of thinking as I've been writing, and I've decided it will be a public story. This is what I am going to do. The story is for you, dead or alive. I will publish it on your twenty-first birthday, in 2003. If you live to read it, half the royalties, whatever they may be, are yours. That won't be much of a gift compared to survival, but

173

it's the best I can do. Then again, is survival a gift? Besides, the real gift is the story.

"How much do I owe you, Festus?" Charlie asked, the darkness gone from him. He nudged the kid roughly on the shoulder so hard he almost fell over.

Festus straightened up, rubbing his shoulder ruefully. "It cost twenty-four dollars and fifty-seven cents." He slipped into a boxing pose, dancing around Charlie.

"Thirty will be good, then?"

The boy lowered his fists happily. "Thirty sounds pretty fine." What was really annoying was that Charlie had passed the grocery list to the kid without Brian noticing. 'When had that happened?'

"Will you stay for dinner?" Charlie yarded a wad of rumpled bills from his pocket and counted out the money.

Festus shook his head, as if other, more boring duties were calling. "I'm supposed to tell you some news, though." He pulled Charlie towards him, and holding the old man by the shoulder, whispered into his ear. Brian overheard something about 'June' and an 'urban fleece office,' whatever that was. The old man nodded impassively. Then the boy was walking across the clearing. "Watch out for that rock," he called to Brian over his shoulder. "It can surprise you."

Charlie stared thoughtfully across the garden at the bay, and the ferry terminal.

***

Brian turned away from the pitiful box of groceries, mostly dry staples, on the table in the treehouse. "I can see why the boy didn't stay for dinner."

"Gawd, you're a complainer." Charlie waved a very large Chinese vegetable chopper at him. "This is a real feast day. I'll bet that's not an organic eggplant. Now why would he buy vegetables for me at this time of year? That wasn't on my list. Festus, he's a real junk food junkie, and he's always trying to poison me, but maybe the pesticides will get you off, give you a little chemical thrill."

Brian sagged back into a chair. "I could use a thrill. My body is starving for real food. I want a pizza."

"Ah, you saw me starting the dough this morning. Peeking through the window, were we? Good guess. Let me warn you I make a fierce sourdough stone-ground tomato and cauliflower pizza. And there's my famous flower petal and seed salad to go with it. Great stuff. It's got borage petals, day lilies, fava bean flowers, nasturtiums, roses, radicchio, cilantro, and cress, with crushed walnuts and pine nuts and sunflower seeds. And my special herbed olive oil and lemon dressing. How'd you like that?"

A fly crawled out from under Brian's jean cuffs and fell onto the floor. The same one from the garden? It had a tattered wing. Maybe it was in love with him. It felt nice to be loved by a fly, different. He leaned back, admiring it. "You said you were going to make a pizza when we were in the garden, about two hours ago, bragging about how early your tomatoes were because you started them inside in January. You're getting senile." Brian laughed companionably. "And paranoid. But I'm at your mercy, Charlie. Make it, and I'll eat it."

"That's what I like to hear. That's what Rita used to say." Charlie busied himself, rinsing in the rudimentary sink the cauliflower he'd brought up from the garden.

"I assume that was before she dumped you."

"She dumped me? Well, I guess you could put it that way."

"That's what she told me. She said you were too old."

Charlie shrugged, dicing up the cauliflower fleurettes. "Yup, that's what I told her. And it was true. What else did she tell you?"

"That you were amazing, the most wonderful man she ever met."

"I could have told you that."

"Then one night, many years ago, you talked in your sleep. You came home, drunk, after being away for a couple of weeks, and you said Coyote was dead. Cement. But you were alive. There was more mumbling, enough to convince her. In fact, I gather you talked in your sleep more than once, according to her. A bad habit for a man in your line of business."

"I recall you mentioning her legs being up when she told you this."

"I exaggerated a little. But sure, she lifted her legs for me."

"Sounds like a cow in rut, not the woman I loved."

"You're right. It's cruel to talk about her like that, yet it's hard not to hate her." Brian turned away, his heavy cheeks quivering momentarily. Then he snapped his head back. "She dumped me, too! Like I was a mercy job — you know — taking me for a lover because she felt sorry for me. We were friends, confidants. Then she met a philosophy professor with a Mercedes and a candy-apple red '57 T-bird for summer driving." Brian primped himself up in his chair, caricaturing a pompous snob driving a car.

"I'm sure you deserved it. Told you I talked in my sleep, did she? That's a good one. She was so young when I met her. She vibrated like a piano string that's always being sounded. And it was a fine, clean note."

"Young for you. Five years older than me — so cool, so knowing, so burnt-out."

Charlie began peeling the eggplant. "Here we are talking about her like she was dead. She isn't, is she?"

Brian looked up at Charlie from his chair, his lip twitching. "Old lovers should be treated like the dead. It's the only way to deal with memories."

"The memories . . . you can't deal with them. They keep growing, grafting onto each other like a meccano construction in the mind. After a while, when you've been betrayed by love, when you murder what you love most, you've got nothing but memories glued together inside your head. Regrets." Charlie examined the naked eggplant as if he were a torturer contemplating what new variation he should perform on his victim. "I've done so many things, seen so many of them come back on me. Rita. The abortion clinic. Tom. The list could go on for miles. All the details that add up to one real big lump sitting on your chest."

"The abortion clinic? You actually did that? I knew it! Even when everybody thought it was a crazed copycat trying to discredit you."

"I never much cared about what people thought. People latch onto an idea and drag it down, re-invent it to suit themselves. So I came back here and settled." Charlie waved the cleaver at the cabin, taking in the outside ground with the gesture. "My family owned this land since before I was born, used to come here almost every summer, plant a new tree and camp out in a cabin that I burned down about nine years ago. It was all rotted out. When I returned I got myself off the ground. I needed elevation — privacy — built this." He tapped his foot on the floor. "The land's a hundred acres of trees and pasture that goes from the deep forest to the sea." He almost looked proud, those blue eyes shining again, as if this land was the most important thing in his life.

"At first, I cultivated it, tended the shrubs, but after a few years, I realized I was corrupting the landscape with the introduced species. I didn't have the heart to kill them, so I left them on their own. I suppose those that survive might become part of the landscape, eventually. Hopefully, they won't be nasty, invasive creatures. Myself, I stick to the vegetable patch, and the few herbaceous flowers I grow for colour."

Brian wasn't going to let the discussion wander into Charlie's obsessions again. "That abortion clinic was an evil piece of business, and it didn't fit with anything else you'd done."

"Look, Brian, who are you? An arrogant, sweating porker showing up with your cigarettes, and telling me lies?" Charlie pointed the knife at him. "You think I'm dumb? You think I don't know this is a game, a misguided quest. For a start, what's with all that sleep-talking nonsense about ChemCity. We'd already split up before that happened. Where did you really find out about me? How did you get to her? It's going to have a bad end, isn't it? Let's just forget the bullshit about a stupid book! What a story!"

"You're being ridiculous."

Something scratched at the door, quiet and tactful. The absurd can easily resemble a beggar, and it often waits politely outside doors.

"What's that?" Brian was suddenly afraid.

Charlie jerked the door open. A large, fat racoon backed away. It held a bunch of mouldy grapes in its paw, a relic from the compost bucket. The racoon seemed to be offering the grapes to the men inside the cabin.

Behind her, there were three kits. The kits thought this was the funniest sight in the world. They rolled joyfully on the ramp while their confronted mother remained frozen with the grapes upraised.

"Ho, ho, what have we here?" Charlie asked.

"Are they real raccoons."

"I should think so. Most raccoons are."

"I mean wild."

"They didn't arrive in boxes."

"What do they want?"

"Crap — what every animal wants. They're looking for heaven, I'd imagine. Watch this." Charlie unwrapped a brown paper bag from inside a jar on the shelf by the door. "I save this, special for them." Sugar cubes. Like a gentleman, he handed one first to the mother and then to each of the kits.

They took the cubes with grace, bowing, nodding their little masks in his direction, before backing away to the furthest reach of the verandah, the mother awkwardly, since she still had the desiccated grapes.

Charlie winked impishly. "Don't worry, I'm not corrupting them. They're taking the sugar cubes to the bucket of water where they'll diligently wash them off before they eat."

Brian's eyes widened with an almost salacious delight. "That's cruel!"

"I suppose it is. I'm beginning to think you expected to meet a perfect man. I'm not, as you should have figured out by now. And I'm conflicted about those creatures, like I am about most of the way our ecology works."

"Why?"

"Because I love them. Because they're so pretty, and they're also one of the most vicious animals I've ever encountered. Besides, it's a relatively harmless form of teasing — it teaches them to never trust people. But you ain't seen nothing until you've seen a coon stripping the neck off a catatonic chicken. I've always had a love-hate relationship with them. They're a bit like us, coons, they torture after they've eaten their fill. I've seen a coon eat five goose eggs; then go rip out the throats of a few chickens, just for the thrill, taking its time on each hen, sucking blood from the neck, yet not quite killing them."

Charlie sidled into the doorway, his head bent morosely, remembering. "This was years ago, when I was a young man. I used to keep chickens for eggs. I loved my chickens, gave them all names: we're dumb creatures who think we're smart — each of us. When I entered the coop there was this coon hissing and burping in the corner while the mutilated hens staggered around like zombies. They were already dead, though they were still moving — their throats ripped out. They were only good for the soup pot.

"I shot the coon, cut off its head, and put the head on the coop, but that didn't make any difference. The others kept on coming. They were out there in the trees like a small, malevolent army of torturers. That sweet mother — you should see the expression on her face when she's holding down a young animal for her kits to mutilate."

"Come on and watch," Charlie said. Brian stood up and leaned over his shoulder, looking.

The raccoons were at the bucket.

In the salal near the edge of the clearing, a small flock of waxwings flushed, whirring into the dusk's half-light.

Charlie stood motionless, Brian behind him. "She's going to do it," Charlie whispered. "Actually, I lied. Most of the time she eats the sugar; only once in a while does she wash it off. Maybe it's because the grapes are so grungy."

The mother took her little cube and washed it in the water until there was nothing left. She turned in horror to her kits. The oddest thing about it, Brian thought, was that she had gone through the same routine several times, according to Charlie. Racoons were supposed to be smarter than this.

Behind her eyes was a resentment bigger than sugar cubes. The kits, being too young to know better, had already eaten their sugar, and now gazed at her with an air of expectation. Everything was gone, except the grapes which the water had made look more unappetizing, if that was possible.

She rocked back and forth on the deck, keening, like a stagey Irish mother; then she hissed at the bucket of water, her children, the two men in the door, and was gone, quickly followed by the kits.

There wasn't much to say after that. Brian tried to appear concerned; he knew he only looked foolish. "I guess you're right, yet it's still ridiculous. And I don't understand why a man with your beliefs would feed sugar to a racoon."

"Time will show us who's ridiculous. You don't have a clue about my beliefs. And you ain't no storyteller. But I did give up raising chickens long ago." Charlie turned back inside.

The parrot had flown in through the open window and was inspecting, contemptuously, the cauliflower fleurettes. Charlie shooed him away and returned to his cooking duties — after he wiped up a big, green-white parrot dump. Then he punched down the sourdough for the pizza crust, and rolled it out on a thin, stone tile. "So there you are. I'm not a hero. I'm not even a good person. Nobody is. What kind of story is that going to make?"

The housefly — there it was in the cauliflower. Charlie's rummaging launched it into the air. Brian watched it land on the sill. "Right now I'd tell any story for a leg of deep-fried chicken."

"Chicken. You're back onto the chicken. Here, let me find a quote for you. Dinner will be a while yet. It's a slow-rising dough." Charlie dropped the knife again, and abandoned the still partially chopped eggplant As he rummaged among his bookshelves his relaxed movements made Brian realize dinner was a distance down the road. Midnight? Charlie found the book he was seeking. He leafed through it, pacing the floor.

"Here it is. Do you know what they give to chickens now? It's like a role call of heroes — our chemical victories. First of all, you've got your basic trace metal contaminations. Cripes, it's stuffy in here."

He walked out onto the porch, as if he were going to declaim this news to the garden or the darkening landscape beyond. And he did. "There's lead, mercury, nickel, zinc, chromium, cadmium, and copper. Your standard chicken has them all. And the levels are growing every year. Hmmm, hard to read in the dark. I used to have good eyes for this." He reached inside and took one of the kerosene lamps and hung it from a hook beside the door.

"And we won't forget the other residues. "Dioxins, PCBs, DDT, etcetera." The parrot flew outside and landed on the railing, watching Charlie with excited curiosity, bobbing its head up and down in a curious dance rhythm. Brian leaned against the sill, thinking about his growly stomach; no doubt the parrot had witnessed performances like this before.

"Alright, here's what our factory farm can give them chickens. The mighty antibiotics: penicillin, ampicillin, cloxacillin. It doesn't say so here. But I think they're also feeding them tetracycline. Oh yes, there it is. Streptomycin. Oxytetracycline, Cholortetracycline. Sounds powerful doesn't it. Take *that,* bugs and fevers."

"Yahoo," the parrot bobbed its head, agreeing, like a drunk in a bar watching a scat player.

Inside the house, on the windowsill, the fly was locked into the back of another, fornicating among the prisms that lay scattered along the ledge.

"Sulfa, all-conquering Sulfa. Sulfamethazine, sulfathiazole, sulfadimethoxine, sulfaethoxypryridazine, sulfaquinoaxaline." Charlie had trouble pronouncing the terms. The parrot didn't mind. It laughed, lifting its claw at him. "The Greeks at Troy didn't have such a list of conquerors. Nitrofurans. Furazolidone, nitrofurazone. Then there's the arsenicals: arsanilic acid, 3-nitro-4-hydroxyphenyl, arsonic acid."

"Whoopee," the parrot said, unaware of the bright eyes of the coons in the tree branches, hypnotized by its loopy movements.

"And let's not forget the hormones," Charlie said with deep meaning. Brian realized he was definitely receiving the regular theatre the old man offered what guests he had. "Melengestrol acetate, Synovex." Charlie was having difficulty picking out the text in the thrown light from the treehouse. "I think, if I'm reading this right, that stuff is a combination of estradiol benzoate plus progesterone and testosterone."

"What?" The parrot did a little circle on the rail.

"Shutup, bird. And we can't forget Ralgro. That's zearalenol. Those chickens must be stoned out of their heads."

"What?" the parrot said again. "What? What? What?"

There, boy, that's enough to give you an idea of the architecture of stunning chemicals we've built around ourselves. Charlie's polemics might sound like an old story by the time you read this. That doesn't matter. The shame is that we ignore all our old stories.

If you live through your own fate this is what you will have to deal with. Our society uses billions, not millions, of pounds of constructed chemicals in its fodder every year. Chow down. Maybe your mother accidentally did that in the months before you were born — then; there it is, the broken gene.

Now I'm sounding like Charlie, but I always did, didn't I?

***

Half a moon hid in the hemlocks east of the clearing when Brian went outside and down the ramp for a post-dinner smoke. The salad and pizza hadn't been too bad, despite the wait. Charlie surprised him, eating so late, and he guessed he'd thrown him off his schedule. Good. A deer browsed at the forest's edge, so tame it wasn't disturbed by the click of his lighter. As he inhaled he grew aware of being observed. It was the rock, several yards away. He blew a little stream of smoke into the cool night air.

In the moon-silvered dark it looked like it was spinning in one spot, solid, black, against the sky — a vibrating mass of molecules compressed so tightly they would break his fist if he slammed it against them. Then it shuddered, and began to move. It floated down the hill towards him while his heart fluttered, and he sucked madly on the cigarette, or was it him that moved towards the rock? Swirling patterns shifted on its surface. Tricks of light?

An alder beetle, more than an inch long, striped black-and-white, crawled across the granite. It moved like a lizard. The beetle waved its long antennae at him, groping. Then it vanished.

He reached out, touching the rock, tracing the hallucinatory swirls. His hand seeped inside, became invisible. Then his other hand. It was sucking him in. He felt his heart begin to slow, as if the rock were making him move to its own beat. Finally, he realized he wasn't in the clearing at all — he was in bed, dreaming. He remembered again the old tales his father told him — if a man dies in his sleep, he actually dies.

He had to get out of here.

He opened his eyes, sweating, aware of dim movements in the gloom. He flicked his cigarette lighter, trying to decipher the shadows — Charlie, pushing something up and down, a rod, a brush. He was cleaning a gun.

Brian lurched forward, knocking his bedside table, a mug crashing, as he scrambled to light the kerosene lamp.

He found the wick. The fire guttered and then burned strong.

Charlie was still running the rod up and down in the barrel of the rifle when Brian put the glass over the wick and the room filled with warm light. The broken remains of the mug leaked cold tea onto the floor. A mouse scurried across the windowsill, past the now-awake parrot which, perched on a chair back, muttered, annoyed: "Time for bed."

Brian was almost afraid to speak. "What are you doing?"

"I'm sharpening my rifle."

"I thought you didn't believe in killing anything."

"Nawww, just harmless animals. I don't understand shooting a pig or a bear or a mountain goat or a chicken, not any more. But people, yes, I can understand wanting to kill people. I believe in self-defence."

"You're going to shoot me in my sleep?"

"No. So why don't you shut out that light. It bothers my eyes. Or are you just going to sit there staring at nothing like a pig shitting in the moonlight?"

"But you would shoot me?"

"If I have to. You're no storyteller."

13
The Last Resort

WREN WAS RIGHT ABOUT THE PARCEL. Someone had driven a forklift through the box. Several folders in the middle were mutilated. Like the victims, Janwar thought.

He spent the next two days going over the material, reams of forensic reports, interviews with suspects or possible witnesses relating to a string of murders in Portland, and two in Alberta. Nothing that gave Janwar any new clues, though there were similarities in the deaths of the prostitutes; however, two and perhaps three of the victims in Vancouver appeared unrelated — possible random events he had mistakenly lumped in with the others. Maybe Blake was correct after all. That night, he had his first headache since arriving on the island.

At the waterfall, the saunas continued, until one morning, after she'd gone inside, he found himself contemplating the shut door. He removed his turban and comb, and placed the *kirpan* on the towel. She pretended not to notice he no longer had the ungraceful towel draped over his long black hair, or that he still kept his *kach* shorts on.

After, they lay side-by-side on the black rock near the waterfall, his dark skin next to her grey skin, their arms folded behind their heads as they dried off in the mottled sunlight of the grotto.

"Did Kirsten send me up here for a reason, outside of my health?" he asked.

"Kirsten always has reasons, but they might not make sense to people like me or you — or maybe her either — she has an uncanny intuition about things. I wondered about her sending you here, too."

"I don't understand."

"Once, in our university days we took an intelligence test in a psychology course we were both enrolled in. She blew it right off the map. The professor's mouth practically hit the floor as he watched her answer the questions. She put the pegs in the holes so fast it made him dizzy. It was funny. You must know what she's like, working with her, watching her trip over her own feet while doing brilliant things. She's had an uneven life."

"So I've heard."

"Her mother was a rough woman. Maybe it was good luck she died when Kirsten was so young. I know that's a terrible thing to say. Then Kirsten was raised by these religious fanatics. Nice people, and I think Kirsten welcomed the change — until she arrived at university. That's when I met her. She had about three wild years before she suddenly changed again. It happened just like that." Wren snapped her fingers.

"She came up to me and said 'I've joined the other side, the right one.' Things have been tough between us ever since. I have this problem, I talk too much. I shouldn't be saying this about your partner." She turned and looked into his eyes. "You carry the *kirpan*, the bracelet and the comb, too."

"Yes. The five Ks: *kachh, kangha, kara, kes,* and *kirpan.*"

"How come you are clean shaven, then? I thought you weren't supposed to cut your hair?"

"When I was a child, I pulled a pot of hot water onto my face, from the stove. It didn't scar badly, and the few scars have disappeared over the years, but I look disfigured with a beard. My elders were kind enough to give me a dispensation — though I have received comment."

"It must have been awful. Was it boiling?"

"I was very young, three-years-old. I don't remember."

"Are you having trouble with your faith?"

"It is a great faith. The trouble is with me."

"Perhaps you should not reflect on that for now. Concentrate on being well. Focus on that while you are here, and take your shorts off for the sauna. They bind up your navel chakra. Think of me as your doctor."

He gazed at the water flowing over the falls, so clean and brilliant. Then he stood up and unrolled his sodden under-shorts, placing them beside the *kirpan* and the *kanga* rolled into the towel on the bench at the door of the sauna, under the hanging turban. Naked, except for the narrow iron bracelet on his wrist, he walked back and lay down beside her, still silent, lying on the warm rock, the sun and air on his genitals.

"Does that feel better?"

He nodded. Terrified.

"You should put your papers aside, too. After all, you are on vacation. Show consideration to your body and your spirit."

"I haven't any problem with the work. It is merely curiosity, something outside of myself to think about."

"Okay. But don't let yourself be wound up in it. Be free . . . loose . . . Remember what it is like to be calm." They didn't speak for several minutes as they rested on the rock, warm under the rare sun of the coast.

Wren broke the silence again. "Old Jake wants to apologize for his behaviour when you arrived."

"Did he tell you that?"

"No, but he's spoken to friends of mine."

"I don't know if it would be good idea for me at this time."

"Maybe not, but it would be for Jake. Just keep away from coffee and sugar, and alcohol, too. That's what he damned near lives on, and they're bad for your candida."

Janwar grinned. Jake? Island politics. Kirsten had warned him. "I'll think this over."

* * *

He went the next day. Since they were ripping up the Low Road beyond the resort, Wren decided it would be easier for him to walk than drive back around the island to the High Road. She told him of a path a half-mile down the beach cutting across both roads to Jake's.

It was a smouldering day, and the path wasn't as easy as she claimed, either that or the islanders were part goat. He'd left after lunch — following his sauna with Wren and a morning considering the herb garden.

It took him hours. The so-called trail went in every direction. What did Wren have against cars? He could have driven here in five minutes.

There was a large farmhouse in need of paint on the hill beyond the well-grazed field that he ambled nonchalantly across, studied by several dozen bored sheep — until he encountered the bull.

Big and speckled brown and white, it had horns. He decided it was a Jersey, and wasn't the Jersey a common, domestic cow? He regarded it for several seconds.

Then it pawed the earth, and he ran, leaping agilely over the split-rail fence. The bull was right behind him.

Janwar performed a cocky little dance as the creature pulled up short — he couldn't resist the gesture, safe on the other side.

The bull, not interested in human definitions of safety, began pushing against the old fence, heaving it, shaking the timbers. One of the top rails fell off. Janwar scampered up the house's back porch, out of sight of the bull. He tapped on the door, noticing the trim on the adjacent window panes was chewed off. Odd. He tapped again. Jake wasn't home. He felt relieved.

He turned to go. The bull was at the bottom of the steps, studying him and the porch. Janwar tried the door. It was unlocked. He stepped inside.

Although Jake was a single man, his wife dead from a cerebral haemorrhage more than fifteen years ago, according to Wren, the place was immaculate: a bright, white country kitchen with a big oak table in the centre. On the table sat a bottle of whiskey. The tidy kitchen made Janwar rueful. He'd been caught again — assuming an old widower would keep a dirty kitchen. He smelled coffee. There was a pot simmering on the stove. Tempting. He hadn't had one in days, but he recalled Wren's injunction.

He didn't know what to do. He sat at the table, inspecting the kitchen, listening. What if the bull came up the stairs? Would it enter the house?

There was a neatly printed notice on the back of the kitchen door.

THERE'S WHISKEY ON THE TABLE
AND COFFEE ON THE STOVE, ABOVE THE FIRE.
IF I'M NOT HERE AND YOU ARE ABLE,
POUR YOURSELF WHAT YOU DESIRE
AND REMEMBER THE HOSPITALITY OF THIS HOUSE.

Janwar poured himself a coffee. There was a mug in the cupboard, milk in the refrigerator, the honey was on the table — next to the bottle of whiskey. What more could he ask for?

He was savouring his first sip when he heard a clumping on the stairs, saw a face in the door window. It was Jake — a huge mouselike head perched on a scrawny body. His salt-and-pepper Fu Manchu moustache hung slightly below his chin.

"So there you are," Jake said, slamming the door. "I thought you might show up. I heard you were parked on the island for a few weeks."

Janwar stood up and stuck out his hand. "Janwar Singh."

"Jake." Jake took the hand, almost crushing it. "Coffee's ready, I see."

"Yes it is, and very good, too. I was chased inside by your bull."

"Thor? Don't worry about him. I've seen fish bait smarter than that bull, and he's terrified of his own shadow. He's only begging for apples, but he does get persistent if you don't give him hell. I guess I have some apologizing to do. I was rude, there's no getting around it, when you arrived at Mecca. And I've got no sympathy for rude people, including myself."

"It was nothing."

"It wasn't nothing. I was rude. Well, I see the sun is past the yardarm. Care for a little nip?" Jake nodded at the bottle on the table.

"No, thanks. I'm not a drinking man."

"You wouldn't insult my hospitality, would you? I leave that out for my friends, for when I'm not here, so they can drop by and have a drink. It slides down smooth with a coffee in the afternoon." Jake rose and pulled two shot glasses from the cupboard, filling both.

Janwar took a sip for the sake of politeness. It was warm, sharp on the tongue.

Jake hammered his back, poured himself another, and refilled Janwar's half-glass. "Like I said, I got my apologizing to do, and I'm not a man who enjoys apologizing."

"Oh, that's not a problem. You already have. Don't think about it."

"Don't fuck me around. I got a job to do and I want no interfering. Have another whack."

"I'm fine. I really am."

"Have another whack!"

Janwar dutifully drank the whiskey, then sipped quickly at his coffee."

"That's better. I like a man who can take his whiskey."

"It's an interesting refreshment."

"I've heard whiskey called many things, but not that." He paused, examining Janwar, indecisive. "So, I should get this over with. I'm a man of few words. I'm sorry. There, I've said it. I shouldn't have been so rude."

"Don't apologize any more please. You're embarrassing me." Janwar was growing annoyed. Oblivious, Jake poured another round. Then he began his story.

In 1987 he'd sold his prize bull, and a great bull it was, to a veterinary professor from Ontario. The vet paid a big price. It went into a semen program run by the institute of agriculture at the University of Guelph. Jake and his son celebrated a few days. They'd bought a case of whiskey and were determined to empty it. Then a mink raided the chicken coop. Seventeen chickens died before the boy went in with the .22.

"Hell, it was a shooting gallery," Jake said. "I don't know if you ever tried to shoot a mink in the dark while balancing a flashlight. They're fast as lightning and slick as a bull's dick."

He was sitting outside laughing, watching the little holes of light open up as his son kept firing at the speedy varmint. The boy killed three good hens and Jake's favourite rooster before he finally shot the mink. He claimed he was aiming for the head, which is silly, considering a mink has a skull the size of a hazelnut. They can slide in through one inch mesh wire. "But we were drunk, and his bad shooting was understandable."

Jake had been involved with his neighbour in a dispute over the large pond on the boundary of his south pasture. The neighbour claimed Jake was taking too much water, mostly because he wanted to use it himself to irrigate what the locals called "a vanity vineyard." This was a strange claim since Jake's farm, inherited from his grandfather, was the oldest farm on the island and had locked up its water rights for nearly a century. The neighbour was a spiteful man from New York who'd scooped up the cheap property next door after lucking into an excellent divorce settlement from his wealthy Brazilian wife. "Americans, they're all assholes," Jake said. The cops, who didn't visit the island much, were unravelling a marital dispute, and found themselves stuck overnight, accidentally missing the last ferry. The "American dickhead," as Jake liked to call him, phoned the detachment at Sweet Water to complain about all the gunfire, and they were at Jake's within thirty minutes.

"My son was still scooping the dead chickens out of the shed when their car pulled up by the porch. It was fucking midnight. I had a few choice words for their intrusion, and so did he. He was holding the lousy little .22, a dead chicken in his other hand. He told them to get lost. They told him to drop the gun. He said he'd drop the gun, sure, sort of wiggling it at them, and not being too polite about it."

"They shot him?"

"They shot him. Claimed it was an accidental discharge in a tense standoff . . . later. This cop just pulled out his pistol and shot Andy in the chest from ten feet away. He went down like a sack of potatoes. And funny enough, at the same time, the chicken he was holding came alive. Maybe it was only stunned during the mink attack. It strutted around, a mad hen in the dark, scratching at the dirt in the headlights of the police cruiser, and the two cops standing there with their mouths agape.

Later, they realized there weren't any bullets left in the rifle. He was only being a little bellicose."

"How terrible."

"That's putting it lightly." Jake uncapped the bottle and poured another round. Janwar saw that his glass was also empty, but he couldn't remember drinking it. Jake filled the tumbler. "Since then," Jake said, "I haven't had much love for cops. But a man's a man despite the uniform he wears. I had no right to insult you like that, especially about that thing on your head, and your skin. I don't go for that racist shit. And I'm sick about myself."

"It's forgotten."

"I can see you're a good man, not your average Mountie. Have another one." Jake waved the half-empty bottle at him, a little wobbly this time.

"No, I'm fine."

"You don't want to drink with me?"

"It's not that at all."

"Then drain your glass and let's get down to business. I'm not the cheap type that leaves a half-bottle on my table."

Janwar knocked it back. He knew he was sinking into deep trouble, and he also knew it was important not to lose face. He had a suspicion the entire island would know about this encounter by tomorrow morning, and it was essential that he held his own . . . or so he thought . . . that is, if he was thinking, correctly . . .

"So, what are you here for?" Jake asked, stroking his too-flamboyant moustache.

"I'm taking the cure at the Last Resort. I've got an overdose of city living. My stomach is rebelling."

"My stomach is always rebelling. I've had the ulcers for thirty years, but that never stopped me from getting my work done. Why are you after Charlie Baker?"

Janwar was silent. His glass was empty and he looked at it. Jake refilled it. "I'm not after Charlie. Baker? That's his last name? I'm looking for a person in Vancouver, and Charlie might be able to provide helpful information. That's all."

"Can't see how that could be. Charlie don't go anywhere much, maybe a few charity trips to help out locals. He likes his treehouse. He ain't going anywhere."

"That's what police work is about, 2,000 questions and maybe one lonely answer that leads to another 2,000 questions."

"You won't get no help out of Charlie. You think I'm eccentric, you gotta meet Charlie."

"I'm sure I will, but there's no rush. He's nearby, isn't he?"

"Down the road; the overgrown driveway next to that pottery woman, Denison . . . I ain't giving nothing away, here, am I?"

"No, of course not. I thought he might fill in some details about a woman he once knew."

"That better be the case. Charlie, he's respected on this island. He's a flake alright, but aren't we all? And he's a big man, if you know what I mean, not physical, well, that, too. He's just big. We call him 'the mayor.' He's got class. Want another drink?

"Really, I don't think I should."

"Come on, don't insult my hospitality. This apologizing is a hard business. Have a little mercy on me."

"I'm sorry. I didn't mean to cause you trouble."

"Christ, quit being sorry, and let's get to work. We've got almost a third of a bottle to deal with here yet. And if word gets out I didn't do my apologizing correct, I'll have every pussy-licking lesbian valkyrie on the island lecturing me. The females, you know, they pretty well run this place. And women, they always want to make everything safe and comfortable, all the way from erection to resurrection."

"You were forced to apologize?" Janwar grew angry again.

"Hey, don't get your shit in a knot . . . your shirt in a kot . . . No-one makes me do anything. You can ask any islander about my temperament. But I did receive advice, I'll have to admit that. Another drink? My chores are done for the day, and you're in no hurry to return to that goofy resort, are you?"

"Actually, I . . . ," Janwar watched, depressed, as Jake refilled the glasses.

✳✳✳

There was a moon. Janwar was sure there was a moon — silver reflections on the road, though he couldn't see their source, concealed by the alder. When did the sun go down? Several hours had vanished. He didn't feel bad, considering how much he had drunk. He couldn't remember drinking whiskey before today, but he was sure he had . . . somewhere . . .

It wasn't unpleasant — he liked the colour in the glass, the warmth when it went down his throat. He didn't enjoy the dizziness. He confronted a clump of salmonberries in the middle of the road and glared at them with disapproval. Why were they growing in the road? Then he realized he had turned sideways.

When he left the farmhouse the old man was snoring loudly, his head resting on the table. Jake's head had hit the oak surface so hard it woke Janwar up, and he realized it was time to go, though it was a little delicate taking the

12 gauge pump shotgun from the old man's lap and emptying the shells out.

Jake had obviously descended from a long line of firearm fanatics, and he certainly hadn't learned any lessons with the death of his son — not being shy about waving the weapon in front of a drunken police officer.

The gun had come out just before dark. There was a pecking, a tapping, a robin chewing at the window. For unknown reasons, every dusk the bird became obsessed with the caulking around the windowpane.

That, and the whiskey, was enough to send Jake to the deep end. He declared he was fed up with that bird destroying his woodwork. Still seated, he reached over and hauled the loaded shotgun out from behind the fridge, and let fire a blast from his chair, almost deafening the terrified Janwar.

The shot missed the bird, showering the porch with broken glass and splinters. In a few minutes the brazen robin was singing in a fir tree beyond the steps. Jake needed a few more drinks to recover from this arrogance. The second bottle appeared. And it was shortly after, or so Janwar thought, that he finally passed out, allowing Janwar the opportunity to empty the gun and get the hell out of there.

The night was warm, the alder branches rustling in a slight breeze. Janwar was happy. He was looking forward to his sauna in the morning. All he had to do was walk off the effects of the old farmer's whiskey.

He heard a rustling. What was it? Deer? Cougar? No, there were no cougar on the island. There was nothing dangerous, no snakes, no predators. He radiated bliss at his sudden discovery of the moon above the horizon, between the branches of two fir trees.

The rustling grew louder. His eyes focussed. It was the bull. Thor.

The low moon was no longer in the trees — it was between the horns of the bull — near the fenced pasture. There was no gate to the road — as if the need for a gate was an afterthought to be sorted out one day. The animal could walk freely anywhere. No wonder it had reached the house so quickly when he'd first arrived. Did that mean it really was tame? He decided he wasn't going to hang around and find out. He ran.

The bull followed.

The next hour was a nightmare of brush, lost trails, strange moons showing up in the wrong direction, and the snorting of the unshakable bull. He staggered up the beach, his heart pounding wildly. He fell on a sandcastle. It represented two woman entwined on the beach. Guilt. Then he was at the path beside the herb garden, and through the twig gate.

The resort was quiet, everyone in bed. He couldn't help a glance at Wren's house. She was there. Seated on the hammock, smoking. A sweet smell. "You shouldn't smoke that," he shouted too loudly. "It's not good for you, and besides, you might get arrested."

She put the joint in the raku ashtray beside the hammock and gazed at him icily, making him feel guilty. He stepped back, stumbling, catching his foot on a vine. It was the Dortmund rose beside his cabin, which she had so proudly pointed out to him. It was a heritage rose. Thorns pierced his calf. He settled onto his knees, wanting to stand up, feeling too drunk, amid more thorns, hurting. Let it hurt. He'd ruined everything.

There was a loud snort on the path.

Wren lurched out of the hammock, instantly recognizing the threat. "Thor! You let him follow you. The gate's open! He'll destroy the garden!"

The bull! Leaping to his feet, Janwar scrambled out of the rose bush and to his cabin door.

Wren picked up a stake, ripping it off a delphinium by her front door and rapped it on the bull's back. It turned towards her. "Get lost, Thor! Go home!" Lights began to glimmer in the nearby cabins. Janwar, confused, stood at his door as the resort came alive. Dimly, he was conscious of the tiny figure of Wren holding the bull by the horns, turning it around. Then she kicked its butt, and the beast fled towards the beach, stampeding through the netted deer-fencing, ripping out a twenty foot section before trampling the sand sculpture Janwar had already wrecked.

***

He woke up, the sun in his eyes, three tiny pots of Wren's herbal infusions on the bedside table, his head banging. He didn't remember her coming in. Was he in serious trouble?

He drank his tisane, his eyes fixed groggily on the pile of papers on the cabin desk. He'd gotten into the habit of browsing through them while waiting for Wren to finish her Tai Chi class. This morning, Janwar didn't have the heart for it; there was a deadness inside his body, one that echoed the sick pounding of his head. His skin was covered with a thin sheen of sweat that stank like rancid whiskey.

Finally, she arrived, tapping quietly on the door. He picked up his towel and joined her. She eyed him up and down. "Feeling rough, are we?"

"I'm afraid so," he said, walking alongside her as they passed the herb garden on their way to the grotto's path. "I believe I made a fool of myself last night, and caused damage to your resort."

"Damage? It's minor. However, you do have a fence to repair this afternoon. The bull came in through the gate — it left through the deer netting."

"I want you to know I am not in the habit of becoming intoxicated. It has only happened to me once before, when my sister . . . went through . . . terrible . . . hard to explain . . . "

"Oh, I figured you were no drinker. I warned you about Jake. I was afraid he'd do that to you. He's a slippery, incorrigible old islander, as bad as that bull of his. It probably did you good, loosened you up a little. Now we must flush all those toxins out of your system. Whiskey is very bad when you've got stomach yeast. And you were as drowned as a newt in a well."

She decided an extra long sauna was called for, and made him drink lots of water before they lay down on the rock to dry, handing him an exquisite celadon bowl that she held under the waterfall, time after time.

Janwar was drained by his extended stay in the heat, glutted with water, and his head still throbbed, though less, as if whoever was hammering on his skull was working further away. After a few minutes, drowsing in the sun, Wren got up and walked over to the sauna, and fiddled with her waist pouch which she'd hung up on the wall. She returned, and lay beside him again.

Then she lit up a hand-rolled cigarette, inhaling long and slow and deep, holding it in before releasing a plume of smoke which rose above their naked bodies to dissipate in the sun.

He lay still, his body stiffening as the smell wafted over him. "That's cruel. You shouldn't do that in front of me. I'm a policeman."

"Why don't you forget you're a cop while you're here?"

"I can't."

"Take a hit." She reached over, the grey skin of her arm above him, her breast, its black nipple, pointing at his face.

"I couldn't feel easy with myself, breaking the law."

"We both know the law is wrong."

"It's still the law, and I'm a cop. Don't be unkind."

She leaned back, inhaling from the joint again, flipping the ash to the black rock. "While you are here, you must think of me as your doctor, and I'm prescribing this. We both know what is wrong with you. You have bottled everything up all your life, always calm and polite. The expectation of your parents, the years of racism, fighting for the law against hopeless odds and in too many despairing situations while trying to be an example for your people, overworking yourself into despair, clinging to a religion you love and yet are losing, eating bad food full of chemicals, worrying about everything, like an alcoholic whose drink of choice is life, hoping that the more you drink the better it will get. And you don't want anybody else to know you're a drunk."

"Whew," he said. "You've been watching me."

"I guess I have. Besides, this will help ease your headache. I like you Janwar, and you're my patient.

Remember, you came here for help. This helps. I learned that during my try at chemotherapy." She took another hit.

Janwar reached over, staring into her eyes as he took the cigarette from her fingers. He leaned back again and inhaled. He choked, sat up gasping, coughing, spitting. She laughed. "Don't inhale so fast at first. Take it gently, savour it."

He stopped coughing, and tried again, sipping at the smoke. It didn't feel like anything, just smoke. He lay back passing it to her. "Now I will have to lie. Another secret. Besides being illegal, it is frowned upon by people of my faith."

"It's called freedom." She drew at the joint, now half gone, and passed it to him again.

He sipped slowly at it, feeling nothing, wondering how the stuff became illegal. He didn't feel anything. "Why is your skin so grey?" he asked, passing it to her, enjoying the touch of her fingers as she took it, desiring her.

"Why is yours so brown?"

"I was born this way."

"So was I. A little over ten years ago I was diagnosed with a rare form of bone cancer. The doctor said I should wrap up my affairs, that maybe I had a year. My bones were rotting. I had a little bit of money — and this property, it was only a couple cabins then, was selling for a song. I managed to swing a mortgage, and I never looked back. Then I wrote a couple of books on healing that sold like hot cakes. I decided I'd heal myself after the chemo failed. I studied day and night. You could say I became obsessed."

Wren's face scrunched up, as if she was holding back a deep pain in her body. "The resort was a run-down fishing camp, going broke as the salmon and the oysters and everything else disappeared. That's where Kirsten came in. We looked at it together. She helped me leverage the financing, twisted those bank managers up in knots. I turned it into a healing place, working on myself first. It's a crazy business. I don't even believe in a lot of the things we experiment with around here; still, it works for a few people. I'm alive. I'm healthy."

"It must be difficult for you." He was crushed by the possibility of her death. How could she live so comfortably with it?

"No, it's become easy. I love my life, but I'm not addicted to it. They tell me I'm a miracle, that I'm in complete remission. This is a cosmic joke meaning nothing."

The sadness was overwhelming, as if it were flowing in his blood. Is this how the marijuana worked? Yet he couldn't deny he was still happy, enjoying this woman, lying beside her naked body. He began to worry that he would get an erection. He looked at himself. No, it was okay. "I think I should go back to my cabin now."

"Yes, that might be a good idea."

At the cabin, he sank onto his bed, sleepy, the distant pounding in his head no longer so painful, a big grin plastered across his face. This marijuana wasn't so bad, after all. At the same time, he considered the stories of people desperate to smoke, looking for mindlessness, blotting out their lives with the drug. Was that what he was doing? What would the officers at homicide think of him now? What if they found out?

Janwar woke up late in the afternoon, refreshed, the hangover faded. He started on the fence. It was good work, redigging holes for two new posts; the old ones had snapped off when the terrified bull tore through. Wren brought him fresh netting and he stretched it between the posts, tying it into the old net. He hadn't done anything like this for years, and it felt good as he sweated the last of the whiskey and marijuana out of his system, and then later, wolfed down his sauteed garlic tops and fava beans nested on a great mound of couscous.

After dinner he dialled up LAWTALK and moused into the SERMUR sub-group, sat back for several minutes in his chair, following the conversation. It was a boring discussion about the credentials of a 'professional witness' who travelled the continent, hired to argue against forensic evidence. His specialty was in confusing and lessening the impact of DNA evidence, a new, powerful tool that had been used in a few cases. Whether the science would prevail in the courts was still unclear, though most officers had high hopes. After a few minutes, Janwar broke in.

JS: Hello from Canada.

Knocker: Hi JS, have you ever had this Wichter on the stand in Canada?

JS: I escaped the honour of watching him in person, though he did scramble a sexual assault trial in New Westminster. It was a notorious case and he's not popular with our prosecutors or police here, either.

Max: Hey. You just missed Cheevers — he signed off half-an-hour ago. Told us everything.

Toad Hollow: He caught his man (and yours) up to the yin-yang in evidence.

JS: Caught?

Max: Cheevers was granted the warrant. When they searched they found a mountain — the geek was an

accountant, he kept records of everything, had the nerve
to write off his stalking trips as business expenses — times
and dates placing him everywhere, plus personal articles
from a couple of the victims. 'Mementos'. And S&M
videos and magazines to colour him for a jury or judge.
He should face Capital after Cheevers lays it out. Cheevers
has a real sense of humour. He even has Revenue lined
up to check phony tax deductions. He doesn't miss an
angle.

Toad Hollow: Cheevers called you up to thank you for
your help but you were on holidays. He commended you
and your partner to your boss. Blake?

JS: Yes, that's him. Encouraging news. I've been out of
grace lately.

Toad Hollow: Well, your work paid off. Cheevers also
sent an effusive fax so there would be paper for your
personal file.

JS: I'm gratified.

Max: But he did mention there were two women,
maybe three, who didn't fit the accountant's itinerary.

JS: It's my opinion that at least two women are another
matter.

Knocker: I thought you had a well-behaved country up
there?

JS: We tell ourselves that. I'm grateful for this
information. I should check up on these new
development with my superior. I promise to return for a
nice chat soon. Goodbye for now.

He decided to call Kirsten on the computer before
talking to Chief Inspector Blake. Or was it because she
was not far from his thoughts these days? It was almost

impossible not to picture her luring johns to their fate on the streets of Vancouver.

Janwar: Hello. Sorry to dial you at home again. I hope I am not interrupting anything.

Kirsten: No, I'm just sitting here, doing homework for my night school course. Have you heard? Sowinki committed suicide.

Janwar: Suicide? What happened?

Kirsten: You don't think he killed her, do you?

Janwar: While we have a case we could possibly put before a judge, I believe he's innocent. Tell me what happened?

Kirsten: Kookoff, either acting on his own or under the orders of Blake, returned to Sowinki's and sprang the news about the threat against Rita he'd made to Variander Singh. This was before we'd heard about Cheevers' accountant, so it looks bad, though the accountant was in Utah when Rita disappeared, according to Blake. I know you didn't want to push Sowinki but Kookoff couldn't resist meddling while you were gone, aggressively enough for Sowinki to eat a shotgun.

Janwar: It's good Cheevers has now laid charges against the accountant, but I suspected Rita Norman was not part of the indictment. And the other student?

Kirsten: No, nor the eviscerated woman. According to Kookoff. He's taken to itemizing who couldn't have been killed by the accountant, to prove that your theory about a serial killer was over-zealous in many of the cases. What will you say to Blake?

Janwar: Nothing. He can sort out with Corporal Kookoff the mess they've got themselves into. It's my file and I was against him interrogating Sowinki again, especially like that, but Kookoff is more eager than Blake. I've been careful enough to make sure my stand is on record, though I assume they will muddy the water, and float Sowinki as the chief suspect.

Kirsten: The media is on their case, serious. That's poetic because they were feeding the press — one reporter especially — information that I would have kept private (But then don't ask me, I'm in the doghouse, too, though I'm going to win my case against Blake, I'm sure of that). Still, all these murders and disappearances and suicides don't make sense — even psycho sense.

Janwar: I'm now sure they're not related. However, the possibility of two entirely different psychopaths is truly disturbing. I'd better sign off and phone Blake at home.

Kirsten: That might be a good idea. By the way, Cheevers delivered a glowing, official letter to Blake — and the stuff you sent must have included my notes because I'm singled out, too. Blake, considering the shit he's waded into, is now remembering us fondly. In fact, the grapevine has it that he's 'looking forward' to my return to homicide once I've overcome my 'inadequacy problems.' How magnanimous. I wouldn't put much hope in that. My hearing on the harassment complaint comes up tomorrow. Any news about the missing phone book?

Janwar: None. Sowinki, if he had a key, might have picked it up, not wanting to get implicated in the mess of her disappearance. Despite my misgivings about the handling of Sowinki, it might be wise to search his residence.

Kirsten: If he stole it and left it lying around that doesn't make him very intelligent.

Janwar: Intelligence and academic skills do not always run together.

Kirsten: I almost forgot. I've emailed you a file. Have a read: it's full of wild and very weird poetry. It was on a disk found in Rita's computer stuff — no usable fingerprints on it, yet I'll bet my bruised coccyx it was written by a man.

Janwar: Okay, and I'll let you know what I learn from Charlie Baker.

Kirsten: You found him?

Janwar: Yes, but my health demands I take a break from this business, at least for a day or two.

Kirsten: How are you making out at the resort? Watch out for Wren. She knows her herbs and good health. She's also liable to have you smoking dope and practising free love in no time.

Janwar: Kirsten!

Kirsten: Sorry. I shouldn't talk that way about her. She is my friend . . . or was, years ago . . . maybe I'm jealous . . . oh hell, dumb thing to say . . .

When Janwar signed off, he loaded his screen dumps into a dated file. Kirsten, at home, did the same, printing hers out, and putting them in the manila envelope she kept in her gun safe.

After Janwar tidied up his desk, there was nothing left for him to do but phone Chief Inspector Blake.

* * *

The moon was full when Janwar went outside. He walked a distance down the glowing beach, inhaling the salty-rich odour of the kelp washed up along the tideline. Far from the resort he sat on a log, and pulled out the joint Wren had left on his tray, displayed like a beacon next to the Thai salad and the water-fried greens she'd brought for dinner.

He lit it, slowly inhaled, and considered the confusion in his life, and how it was increasing. Aside from developments at the resort, the investigation was a rat's nest. He wasn't sure about anything now. According to his stiff conversation with Blake, the American accountant was wrapped up, barring an unfortunate incident or legal technicality at his trial. The two students were not on the list of victims, nor the mutilated women, and there was clear evidence the accountant was in Utah when Rita vanished. Blake considered this a confirmation that he'd been on the right track, yet he was still catching heat from his superiors. Only this afternoon did he finally learn why. Sowinki had a cousin in the prosecutor's office, a very unhappy cousin, and now Blake was unsure how Janwar would testify if there was a hearing.

Janwar knew the Chief Inspector wanted to cook the investigation a little. He ignored the unspoken suggestion. In fact, feeling annoyed, he suggested to his superior he considered Kookoff's forceful visit inappropriate. On top of everything, Blake was inordinately worried about Kirsten's harassment complaint to internal affairs. It should have been a brush-off — unless there was substantiating evidence or other claims. Janwar decided it was best to avoid contacting the office for a few days.

He lay back on the log, drowsy, despite the cool night-breeze sliding off the ocean, rippling the water, as he inhaled the last of the joint. In a couple of days, he would visit Charlie Baker which, hopefully, would be an improvement on his encounter with old Jake. There was no hurry, and besides this was supposed to be his holidays.

For now, he should deal with his own health . . . and state of mind — it had become clear they were inextricably interwoven, like the DNA in a cancer cell. The dope was working through his blood. The idea of cancer cells made him think about stars for some reason, the Milky Way radiating across the night like an infection. And Wren, her skin, most of all those deep gentle eyes. The thought of them being snuffed out brought a lump into his throat. He looked up again and surveyed the glittering sky for a long time.

14

A Red Porsche and Moral Discussions

LOVE — THE SWEET BONE WE ALL CHEW, the rush when a name is uttered; the emotion when your head hits the pillow and you glance sideways, realizing her face still delights you after thirty years.

I've not forgotten my promise at the beginning — the romance that everyone demands. Life is becoming intense for our stressed inspector and the grey lady, but I also want to talk about another romance.

Since this story is growing beyond your tough request, Festus, I'm going to use the term 'reader' sometimes. Count yourself included, of course, because you asked for it. But it's for me, too, and your friends — it's a story with few borders.

Those interested in the gory parts, or who want to find out who kills who, can skip this section. I wouldn't recommend it. I know that you won't. I saw the hunger in your eyes the day we first met. The threat of death exposes so many desires, especially the desire to understand love, in all its forms.

So, love — here it comes — though we must begin nearly twenty years in the past, and its complications reach into the future — love shows its face everywhere, in the garbage dump, at the checkout counter in a supermarket. Love, the melodrama, the grandiose, the silly and the stupid. Witcher of young and old — posturing, silk-shirted, dumb love . . .

The red Porsche convertible tacked around the curve too fast, squealed, snake-slithered, and straightened out.

She stood, hitchhiking, in the downpour, wearing almost nothing but blue jeans and a near-transparent scarlet blouse plastered to her skin. "Awesome," Charlie said, slamming on the brake and skidding again. The collie dog in the space behind the seat, lurched forward, driving its wet nose into his ear.

Man and dog regathered themselves and beamed and panted at the woman as she surveyed this unlikely pair in a roofless car in the rain. "What am I getting into?"

"Open the door and you'll find out."

"I assume you're going up the hill to the university?"

"Sure, me and my dog need an education."

She climbed in and slammed the door. A shower of droplets from the windshield fell onto her lap. "I'm Rita."

"Charlie. The dog's name is Charlie, too. I figure everything in the world should be named Charlie. That way nobody will have to introduce themselves." He engaged first gear and squealed up the straightaway, towards Simon Fraser University.

"Do you always drive with the top down in the rain?" she asked as she rummaged in her purse for her sunglasses, the torrent pummelling her head while she searched. It was now obvious why he was wearing his — to keep the driving rain out of his eyes. He thumped the car into second, and left another streak of rubber on the wet asphalt.

"Most of the time. But I also keep the top down when the sun shines. It usually evens itself out. Who could ask for more? Do you always wear nothing but a thin blouse in the rain?"

"Well, I get rides fast. Men are predictable, especially guys that drive red Porsches."

Charlie wheeled the convertible into a u-turn in the middle of the highway, driving the dog's nose into her ear this time, and began descending the hill.

"Hey, what are you doing?"

"My mother owned the Porsche. She left it to me in her will. My purpose in life is to destroy it so I can return to riding my bicycle. Why don't I leave you where you started, and you can massage the more predictable types?"

"I'm sorry. You seem cool. I've been picked up by so many over-heated middle-aged guys I've learned to be defensive. I'm sorry about your mother. I went weird when my mom died."

"Forget it. She lived a full life, became old and sick, and then she died suddenly in a boating accident. I should be so lucky when my time comes. However, I object to your making snap judgements about offensive people, especially when those points under your see-through blouse can be as much a weapon as any I've encountered in a war zone."

"War zone? You've been in Nam!"

"Sure, I'm part of the Viet Cong plot to infiltrate North America." They reached the stop sign at the bottom of the hill. He pulled over. The dog thought this was an impressive tour but clearly wondered where they were going.

"Do you want me to get out?" Rita asked.

"No."

"It wasn't raining when I left home. I wasn't out to play the tart for men."

"Strange," he said, "it wasn't raining when I left home either; besides, it's not going to rain much longer, and I'll be damned if I'm going to cover myself at this point with the top." He turned the car around.

There was a cluster of teenagers near the corner, standing beside a sidewalk extension newly planted with flowering Kwanzan cherry trees. One of the boys, talking to a girl, unconsciously broke off twigs from the young tree beside him, folding them up in his hand, and tossing them away. Charlie watched, long enough for the group to become aware of him. One-by-one, they turned towards the Porsche. "How'd you like it," Charlie said to the boy, "if I broke off a few of your fingers because I was bored and had nothing else to do, like you're doing to that tree?" There was enough threat in his voice to make the group stir uneasily. "Kids are so oblivious," he said loudly to Rita, flooring the gas pedal and speeding away while the teenagers glared at them.

"Not as much as you think. If they see your car again they're liable to drag their keys across the paint."

"I should have said nothing?"

She grinned and shook her head. "I would have done it differently. I'll bet you're going to the big rally in support of the Khmer Rouge, the one to celebrate the end of the bombing of Cambodia."

"No, I don't support the Khmer Rouge, nor the American Army, nor the Viet Cong. They're all the same enemy. I'm returning a few library books, and then I'm going to a poetry reading in the quadrangle — a French medievalist who's a hot translator."

"That sounds boring to me."

"You shouldn't insult what you don't know."

"You aren't a student, are you? You're too old."

"I'm forty-six. Any more insults?"

"Wow, you're almost twice as old as I am. I'm twenty-four."

Yes, she was young, and the sixties were over, yet the decade's luggage packed more than its share of innocence. When he first met her, Charlie was still dealing with the awful inheritance of his parent's death. He'd already begun his campaign a few months earlier, and he was now researching the mistreatment of animals at the university library. When he returned to Artemis in a couple of weeks he would give his dog to Old Jake the farmer.

The love affair didn't take long to begin; it flowed naturally out of words and rides and conversations. Then, one day, Rita realized, apart from Charlie's 'regeneration absences' to the island or elsewhere, they had been living together almost ten years. It hadn't taken her long to learn of his other role, and though she never joined him on any expeditions, she provided help and advice, since she agreed with his motives — until her pregnant belly turned into a battleground, and they discovered neither knew who the other person was, and she returned home on a hot afternoon, no longer pregnant.

That's when the arguments became bitter — so she took off down the hall, and out the door. Gone. She was a runner. Smart woman. Only she didn't run far enough. She was also silly and melodramatic. He found her less than a week later, after a phone call from a friend who'd spotted her drunk at a hotel bar frequented by university students. By the time Charlie arrived she'd been evicted, and was weeping on a curb near the cheap hotel fronted with a neon sign depicting a long-necked swan defending a nest. It was ludicrous, the sign, like the situation. Had she designed her own discovery?

She staggered to her feet, knocking away his hand, straightening her soiled clothes with the comic grace of a drunk. She wiped her eyes. "Detective Charlie, you're a bloodhound; you found me, but you can take off. If I want to end up in a ditch, that's my right. I don't like men who talk in their sleep. The stories they tell. How moronic can you get, talking in your sleep — or were you, asshole? Did you want to make sure — in case I was too stupid to figure it out?"

This was after the fire-bombing of the abortion clinic, the attack that so troubled Coyote's advocates, as well as Rita, for obvious reasons. Once suspicion takes root, it runs in every direction.

"I've got no idea how I ended up here, but I'm never going to drink whiskey again." She hiccuped for effect. "We should go home. I need to sleep, sleep forever, because when I wake up, I will leave you." She did. And he helped her go.

Love in our species. We spend a lot of time thinking about it, writing it, filming it, painting it, documenting the permutations. Everyone wants a love story.

Love stories have a bio-social purpose. Take at look at science fiction — all those stories set after Armageddon, after the last (but not quite) end of the human race. Love in the ruins. We always end and begin with a single lonely couple surviving and ready to procreate. It's the simple, relentless genetic drive of a species determined to reproduce, even in a ravaged landscape. All other variations on this, the only real love story, are merely packaging, refined by history, but still packaging.

The last woman in heat. Don't worry, the last uncontaminated man will find her. These stories are pumped out with a compulsive monotony. For Coyote, also the victim of this conditioning, the next step in his ecological escapades, saving the produce of this organic union, had been inevitable. If he fought for the animals and plants that were being consumed, if he argued for the children of the fox and the necessity of sequoias, he had to argue for the foetus. His logic demanded that any enemy of natural life was an enemy of his. Besides, revenge always invents its own logic — and she did abort the baby . . .

So this is what happened a little more than a week before Rita went on her drunk. It takes place in one of my favourite locations, a shopping mall.

Yes, the mall.

The treasure horde of American civilization. The consumer paradise on earth, the malls, around which the suburbs circle like protective wagon trains.

Run.

To the mall.

Coyote paused under the sodium lamps in the empty lot, listening. Apart from the background hum of the lights the mall was quiet. In a few hours the daily slaughter of the city would begin — regiments of men and women rising and putting on their clothes; then driving to work, wrapping meat, flopping tons of dead fish onto the stainless steel sinks, lining up outside the chicken-killing hall to don their laundered smocks, and begin murdering hundreds of thousands of animals for breakfasts, lunches, dinners, and delicate little snacks in the evening.

A low berm of mugo pines divided the car parking stalls. Most of the pines had survived, but one was crushed and mutilated. Too many feet had stepped on it; yet they'd also made it beautiful. A lost bonsai in plastic land, its last living branch reaching towards the distant high-rises behind which the sun would rise — a scraggly little tree that should have clung to a wind burnt-cliff facing the sea.

Coyote straightened his heavy pack, stepped over the pine tree, and approached the building.

The doctor who'd originally leased the clinic had tricked the mall owners. He'd applied to set up a medical clinic, fulfilling the mall's policy of providing a variety of services capable of luring people to a centre where they might purchase all their needs. Only he'd failed to mention he would specialize in abortions, and that brought protesters and controversy, to the horror of the managers who now had to wait four years before they could find an excuse for failing to renew the lease — which would also bring another onslaught of protestors — and that wasn't good for business, either. It was a mess.

Coyote scuttled along the side of the cinder block supermarket, past the glassy post-modern facade of the entrance — to the rear alleyway. There wasn't any life anywhere — not even a rat.

The clinic's back windows were a row of eyes overlooking the service lane and the rear of the fast-food restaurant. He wanted to move, not think. His thoughts made him nervous, clumsy — a dangerous state for a terrorist. 'I come here to defend a biological attitude I don't understand.'

'Don't think.' He lowered his pack and opened it. Molotov cocktails — they made him feel amateurish.

The clinic's night lights shone through the high yellow windows. Scrawling his chalk note across the pavement he felt wrong, knowing it was a telegram to Rita. COYOTE WANTS THE CHILDREN TO LIVE AND DIE ACCORDING TO THEIR ELEMENT. The question was too complicated. There were no white and black hats here. Instead, there were images of tiny foetal pieces — arms and legs filling garbage bags, young women with their choices restricted, rapists laughing at the ultimate revenge, righteous preachers proclaiming the sanctity of life while wolfing their pork chops, and housewives breeding heirs — then drowning on martinis in the suburbs.

"But you can't kill the children because we aren't able to take care of them." That was corny now, here. Coyote pulled the nylon stocking over his head. Ready, he lit the first rag, the second, the whole shebang. Cradling them gingerly, he made his run, and as he ran Rita's voice mocked him.

"You don't know what you're talking about. You aren't a woman. It's not your choice."

"It's not yours, either. It's another life."

"That life couldn't survive on its own. If I pulled the plug, it would die. I'm not killing a life. I'm killing the potential for a life. And you don't have any say in the matter. If you want a breeder, find another woman."

So she'd done it — had herself vacuumed out, despite his feelings. Now he was here.

The first window shattered. There was a poof inside, flames running up the wall. Another window, and another. He ran down the line tossing the cocktails inside until every window spewed fire.

He stopped, out of breath, facing the young night watchman. Both men froze, wondering how the other had appeared so suddenly. "You don't want to mess with me, kid. No, you don't."

The nightwatchman's eyes widened. A lock of blonde hair had escaped from under his peaked hat and curled into his cheek. His mouth was a vivid red in the glare of the lamplight. "Who are you? Why are you doing this?"

Here's another story for you man-child. I'm one of those who would now be aborted. I suffer from a chromosomal syndrome that has disrupted my life, and it's also supposed to be toxic. At first I didn't want to tell you because you've already got enough problems. Why do you think your request hit me so hard?

I'm told my syndrome has been added to the list for recommended deletions (thank God, you may say). True, it's not as rare as yours, or as potentially fatal — at least not yet. When I was young, a doctor told me I'd be dead before I turned forty. Here I am, still kicking. Should I be grateful? I suppose so, yet often, I don't feel grateful. By the way, your kind will be deleted, too.

Right. This the story of one diseased man explaining the nature of disease to another. Let's call it a mystery.

I need a needle to keep me going. I get stabbed in the buttocks every week. Though I have survived my life, those first twenty years of pain, and the next twenty-five years of survival tactics, I wouldn't wish it on another. Looking back, I have to favour the destruction of my kind.

Murder them before they're born.

Murder. It's a tough word. Occasionally, like every victim of the cellular necessity for reproduction and survival, I want to believe there should be more Brians; that we are fine, despite our misshapen bodies, headaches, sexual dysfunctions, bone pains, manic-depressive emotional turmoils, and dead glands in our skulls. I also understand this body is a mess — which puts me in conflict with many other 'handicapped' people who want to call themselves 'otherwisely enabled,' or similar nonsense. They don't like being called crippled or spastic or retarded, although they are.

Words should mean what they say. Sometimes they build up a lot of freight, so it's a good idea to invent new ones, but please, let's forget the ones dreamed up by committees.

In our search for decency, for courtesy, we reach for euphemisms. I'm a cripple. I'm screwed up. I was born terribly wrong. Although I'm disabled, you can't tell it from looking at me. Others are not so fortunate: the spastic, the limbless, the blind, etc., I can't speak for those in worse shape than I am, yet I will. After all, this is just a story, and I can say anything I want. Watch me.

Just a story? Ha! You had no idea what you were getting into. Well, neither did I when I began.

The cripples? I suspect many of them feel similar to me. We are cripples. We are born to be fatalities. So is it wrong to ask if society should eliminate us before we have the chance to live? Scary stuff. It can lead directly down the road to eugenics and Buchenwald. Yet, should we breed the legless, the brain damaged, the spastic, because to do otherwise is to say they are no good — that we're discriminating against them?

So let's discriminate (discrimination can also have a positive meaning). Let's say the legged are in a better position than the legless. Let's say the brain damaged and the spastic and the sexual indeterminates are what they are. If we had our rathers, we'd rather be something else. To be disabled is to be diseased, is to be wrong — this doesn't mean we can't live with it, even take pleasure in our condition. It's just not a state I'd recommend if our technology gives us the foresight to prevent it.

Looking back over this passage, these facts seem clear. Yet, we feed ourselves lies that deny them. To decree that being disabled is as good as being enabled sends us down another immoral road, the one that can lead to crippling the healthy in order to make everyone equal.

How long before we try to breed deaf babies for deaf parents who want to honour their child with the glory of silence?

The abortion issue is a mess, a logical conundrum. Our reactions depend on our cultural conditioning. And these moral discussions are merely my culturally programmed theories and feelings being offered to your own culturally programmed world view, and to any other readers crazy enough to wade into this mess.

We justify these arguments by calling them logic.

We could call them stories.

Take another classic argument for abortion. No man has a right to decide what should occur within a woman's body. I agree; just as no man should have the right to decide what occurs within my body. I'm in possession of this bundle of flesh, good or bad, and for you or the government to control my body is theft. The same goes for all of us, women, children, drug-addicts, suicides.

Drug addicts? Suicides? Whoops! They are not culturally acceptable.

Why shouldn't we have the right to control our own bodies? Cut off our hands if we choose. A little self-mutilation? Or how about selling organs and body parts? Have I ever got a bargain basement heart for you. I give it away all the time, so I might as well sell it cheap. Why don't we have the right to commit suicide, celebrate it?

In the end, all we'll reach is a decision decreed by the vagaries of cultural swings and fads. Right, I can present you with arguments on either side, to support or oppose. I want to deny both. This aside is not about whether abortion is good or bad, but about the process that leads us to the making of that decision.

There is no right answer! That's my answer.

Abortion. Suicide. Substance-abuse. Prostitution. After a few thousand years of dealing with them we might yet conclude they're metabolic, chemical, certainly undeniable, and finally — impossible to solve.

Let's line up both factions in the abortion debate. There are many side issues; however, I'm going to arbitrarily cut it off at the five major ones that interest me most (I can get away with that since I'm writing this story. If you don't like it, as I said earlier, you can read another story).

Hang in there for one more round.

In order to see a motionless lizard on a rock we might have to pass by it a number of times via different routes. That's what we're doing. Consider this a plan that's not a plan; an unplan. Stick with me, kid, as we grind our way through this section, and I might tell you one hell of a story, yet. Here're the factions:

FOR ABORTION:

1. Abortion is not killing a child, only a potential child that couldn't survive on its own (Generally, there are no abortions performed after viability of the infant, at approximately 20 weeks). It's also useful for protecting potentially deformed children from a life of horror. Plus, pregnancy and childbirth can be fatal for some women, either psychologically or physically.

AGAINST ABORTION:

1. Life begins at conception. Society must protect the rights of everyone, such as stroke victims or children born brain damaged and needing support. To destroy a child is murder; because a body is being nurtured by another doesn't mean it should be deprived of its right to live, especially for selfish reasons.

2. No one has the ultimate right to control their body in

2. A woman has the right to control her body. No government has the right to decide what she should be doing with her flesh. Knowing this, many women, if denied legal access, will use illegal abortions at great cost to their lives and health.

3. Abortion should be legal for rape victims. No woman should be punished for having been attacked.

4. The majority of those opposed to abortion use Christian rhetoric on the sacredness of life. They are attempting to promote their religion and not a real moral position. But Christianity also has a history of intolerance, and despite the claims about the so-called Christian belief in the 'sanctity of life,' Christians have also systematically persecuted and murdered millions of Witches, Jews, other Christians, and aboriginal people.

our society — if we regard suicide or substance abuse as crimes, and protect or institutionalize those who intend to damage themselves, then this should also apply to mothers of unborn children.

3. To legalize the murder of the child because the mother was mistreated is to add one crime to another. There are many homes eager to adopt children now being aborted. Besides, these are rare cases, and the entire issue shouldn't be tainted by them. There are approximately 1.5 million abortions every year in the United States alone. Abortion is being used as a method of birth control, not a treatment for a few terrifying cases.

4. Christians aren't the only ones opposed to abortion. But because Christianity, like other religions, has suffered from opportunists and fanatics, that's no reason for hate literature

5. *Men like me should not have any say on the question. The history of the manipulation of the female of our species is so strong that we are tainted by our cultural conditioning, and more often than not, we have ulterior, unprogressive motives when dealing with the issue (Yes, I do, but they're not your standard, ulterior motives).*

against it like the argument on the other side of the page.
5. *Everyone, male and female, has the right to address every issue. Only through free speech and the opportunity to express opinions and knowledge will we progress as human beings. To say that men shouldn't have any input is sexist censorship and restricts their rights.*

And so this ancient story goes on and on and on and on.

My argument is with our unnatural assumption that we will find answers — that there is progress — that we can solve the dilemmas we invent for ourselves.

Meanwhile, we are left with an opinion typical of our society, typical because it doesn't make sense. I am in favour of abortion, although I believe it's wrong; a position guaranteed to get me in trouble with almost everyone, plus I suspect it's as fuzzily thought-out as most arguments.

A pox on all of our houses! However, my position does have one positive aspect. It believes in guilt. We spend too much time telling ourselves that old-fashioned guilt is unhealthy. Yet, it keeps us in check. It makes us think: 'Well, maybe I won't try that one again.' Sorrow makes us mark our routes, and learn.

We cannot sanitize abortion. It is not as simple as taking a crap. It is a more complex issue than the advocates of free-abortion want us to believe. On the other hand, while researching this story, I encountered enough garbage written by religious fanatics and screwballs to turn my stomach. The tactics and moral arguments are so awful they disgrace their claims to the moral high-ground.

We live in the world that Charlie discovered through his misadventures as Coyote — the world where you can't be right or wrong any more. You can only limit the extent of your damage. That's the contract with our environment we've broken, the one we never understood. Take that.

Yes, take that. And run with it.

Run back to Coyote facing the young guard at the abortion factory.

"I'm the Coyote. You could have been aborted, too."

"Aborted?"

"We're all victims." Coyote advanced on him, his hunting knife glimmering in the electric light, his face mutated by the nylon stocking.

The bewildered young man, as thin as a rail, was frozen on the pavement. "I'm not a nightwatchman, really. I'm an actor working my way through theatre school. I only do this for the money."

"Try and put out the fire. You'll look good in the newspapers tomorrow."

The watchman ran towards the fiery eyes of the building. Coyote didn't wait around. He ran also. There was a crash as the kid broke the glass on the alarm beside the fast food restaurant. Feeling betrayed, Coyote dashed across the ghostly parking lot, through the sparse trees of the seniors' park, and beyond the roadway to the waiting truck. He'd forgotten to snatch the valiant little bonsai pine.

"Nothing . . . ," he said to Tom, slamming the door. "Nothing ever works out the way I think it will."

15

Last Rites and Eagles

SEATED ON THE THRONE IN THE OUTHOUSE below the pond, Brian gazed through the south window at the garden where Charlie grubbed among his vegetables. Just like grandfather — another old geezer always messing with his gladioli and his garden until he had a stroke two summers ago, climbing over his fence while in pursuit of a laughing teenager clutching one of his prized watermelons.

***

There were geraniums everywhere, abundant and overgrown, almost climbing up the walls on both sides of the carved cedar doors of St. Paul's — a dowdy little church, its dirty stucco walls cracked and chipped — the same church where Grandfather was baptised.

Brian's father shambled into the church like a circus bear, maltreated and defiant. He glanced away as his wife genuflected and slid into the front pew. Grandfather was in an open coffin, his face pale and pasty despite the makeup. The priest entered, bearing the chalice, and the mass began.

Brian, seated beside his father, compulsively tried to memorise the details — they were important, part of a life he felt cut off from, a closeness to Mom who'd buried her childhood dreams when she married Dad. Later that evening when he returned to the university, he spent hours reading about Catholic rites, as if they were as important as the death. They were a method for concealing death, translating it.

The chalice, the veil, the priest in his alb and girdle; a spectacular pagan rite, though, saying that would upset Mother. Suddenly he hated her for the years she'd held the Church secretly to her heart. Now she was determined to carry on, see it done properly — whatever properly is.

"Requiem aeternam dona eis, Domine: et lux perpetua luceat eis."

His father fidgeted, looking old and like a trapped child at the same time, scrutinizing with impish curiosity the progression of the mass. "Gawd, he sure is knocking that wine back." Mother had never gotten through to him — a church hater to the end.

"Psst," Mom hissed. Beside her on the bench, Brian's younger sister Elizabeth was flushed with shame. She was such a stupid cow it didn't matter. The only pleasure she gave him was in lying about her. He enjoyed telling his few friends he had a sister who was a prostitute, who was brain damaged at birth and drooled when she talked, who was a lesbian activist with a moustache, who married a rich stockbroker and gave Brian money whenever he needed it, who was a missionary killed while being raped by an entire lost tribe in Paraguay. That was all she was good for — goofy stories.

Brian grinned. Father, noticing the grin, assumed he was amused by the priest, and winked.

"MY SOUL IS DEPRIVED OF PEACE,

I HAVE FORGOTTEN WHAT HAPPINESS IS;

I TELL MYSELF MY FUTURE IS LOST,
ALL THAT I HOPED FOR FROM THE LORD."

A red ant marched across the open rim of the coffin. Would it crawl inside and be buried with the old man?

Mom's hands were clenching and unclenching in slow motion on her lap while Dad tried to appear casual and respectful — he must have really loved Grandfather to put up with this.

"Dies irae, dies illa, Solvet saeclum in favilla . . . "

The air was thick with incense and the priest did his mumbo jumbo in every direction. "This is real magic," Brian thought, "It has meaning." There was a hole in his life, and he couldn't understand it — maybe it was simple — the desire for God.

Father was still mesmerized by the numerous sips at the chalice. "That priest is going to get pissed," he said, earning another dirty look from Mother. When it was time, Mother took the host. Brian didn't have the nerve, not with Father at his side, though many mourners came forward. He noticed Elizabeth also avoided it. "What's the magic act with the crackers?" Dad whispered, but Brian didn't dare reply. Mom was too close.

Then they had to shuffle past the coffin. That's when Mom said: "Kiss your grandfather goodbye." And he did. The lips were cold clay. He recoiled, aware that Dad's eyes were on him.

Outside, the sun shone on the geraniums. The mourners shambled around as if they were lost kids who'd been refused entrance to a deeply significant circus. Nobody knew what to do with their hands, so a lot of cigarettes were lit. Dad kept up his routine. "That old priest must be a real lush."

Unfortunately, Mom was behind, and overheard. "That's the blood of Christ. And besides, it's watered down." Her final point was almost too emphatic: "With holy water!"

The old man grimaced, defiant.

"Where's Rose?" Mom asked.

"Rose?" Brian was at a loss, startled.

"Yes, why isn't she here?"

Brian shrugged. Rose was the only woman Brian had ever introduced to Mom, and he regretted it. She was normal enough, and looked good, so he'd brought her over to meet the old lady. Unfortunately, she'd performed too well at that one forlorn dinner. It was a big mistake. Ever since, Mom was always asking about her, hoping.

"She got hung up."

"Hung up?"

"In her closet, reorganizing her life. You know how it is Mom . . . modern women. She wasn't interested in attending a Catholic funeral for a man she never met."

Then the coffin came out. Brian had always assumed it was supposed to leave the church first, followed by the mourners, not met by them outside, but maybe they'd changed things, especially since the traffic was whizzing by the church which, though built years ago in a quiet corner of the city, now occupied one of the worst intersections.

The crowd hovered around the coffin, keeping a five foot space, waiting for the hearse to ooze through the traffic and double-park in front. The cars on the road dutifully gave it a wide berth. The pallbearers picked up the coffin and carried it to the back door, sliding it inside.

There was another awkward pause, a wait for the priest, the announcement that would scatter the mourners to their cars, but it took too long, became almost scary.

Suddenly, everyone was silent, waiting, and just as suddenly, the silence was broken by a loud, nasal honk — an odd noise that resembled a cross between a gasp and a big man blowing his nose.

Dad stood by the back of the hearse, his hand touching the coffin. He turned away, glaring at everyone, and shambled through a geranium bed to the lane where his car was parked. Brian following quickly, to drive him home.

They'd gotten Dad into a church, but they'd never get him into a cemetery — not until the day they planted him, one year later. The hush among the mourners was palpable, echoed by the traffic which became non-existent for one weird second, as if the entire world was startled by the old man's single display of love for his lost father-in-law.

***

Brian wiped his bottom with the glossy business magazine paper. When he'd complained about the rough facilities, Charlie had just said: "Tender-ass. You should learn to accept what you get in this world."

Pulling up his pants, he ambled down to the garden.

"You look depressed," Charlie said, leaning on his Dutch hoe. "A good dump always makes me cheerful."

"It's the wipe-up I can't take." Brian nodded disapprovingly towards the outhouse. "I was thinking about my grandfather, a great old gardener who died two years back."

"Too bad. But we all have to do that . . . die . . . so maybe it ain't bad after all."

"Tell me about your brother."

Charlie took the hoe and began hacking at the quack grass. "There's not much to say. A lovely man, so sweet, but not all there." Charlie bent down among the cabbages, hilling up the stalks where the root maggots had down their work. The parrot, nearby, wandered among the broccoli, searching for juicy cutworms, or whatever bug a bird would enjoy. Charlie nudged a plant with his forefinger, sorrowfully. It wobbled, its riddled, swollen roots decimated. "Whoever or whatever made him, forgot one of the switches. The last light wasn't turned on — the one that would make him whole — it was a big light that got missed. Still . . . he enjoyed his life. He had a delight in things I never achieved. He got along pretty well. I bought him a little house in Vancouver, where he took care of himself as well as could be expected. His needs were always few. I wish I'd been like that when I was younger."

A shadow fell over him and he glanced up at the sky. The parrot was already watching. Two turkey vultures were gliding on the thermal above, their wings bent back. Charlie raised his hand and gave them the finger. "I'm not ready yet! Come back when I'm ripe."

The vultures drifted over the trees, toward the shoreline, Charlie watching until they were gone.

"What made you decide to take direct action?"

Charlie swivelled around, examining Brian with flagrant contempt. "Kid, you come from a different universe."

"Is your brother the reason you became an eco-terrorist?"

"He had nothing to do with it."

"I think he did." Brian knew he'd discovered something.

"Direct action? What kind of childish crap is that? That's pretentious politico kids toying with fart bombs."

"That's you twenty years ago."

"No, that's not me. Sure, I belonged to a group, but it was really just me, alone, for my own reasons. It wasn't revenge. It wasn't politics. It was what had to be done, the way you back up the truck and crush the kitten's head after you've already run it over. I did that once. It was all mashed up, and I tried to snuff it out but I kept missing because it wriggled around too much while it was dying."

"Like a sperm cell, was it? If all life isn't sacred, who decides?" Brian was pleased with himself. He'd brought Charlie to where he wanted him. "You?"

"The clinic was different, altogether different."

"A lot of people lost faith in you."

"I don't care. They don't know. They also put their own reasons on other things I did . . . the zoo . . . the dam caper . . . the rabbits . . . Yet when one wasn't politically correct . . . I know a lot of people pretended I hadn't done it, that it was fake perpetrated by the cops, or a misguided 'Son of Coyote' — all those amateurs running around, dumping sand into bulldozer gas tanks or cutting off the electricity to smelters."

Brian bent down and picked up a clump of quack grass and tossed it onto the pile Charlie was building on the path. He felt a sharp pain in his back, as if a disc were rubbing. The pain made him feel old. "I always knew it was the real Coyote who fire-bombed the clinic.

"When you believe in the sacredness of life, there isn't much choice."

"You're being a little theatrical, don't you think?"

"As theatrical as any child in the womb. Life, if you worship it, you're committed. You have to follow everything to the end, even if you don't always understand what you're doing."

"You left her, didn't you? Rita never dumped you!"

Charlie began weeding again, wielding the heavy hoe with an easy fluidity as he yarded out the grass. "I'd guess I was the only man who ever walked out on her, despite her always saying she'd be the one."

Oh what a liar, that Charlie! Where is he leading Brian?

"She walked out on me."

"I don't blame her."

"But I had the last word."

"Was it only a word?"

Brian sneered with as much as he could muster. "Sometimes, I think you've forgotten what it's like to be young and full of hormones."

"Naww, I think young, and I've got my share of hormones yet."

"For God's sake. You deny everything I say."

"Only the stupid things. And don't use God around me. God! The God of tooth decay who murders babies at childbirth, so that we will know his power? If there was such a God, I'd join Satan and fight him to the end. I'll never believe in a pompous old nobodaddy on a throne — inflicting pain on every living creature for his greater glory. But a god that is everywhere, energy and life, confusion and craziness, the non-thinking and beautiful god inside the cabbage leaf — the god of blind and directionless pain who lives alongside joy and vision, now that's a god I could love."

"Even someone as saintly as Christ, you would deny?"

"Naw. I'm being cranky. It's unfair to criticize the ointment others put on their wounds."

Brian considered this as Charlie finished the row and moved over to the next one. The old man was unrelenting. Maybe that was his ritual, his religion. Years ago Brian had pored through as many sacred texts as he could read, both eastern and western. He'd spent an entire summer studying the Jewish world, all the ceremonies, the *halakha*, the dietary laws . . . "My mother was a Catholic — until she married my father. He made such a production of hating religion that she gradually gave up going to church for years. But it came back stronger as Dad grew weaker. Now you should see her working her rosary. But it hasn't made her world any prettier."

"I praise the world every morning when I wake up. Yet each breath, each footfall I make, kills something."

"So what's the answer, suicide?"

"That's a denial. That's 'no.' I prefer 'yes.'"

"What kind of an answer is that?"

"That's your big problem, Brian, wanting an answer. The answer is that there is no answer. We can only limit the extent of our damage." Charlie dropped the hoe and knelt down and began shaking the dirt out of the piles of grass clumps.

"You believe in fate, though, don't you? — that the collisions which happen to us are inevitable?" Brian felt a surge of power in his blood. This was good.

Charlie let the rich earth flow through his fingers as he loosened it and heaped it and scooped it back under the stems of the bush beans. He pulled a hand fork out of his back pocket and used it to loosen the last few weeds while mounding the earth around the plants. "I suppose so."

"You've interfered with my life three times over twenty years. First, when you sabotaged the pulp mill. I was summer jobbing my way through university at Sweet Water. Your action got my shift supervisor canned and me promoted."

"I'm glad I did you a good turn, but I should think it was you and your supervisor who . . . " Charlie sat back on his haunches with a bemused expression. "I recognized you as soon as I saw you come across the field here, but I couldn't remember where from. You're the asshole kid in the bar bragging about another man's misfortune and how you got his job. I was there, listening at the next table. You haven't changed much either, still an asshole, only fatter, and you talk better."

Brian flushed. He didn't remember sitting in any bar, or bragging about his promotion. He might have. He had to keep going — now was the time. "Years later you interfered with my life again. Let me tell you about a young girl named Elizabeth.

"She was seventeen-years-old, funny in the way seventeen-year-olds are, full of life, good-looking too. She wanted to be a nurse. One night things got carried away with a slightly older guy she met, a construction worker.

When he found out she was pregnant he dropped her like a hot potato. She didn't have much money. Her mother was a Catholic, her father too scary. Luckily, her brother got her an appointment at an abortion clinic, the only professional one in town that shuffled under-age kids in through the back door. The day before her appointment, it was burned down."

Charlie stabbed his garden fork violently into the earth, and pulled, accidentally lifting a bean plant.

"So she panicked, went to a bargain-basement butcher another friend told her about. She doesn't have to worry about having children any more. She nearly bled to death that same day. Now she's sterile."

"I'm sorry to hear that."

"It was a good cause, Charlie; that's all you thought. You ruined my sister."

"And Rita?" Charlie ripped off a piece of green cabbage leaf and began chewing on it defiantly. "She must be number three. You don't have to tell me what I did to her; I know. She was alive when I met her, one of the most naturally happy people I ever met. By the time we split up she was a walking, talking, overweight depressive who drank too much. She said I made her think all the time about the dark things, weighing her down with the world's pain."

Brian was afraid he was losing the thread. "She wasn't that depressive when I met her, and I fell in love, but yes, that's what she told me, that you killed her, made her hate the world. You've been a ghost haunting my life."

"What crap. No, not me. I'm merely the blind instrument of chance that hurt you . . . or maybe didn't hurt you. You're a liar. And you want the truth? Truth is nothing but a lot of hand washing — an excuse for you to come here to kill me."

"Who said I came here to kill you?"

"You didn't come here to write any bloody book!"

Brian shrugged, attempting to look mysterious.

"What happened? I'm still alive. Change your mind? Or don't you have the guts?"

"You'll know that when I'm gone."

"And what happened to Rita? Tell me what happened to Rita! How did you get to know her, anyway? You weren't searching for me, were you?" Charlie was almost screaming now. "And don't think I believe for a minute that crap about your sister! I doubt an animal like you could have a sister!"

Brian stood up, moving suddenly, so that Charlie, still on the ground, shifted to face him. "I hope," Brian said, "you're proud of yourself."

He stalked out of the vegetable patch, his blood surging to his face. He could feel a popping in his skull, like dripping water. He was giddy, faint. Was he having a stroke? It was dreamland here, an askew nightmare he had to escape. Finish and escape. Yes. Only he couldn't. He turned around and walked back to the garden, still dizzy with anger. Then he wanted to giggle. He didn't know what he wanted. "No, you old fart, I don't have a sister." At least he wished he didn't have a sister, not after that incident last year — and now her husband was threatening to have him charged if he came near them again.

So there's Charlie kneeling among the beans, the truth slipping out in the form it knows best — lies. For so many of us the truth is only the lie we believe at the moment.

The old man remained seated on the garden earth, as if waiting for Brian to pick up the mattock and split his skull, but Brian wasn't going to try that, not now, not here. Charlie was too fast, despite his age.

This wasn't working out the way Brian planned. He stepped between the old man and the sun. Charlie ignored the shadow, and definitely wasn't frightened.

Brian felt his hand close on the mattock handle. It wasn't supposed to be like this.

"Why have you come here?" Charlie began weeding again, calmly.

"We'll get to that when we finish your story."

"My story?" Charlie harrumphed. "It's your story that I'm after." Suddenly, his head jerked up and he considered the sky, squinting.

Brian didn't see the black shape racing above the trees beyond the meadow's edge, towards the raspberries, but he knew it was there. He could hear the whistling of its wings.

"Congo!" The old man screamed. "Congo!"

Down below, at the low end of the garden, the parrot, messing about with a dead June bug on the path between the berry bush rows, snapped to attention.

"Look out," Charlie yelled, "it's an eagle! An eagle!"

The parrot screeched and dived into the raspberry brambles.

The stooping raptor boomed onto the now-empty path, wings arched — the lowered talons mechanical and powerful, like the wheels on a jet making a landing. It hit the ground, tearing up leaves and dust, the dead June bug floating into the air as if it were an errant, tossed coin.

The parrot tangled itself in the raspberries, ramming through the prickly stems, twisting around, brandishing its defiant but hopeless claws and beak at the eagle, screeching and helpless.

The eagle, frustrated by the failure of its dive, gathered up its pride and swaggered into the stalks, beating the stiff stems aside, lunging for the parrot.

Charlie ran towards the raspberries, waving his arms and hat. The eagle glared at him; then continued after the thrashing parrot. Congo screeched again, snapping through the raspberries, terrified, yet still threatening retaliation with strangled gasps and his ineffectual beak.

The eagle caught hold of his wing, ripping out a flight feather as Congo lurched backwards into another tangle, unleashing an ear-splitting howl of despair.

Charlie rushed down the path. The eagle realizing this hunt was over, backed out from the brambles, attempting to depart with dignity.

The slow beat of its wings thumped through the air as Charlie charged after it, close enough to touch its white tail. The parrot kept screaming and struggling, meshed between the branches.

Gasping for breath, Charlie sat down in the dust of the path, and slammed his hat back on his head.

Tears rolled down the old man's eyes. "Congo?" His voice was so despairing it made Brian want to turn away. "Congo?"

The parrot disentangled himself from the raspberries, and hesitant, shambled out, dragging his wing. He considered the old man's knee for a moment before digging his beak into Charlie's pantleg and pulling himself up until he gradually reached Charlie's shoulder, where he huddled beneath the straw hat, and carefully folded the injured wing back into his quivering, grey chest.

Charlie recovered his composure, and fixed his attention on the vegetable garden, as if he were ashamed he'd broken down so completely.

When the parrot spoke his voice was stripped of its usual defiance; he had become plaintive, almost questioning. "Watch that hawk? Roll that rock?"

16

"HOW ARE YA?" BRIAN ASKED.

The rock didn't reply, occupying like an emperor a skewed, bristling throne of bars and wedges. Unmoving and resolute it had refused to roll over this morning, despite its awkward angle and the effort Charlie had put into dethroning it.

"Not talking?"

The rock definitely wasn't talking.

"I've decided we should make peace. You scared me at first, coming up the stairs in the night." He gave it an affectionate pat, admiring the flecked mica on its surface. "I thought you were malevolent, but now, after watching you, I realize I was wrong. Will you forgive me? Forgiveness is everything, isn't it?"

The rock still wasn't talking.

Brian shrugged. "I understand — you're the silent type. By the way, I might write that book yet. Charlie got me thinking. Can a rock be a character in a story? I don't know. It would have to be a little more articulate, or at least more active than you — or are you just waiting to make your move? Do you want to kill me?" He leaned against it, his eyeball close to the black mica flecks, and it seemed he was falling inside, caught by a weird, immobile rain of dark spots. "Are you alive?" Then his eye focused on the fly. It was the same one. The wing. He slapped at it, and it was gone, buzzing away. The rock shifted, rolling over. "You son-of-a-bitch!"

The rock lay silent on its side.

"Is that supposed to be meaningful? Is that the way you talk?" The same anger, the uncontrollable surge that had overtaken him earlier, swelled in his temple. He grew dizzy again. He sat down with a thud against the rock, and put his head in his hands. He wanted to cry. This was bullshit.

Charlie marched up the hill. He stopped at the rock, studying Brian's tearful eyes. "How the hell . . . ? I spent all morning trying to do that."

"The bloody thing moved on its own. I was only leaning against it. And then I slapped a fly . . . "

"Well," Charlie said, "I've never heard such nonsense. I think you're getting bushed, lad. Why don't you put on your dancing shoes and let's go to a party."

Believe me, man-child, this rock is no symbol, or fancy literary allusion. It's a rock, real — like the big one behind my house. As Charlie would say: "complete in its rockness, and nothing else . . . " Think of it as a character within a story that distrusts storytellers.

"A party?"

"Yup, the monthly dance at Terminal Hall. I never miss one. Come on, a body needs a fire inside every once in a while."

"What about the rock?"

"The rock can come, too, if it wants, but I doubt it will."

"This isn't funny. The bloody rock moved on its own."

"Don't be an idiot," Charlie said, and his grin was scarier than the stillness of the rock.

***

There's nothing like a shower and a change of clothes when a man spends his day working in hot weather, even if the shower is a bucket with holes in it hanging from the deck of a treehouse, and the water has to be heated on a stove. Charlie pranced down the path like a peacock, wearing an old but immaculate set of bell-bottom jeans, a leather insert widening the bell further, a white Nehru-collared shirt with open chest and poet's sleeves, and on his pate, shadowing his red forehead, a cockily perched Donovan — the remnants of his hair gathered in a tiny ponytail. He was almost pretty for his age, and the kinky sunbleached chest hairs added the final touch.

"You look like an escapee from the sixties."

"Ah, the sixties," Charlie sighed, "that was fun."

"Free love, the drugs, that sort of thing?"

"Love ain't ever free. If you're gonna play you're gonna pay. I played and I payed. As for the dope, those were the days! I'm no innocent. I smoked my smoke. I drank so much whiskey I could feel the fat growing under my armpits, and my sweat smelled like liquor.

"I went deep and fast and hard. Down to licking the last fragments of my last line of cocaine off the cover of a paperback copy of *Steppenwolf.* I was desperate for every grain of it. Hell, I wolfed so much mescaline and acid and peyote I glowed in the dark."

What Charlie said about fat under his armpits disturbed Brian. He could feel it under his own arms, growing thicker every year, like his belly. He walked faster, striding ahead of Charlie. Then he stopped. "Aren't you going to lock the place up?"

"There ain't no lock. Besides, somebody might want something."

"Want something?"

"Sure . . . a tool . . . a can opener . . . tea or sugar . . . How else could I give it to them if I wasn't here?"

"What if they stole it!"

"Son, if any islander stole anything from my place, they'd come to regret it for the rest of their lives, and then some. Everybody would know. They'd never live it down. They'd have to move away. Besides, they can just take it and tell me later. Why bother stealing it, city boy?"

The car gleamed like an odd-shaped moon in the dusk among the trees. Charlie touched its skin, running his hand over it, stroking it. "Very pretty." He climbed into the passenger seat. "Take the High Road. The road crew has destroyed the Low Road again. They ain't got much else to do around here, so they keep ripping up everything and fixing it worse. I used to love cars, worked on them myself, rebuilt motors and turned brake drums. A good machine is as beautiful as a tree. It thrives out of its own necessity. Mind you, they've got all that computer stuff now, wrecking them. They're not real machines these days. Before, you could say: 'if this pushes that; then that must push this.' Mechanical parts have a visible logic. Electronics use invisible logic."

"Do you want to drive?" Brian held up the keys.

"No, I couldn't find it in my heart to pollute the air any more, though the smog makes for lovely sunsets. When the light hits the sky beyond those islands there's fabulous marmalades and scarlets. On good days all the shrubbies head down to the beach at Opportunity Bay to blow a little dope and cheer the sun into the horizon."

"But you will ride, won't you?"

"Since you're going that way, I don't mind if I do." They started off, Charlie ebullient. "Yup, now that men can't rape and pillage so much these days, they've only got cars. The driver's seat ain't called a cockpit without reason."

It was about two miles to the hall. The old wood-framed building stood sentinel above the chute to the ferry terminal — it sure was a mean piece of hill. Brian hadn't signed the petition because he didn't want to tag himself, even with a phony name (he kept his name changes to a minimum); yet here he was going to a dance, steering the white Miata into the dirt parking lot of a hall that resembled a haunted house. He knew the locals would be curious, and he sat behind the wheel as Charlie wandered towards the crowd. Then, afraid to miss anything, he climbed out and followed.

Charlie sashayed like a hero through the throng at the door, where an agile old woman grabbed his hand. He gave her a twirl on the floor while the Celtic-Bluegrass-Rock-Country band fiddled a jig. Then he left her in the embrace of another, greeted a few men at a table, and made a comment which obviously amused them. A second woman, middle-aged, confronted him with smiles and granny glasses and a gingham dress. She would have been pretty if her teeth weren't crooked. Bad teeth are a common phenomenon beyond the reach of the big cities and dental plans. Charlie danced an entire song with her, and after it ended, spun her around a few more times until she walked away, graceful, dizzy, laughing. She was familiar. The woman in the double bust on Coyote's table at the treehouse? Elvira, the boy's mother.

"The dirty dog." Brian surveyed the dance floor — Charlie was at home here on the island; he wasn't a secretive relic or recluse. The last vestiges of the sixties' back-to-the-land movement had come to these bays and farms, and hung on. Charlie was one of them, and popular, too.

Charlie returned across the floor, beaming, his Donovan askew. He was also an impeccable host, introducing Brian to numerous people, making sure his guest wouldn't feel neglected before he went out and danced with the women again. He paid special attention to Elvira. Brian wondered how much self-protection there was in the old man's performance. Brian was identified now. But that was all right; he had a few tricks as well. Charlie's innocence disappointed him.

The band launched into another foot-stomping jig. Their tunes mostly had one speed, *allegretto*. Then, cadging a cigarette off a bearded long-hair, Brian found himself inheriting half a deck. The good-hearted man, one of the last smokers on the island, was well-supplied and understood life without tobacco. Brian fled with his treasure while Charlie continued dancing on the hearts of the ladies.

He meandered across the lawn, inhaling the first cigarette, happy, holding a glass of wine with his other hand. There was nothing else he needed — paradise is one more cigarette when you think you're quitting.

A figure stepped out of the shadows. In spite of his near hopeless sense of smell, Brian could whiff the marijuana. The boy wore a black T-shirt — an enormous, red tongue hanging down the front. The gathering darkness obscured his face. "Festus?"

"That's me."

"How come you're not inside, partying?" Brian lit a second cigarette off the first. This was more than heaven.

"I'm busy fixing up a man's life."

"And how do you do that?"

"It's a lady he wanted to meet later. Only he's not very popular right now. But I think I set him up. I'll find out tomorrow." There was a rustle and a figure departed from the back end of the brush, heading behind the hall. "That was him in the bushes, there. People call me Festus the Fixer, 'cause I fix everything. I can fix your car, your love life, your barn. What do you need?"

"You sound very mature for a boy of your age. How old are you?"

"Younger than I look and older than you think."

"And you can fix everything?"

"Except myself."

They sat down on the grass under the rising moon.

"That needs fixing?"

"Everything needs fixing." Festus reached for the cigarettes in Brian's shirt pocket, pulled out the deck and took one for himself. Brian, greedy, despite his bonanza, reluctantly held up the lighter and lit it for him. "You're a little young to begin a life-long addiction."

There it was again, that too-wise birdman look in those unearthly and unbirdlike blue eyes. "I only smoke at parties. You looking for dope? I can introduce you to that fellow from the bushes; he's got great bud. The main crop won't come in for another six weeks at least, but you should see the colas on his clones. Mega. They'll mature as big as my forearm. And it's not harsh, either. Very smooth. Primo."

"Many people grow it here?"

"Sure, smoke is about the only cash crop on the island. That, and sheep, and you get sick of eating lamb after a while. You should meet my friend. He's lonely. The men are scared to talk to him in public, and the women are on his case."

"Why?"

"Jim — his name is Peacock Jim because his father brought the first peafowl to the island, and Jim, who's kind of impetuous, freed them all one night, years ago. Now he's in trouble with the ladies. At the solstice there was a woman's night — where they celebrate the goddess. Dancing and singing and kissing and praying — channelling and invoking — all that New Age stuff.

"It was down at Harpoon Bay. And there was a moon, too. That made it a big-time solstice. I saw everything. When I heard my mother mention where 'the woman's night' was going to happen I snuck down and hid below the arbutus in the rocks — that's scary. I don't like spending long under the arbutus, because they're a good place for ticks, and we've got Lyme's disease on the island. The ticks carry it."

Brian felt itchy. Ticks gave him the willies. "Have you ever had a tick on you?"

"Lots of times, but I never got Lyme's. Are you going to let me tell my story?"

Actually, Festus, not many people tell long, structured, stories except in novels, but I'll give it to you because you asked for it. I think you should have the honour of telling your story, don't you?

*— in the way that you would tell it if the world didn't keep
interrupting you. Oh, you're going to hate me ten years from now.*

"I had a good view. I only went down there to watch
the women show their tits. They get naked around a fire,
drink wine, smoke grass; bonding and sharing and all
that. Pretty soon they're dancing, shaking themselves at
the moon, bonding away, especially the lesbians; they were
sticking their tongues into each other's mouths, and
anybody else's they could get hold of, including my
mother. Mom doesn't like these parties much, but she says
it's good for community relations. Most of the younger
women go. I think they're afraid of what the fembos will
say. A few of the lesbians are real creeps. Don't get me
wrong, I don't mind them, except there's this gang of
heavy political ones — we call them fembos — they sure
can abuse people, especially the fellas. They're always
spreading malicious gossip.

"So everyone's having a good time. Me too, 'cause I'm
seeing all their breasts. A group of the women are kissing
and playing around, dancing, or talking seriously, away
from the fire. One of the woman was crying, and her
friends were giving her lots of sympathy.

"Then, out of the rocks in the shallow water, comes this
black sea-monster thing, draped in seaweed, waving its
arms about. It looked like the creature from the black
lagoon, and it made strange noises, too, as if it were playing
a didgeridoo. The women went nuts . . . screaming and
freaking and running for their clothes, and into the bushes
until there was nothing but the fire and me and the
creature. I was scared shitless. Except I was too scared to
run anywhere in case I ran into my mom, and she can be
as hair-raising as any sea monster when she gets mad. But

the creature subsided back into the water. Soon, I saw bubbles going away across the ocean.

"Rumours about this spread like wildfire. Only nobody knew what happened — until a week later. Peacock Jim opened his big mouth at the bar in Sweet Water. It turns out he'd gotten wind of the big event, like me, and dug up a creature suit somewhere, and scuba dived to the site. He dumped his gear underwater, and came up, scaring the women; then went down again, grabbed his scuba gear and swam off. He's supposed to be a Buddhist, but he's got a twisted sense of humour — I guess he's real Zen.

"A thing like that REALLY gets around. The day after he opened his mouth everyone on the island knew what had happened. The men roll up and give themselves stitches at the mention of it, especially when there's no ladies about. A lot of the women, my mother, too, think it was pretty funny. You know, awful at the time, yet when you look back upon it . . . But the fembos, are upset, and they're gyrating the island. So people have to leave Peacock Jim out in the cold for a while. It's not that bad, but Jimbo's got a taste for melodrama so he's pretending he's a real outsider, practically a shrubbie — those are all the eco-radicals from the city who come here with no money in the summer and live in the bush. Jim will find a way to make it up soon, and be forgiven."

Brian nodded. "That's a pretty good story."

"Talk about it has kept islanders cooking for a couple weeks. It should be worth one more cigarette."

The request made Brian's smile sag. The half-deck was disappearing at an alarming rate. Oddly, the boy's request made him recall a spy novel he once read, where a secret agent died after his first puff on a poisoned cigarette. What was in it? He couldn't remember any more; something exotic — atropine or epinephrine. He withdrew another smoke and handed it to Festus, who lit it after striking a wooden match on his zipper with too much ostentation.

"This Jim, he's an eccentric fellow?"

"Yup. An old islander, born here — fled for a while when he was a kid in the seventies, came back and decided he was a Buddhist. Then he launched a towing company, claimed he was everyone's salvation. After that he got the government road contract, which worked out okay, because he decided all the potholes were products of the world of illusion, *samsara*, and never fixed them much until a local threatened to throttle him after losing a muffler. But it works out fine for the island, too — the rough road keeps the tourist count low. Occasionally, the government gets on his case, so he has his crew rip up a section and put it back, like they're doing on the Low Road right now. Usually, they do it in the tourist season — tourists are like road dust, you have to damp them down occasionally. Otherwise, they'll multiply so fast they'd pollute the place. Jim provides employment before the marijuana crop comes in — when the local boys are broke and need work. But mischief is his second cousin, and he has to find trouble once in a while, otherwise he gets depressed and threatens to become an evangelist or Jehovah's Witness or scary stuff like that . . . which we sure don't need around here. This island is too nutty already."

Both their heads snapped up. Charlie and a big-bossomed woman, feathers dangling from her hair, trampled laughing down the darkened steps of the hall and disappeared around the back.

Festus said: "He's got the grace. He's a gentlemen. The women love him."

"What's you're father like?"

Startled by the question, Festus was silent, his child-man face waxlike, studying him. "My stepfather. He's a good fella, but he has to work off-island too much."

Brian lit another cigarette. "Have you been abused?"

"Abused? What do you mean, abused?"

"Hit. Hurt or molested."

"Why don't you screw off, mister." Festus climbed to his feet and threw his cigarette onto the grass between them, and stomped off. The boy's island sense, the fear of tinder-dry summers, turned him around. He squashed the cigarette until it was dead. Then he stalked away, towards the trees.

"It's written all over you, Festus," Brian called out. "He hits you. I know that."

"You don't know nothing, mister." Festus evaporated into the trees.

Brian lay back on the lawn with a groan. That altercation was worth another cigarette. Lighting it, he lolled back in the grass, high on carbon monoxide. "Poor kid."

***

The wine was gone, and so were the cigarettes. Had he passed out? The hall didn't sound like many people were left inside. He felt green with all the smoke he'd inhaled.

Staggering around the side of the hall to the back of the near-empty parking lot, he heard a giggle. There was a peacock feather at his feet. He picked it up, and walked to the car, aware, despite his nausea, of the couple groping and laughing under the tree in the dark at the end of the field. A solitary, erect feather and the Donovan mingled in the shadows. And that seemed to be all they were wearing. The pair leaned against the tree, Charlie's wiry frame like a thin, red rod between those great breasts.

Brian, in a fit of decency, walked back to the car, but he couldn't resist peeking. He climbed in and waited at the wheel, hooking the feather onto the rear-view mirror. The couple was still going at it. Festus lurched into his consciousness, barely a foot away, leaning against the fender, angelic, yet frightening. "So you think you know everything?"

"I don't know anything," Brian said. "I just don't like pain."

"You got pain?"

"We all got pain."

"I can fix it for you. I'm Festus the Fixer. I can fix your car, too. It's a nice car." He stroked the Miata's hood. The gesture was obscene.

"There's nothing wrong with my car."

"That's okay. I'll fix it anyway."

Brian laughed. "You're a beautiful kid."

Festus posed artfully in his baggy Stones T-shirt, legs crossed, arm behind his neck, an innocent model for a sculptor, except for the grotesque red tongue on his black chest.

Charlie emerged from the dark, breathless, cheeks lipstick-stained, his shirt hanging out of his pants. He climbed into the passenger seat. "Let's get outta here before I end up married." He gave Festus a wink.

Festus, still posing, winked back. He stretched and wandered away. "I can't get your groceries tomorrow. I have to go to Vancouver with my stepfather."

Charlie shrugged. "Next week?"

"I'll check my calender."

"You do that."

So there you are. I can't help painting you the way I see you, only it will be ten years later when you read this. Is it embarrassing? Fascinating? Or merely gone the way of so many things once important? Gone — like the stars in yesterday's midnight sky.

17

The Loaded Parrot

CHARLIE'S FACE WAS RAINBOWED BY THE PRISMS IN THE WINDOW, the parrot tugging at a sheet of paper in his hand. The paper ripped and the parrot lost, clutching only a shred in its beak, which it spat out.

Charlie handed the ripped page to Brian. "Since Festus is gone, and you've got that fancy car, you can do the shopping.

Clutching the nearly illegible scrawl, Brian felt like he'd been released from jail. It reminded him of his school days, being given permission to go to the washroom, and then not stopping until he reached the pool hall. There was no telling what hell could break loose. Maybe he'd buy a steak and eat it raw.

At the store, the woman, her elbows propped on the counter, held up a book she was reading, *Ayahuasca For The Novice Shaman*. This way anyone who entered the store could see what she was studying. She closed the book and sat up straight, ramrod stiff. She wasn't wearing a bra again. The magnificent breasts under her shirt and that long, scrawny horse-face still didn't match up. She remembered him, and pursed her disapproving lips. She only smiled for real islanders.

He pictured her naked and dead behind a bush, flies laying eggs on her. A wave of nausea swept through him — where did these thoughts come from?

Noticing there were no feathers today, he gave her a big beaming grin which confused her, and she was forced to return his smile.

The most interesting thing about the store was that it had liquor. Before he checked out the vegetables, Brian picked up a mickey of Glenlivet and a bottle of Chateau-neuf-du-Pape, and placed them on the counter beside her book. For such a tiny, two-bit store it had an excellent stock of quality liquor. The islanders were a discerning lot.

Ogling the shelves behind the storekeeper, he didn't have the heart to purchase cigarettes. That was carrying betrayal too far. Besides, all that smoking last night had nauseated him. "I can make it," he whispered to himself. "I can quit." He picked up a Vancouver newspaper.

The organic section of the store was pathetic. He contemplated the withered eggplants and apples with disdain. Across the aisle, the fresh, almost plastic oranges beckoned. He picked out a dozen, immaculate, except for one, which had a brown spot near the crown. "You look like a killer to me." He polished the orange against his cheek. The brown spot didn't rub off.

Outside the store, the note about the wandering ram had a little scrawl added. JAKE FINALLY CHECKED HIS SHEEP. IT TURNED OUT TO BE HIS RAM BUT I ALREADY HAD IT IN THE FREEZER. TOUGH GAMEY MUTTON FOR SALE. CHEAP. GREAT FOR STEW.

There was a fresh, small bullet hole in the window, bulls-eying the petition demanding stiffer penalties for juvenile delinquents that was taped to the glass.

Across the grass, Mecca was in full glory — middle-aged women in flower print dresses that brushed the dry ground, old long-hairs with scraggly beards sitting on benches and sipping their cappuccinos, kids flying a kite over the beach beyond. An extraordinarily tall gaunt-looking teenage boy who resembled Festus slightly, danced on a blanket; pulling gaudy scarves through the air, being watched by a couple of young women — shrubbies — bare-breasted and seated cross-legged on the dead grass, their dirty feet sticking out from their dirty jeans as they sipped from ceramic tea-bowls. Nobody paid any attention to their toplessness. It was almost tempting to stay.

He stashed the liquor in the shrubs beside the ramp before he entered the treehouse with the groceries and dumped them out on the table. Charlie gawked at the oranges. He picked up one, and rolled it in his palm. "Crap," he said. "Death. Imported fruit picked green and treated; that's after it's been sprayed; then they hit it with the ethanol, to change the colour, make it appear real. We're the eaters of unripe fruit. Nothing ripens naturally in our food economy." He sunk his teeth into the orange, tainted rind and all, spraying a mist of juice. "Let's live dangerously." Charlie rolled back in his chair. "Aw, it's evil, but it tastes good — like most evil things. As sweet as ice cream."

As sweet as ice cream? Rita was seated on a stool in a small ice cream shop near Kitsilaino Beach last summer in Vancouver. She'd bought a pecan waffle cone. There was so much life in her face — as she told him how a man named Charlie had ripped her heart out and killed her spirit. It had taken Brian a long time and a lot of work to stumble upon her, and then it happened so easily.

She was sucking the ice cream out of the cone, gazing at the beach when a strange expression swept over her. From beneath the table an invisible force possessed her, moving up the length of her body, until she shivered on the stool. "I just had an orgasm," she said.

"You what?"

"I had an orgasm eating my ice cream cone."

It shocked him. "Here? Now?" Her erotic innocence, despite the fact she was at least five years older than him, was disarming. It also belied her claims to internal sorrow.

"Why not?" she asked, sticking her tongue inside the cone. Brian was overwhelmed by a surge of lust.

Then he was back in the treehouse.

Charlie was scrutinizing him, as if eavesdropping on his thoughts. "Come on, he said. "You're getting weird on me. Let's pack a lunch and go for a hike. I want to visit one of my favourite places."

In the forest the air grew heavier, thick with summer humidity. Brian was high on it. Maybe all this fresh island air was improving his sense of smell. He lurched down the pathway behind his guide. A red-shafted flicker sang out — a creepy lilting chatter. It dived off its branch and glided through the cedars. The parrot perched on Charlie's shoulder, letting the old man do the work on this walk, kept its eye on the disappearing flicker.

After a while, the trail pointed down. They'd passed over the central hump of the island.

Arriving at a low bluff, they scrambled the four feet down to the beach below — rough stones tumbled together by the wind and tides. "This is the spot," Charlie announced, as if he'd taken a short stroll to the outhouse, not a gruelling hike through the island's heart. "No one comes here, not even the Indians. The local Salish say cannibal spirits inhabit this beach. Maybe that's why they threw a land claim at it, although it's privately owned. If they get possession they can turn it into a tourist spot for whites, and have the last laugh on the evil spirits."

Finding a good picnic spot on the beach, Brian, exhausted, loosened the Moroccan leather packsack and settled it among the rocks, the clink of the wine bottle echoing across the bay. The parrot flew from Charlie's shoulder and began poking about the rocks, playing a self-important tag game with the baby crabs scuttling among the barnacled litter. When it caught one it would quickly crush the shell and toss it into the air, cackling.

Brian emptied the bag onto the stones, the granola and organic grapes and peaches and carrots for Charlie, and the salami and cheese he'd bought at the store for himself.

There were rock oysters cemented to the stones. "Hey! There's oysters. Have you got a knife?"

Sceptical, the old man pulled his pocket knife out. "Don't damage the blade." He handed it to Brian who crouched among the rocks and began prying oysters free.

When Brian looked up, Charlie was naked, wading gingerly around the barnacles into the sea. For a moment, waist-depth, he faced the strait, all sunburnt and grizzled. Quite a sight. Then he dipped into the water and began swimming across the bay.

Brian slid the mickey of scotch out of the pack and took a long drink. He hadn't been able to resist bringing that along as well. Now he regretted it. It wasn't the same.

Whiskey didn't belong to the natural landscape, except perhaps after a hard run in a canoe through fast water, or maybe a dash tossed into the camp coffee late at night in the mountains. He took another pull.

The parrot skittered over to his side, curious about the bottle. "Cookie?"

He poured a capful and offered it to the bird. The parrot sniffed contemptuously at the whiskey, and turned its attention to Brian's sneakers, chewing on the lace ends, attempting to undo the knot.

Brian opened the first oyster, breaking off splinters from the shell. The knife was going to be a mess. Holding the half-shell to his mouth, he slid everything in — oyster, juice, and bits of shell, worked it around a little, savouring, before spitting out the little white pieces and swallowing the raw oyster whole. "Aww, that's good." Yet a little icky. "It was a brave man who first ate oysters." He belched — a curious whiskey and oyster taste.

The parrot belched in sympathy. Tilting its head, it inspected him, debating whatever a bird debates inside its head. "Cookie?"

Beyond the bay, Charlie was still swimming — a dot in the smooth, blue water. The upper orange haze of the polluted air that ringed Vancouver played out a narrow drama of exotic tangerine and scarlet, though it was a while yet to sunset. Charlie's right, Brian thought; there is something to be said for polluted air. "It sure can look pretty."

The parrot waded among the growing pile at Brian's feet, picking at the cone of muscle attached to a shell. This gave Brian an idea. He saved as much of the juice as he could from the next oyster, and poured it into an empty shell. He added a dollop of scotch. The parrot sidled up to the concoction and took a sip. It gargled the drink briefly; then swallowed. It looked at him for a moment, belched, and began to laugh. It struck the shell with its beak several times in appreciation, and lapped up the remainder of the drink, its thick black tongue shooting in and out.

He mixed him another. "Hey bird, I think I just invented a new drink; maybe I'll call it a shelltail. An oystertail?"

When Brian glanced up he saw that Charlie was returning. He nudged the parrot away from the oyster shell, but the bird would have none of that; it shouldered its way back and finished it off. Brian scattered the shells down the beach while the bird watched with disgust.

Eventually, the old man stumbled his way through the stones and barnacles, and sat heavily on the rock beside Brian. "Swimming is a beautiful thing. Since you showed up my routine has gone to hell. I try to swim three times a week, all year around."

"The winter?"

"It's better in the winter. At least on these islands. The weather doesn't go much beyond freezing, and the chill makes me feel alive."

"You look like a mangy old predator on that rock. Why'd you call yourself Coyote?"

"The coyote can live in urban areas, yet it's got a wild heart. It's a survivor."

"He's the trickster, too, isn't he?"

"One of them. Along with the raven and the rabbit. Deep inside, I must have known how my tricks were going to turn out, right from the beginning; you know how the stories go — Coyote always trying to help, to find new good things for the people, and then accidentally setting his asshole on fire, or stuff like that. Then there's Charlie E. Coyote — his modern face — always getting blown up by the roadrunner."

"And now he's dead."

"Coyote is dead. Long live Coyote."

"In ChemCity?"

"In ChemCity."

Coyote turned his attention to the small islet at the end of a narrow land bridge from the beach. "Everyone calls it Erection Island, because that's what it looks like from the air when the tide is low. It extends from the crotch of Artemis — I guess that makes her a hermaphrodite — and it's full of rare plants. An American millionaire owns it — they own most of the good waterfront around here. No doubt he'll build his dream hideaway one day, and ruin everything. Unless the land claim shuts him down."

"Rare plants?"

"Rare enough. Cape Blanco sedums and an uncommon variety of monkey flower, prickly pear cacti. It's hard to imagine cacti this far north, but they're real — pronged my feet a few times."

Charlie, still damp, dressed. Then he bent down and held out his arm; the parrot clambered unsteadily onto his shoulder, where it perched at an angle.

They walked across the low-tide gravel bridge to the island. Its dry yellow moss was shaded by arbutus trees and twisted fir. At their feet, cacti and blooming mimuli and yellow sedums. This was intrusive; the islet did have the atmosphere of a sacred territory.

Ahead, Charlie stopped, as if he knew what Brian was thinking. "I can never forget that every step I take, every breath I make, kills something."

The parrot nodded in agreement on Charlie's shoulder; then it almost fell off. Brian ignored it. The men stopped and lay down on the moss, gazing at the strait, and were silent for several minutes. Charlie let his head rest on a rock while the parrot meandered about, inspecting the moss for insects. "This would be a good place to kill me, but you haven't got the nerve to do it here and now, do you?"

"Maybe you're changing my mind."

"When I was younger I still ate fish. I caught rockfish, and ling. Once I hooked a big ling. It hung onto the hook like the ultimate old boot. When I pulled it up there was this huge wide head; it resembled a shark. The thing was maybe ten feet long. It burped up a small rockfish, about a two pounder, and turned around, went back down. The rockfish must have taken the hook and then been swallowed whole by the ling. The world is strange. I took the rockfish home and cooked it for dinner. It was delicious.

"It was off those rocks below us — to the left there's a deep pool. Now, I hear the cod are full of tumours. There's so much poison in the strait. Cadmium . . . dioxins around the pulp mills. That sort of stuff. A school of grey whales got whacked a while back. They say a paint company lost a couple of thousand gallons of pentaphenols in a river and it flowed down to the bay where they fed.

"It used to be wild here." Charlie's arm swept out in a gesture encompassing the entire strait." Once, I was swimming nearby; a mist appeared around me, and a deep gurgling. Killer whales. A whole pod. They were curious, I guess. They swam alongside for a few minutes, and I was frightened. I've never been afraid of dying, but the size of them scared me. It was a different kind of fear. And their breath, that mist, stank like hell."

"I'm afraid of dying."

"Why?"

"It's not as if it'll make much difference, but I want to do things."

"Write books?"

"And make love to women. See different countries."

"You want to be a tourist?"

"Aren't we all?"

"Not me." Charlie stood up, disgusted. The parrot flew awkwardly onto his shoulder and the pair walked away, Brian following them. "I'll take the guilt," Charlie said, scrambling up the rocky slope. "The pain and the joy. I ain't no tourist and I don't think of loving women and going to exotic countries in the same breath. I take my responsibilities serious. Why do you think I'm rolling that bloody rock?"

The quickly rising tide had obscured most of the bridge to Erection Island, and they waded across while the parrot went nautical. "Avast mates!" it screamed.

"Where'd he get that from?" Brian asked.

"Must have watched too many pirate films in his younger years."

On the beach, Brian gathered more oysters. When he looked around he saw Charlie, now seated, holding the bottle of wine. Brian handed him the knife, and with an impressive dexterity, the old man carved out the cork, hardly breaking it up at all, before handing the knife back.

Charlie looked at Brian, and nodded sagely. "The body is a temple, and every temple should be washed with wine once in a while. Besides, I was too busy dancing last night. I forgot to have a drink, and now I'm so dry, I'm farting dust." He took a deep chug of red wine, and set the bottle down so hard on the rocks Brian thought it would break. He gargled briefly, swallowed, and belched. A hell of a way to treat good wine.

Dumping his oysters, Brian stretched out, squirming and pushing stones out of the way. "Oysters and red wine. Salami and cheese and good bread. It's all I could ever want."

The parrot clucked behind Brian's ear while he shelled the first oyster. Charlie was relaxed, looking ready to doze off as he faced the strait in front of him. Brian splashed a little scotch into the juice remaining in the oyster shell; the parrot lapped it up. He gave it a piece of bread, which it threw away. Brian shrugged and wolfed down a chunk of salami and bread.

"I don't understand what you want from me," Charlie said, his broad, gnarly back rippling, old, yet well-muscled. He picked up a carrot from the pile of uneaten ones at his side, and began chewing on it, contemplating the water.

"Only your story."

"You've worn that line out."

Brian laughed, leaning back against the rock pillow he'd made, while Charlie dealt with his vegetables. Brian poured another big shot into the shell for the parrot, and pried open an oyster, leaking its juice into the drink. There wasn't much scotch left. 'One for me and one for the parrot.'

There was a moment of inner quiet, a loss of tension between the men. Charlie picked up another carrot. He'd finally understood Brian's appearance didn't need a reason; logic had nothing to do with this. It wasn't supposed to make sense.

And Brian was comfortable about who he was — a hunter. Not all hunters need a justification to hunt — they only need the hunt itself.

The sound of the old man chewing on his carrots grated at Brian's nerves. He finished off the whiskey, drinking the parrot's share while the reeling bird gaped at him.

Time passed easily. Charlie finished eating. He stood up, stiff; there were things to do, like the long walk back. The sun had begun to bury itself in the far mountains of Vancouver Island. "Let's go, kid."

Brian realized he was drunk, and there was an empty bottle on his lap. Alongside him, the parrot tightrope-walked across the rocks, its wings held out wide for balance.

"Where'd you get that?" Charlie pointed at the empty mickey.

The fog had come from nowhere. Brian couldn't get it out of his head. "What?"

"You're drunk."

"Yup, and proud of it."

"More shame on you."

"Fuck yourself, you old fart."

Charlie's mouth appeared an inch away from his eye. "Think about it, boy. I could kill you now." He straightened up. "Come on, bird, let's leave this relic here."

The parrot lurched towards him, attempting dignity. For the first time in its life it understood the geometric and muscular difficulties of normal movement, and it stopped moving, gawking open-beaked at Charlie, frozen in space. It began pounding its head against the boulder it was standing on, as if trying to drive out the monster inside.

"What did you do to him?"

"I didn't do nothing," Brian slurred, "The bird tempted me."

The parrot performed an odd pirouette, held itself steady for a moment, wings akimbo, and looked up at Charlie. "Asshole," it said, before it fell head first off the rock, where it lay on the beach, breathing heavily, its eyes half-open.

Appalled, Charlie lifted it up and settled it gently into the big side pocket of his knitted vest, the head lolling out, thick tongue hanging down like a dead lizard's tongue.

"I think we've done enough damage for today." Charlie picked up the empty wine bottle and stuffed it alongside the flask and the remainder of the food in the pack, which he slung over the opposite shoulder, and started walking.

"Hey, wait for me!"

The walk back was brutal — lurching over roots, through mud, up and down hills, across meadows and back into deep woods. Was this the hard route? Brian wanted to vomit at the trunk of every fat cedar, and when he focussed on Charlie marching purposefully ahead, he wanted to vomit all over the parrot in his pocket.

He fell further and further behind.

The sky grew dark. Or was it the fog?

And then he was in the clearing once more, beside the rock. It was pulsing hypnotically, like it was sucking the energy out of him. He had to get away.

Did he hear a voice, Charlie's? "You should be ashamed of what you did to that bird!"

Brian, defiant, rested his hot face against the rock's cool surface. "Tell me your story," Brian whispered, "Dance for me, dead thing."

He awoke, cold, in the hammock on the verandah, an old Mexican blanket thrown over him. There was a wild, full moon playing tag with werewolf clouds, and a tiny owl on a near branch. The owl inspected him with its fake wide eyes and asked "Who?"

Inside the building, a house cricket struck up its lonely song. The clouds fled beyond the moon, releasing the meadow from darkness. There was the rock — humming, dancing again. Beside it a crazy figure capered, a man leaping about, animalistic, angular limbs in fluid motion, menacing, like a prehistoric warrior gathering energy before the big hunt — Coyote dancing alongside the rock — and Brian, instead of being afraid, was filled with wonder.

18   White Hats/Black Hats

WHAT HAVE YOU DONE TO ME?

Janwar waited. It was eleven P.M. She had to be home. After several minutes, she finally responded to the computer's alarm. Her name jumped onto the screen as she began typing.

Kirsten: So you heard the news? I think you're about to be promoted to chief inspector.

Janwar: I will refuse it. I'd rather have the respect of my fellow officers.

Kirsten: You already have. You're the man.

Janwar: Not any more. I'm told everyone in the department believes I also denounced Chief Inspector Blake. Would you please inform me of the full details of yesterday's developments?

Kirsten: It's supposed to be a confidential inquiry, but everyone knows everything . . . and since you were a central figure . . . It was abrupt, to say the least. I was shocked myself. My testimony followed Kookoff's at the Internal Affairs inquiry. He saved his own butt and testified that Blake forced him to return and put pressure on Sowinki despite his and your misgivings. It's tiresome typing all this out. Why don't we just use the phone?

Janwar: I prefer typing, besides the phone receiver in my cabin is malfunctioning. Full of static.

He disliked lying, but he needed the antiseptic distance of the computer screen — the time to think, along with the printout. And the sound of her voice . . . it would melt him.

Janwar: As I recall events that's not true. It was Kookoff's strategy to strongarm Sowinki. Though Blake might have approved the second interview because he'd gotten it fixed in his head that Sowinki was the perp. He always favoured the direct approach.

Kirsten: Whatever. By the time I testified I was hardly necessary. It turns out Blake has already been on the carpet twice — formally — for tactlessness with coloured people and women. Kookoff really bailed on him, implied that Blake relished tagging a wealthy Jew. They barely had any questions about my testimony and documentation before they told me he was being demoted to inspector, and would be suspended for a month without pay. It was almost fun sticking it to the bastard, though I was surprised. I mean the review board never does anything fast, do they? They were obviously gunning for him. It worked out fine for me, though; I'm returning to the department. You're stuck with me again.

Janwar: I witnessed one of the complaint incidents last year. It was spurious.

Kirsten: Why do you insist on defending the man? He's a dinosaur. I almost enjoyed crucifying him.

Janwar: He might be a dinosaur in your mind but he has performed his duties excellently for many years. No one has a perfect career. He has come to my rescue on several difficult occasions.

Kirsten: His mouth is full of garbage.

Janwar: His manner of speaking might be old-fashioned. It sounds harsh to those who don't know him, yet the man has a good heart, and he has my respect. Now would you mind explaining the transcripts Internal Affairs received.

Kirsten: Oh, them. You did discuss the matter of Blake's systemic racism and sexism several times with me. I merely gave them copies of the germane parts. Sorry, it was self-protection. I nailed that asshole. And he deserved it. That's what's important.

Janwar: I don't believe I made such comments.

Kirsten: They're on the record.

Janwar: Then they have been taken out of context. I will go to the committee with my own records.

Kirsten: You recorded our computer dialogues, too?

Janwar: I most certainly did.

Kirsten: What a snake!

Janwar: For performing the same actions as you? I had my suspicions, though I now see I wasn't suspicious enough . . .

Kirsten: I trusted you. I thought you were on my side.

A hollow filled Janwar's chest, and he couldn't help picturing her at the desk, his own conflicted desire, her goofy smile when she shut off the vibrator in Rita's apartment, and the hunch that she was right about Blake, had been right all along.

Kirsten: You aren't recording this, are you?

Janwar: I most certainly am.

Kirsten: Are you going to nail me?

Janwar: I will let those in the appropriate position decide appropriate actions.

Kirsten: What a mouth I've got, haven't I? Sometimes I don't mean what I say. It's worse than that. I knew all along you'd keep copies. I've got this real masochistic streak in me, and don't worry, I'm not going to blame it on my mother. I like you. I like working with you. I guess I deserve everything I get for being so stupid. Maybe I couldn't believe that you'd shaft me back. What chokes me is that I'm right about Blake. I'm finished, then?

Her typing had flooded across the screen, and Janwar's heart sank as he read it.

Janwar: That's not my decision, but I hardly think so. No doubt there will be a reprimand . . . It's hard to believe you would give my personal correspondence to them without my knowledge or approval. And so foolish.

Kirsten: I just can't talk to you. Why am I so bad at reaching out to you?

He pushed himself back from his desk, feeling like a total crud. Then he pulled up his chair again.

Janwar: We have our duties. I expect we shall carry them out. Thanks for being candid. I'm sorry this has turned into such a train wreck. Try to continue as if nothing has happened until I think it all over and decide the most honourable way of dealing with the mess. Despite everything, I am not your enemy. I enjoy working with you too. I enjoy you. Signing off now. Bye.

Janwar mouse-clicked himself out of the chatline, and leaned back; his head full of mud. He went outside. Why had he behaved like a pompous prig with Kirsten? The clouds were there — backlit by the waning moon — shuffling across the night. There was a sacrificial quality about several comments she typed. She remarked on it, herself. Yet, she was no victim. Was she daring him to hurt her? She was reaching out to him, that much was sure.

It was late, and there was no light in Wren's house.

He was trembling, not from the cold, the night was warm. This was something deeper, a looseness in his limbs. Decisions had been made within his body without his apprehending what had happened. There was no headache, no aching knees, no bad stomach. Despite his confused emotions he felt younger, as if he were becoming alive again.

* * *

The sun was pouring through the curtains by the time he returned to the cabin. It felt sinful. He couldn't remember ever staying up all night to think about himself and his life, let alone while walking on a romantic moon-flooded beach on a warm summer night. This was good. He'd have to do it again.

There was a bowl on the table filled with whole grain cereals dusted with various powders, beside a glass of soya milk and two hot silver pots of herbal infusions. A little raku dish of pills. Acidophilus, caprylic acid, biotin, pancreatic enzymes . . . who knows what else? There were enough of them. Janwar was amused. Despite his sleepless night, he was already anticipating their sauna.

For the sake of his conscience, he decided to read the file Kirsten had sent over, the one on the disk found at Rita Norman's apartment. He pulled it up on the screen and translated it into his own word processing program, retaining the original codes.

CRY MURDER
THE FIRST FIRE
• • •

**in the beginning was nothing it was perfect because
it was nothing and we could call that nothing god if we
wanted to name it and it perfectly was and we have
always wanted perfection so what could be more
perfect than nothing except more nothing and all this
would have only been a great dream by an unknown
dreamer until a sudden change occurred and at that
point was made tangible so it all broke down and we
called it god because it had thought itself into existence**

There were pages of it before God even got around to
inventing the first living cell. Then it struck him that the
opening was like a monstrous parody of the Sri Guru
Granth Sahib, the Eternal Guru. He continued reading.

**naming is a pathetic form of limitation and nameless
goes far better in the night and should have remained
that way but everything has one force built into it and
that is change which is the enemy of nothing because it
is always attempting to create so you might call
mutation the devil for everything that changes is always
less than what is changed having become different and
usually more complex which is the second force the
push to complexity as the planet sun galaxy god
devolves from perfection to increasingly more delicate
and complex forms**

END OF THE FIRST FIRE

'University people, the things they can write!' Thankfully, it wasn't a slander of the faith. The only interesting item was the ominous title. He'd finish it later. Wren should be arriving. He closed the file and shut down his computer. 'How very strange the world is.'

When she came to collect him, he was sitting on the bench in front of his cabin, towel on his lap.

"You look cheerful today," she said.

"I feel good. My stay here is beginning to have beneficial results."

They walked through the garden, past the monkshood, the foxgloves, and the lobelias; the very clearly identified poisonous plant bed. "I can't believe," Wren said, "my treatment is entirely responsible for your recovering so quickly. One goes through many changes when working with systemic ailments of the body. I'm sure there will be relapses. The moon goes through different phases. The stars change. Your chakras re-align."

She took his hand in hers as they walked. "You've just hit that first surge of wellness which occurs when combatting a yeast infection. It might take many months before you are fully cured, depending on how you continue your diet and treatment. A lot also depends on your mental condition. Is that improving?"

She looked into his eyes.

"It certainly is. Though I've brought my work with me, being away from town has given me new perspectives. Why do you keep a flower bed of poisonous plants?" They closed the rustic gate behind them, and entered the deep cedar forest.

"Mostly for contemplation. Good health lives next to pain. Besides, what's poisonous in one circumstance is not poisonous in another. It's a matter of balance." She performed an odd, graceful gesture, like a Balinese dancer. "A philospher once said: 'There are no poisons, only different strengths of medicine.' Though I do have to put warning signs on that section of the garden. City folks will nibble anything. Understanding what belongs where is part of the healing process."

Janwar nodded. "I am learning that. I think I've been racing through a forest when I should have been lying on a bed of moss, enjoying it."

"There's a time for forcing and a time for contemplation."

At the sweat bath Janwar stripped completely, piling his clothes in a neat bundle on the twig chair by the door, and followed her inside, stopping for a moment to listen to the water tumbling into the pool. Being naked here was so glorious.

It was a long sweat bath. They settled in comfortably, gazing at each other as the sweat poured off their skin in that ancient unspoken game of who could survive the heat the longest. "Why did Kirsten suggest I stay at the resort?" Janwar asked.

"I don't know. Nor why she came up here last year. I think she was lonely."

Her head hung down and little drops of sweat collected on the ends of her short hair like clear pearls. She looked sideways at him — those dark, deerish eyes. "I've a confession to make. We became very close in university." The words gushed out of her. "I've never loved another woman, nor has she, as far as I know. It was so powerful. We'd gone to a boring art gallery opening, returned to my place, got giddy drunk, and *whamm* it happened. A single night. Wow, it was great. And only the once."

Janwar saw that her nipples had grown erect. He looked away, towards the *dogen* resting on the windowsill.

"We felt strange about it, and avoided each other for a couple weeks. That's when my tests came back and I learned I had cancer. She'd been alone for three months, after shacking up with this wild performance artist for a couple of years. She finally dumped him because he was nearly psycho."

Wren shook her head, splattering both of them with sweat. "Sorry." She leaned back against the hot wall.

"I was so upset I rushed over to her apartment and told her. I needed solace. Instead she went hysterical. The news of my cancer was the last straw and she guilted out — confessed that she'd been having an affair with my guy since shortly after she'd split with hers. After I slapped her we had a huge spat. I mean, this was just too complex.

"The next day she phoned me up and said she'd joined the other side — that she had behaved so badly she was changing her life. We were distant after that, though she helped me when I needed mortgage advice to buy this place. She's terrific at figuring out stuff like that. But we drifted apart, as if she weren't comfortable around me. She switched to criminology at university, became a cop, and turned into a hermit. That was the last I saw her until she phoned up and said she wanted to come to the resort, eight years later. We had a lovely visit, but the distance between us remained — we couldn't overcome it."

She ran her finger along her arm, collecting the sweat and flicking it towards the stove. "There; I've told my deepest, darkest . . . You owe me a secret now." She laughed and dashed outside, pausing to look back at him through the open door, before she dived into the pool.

Janwar staggered behind like a drunk.

They splashed around in the cold water, scrubbing their skin, dousing their heads to release the heat from their skulls. Wren was acting shy, almost abashed, after her confession. When they crawled out they took their towels and spread them on the flat crest of the rock where they stretched out, letting the sun and breeze dry them. Janwar found himself humming an ancient Punjabi melody.

"You're in a fine mood this morning."

"It is a beautiful morning, and I feel wonderful, relaxed."

"I'll make an islander out of you yet."

"You might."

"Did you smoke that joint I gave you the other day?"

"No. I threw it away."

"That was a waste."

Her eyes were shut, the sun bright on her forehead. This was not the landscape for lies. "I smoked it."

"Did you enjoy it?"

"Yes." They grew quiet again for several minutes. The tock-tock-tock of a woodpecker drilling at a maple snag echoed through the forest beyond the grotto. "Since I've been here, in less than two weeks, I have betrayed both the work I love, and the religion of my people."

Wren touched his fingers with hers. "I didn't set out to corrupt you, and you shouldn't feel guilty."

"I know, and strangely — I don't feel guilty."

"I'll have to admit, though, you sure were easy." She turned her head towards his, resting her cheek on the towel, inches from his shoulder. "Let's be quiet . . . listen to the forest . . . " The woodpecker had ceased its hammering, and moved on. Now only the morning breeze shuffled through the evergreens and the salal.

"I'd rather talk."

"Then let's talk."

"I am attracted to you."

"I know. I feel the same. I knew it as soon as you came in the door of the office with your bleeding hand."

"I have never felt it before. I thought that nonsense was in books, in films; the long, smouldering glance and its all over . . . What are we going to do about this?

"I don't have an idea." She shrugged. "It's rather complicated for you. We should just see what develops."

"I'm changing," he said softly. "There's a miracle happening all around me, a magic I don't understand. And odd events . . . This island, so many flowers I've never seen . . . a bull charging . . . a box of papers run through by a forklift. Everything has become electric with meaning. I don't know if I want to understand it. It's beautiful indeed. All the murderous crimes in the city, and wrong suspects, wrong reasons, right solutions, and loose bowels, and now love. It's a mystery."

"Speaking of mysteries, why haven't you talked to Charlie yet?" She slapped at a mosquito on Janwar's thigh, startling him out of his dreamy state.

"Tomorrow afternoon."

"I don't know what you're investigating; I'm not much interested in it either, but you should talk to Charlie. You've got half the island in a panic about it."

"I do?"

"Sure, you ask for Charlie when you arrive, let everyone know you're a cop, and then don't go near him. The phone lines are burning. Old Boomer Baggins was yakking it up so much she came down with laryngitis."

"I had no idea. It's a side issue, hardly relevant; I only want to find out more about a woman he used to know years ago."

"That's a relief. Charlie is much-loved on the island."

"Is there any reason I should seek him?"

"None that I know. He's a cranky saint, eccentric as all-hell, lives in a treehouse. But he's not loved just because he's rich."

"He's rich?"

"He's always making donations to the local church groups and community service organizations or ecological projects. His family had money, I'm told, a lot of money, though he doesn't think much of it. He'll take sick kids to New York hospitals, and he'll build your barn for you. He's helped nearly everyone on the island at some point. He built one of the cabins at the resort for the exercise, or so he said. That was when I was going through a real broke period. And he's a soft touch for children born with problems. I think he has a retarded brother, though no one's seen him around in years. His neighbour's boy has a genetic disease that causes premature aging, and Charlie has practically adopted him, making sure he gets the best medical care, and so on.

She sat up with a jerk, running her fingers through her hair, flicking a spider onto the rock between them. It didn't move, stunned; then it skittered towards the edge of the pool. "Would you like me to tell you a story?"

"A story." He thought about this. "I love to be told stories. My father used to tell me magic tales about his homeland when I was a child."

Yes, a story. You're not the only sick child who needs a story, who is a story. We are all stories. That's why we love them so much. And since I gave you an uninterrupted story we'll give this one to Wren.

"There's another sick child on the island. You might have seen him at Mecca. He looks like a tall, older version of Festus, about eighteen, has this amazing hawkish face and eyes nearly as black as Kirsten's. He's always dancing. In fact, that's what his mother soon called him, Dancer Day, when she saw how he loved to perform.

"Her name is Opera Day. She likes the opera. Her name used to be Betty. In the sixties she met this guy and they changed their names. He became Forest King and she Opera Day. They wanted a different numerological match up, like I did when I arrived here. In fact, I partially named myself after the boy, out of respect for his desire for grace.

"Opera lives in a log cabin with the boy on Day Bay, which her grandparents homesteaded at the turn of the century. Forest and her didn't have much money and lived poor, eating whatever fish she could catch. She's a master with a hook and line, knows the best fishing holes around the island, only uses a rowboat and a handline. They grew vegetables, too.

"Forest was the island expert on edible mushrooms; however, he screwed up big time, and they ate a bad batch. This was nearly a decade before I came here, but I've heard the story several times. He never recovered from the coma. She woke up confused, and stayed that way. She was released from the hospital at Sweet Water, returned home, and went on welfare. None of the islanders had the slightest idea she was pregnant until seven months later. Nobody had seen her around for a while. She reappeared with the kid, Dancer. There's nothing going on inside his sweet little head either, that's for sure. Still, he has the temperament of an angel, and he loves to dance. No technique, of course, yet he's beautiful to watch, those vacant black eyes, that elegant, nimble body.

"My heart goes out when I see him. He earns almost all their spending money with a hat beside the blanket where he dances at Mecca. Nobody could figure out how she kept possession of Day Bay all these years while on welfare, but one day she let it slip that Charlie has been quietly paying the taxes. He does things like that. Mind you, everybody has taken to renaming Day Bay, Opportunity Bay, because the island boy who marries her is going to inherit a lot of valuable, undeveloped real estate.

"Lately, I hear Social Services has been threatening to cut her off unless she sells the land. That's her home. She won't sell. Maybe Charlie will support her. Meanwhile, Charlie has a standing offer for anyone who goes to Vancouver. He'll pay all the fares and hotel bills and expenses if they take Dancer, and escort him to a ballet performance.

"Couples go down every year. It's great. A big night in the city, accomplish their own business, and do a good deed at the same time. That's the way Charlie thinks. That's why the islanders respect him so much. We call him the mayor."

Janwar shielded his eyes from the sun, watching her as she laid back on the towel. "In that case, I'll definitely interview him tomorrow, if that will set the community's nerves at rest. It's nothing really, nothing. I've already encountered the machinations of this island once, and I'm eager not to see it happen again."

"How so?"

"The incident with Jake — his being forced to apologize."

"He wasn't forced. He was talked to."

"That's what he said. Then he saw the light."

"He did. No-one can force Jake into anything he doesn't believe."

"So he said."

"Believe him. The world is not as complicated as you think. That's one of your problems, Janwar. You try and look behind everything."

"It's my job."

"It's more than your job. It's your way of life. It's why you took your job."

"You know a lot about me in less than two weeks."

"Sorry, am I being intrusive? Or do I have that right because we're in an awkward situation, together . . . "

He looked over at her; all he could focus on was the dark nipple and the grey curve surrounding it. He jerked his head back and was blinded by the sun.

"How much does it bother you?" she asked.

"Huh," he said, startled. Could she read his mind?

"That kind of stuff, like you got from Jake. Do you get it often? Is that what's driving you?"

Irritated, he fell silent. But he knew he had to reply. "No, it doesn't much," he lied. "What does bother me is all the well-meaning individuals who think it's important, and their questions, or worse, their pity. People like Jake, I can handle. I have trouble with those who worry about me because of the colour of my skin."

"All of a sudden, I'm really putting my foot in it — or maybe my mouth . . . "

"No, I want to talk. I have to talk. I need to talk. Thank you. Hit me again."

"Kinky!" She laughed. "All right, why do you hate those who hate racists?"

"Because I come from a racist family."

"I don't understand."

"Perhaps it's my turn to tell a story."

Oh no! Not another story! And we'll let him tell his the same way Wren told hers.

"My country, Canada, my people, my community, they all assume that you have to be white to be racist. My father came over in one of the early immigrations. He worked in sawmills. He got his pay cheques handed to him wrapped in toilet paper because the locals assumed anyone who wore a turban used water to wash their bottoms after excretion — the left hand, untouchable. It was a cruel joke. And many were so ignorant then they couldn't distinguish between Sikhs and Hindus and Muslims — called everyone Hindus or rug-riders.

"He had friends who'd witnessed the *Komegato Maru* incident, the shipload of Sikhs that wasn't allowed into Canada, all the horrors our people suffered. Yes, he was treated badly, and he reacted badly. He hated the whites — "the ungodly people" — because of the poor behaviour of a few. My mother was the same. She returned to the Punjab to bear all her children, wanted them born on home soil, despite the fact she and Father were legally Canadians by then.

"My parents hated white people, spoke against them in the *gurdwara*. Yes, they became Canadians. They were earning so much money they didn't dare endanger it by refusing citizenship. But it was begrudging, because of their contempt for white Canadians. And when my sister began dating a white boy, I was young then, in high school, my father took her aside and spoke to her. She disappeared the next day, without a word. My father — everyone — knew she killed herself. The police were no help. Father walked across all the bridges in Vancouver for weeks, looking over the rails for her body. I don't know what he said to her. I assume he threatened to send her back to the homeland for betraying her people.

"My father was heartbroken. He retreated to the *gurdwara*, ceased working, abandoned the world. He had killed his daughter. My people — you have no idea of the strength of our community — they looked after us, made sure we had food and an income while they dealt with Father.

"It was no good. He died within a few years, convinced he had murdered his daughter, the sweetheart of his life. I think Mother was behind his threat to my sister. She's never admitted it, seeking refuge within the faith and the prophets. The community looked after us, and I owe a number of debts, the toughest kind, those that don't involve any fixed amount of money. I've been repaying them ever since he died.

"I know it sounds like a soap opera. I waited a couple of years after I had become a police officer, before I went into the computer. It's illegal, you know; well, not illegal.

Still, I could be fired for improper procedures. I found her. It turned out she'd ran away and after a year, once she was legally old enough, married the white boy in Thunder Bay. I guess her boyfriend followed her east when the ruckus died down. They have two children, and are still happy together. I phoned them last year, finally. She was cordial. She won't speak to Mother, never again. She's a real Canadian now, she says. As for Mother, she thinks I am doing something with my life, proving our people to the whites. She prays every day in the temple for our people, for my success, and that the world will rid itself of this plague of racist white devils, and she prays for the souls of her dead husband and daughter. I've never been able to tell her my sister is alive and married to a white man. I'm too weak."

"Wow," Wren said softy. "That's a hell of a lot of baggage."

"I have nowhere to unload it."

"Try me."

"I just did. Do you get many neurotic police officers up here?"

"You're the first. I don't think I could handle any more."

She grew thoughtful, her eyes almost vacant. Then she spoke: "You've never had a lover, have you? You're still a virgin?"

"That's private." He blushed.

"You are a virgin!"

Janwar cleared his throat. "I'm afraid I had too many responsibilities. I don't know. I'm sorry . . . "

"It's nothing to apologize for, but I think we should rectify this mishap right away. Wow, a real virgin. What a treat."

Her eyes lit up with mischief. "I'll be gentle." She leaned over him, her short black hair framing her grey face, her nipples brushing his chest, her small wet mouth finding his. It was so sudden he lay paralysed like a rabbit on the rock.

Her lips left his mouth, dragging across his chin, his neck, down his hairless chest, towards the groin. "Wren!"

Wren lifted her head, grinning. "It's fine, relax. Think of me as your doctor."

"My doctor?"

"Don't think, just do." She kissed him on the lips again, and he thought he was going to faint — everything rushing with blood, his body tensed all over. Then she sat up, easily slung her leg around, and sat on him, an almost pained expression racing across her face as the chute in her groin engulfed Janwar with the grace of a Tai Chi move. She was dancing with him inside her, and he began to move in matching rhythm, his hands slipping onto her hips, holding her close. The concentration in her face made him think of angels; that expression which signified a spirit possessing a woman in rapture.

She began to move faster. He'd always been afraid he wouldn't know what to do if sexual love ever arrived.

Suddenly, his blood became hot, too quickly, a release, and he flooded into her — surging once — twice — three times, and each time her belly contracted as she let out small gasps, like a bird that had been caught in the hand, trying to breathe.

"I was too quick," he groaned.

"I was quicker."

Her eyes went drowsy, soft, and she relaxed, stretching onto him until she covered his body, his hands wrapped around her back, holding her hot, damp skin against his. "That was a good start," she whispered in his ear.

He could feel her heart against his chest, slowing down, his cheek against hers.

They lay on the rock, holding each other, murmuring meaningless phrases, listening to the wind in the evergreens, until she rolled over, back onto her towel. Her knees were red, scratched, and her face had become tight, almost pained, and he wondered if she was going to cry. He didn't think he'd said anything wrong.

Her face altered, as if she was consciously reforming it. "I don't seduce my clients. I never have. And my blood's been tested. You won't get anything."

"I didn't think I would."

"I'm sorry."

"Please, it was too wonderful for sorrow. Now you're the one apologizing."

"That's funny, isn't it? I don't want you to think I'm a flakey new age tart, which I guess I am. I just acted like one. And right after I told you about seducing Kirsten. What you must think of me."

"I don't want to talk any more." He smiled at her. "Let's be quiet. I feel good, happy — in love."

Her hand slipped over and took his fingers, clutching them the way a child would.

***

The laptop on the table was an alien instrument — a refugee from another planet. Janwar sat in front of it like a zombie, wanting to unplug it and slide it into the garbage can. That would never happen. 'What should I do now?'

The computer answered his question with a faint ring.

Kirsten: I've been trying to reach you.

Janwar: I was involved with my treatment. How are you?

Kirsten: Terrible. I'm hated at the department. I'm sitting all alone in my very cute and very lonely little house, with a slightly sore butt, I might add, and you are about to betray me. How the hell should I feel? But I won't bore you with the horrors of my messy, personal life. Besides, I'm sure a big-mouthed little bird has already told you everything about me, hasn't she?

Janwar: Not at all. She's been the soul of discretion. We haven't discussed you.

Kirsten: How do you laugh with a keyboard? Forget it. I have some new stuff to report. A thorough search of Sowinki's home and office failed to find Rita's phone book there. That leaves open the possibility of another player. I also back-checked on the student who hung herself from the door knob. While her birth certificate places her town of birth as Sweet Water, her family came from Surrey. She was born prematurely during a camping trip. A rousing story in the family annals — a bear in the campground — her mother went into labour early. Absolutely no connection with Sweet Water outside of that. Are you sure you're on the right track?

Janwar: No, I'm afraid not. I've merely been trailing an odd string of coincidences, but since I'm here I'll wrap up the thread. By the way, I glanced briefly at the file you mailed over, the one that forensics discovered in Rita's disks. "Cry Murder." It's sophomoric gibberish.

Kirsten: Weird, eh? Forensics thought we might want to check it out. I skimmed through the first section, couldn't tell which end was up, but I thought the title interesting. So you haven't interviewed Charles Baker yet, sir?

Janwar: Tomorrow. After all, I am supposed to be on holidays. It's not necessary to call me sir.

Kirsten: I'm beginning to think we should deal in a formal, businesslike manner at this point, considering the circumstances. Have you spoken to Internal Affairs yet?

Her drift between confessional and official was making Janwar nervous. And why couldn't he escape the guilt in his heart?

Janwar: No, I will do that upon my return, once I've had time to evaluate the situation. There's no need to take this personally.

Kirsten: Well, I do.

19

MORAL QUESTIONS. THAT'S WHAT WE'RE TRYING TO EXPLORE — *the answers to moral question that might not have answers. Some people would call them stories.*

How else can we understand fate and luck and decisions if we don't tell stories? And we've encountered fate, haven't we, Festus? — and luck . . .

Questions? Answers? Ha. There's nothing but stories running in every direction.

Right. We take a direction, and we run along it.

The rain, the sweet rain tapped drowsily, at first, on the night. Then it hammered against the treehouse roof, slaking the thirst of the cabbages in the garden, pounding the leaves of the arbutus at the trail head, working over each inch of landscape until everything was saturated, drowning the morning and seeking the afternoon.

Brian was trapped and sick, sitting on his bunk. There was nothing to do in the tiny cabin but huddle in his blanket, leaning against the wall and glaring at the rain-streaked window as the drum on the roof signalled the ancient code of the hungover.

How had he ended up in the cabin last night — in his cot? The last thing he remembered was sleeping on the deck. And was that horrible rock dancing with Charlie in the clearing?

Brian stiffened. "Damn!" The blowing rain came sideways at the windows.

Charlie looked up from tuning his lute. He'd spent hours fussing with the thing already. It was almost impossible to tune in this climate. At last, deciding to fight the dampness, he'd got up and lit the stove.

Too much wine, whiskey. Too many oysters. There was a war inside Brian. He gazed at the mound in the fruit bowl. The orange with the brown spot. And he was reassured by the crumpled Vancouver newspaper clipping in his pocket. A professor of philosophy had committed suicide.

It was lucky going for groceries and picking up the newspaper, which he hardly ever read. He'd already left the store and was sitting outside on the bench when he realized the paper was almost a week old, abandoned on the bottom of the shelf. He was about to return inside and demand a refund from horseface when he noticed the small headline on page three that was meant for his eyes. He tore out the article before dumping the paper in the garbage.

The professor had been under scrutiny by the police, due to a missing woman, a semi-permanent student and instructor at the university, and he'd been interrogated the day of his sudden death. It was a long article, well-written, Brian thought, for a tabloid reporter.

He stretched in the cot, luxuriating while the rain pounded on the roof as he allowed his imagination to embellish the scene.

This is where Brian, fateful Brian, has his chance to tell his story, and since he's Brian, he will have to tell it to himself.

Professor Albert Sowinki, owner of the Mercedes parked in the garage of a spectacular glass-fronted West-Coast-Style house overlooking Deep Cove, shut the carved cedar door as the young corporal marched purposefully away down the sidewalk

Sowinki retired to his expansive, basement study. That was the second interview by the police. A third visit, he speculated, was inevitable, and it might end with handcuffs. Everything had gone wrong from the beginning. He'd become nervous when the corporal told him Rita had disappeared — the news had an instant effect — he started rethinking his life, wondering why he'd invited her to share his bed in the first place, only it probably looked different to the officer.

The corporal, a decent cop, had shown up with "a few questions" — and stood at the door, uninvited into the house, admiring the ornate *mezuzah* that Albert had embedded in the door to please his mother. Albert answered the questions poorly; his relationship with Rita had become mortifying. She was the wrong one, yet when she'd been beside him there was so much laughter.

Apparently, the corporal had been to the university and questioned not only his associates, but the dean, who Albert was angling to supplant.

Of course, Brian has everything confused, since it wasn't even Kookoff who'd interviewed Sowinki the first time — though the article was in-depth for a newspaper, there was a lot missing. But what is the truth? What use is it to Brian who is merely practising his story-writing (as well as his amateurish research on comparative religions and rituals)? His fantasy is more about

him than it is about Sowinki, or anything as mundane as the
real facts, whatever they are, if they are . . .

It was beyond Albert's comprehension how the dean
had attained his position, let alone that the cop would
give any credibility to the lies the man spun. After all, it
was on record with the university's Human Rights
Committee that Albert had taken an unfavourable
position to the dean when the man was sleazing out of
the sexual harassment charge two undergraduates had
brought against him.

Things had become sticky when the dean accused him
of similar misdeeds, but Albert had demanded and
received, due to the seriousness of the charges, an
opportunity to speak to the committee again. He testified
that he'd only had one relationship on campus, and that
was with a graduate student from a different department.
That made the affair legal, though dubious, but it would
have been hard to deny, as his alliance with Rita was well-
known.

Both men survived the charges and counter-charges,
a little tattered, yet still jockeying in the department. Then
Albert made the fatal mistake of taking Variander Singh
to the campus pub for a beer and a conversation. Singh
was, until then, a non-political vote on committees,
important because he was a visible minority. It began
badly when Singh insisted he only drank tomato juice.

Albert wanted to help the man out, buy him a few
drinks, explain the ropes . . . build bridges . . . At the time
his remark about Rita was innocent enough, one man of
the world talking to another. "I've invited her to live in
my home, yet sometimes I'd like to kill her." It was only

man talk. How could he know Singh would use it against him?

The dean had gotten to the man. That was the only answer: Singh was manoeuvring for an early tenure. Now Albert was finished, especially when the remark appeared in the newspaper. Some jerk reporter was feeding off the cop. Real news must be tough to get these days. A complaint should have been laid against the corporal. Everything was blown out of proportion. No one knew if anything had happened to Rita. There were only the keys in the car ignition, the vehicle parked oddly in front of her empty, unlocked street-level apartment, her purse found in the river rocks at Sweet Water junction, and he'd never seen this missing phone book everyone was prattling about.

Brian could have told the professor about Rita's forgetfulness. She was always in a hurry, dashing about recklessly, often leaving her car unlocked with the keys in the ignition. Oddly, our investigating duo hadn't discovered she'd filed two stolen car complaints over the last decade, and then withdrew them. Now, the abandoned car added to the professor's problems.

That first visit from the cop was a surprise. Albert thought he'd been stood up by Rita. He was used to it. He'd lost a few grad students who developed cold feet over the years. When the cop asked him about Sweet Water, he'd blurted out that, yes, he had been there with her before. It was a nice place to die.

Where did that come from? Such a bizarre thing to say? But where does it all come from? Then, on top of everything, his sister, Marian, after reading the paper — that unscrupulous reporter's libellous diggings into Rita's past and her many 'relationships' — had decided Albert was a prime candidate for AIDS. The bimbo!

Brian's imagination is really stretching here, as he cranks up his little fantasy. This is his delight. He's a dreamer, and we know how twisted dreamers can be.

Albert hated the reporter more than the cop. How did the man get away with printing that stuff about people's past love lives? Albert's lawyer told him it was legal, but dicey. Maybe he'd try charges through the Newspaper Guild. Still, that was secondary to the tenacious cop who'd decided to make a "woman's case" out of Rita's disappearance.

But the worst was Albert's mother, who by the time Marian had finished with her, was convinced he was infected with AIDS. There are Jewish mothers, and then there was Mama, the queen of paranoia. Four days ago, Marian had shown up at the door with a plastic bucket full of frozen chicken soup stock, and although she wouldn't step into the house for 'fear of contamination', she told him that Mother had sent it along. It might help him fight off the HIV virus. Albert knew his sister didn't believe that guff — she was pandering to the old woman, and digging the knife into Albert, whom she'd always disliked.

Albert drop-kicked the bucket of frozen soup stock into the Japanese entrance garden, whacking his shin, screaming "You're both nuts!" And there it had stayed.

Now the cop was gone again, his car pulling out of the driveway, but he would be back. Sowinki locked the door to his study, and stood by the open, ground-level window, inhaling the salty air from his beachfront. Above his desk on the white wall was a signed Salvador Dali print he'd owned for so many years he hardly ever looked at it any more — an accusing woman, her cartoon mouth distorted with pain. How appropriate, he thought. He'd bought it as an investment. It turned out to be another Dali forgery. Albert never had been good at art speculation. Outside the window, the bucket oozed its bubbling and now rancid contents onto the leaves of the last blossoming Japanese iris, the sole flower in the austere garden.

Albert locked the window and pulled the blinds. Then he donned his *tefillin*, binding his wrist and head with the little black boxes, their enclosed prayers. He blessed them as he wound their leather straps into place. "Blessed art Thou, Lord our God, King of the universe who has sanctified us with His commandments and commanded us to wrap ourselves in the *tzitzit.*" This was almost shameful. He'd given up on orthodoxy, and his mother, years ago, after his father died and she'd put the screws to him, attempting to bring him back to the fold — when she became obsessed with The Law. That was the year she'd remade herself, turning her life into a racist cartoon of Jewishness. None of it worked on Albert, not until now.

Brian, pulling all the stops out now, converts his sad Catholic mother into a Jewish caricature. Dreams are fun for the twisted.

Lighting the candles in the menorah which Albert used to think a great joke because he'd purchased it cheap in a garage sale, he blessed them. He blessed his mother, Marian, the dean, Singh, Rita — the bitch — and whoever disappeared her. He blessed his bruised shin, still hurting from its assault on the bucket four days ago, the mat he knelt on, and the Dali print. And he gave thanks to God. After all, it was a magic world.

"I'm innocent. I've been harassed. They're going to suck me down, ruin me. I wanted to be loved." Then he cut the *tzitzits* off his shawl.

Beside him, the print cabinet — the bottom drawer and the twelve gauge Browning single shot. He withdrew it tenderly. An antique, worth a lot of money, useless to anyone but old-fashioned skeeters and suicides. Mother had given it to him after Father died — an unspoken challenge. Skeet shooting, the old man claimed, had taught him discipline. Albert accepted the shotgun politely, while Mother doled out Father's more lavish inheritances to his sister because she'd married a poor, working guy. Now the gun was enough.

He fumbled with the locked desk drawer before the key clicked and he pulled it open; the blue cartridges rolled among the nicotine gum and the pipes that were going to help him quit cigarettes, and the scattered business cards from associates and plumbers and jade carvers.

He pushed the barrel of the gun into his mouth, closing his lips on it as if it were a nipple. Tears welled into his eyes. The print on the wall dimmed. He squeezed his eyes shut, and opened them, wet with salty liquid. Underwater in his study, he was with Rita, gone beyond where her purse was found near the river mouth, into the ocean. He watched the ceiling mutate, swell, darken, develop a multitude of tawny colours as something descended, enveloping him with arms and tentacles stretching out, an octopus, sensual . . . swarming overhead . . . sucking him deep into the great green dark of the ocean, until he pulled the trigger.

Brian, warm and comfortable at last, yawned, all swaddled in his blanket while the rain terrorized the roof and the stove's heat permeated the cabin.

"You're not the decadent fool you pretend to be," Charlie said.

"Naw, you would have kicked me out right away if that's what you thought."

"Are you really here to murder me?"

"Of course I am. Afterwards, maybe I'll strangle a few children, and then crack open the canister of anthrax hidden in the trunk of my car."

"You're a decent young man, screwed up, but decent."

"Why do you let me stay, if you 'know' I want to murder you?"

"I'd rather have you in my line of sight. Maybe I don't think you will."

"You don't think I have the guts?"

"I'd like to know what happened to Rita."

"Suffer." Brian lurched out of the bed, and shrugged his legs into his pants. The jeans were beginning to feel slimy. He had to get to a laundry soon. Handwashing them just didn't cut it.

A wind blew open the window by the door and the bedraggled parrot plummeted into the room, skidding onto the table. It surveyed the scene before it focused on Charlie. "Roll that rock. Watch that hawk." It didn't look too eager. Brian figured it had a hangover as well.

Both men sighed simultaneously, and the parrot laughed. "He never stops, does he; he never stops," Brian said.

"Nothing ever stops. It merely moves to another place."

Suddenly, Brian said: "You don't believe in democracy, do you?" He was astonished by this realization.

"No, of course not."

"Neither do I. I always considered government an independent organism. Sure, we can influence it, push it around a little, but it lives for its own reasons."

Charlie guffawed. "Cripes, we agree for a change. I never voted, except once — for myself, when I ran as a nuisance candidate against the mayor over in the town of Sweet Water. He believed in progress. People still believe there's such a thing as progress, where the world always gets better and the money keep growing, though, that defies the first law of thermodynamics. Permanent growth is impossible."

Belief in growth is what Edward Abbey called: "the creed of the cancer cell."

"I used to think politics was a conspiracy," Charlie continued, "but it isn't a group sitting around a table dividing up the pie. No, they'd cut each other's throats at the drop of a hat. It's a conspiracy of attitudes. They all think the same, those baby kissers and hand shakers. Our politicians are responsible for the real crimes against humanity; they're elected terrorists, pigs in suits, with ties hanging from their necks like nooses — all preaching controlled development which translates as the right to ransack in the name of the holy tax base and economic prosperity for them and their friends."

Okay, we know where he's going, and that's not where we're going. This isn't only a story about moral discussions, and the cultural conditioning behind them. It isn't just about ecology and romance and murder either. Or bad genes. Fooled you, Festus.

Actually, I fooled myself, and might do it again, because I'm not finished yet. Yes, you're on your own.

Aren't we all? So you might as well keep on running, along with the rest of our readers, whoever they may be. Because I'm assuming, Festus, that you'll survive, and we'll publish this story. The meagre income from its sales will be your inheritance. I'd hate to waste the money putting flowers on your grave.

As a gesture of good faith, I'll return to the murderous aspect of our tale. Maybe that'll buck up the sales. Everyone enjoys a good murder story, although personally, I find the concept repugnant. Besides, the mystery here is not who kills who, but how we learn to live in our world. Now that's a mystery.

"You'd kill," Brian said, "if you had the chance. You'd kill, wouldn't you?"

"You still don't understand. I'm no better than anyone or anything else — protecting my territory, like a sparrow or a wolf eel. Yes, I could kill, if anyone tried to destroy it."

"Even me?"

"I don't understand why you think you're so important in the scheme of my world. You're only another animal pissing on my territory." Charlie was thoughtful for a few seconds before he continued, resting his wrists on the louse-shaped body of the lute. "Brian, I don't understand what good killing me would do. If I wronged you in some horrible way, which I'm assuming I have, there's no point in killing me, unless I intended to do it again. And it's obvious I haven't the inclination or ability to do anything that would interfere with your world. I understand killing in self-defence. I'd do that. But you've got problems, young man. I think you need serious psychiatric help.

This crazy business is a shame because I'm starting to like you."

"What if I decided I didn't have to murder you, maybe walk away and not talk about this, not write the book?"

"That's the rub, isn't it, Brian? You can't walk away. One of us is going to take a dirt nap in the bone orchard."

"You'd have to trust me."

Charlie sighed. "The last person I trusted, died."

"I'm not the wimpy useless creature you think I am."

"I never thought that."

A gust of windy rain howled through the open window by the door. Brian walked over and latched it ostentatiously. His face felt weird, the veins standing out, and he hammered his fist through a pane. The tinkle of glass echoed across the clearing. Brian withdrew his gouged hand from the hole. Little bubbles of blood surfaced and began to drip. He held his other hand underneath, catching the blood, watching it with a blank expression.

Charlie set aside his lute, also angry now. "That's nothing, that's mere blind rage. You can't impress me. I've got everything you've got, sorrow, guilt, only worse. Plus, I've got to fix the frigging window. I'd make you do it, but you're probably useless." He stood up and began collecting the broken glass, dumping it in a paper bag. "I'm tired of this stupid conversation, and I'm getting tired of you." He threw Brian a rag.

Brian was ashamed, speechless, wrapping his bloody hand. The cuts were shallow. "Sometimes, I can't bear being alive." He was lost.

"Sit down and I'll play you a tune." Charlie took the lute off the bed, and turned to the parrot who was still on the table, scrutinizing the shattered pane. "Give me a G," Charlie said.

The parrot fanned its wings. "G gets me a cookie!"

It whistled a note.

Charlie sat down on his bunk, and strummed a pair of strings. "Again." The parrot whistled out the same note. Charlie tuned the G note. "He can't sing, he's got no sense of time, but that whistle of his, it's a perfect G. It never varies. Once I figured that out, it was always worth a cookie for him." He leaned over and pulled a cracker out of a tin and threw it to the bird, who happily picked it up and began to munch on it.

It dropped the cracker onto the table. "Yuck?"

"Gawd, you're a pain." Charlie put the lute down again and found the covered butter dish on the shelf above the sink. He spread margarine on the cracker and handed it back to the bird who, taking the cracker in its claw, nodded happily, transferred it to its beak, leapt with an absurd grace onto the window ledge, and popped through and outside.

Charlie returned to the lute, and began to play. "This is called Orlando Sleepeth," he said.

***

Brian slipped on his mackinaw and shut the treehouse door once the old man had settled into his afternoon nap. The weather had slowed to a drizzle.

There were still a few pieces of glass on the windowsill. That was a silly, useless gesture, and now his hand hurt. One of the cuts was deeper than it had first appeared. It should have had a stitch. Another scar.

Past the rock, Brian found the trail, and followed it to the swamp, where he located a suitably private, marshy spot, and shoved the fingers of his unbandaged hand into the rank earth. He hollowed out a cavity and dropped the syringe and the vial into the hole while a long, pink earthworm attempted escape. The empty vial smelled faintly of almonds. His sense of smell had been wonky since a pipe fell off a walkway at Sweet Water, and hit him right between the eyes. Another handicap, like the aphasia of his childhood — at least that one he'd overcome through nothing but force of will. He'd been dealt so many shitty cards, but he was winning now, wasn't he?

Brian got the syringe-and-orange idea from his teenage years, injecting watermelons with vodka so he and his friends could drink while eating, free from harassment by the police who never found liquor bottles when they searched the drunken kids on the beach.

He couldn't resist pulling out his lighter, igniting the newspaper clipping, and releasing the crumpled little torch, making the worm writhe ecstatic with pain. It was almost sexual. Then he threw the black phonebook into the hole, followed by a pair of latex surgical gloves.

He shoved the earth back, smothering vial and ashes and phonebook and gloves and syringe and barbequed worm. Returning to the path, he was careful to pat the jelly like ground smooth and spread a few leaves and branches. The swamp had become a swamp again. The drizzle stopped; he could see the clouds breaking above the trees.

Turning, he faced the parrot perched on a branch at eye level. It cackled evilly, and for a moment, Brian wanted to retrieve the contents from the hole. Paranoia. He shooed the parrot away, and continued down the trail while it squawked along behind him until, growing bored, it disappeared into the trees.

Further on, there was another frightening moment when an enormous maggot hobbled through the trees. It was a sheep, a ram, followed by an ewe and lamb, their wool lumpy and their tails undocked — hanging like shit-festooned towels from their rumps. He'd heard of wild, feral sheep on the islands, but had never seen them before. More of Jake's, probably. They were not that wild. As soon as they saw him the sheep turned onto the path, following on his heels, bleating, plaintive.

"BAAAAAADDD," said the ram. Brian stopped with a shock and looked over his shoulders at the animals. "BAAAAADDDDD." All three chimed in together. Brian ran like a maniac down the path, leaving the sheep far behind.

It didn't take long to arrive at Erection Beach this time, not at his reckless pace, leaping over fallen logs and narrow creeks. Still, he was amazed by its sudden appearance. Had Charlie navigated a circuitous route during their first visit — to make their arrival at the beach more magical?

Coming out of the trees, he saw a lone kayaker paddling towards the island, disappearing around its point. There was no more privacy, people were everywhere. This angered him. Maybe too many things angered him. He had to put himself under control, practise his discipline — after he left Artemis.

"I really must kill him. It's too late for anything else." He imagined Charlie in spasm, staggering down the ramp from the treehouse towards the vegetable path. It made him sad. Then he realized the grey-white boulder that he'd been staring at, twenty feet away on the beach, wasn't a boulder at all. It was a skull. A small whale's skull.

He traversed the narrow spit of gravel to the island, following a line of dark black kelp like a gunpowder trail leading to a potential explosion beyond the point. Hiking around the bluff at the south end of Erection he saw movement. He stopped. The kayaker. She was naked, her eyes shut. Oblivious. She was performing Tai Chi, her grey skin against the grey sky, the skin stretching as she moved. She was small and very skinny, no fat anywhere — small breasted, black nipples erect in the cool air. Her tiny patch of pubic hair excited him as much as her gestures. There was something beyond physical — unearthly, spiritual — that belonged to this ghost on the bluff.

The woman posed and blocked and gracefully struck out at the world of scrubby, dwarf oaks and sand. Then, as if she'd been in a trance, her eyes snapped open, and she saw Brian. His approach hadn't been as quiet as he thought. Brian gave her a weak nod. "Hi," he said.

"Why are you spying on me?"

"I wasn't spying. I was watching." He wished he could have been closer before she saw him.

"Take off, creep." She snatched up her clothes, dragging them on as she marched back to her kayak. Once dressed, she pushed her kayak into the water. Stepping in, she turned long enough to give him the upraised middle finger, before paddling away around the point.

***

The walk back was almost as quick. He stepped out of the trees into Charlie's meadow and saw him immediately, among the vegetables, meditating. Charlie was seated on the wide homemade bench, cross-legged, fingers outspread on his lap again, holding his traditional Buddhist position. A hummingbird circled him, followed by her young. The baby hummingbirds were tiny — a string of slow-moving shotgun pellets. The mother veered away, rocketing towards the tall, woody fuschias by the netting.

"Are you a Buddhist?" Brian stood at Charlie's side. A dumb question.

Charlie opened his eyes. "I am Buddha. How'd you expect him to behave if he were born in this age? For that matter, you're Buddha, too, but that's a different story."

The garden was luxuriant with the unearthly green of the West Coast after a heavy rain. Everything was so alive. "It's beautiful here."

Charlie closed his eyes again. "I enjoy listening to the vegetables sing after a rain. Each has its own tune. And, all together, they make a symphony."

Brian felt a great sadness. "You love even them, don't you?"

"Even them? You still don't understand that the world is wild beyond what we see. They're full of life, the cells electric with energy, the chlorophyll chewing on sunlight. Listen to them sing!"

There was the startled cry of a peacock, and both men looked up. They saw an orange object bobbing above the shrubs at the edge of the clearing. It was a turban, following the path from the road.

"Who's that?" Brian whispered as the intruder hesitantly crossed the meadow of wild oregano.

"I would suggest," Charlie said, unwinding his legs until he sat normally on the bench, "that we say as little as possible, and show care in what we say. He's a cop."

"How do you know he's a cop?"

"Word gets around on this island. You should be more attentive." Charlie watched Brian. Was he waiting for a sign of weakness, a little squirming?

Janwar noticed them, waved politely, and ambled in their direction. He nearly glowed by the time he reached their side. "My, what a lovely garden you have here."

"Thank you," Charlie said politely. "It provides me with many comforts."

"I am Inspector Janwar Singh of the RCMP." He briefly showed his badge, and stuck it back in his shirt pocket.

The old man, still seated, took his hand and shook it roughly. "Charlie Baker. And this is Brian. He's a writer fella, been up here a couple'a weeks researching a book on old farts like me."

"Glad to meet you," Brian took Janwar's outstretched hand and shook it politely.

"How can I help you, Inspector?" Charlie pushed up the rim of his hat with his palm.

"I don't mean to interrupt, but I was hoping you might provide me with information concerning a woman you used to know, a Miss Rita Norman."

"Rita? We lived together for close to ten years. She isn't in trouble, is she?"

"It's hoped not. However, I must tell you she disappeared in odd circumstances? We are aware of your relationship with her and were hoping you might provide us with a few leads about her acquaintances and life style."

"Disappeared?"

Janwar took out his notebook. "May I sit down?"

"Certainly? Would you like tea or juice or water?" Charlie waved towards the treehouse, which Janwar admired for a couple of seconds.

"No, I am fine." Janwar sat on the bench beside Charlie while Brian stood across from them, watching awkwardly. Feeling stupid standing there like that, he sat down next to Charlie.

"This might be private," Janwar said. Not wanting to upset the venerable old islander, he was smiling too cheerfully.

"I don't keep secrets. Disappeared, you say? What does that mean?"

"We have no idea at present. We do have concerns about her well-being."

"You're making me ill," Charlie said. "There's nothing more definite?"

"I'm afraid not. When was the last time you saw her?"

"I don't know . . . several years ago . . . when we separated and I came to live here on Artemis."

"You were on the island between the fifteenth and twenty-second of May?"

"That's when she went missing?" Charlie stared ahead, not looking at Brian. But his voice went slightly more formal, thoughtful. "No, I wasn't. I was in New York." Both Janwar and Brian looked more closely at him following this news. It was hard to imagine Charlie in Manhattan.

Charlie shrugged. "The neighbour's child, Festus Denison has an extremely rare chromosomal syndrome that causes premature maturity and aging — it also causes bone problems that become excruciating when puberty arrives. He's aging five years for every one. However, there's a treatment for this. Growth hormones. In a few, odd cases they will brake the premature aging process, kickstart his body into producing the necessary enzyme, whatever it is, and he will be healthy. That's the theory.

He starts the treatment as he approaches puberty, which will be soon. Already, he's got the mind of a twenty-year-old. In two cases out of ten the child survives. I have independent funds. I took him to a clinic there for three weeks. May seventh to the twenty-eighth. I don't travel much any more, so I remember it well."

"You are a generous man."

"I do my best. Festus and his mother and stepfather live on the neighbouring piece of land. You can verify it with them."

"No, no . . . not at all. It won't be necessary. It isn't my intention to make you believe you are the subject of suspicion."

"Well, it sure sounded like it."

"Was Rita Norman of a nature that she would suddenly disappear?" One of the baby hummingbirds reappeared and floated directly in front of Janwar's nose. Distracting him.

"You could say that. She took off on me a couple of times. If domestic life got too stressful, she would run. She always came back, except the last time, but that wasn't a runaway. I helped her pack."

"I'm afraid she hasn't returned this time, not yet." Janwar's voice trailed off, his eyes following the hummingbird across the meadow.

"So she could be okay — merely gone?"

"Yes."

"Despite our separation, I still have a great affection for her."

"Are you aware of her movements recently, any acquaintances I could contact?"

"No, it's been years."

"Any favourite locations or places where she would go, maybe recollect herself if she was stressed. Sweet Water River?"

"No. I'm afraid I'm not up to date, like I said. We used to picnic near the upper reaches of Sweet Water River, so she knows the area, if that's any help."

"Help often comes from uninteresting details that lead in new directions."

Charlie nodded sadly. "Are you sure you wouldn't like tea or juice?"

"Thank you, no. I don't mean to take up your time, nor am I happy to cause you unwarranted fears; it's necessary to check out every avenue. My apologies if I have created needless worries. And you, Brian, do you have any knowledge of Miss Norman?"

"Me? Hell, I drove up here from Vancouver to hang around and grill Charlie myself, for my book."

"And what is your book about?'

"It's difficult to explain. I want to write a story on those who live a healthy life at the edge of civilization and the modern social order. I was thinking of calling it *Coyotes*, or maybe *Coyote*. These animals are all around us, you know, living on the edges and doing well."

This announcement made Charlie's brow wrinkle, his blue eyes sparkling.

"I guess I didn't tell you that part." Brian grinned. "There's certain animals, 'weed' animals, that have an ability to adapt to any environment or lifestyle, like cockroaches and coyotes and racoons, etc., I intend to draw parallels with human nature."

"*Coyote*? It sounds interesting. I will do my best to read it when it's published."

"It'll be a while yet."

Charlie interrupted. "So you think Rita was abducted — or worse?"

"I really can't say that. We have no suspects, no definite evidence."

"No suspects?" Brian asked, his voice rising. That wasn't what the newspaper said. "It doesn't sound like much of an investigation to me. Maybe she's taken off on a holiday, sunbathing, warming her bones on a beach." He wished he could keep his bloody mouth shut.

"Let us hope that." Janwar shut his notebook.

"Well, if you hear anything," Charlie said, "I would appreciate knowing. I've got no phone, but you could call the store at the ferry terminal, and tell June, and she'll get it back to me. I'd be grateful."

"I'll do my best. My apologies if I have caused you distress. Let us hope there is no problem. Thank you for your time. And if by chance you should hear from or about her, don't hesitate to call." He proffered a business card which Charlie accepted and casually tucked into his hatband. "It was good meeting you, and you too, Brian. This is a charming and unusual home you have, Mr. Baker."

Janwar stood up and shook both men's hands. Neither rose from the bench.

As he walked across the meadow and down the path that gradually became a driveway, he considered his conversation. Nothing useful, though he didn't regret coming to the island. It had changed his life. He saw the white Miata pulled into the shrubbery alongside the road. A beautiful little car. It must be Brian's. It most certainly wasn't an island vehicle. The first numbers of the license plate signified it was a rental. Odd that a writer would rent a car to drive up here and park for a few weeks. The writing business must be more lucrative than Janwar had been led to believe. He'd missed taking Brian's last name. How unprofessional that would look in an inquiry. He pulled out his notebook and wrote the license plate number down. It might be wise to phone Kirsten tonight and have her trace the name and address.

***

At the cabin, Janwar was energized, tingly from his brisk walk back to the resort, unable to relax. He decided to browse a little more through that epic, crazy file Kirsten had sent.

He opened his laptop. There was a tall glass of slimy-green liquid beside it on his desk. A new concoction from Wren. A fly struggled on the drink's surface, drowning. It had a tattered wing that made him feel sorry for it. He slipped his spoon under the fly and scooped it onto the desk surface where it continued wriggling. It recovered, shook its wings dry, and flew away. Janwar smiled, sipping the putrid-looking drink, which was very good despite its resemblance to pond slime. He smiled again. Should he go visit Wren? He began to read.

THE SECOND FIRE

. . .

thus began the great construction of the great destruction of the simple which was born out of the perfect as chemicals strange brooded in the muck of the aminos in pools and that fateful electric sky shot it with lightning and evil oh evil the first cell was born then more cells then millions of cells each one glorious

and clean but then continued that awful urge towards complication and the cells divided and warped and mutated and changed as the planet declined at an accelerating rate and suddenly oxygen the monster oxygen spread its elemental tentacle and time accelerated and oxygen multiplied and the cells multiplied and their mutations multiplied until we arrived at the mad bad diversity of today

Janwar looked away from his screen for a moment. Was this a code? Code breaking was a hobby of his, and this kinky prose poem made him nervous. Was the disk a plant, a dare, a clue? Unfortunately, all his cryptography software was on disks at the apartment. Slipping out of his daydream he looked at his drink. The fly had returned, and was dead in the residue at the bottom of the glass. Sad, he continued reading, skipping a few pages to see if the style changed. It didn't.

the endless endless life too much life had overcome the earth like maggots of death only it was life and maggots and the awful trees spewing out their oxygen that enemy of stillness and simplicity a process so unlike anything the universe had seen and so unlike anything that could have been dreamed in the initial stages of god dreaming when the night was perfect when only the dream had its dreamer and nothing else existed so that the full horror of god looking now at this monstrous spewing mass of mouths and feathers and electrolysis and atoms is untimely in our bones and irrevocably its own unholy devil god backwards angel named ecology

END OF THE SECOND FIRE

"This is delightfully mad," Janwar said, leaning back in his chair. The prose was too pretty to be cryptography. Was Rita Norman involved in a cult? That might be an interesting avenue of approach. Yet Kirsten was right — this was written by a man. It reeked of testosterone.

There was a knock, and the door swung open. Wren. "I see you finished your spirulina drink. Did you enjoy it?"

She picked up the glass and looked down at the fly. Tilting the glass she stuck in her finger and scooped out the insect. "I've been working on the formula for years." She blew on the corpse of the fly for several seconds, pouting out her cheeks so cutely that Janwar melted in his shoes.

The fly shrugged back into life as her breath dried it off. It stood on her fingertip, hesitating. Was it going to collapse again? Then it was gone out the open door. Wren wore the benevolent face of an angel. "The drink has the enzymes you need, and the spirulina gives it a real snap. And most importantly, the ph is balanced exactly. That's crucial for you."

He shut off the computer. "It was strange tasting at first, but yes, it was delicious." Almost as delicious as the sensation that rushed through his body at the sound of her voice, the sight of her unkempt, spikey black hair against her forehead.

20

Adventures in Non-Euclidean Living

IF YOU ARE ONLY INTERESTED IN NARRATIVE you may skip the next few pages though I suspect you, Festus, at least, will hang around. This passage doesn't have much to do with who murders who, or even why. As I said earlier, this story is not an exercise in linear thinking.

Brian, of course, is not me. Besides, the chances of his real name being Brian are about the same as unicorns being born on New Year's Day. Plus, he's a fictional character. He doesn't exist. That doesn't matter. So why do I give him my name, and sneakily imply at first it might be him/me writing these words, as if they were a confession? Sure, we like to hear ourselves discussed, especially if the remarks are flattering, but Brian, although he resembles me superficially, or at least a younger version, is a very bad person. I've done my share of misdeeds on this planet. But I'm not in his league. This is a good time to disown him.

But why did I play briefly at the beginning with the conceit of a main character possibly telling a story who is not actually telling the story, and keep using it, only now with irony? Do I want to examine the potential for corruption inside myself? Or do I imagine a monstrous version of myself in order to understand the monster in all of us, the monster at the heart of life's entire eco-system — the one who gave you a terrible disease and the threat of an early death?

Those who've been hurt will sometimes study the world of those who cause hurt, hoping to stop it from happening again, or at least understand it. I also know this is adult material, not for a boy your age, although your premature aging is the question that ignited everything. That's why I'm writing it for your future — down the road — hoping that your road doesn't end too soon. If I could invent an answer in a few, neat sentences I wouldn't have to write this story.

A request for a story, simple enough in the beginning, unfolds like a Chinese puzzle, pieces inside pieces. Worse, the narrator (the one who keeps saying 'I' and uses this italicized type) is not me either. As the fiction runs, so have I run, and the narrator speaks what I would not speak although it is me choosing the words.

Yes, I'm now being written by my own story.

I am not me. I am a story.

I am no longer the author. He's your friend, the one you originally asked for a story — the guy facing the keyboard, the one who made me. The one who might or might not have sat down to answer a straightforward request from a mutant boy. I am what they call "an unreliable narrator." Hey, aren't we all? Sadly (for me), I, the narrator, will die when you shut this book. I will be memory. Yours.

Is Coyote real? No. But it will please me if you believe in him, or believe him, or believe the lies I am telling you in a work of fiction attempting to understand a boy with a birdlike face and thinning hair. The truth? Non-existent, except perhaps in a few mathematical equations, and there, too, be suspicious. The truth? Reality? Logic? They're claptrap — rhetorical weapons we use in arguments for power. Power, is what we are seeking, the real secret of a good story.

What we're also talking about are the instruments of our culture. Mental weapons that have been used historically in a skewed manner by those we usually assume are lesser beings than ourselves — our primitive forefathers and foremothers. We use the term logic like a knife, and with it we devise the atom bomb to create peace. We use logic to tell ourselves we are superior to animals, trees, other men and women and children, different races, or rocks, whatever. Certain practitioners of analytics will tell you this is only a bad use of logic, and has nothing to do with the actual process. They tell you that because they have to preserve their jobs and belief system. Don't listen to them for a minute. They would've had to invent Euclid if he wasn't born. Fuck the isosceles triangle! The philosopher who came closest to getting it all right was Godel, the Kafka of math, with his notorious equation — that sweet piece of twentieth century mathematical nonsense — which proved that nothing can be proved.

There are no answers if you use logic, only more questions. It is merely a process. Yet ,it is our major tool, one I've co-opted often in my own eccentric and non-linear, non-Euclidian fashion, in order to create this story for you. What is the answer? As Gertrude Stein said on her deathbed: What is the question? That's the trick! As soon as we postulate a question we presume an answer. What if there is none? What if the question itself is a trick of the imagination? And none of this has any relationship whatsoever to an imaginative concept called truth?

Since truth is merely a social construct, and if we believe we are moral creatures, it's our job, no, duty, to invent the best truth we can in the circumstances we are given.

We've got a long route to go down many twisted roads. We're certainly not going to make it all the way in this story — maybe wave at a few bystanders on the roadside and give them ideas.

That will have to be good enough for now. So I'd recommend we use a little common decency along the way, a little respect for our companions under this weird sun that gave us life — such a dazzling spectacle of confusion. I'd recommend it, but that doesn't mean I'm going to practise it. After all, I'm nearly as hapless as you.

No! I'm lying again. Sorry. I am Brian. So are you. Everyone is Brian. Brian is Buddha! Perhaps a tad low on the ladder of reincarnation, somewhere close to a slug — though that might be insulting to the slug kingdom.

I'm a creep. I'm a monster. We all are. Our monstrousness is not a question of good or bad, but how bad we are — the extent of our damage — the difference between a cheap insult at a dinner party and the slaughter of the Albanians.

Remember, a poison is only a medicine that's too strong.

You, Festus, would never have sprung your request if you didn't trust me. Well, don't trust me. As for our other readers, if there are any left, I'd suggest they don't trust me, either. Let's just call me Brian. Sure, I haven't done any finger-burning, poisonous misdeeds. My crimes are minor social ones, hurting those I love, kicking a dog in a rage, insulting neighbours over local politics, and slaughtering chickens for my dinner. That sort of crime. But that's irrelevant. Brian is me. At the table of my life, he sits next to the narrator. He sits next to the man you believe is your friend and protector. Brian, like me, thinks he's a priest to the world. Somebody who can explain it. Yet I can't. I can only tell stories, and maybe strive towards the goodness I haven't found yet in my life.

I was a nutcase when I was twenty, a fool when I was thirty, an arrogant idiot when I turned forty. I keep looking back, and all I can find is sadness at my own misbehaviour, my own stupid justifications, and a personality constantly dividing itself into multiple personas. At the same time I still want to believe I can be good. I used to have apocalyptic fixations. I thought I could change the world. I can't change myself.

Perhaps, at least, I can tell you a story, and since you've survived into the heart of it, let's take a few more runs. According to the Navaho people in one of their chant systems: Everything is beautiful.

Everything.

Janwar picked up the phone and dialled headquarters. It took a few rings for the switchboard to connect him. "Kirsten? This is Janwar. Any news?"

"None, sir."

"I'm coming back on the Monday morning ferry. We can go through everything Monday at the office. I might not be laying a complaint against Kookoff's actions, despite my initial misgivings. Who am I to second guess the actions of another officer?"

"I figured you might come to that conclusion."

"We'll see. Meanwhile, Rita's disappearance continues to haunt me. I can't escape the feeling she is the key to our investigation. This trip was a dead-end; but your friend has done wonders for my health with her herbal tonics."

"Tonics? I thought her healing techniques involved the 'whole body.'"

"Did you trace the writer's name and address from that car licence number?"

"I'm sorry, I forgot. How come you want it? I thought there was no interest in Charlie Baker."

"It's not important. Still, thoroughness never hurt. I want to check any New York flight passenger lists for May seventh and twenty-eighth as well. You can do it Monday. Talk to you then."

This is almost fun! Yes! Janwar, with his meandering-around-the-mountain-approach is trudging closer to Brian — and to Coyote . . . Meanwhile, life is becoming scarier at the treehouse.

"Have an orange." Brian picked a pair of them out of the bowl, juggled them adroitly, grabbed a third, and managed to keep two afloat at once. "Here." He tossed Charlie the brown-spotted one, before he put the second one back, and began to peel the third.

"Naw, not right now." Charlie dropped the orange into the bowl. He peeked outside through the curtain. The rain, after that too-brief clear patch yesterday afternoon, was pounding against the glass again. Charlie played his lute.

The visit from the cop yesterday weighed heavily on both men. A damp and unhappy peahen stood on the deck, sheltering under the eaves.

"So," Brian said, "what's the story on these peacocks? They're all over the place. And this Peacock Jim?"

"It ain't much of a story. An islander raised them in big pens on south island, and when he died, his son, Peacock Jim, who hated them because of the noise, released the birds — he was a kid then — and they went feral. They're good foragers and survive, despite the racoons killing females in their nests. There's a big white one. A real granddaddy. You probably saw him by the ferry terminal. He's developed a taste for the tourists' fish and chips."

Another gust of rain blew against the big window above the table. "Since we're stuck, why don't you tell me more about Coyote."

"I've told you enough. Why do we keep on with this farce about a book. You don't even make notes. Besides, it's your turn. Why don't you tell me about Rita?"

"Later. It makes my heart sick to think about it. I'm not ready yet."

"We're all so greedy." Charlie sighed, settling back in his chair, leaning his head against the damp window pane. "We want everything for ourselves. It's too hard for us to share. Most people's concerns with the environment are only greed for old memories. We all want to cling to our past, including me.

"When I was a kid, the world was so rich. We'd steal from everyone's gardens — corn, pumpkins, watermelons, sunflower heads, carrots, too, which always tasted good if they were raided from an old coot's backyard. Kids can't steal from gardens today. They're liable to get poisoned by some fool's pesticides. Or we'd go down to the beach and dig up buckets full of clams, and have clam-eating contests, daring ourselves to quit. The one who quit first 'couldn't take it.' The same with fish.

"There are pictures of me in the family album, standing behind strings of fish, more than we could eat. The carnage was unreal. We used to shoot everything in sight, practise on robins and squirrels and gophers, and kill bears for their hide — rugs, an ornament, while the bear's meat rotted in the bush. A lot of people would like to see everything brought back so they can pillage it again. That's the way you think about Rita, not about the richness of her laugh, but wanting to possess her again, as if you could ever possess a human being, or a landscape. You can only work damage."

"She didn't run away. Rita's dead."

"I know that. Did you kill her?"

"You killed her first. I merely finished the job. It was an accident."

"I won't go to the cops — our polite inspector . . . " Charlie gave a wry, teasing laugh. "You can tell me."

Brian squirmed in his chair. "There's no evidence. No one knows. Rita was a woman who could tell me she was dumping me for a philosophy professor who owned a fancy house on the waterfront and drove a Mercedes — after we made love. And worse yet, not out of cruelty. She was actually unhappy when she told me she was dumping me. She talked about you, said you ruined her ability to love, so she might as well live in luxury. There I was, lying in bed, listening to this stuff in a dingy east-end apartment, all I could afford. I'd spent more than twelve years of my life getting an education, working part time, studying for more degrees — what everyone calls a permanent student, like her. Then I just drifted for nearly a decade before I met her. She never cared much for me — maybe I was a sympathy case.

"She was going to leave in the middle of the night. 'Let's have a day,' I said. 'Stay with me until tomorrow night. If we're going to part, let's do it well — go for a picnic at your favourite place, Sweet Water.'"

"'How circular! That was Charlie's favourite spot,' she said. 'He took me there years ago. It had a special significance to him. Maybe that's why I brought you there that first time — and Albert.' She could be so cruel without recognizing it."

Memory — the most perfect manipulator of thought ever conceived. An organic hard drive constantly rewriting its history.

It weeds out the dross, and feeds us what we demand — self-justification. The memories, ah yes, the memories . . . We'll call them a story, too.

There's a naked woman doing Tai Chi, posing; yes, another one, not the grey stranger on the beach, a different woman . . . location . . . time . . . several weeks ago.

Rita — her skin tanned, her hair long, her face cherubic, her breasts large and jutting — beginning to face the defeat of middle age and too many years of wine.

Rita was fooling around, running riot between the cedars, barefoot on the moss, too bawdy for a dryad, yet possessed of the grace that runs alongside desire, practising her moves with a poise that had no resemblance to skill.

She struck out, threatening the cedars, strutting along the cliff edge above the water. Soon, she forgot about Tai Chi, and just danced. Was she flaunting what he would lose, the flesh of a desirable woman? Her feet disappeared to the ankles in the lush moss. When she ran, her toes and heels were stained green. She used the descending strands of old man's beard like veils. It was a goofy dance, full of power and life performed above the river while he sat on the blanket and drank from the wine bottle, knowing what he had lost. And this was such a perfect place to lose her.

"I'm going to miss you, though you are weird," she said.

"I can't be worth that much; you're trading me in for waterfrontage and a Mercedes. I thought money didn't matter?"

"I wouldn't put it quite that way. I'm getting old. Look, I'm sagging." She stood graceless, innocent on the bluff in the diffused sunlight, letting it reveal the marks of her age. "I've lived for love. Now I want to be quiet. I don't want to endure any more dumpy apartments with shorted-out lamps, or wild men telling me they're going to burn for their dreams. I want to be quiet for a while."

"Go where you want to go. I can't stop you."

"I want your blessing."

"You aren't going to get that. Did I tell you my last lover abandoned me for a closet full of clothes?"

She flitted about again, talking as she paraded. "I guess you're an unlucky man. Maybe you should get a decent job one day." She could tease so artfully, make everything a great joke.

"I'm very lucky to have found you and become your lover. You have no idea how fortunate I consider myself."

"You remind me of Charlie. A nastier version of him — pushing, always pushing. Alright, push!" She bent over lewdly, her wide backside to him as she faced the river below. "Have your last shot!" She patted her buttocks.

He lurched to his feet, grinning, drunk from the thick, black wine. He stumbled through the moss and stood behind her, resisting the urge to give her a good, swift kick.

He pulled his zipper down, a mechanical sound in the hushed forest above the river. "Is that what you wanted to hear?"

"That's what I wanted to hear. Go ahead. Use me. Be like everyone else." She was choking on her tears, raging and crying at the same time. It was pathetic.

He pulled up his zipper. "But I'm not the same as everyone else. I'm real. And you're dead." Then he saw his boot lifting out of the moss, extending forward, contacting her buttocks, pressing into the flesh, pushing her ahead, and over the bluff, out of sight.

It took him several seconds to gather the courage to peer beyond the edge, knowing he'd see what he did see. She was spread-eagled on a partially submerged rock, the water streaming around her, tugging at her hands; blood leaked from her skull. Her eyes were open, unblinking. 'A direct hit,' he thought. The river surged, tugged harder, loosened her, and she flowed away with the current, wallowing among the waves before she sank, a breast rising lewdly in the foam like a last taunt.

Panicking, Brian gathered her clothes and threw them after her, the scarf, shoes, dress, purse. Why did it always have to be like this? Then he collected the food and empty wine bottles in the blanket and dragged them to his old car. He drove the long, rough road past the new, well-fortified junction which diverted part of the river into a culvert leading to town, the mill and the hospital. When he reached the highway he stopped at the bridge above the heart of the river surging into a lonely man-made estuary, a mile from Sweet Water.

There was a red shoe on the rocks, and further down amid the boulders at the bend, a scarf snaked its way towards the sea, as if it were a lure leading him to the hook, as if both objects had raced all this way to greet him. Beyond that there was nothing, a sailboat on the horizon.

He tried to imagine the river a deep cobalt blue, the colour of the scarf, the way it had been the day Coyote sabotaged the mill, many years ago. That was when this was a small creek, the major flow going through town, before the bridge made necessary by the diversion project. Blue. Coyote blue — like the scarf of a murdered woman. Yes, there was a duty ahead, the main project — phase one was completed.

He drove back to Vancouver, his emotions alternating between guilt and the fear of being caught. His relationship with her was unknown — the shadows she had always demanded were a help; there was nothing to link them. That left only the guilt. He could live with that, though he did love her, even if the relationship only began with a name given to him by a tortured old woman whose fingers were burnt into claws.

***

"So what happened?" Charlie asked. "How did she die?"

Brian shrugged, unhappy, his face emotionless. "What do you think happened? You know Rita. We had a last picnic at Sweet Water. Coming back, we stopped by the bridge, went for a walk, and an argument erupted. She told me I was a jerk, I told her what I thought of her shacking up with a wealthy professor with a Mercedes, and she pushed me. Hurt me. I pushed her back."

"Over the bridge?"

"It was odd the way she fell, almost unnatural, a dream. When I looked down all I could see was a shoe in the rocks and her scarf, like an eel — a snake — moving through the water."

"I kept hoping that she wasn't dead."

"She's dead. The last I heard, the police — our inspector friend, or one of his partners, were investigating the professor she dumped me and her other boyfriends for. You know, I didn't mind her secretiveness, or learning she had other lovers as well as the professor. I didn't mind that. Besides, she was always clear with me. We were odd companions. I think I gave her the creeps. She did the same for me. I loved the ghostly knock at the door in the night. I loved whispering in her ear: "come tonight," telling her my door was always unlocked, and having to keep it that way in case she came. She kept me so apart I never met her friends. Maybe she knew from the beginning it was a doomed affair." Brian scrutinized Charlie sitting downcast by the window, his chin resting on his chest. The face was so long and haggard it could have belonged to a different man.

Charlie sighed. "Some women, like some men, bruise without effort. She was easy to hurt."

"She pushed me first!"

This was too much for the old man. "Who are you! What are you!"

Brian was overwhelmed, haunted. "I'm everyone. I'm everything. I'm the devil. I'm the crazy darkness full of animal noises." He spoke with such forceful, tragic sadness that Charlie's eyes began to cloud. He released a great honking sob, and the tears followed the creases in his weathered cheeks.

Learned people might call it a sympathetic reaction. It was and it wasn't when Brian began to cry also. The two were lost now, enveloped by personal sorrow.

Now the time has come. Yes, now that we've started this story, let's keep on going into a new universe. We go under the water. The dead woman should be allowed her say.

Let yourself imagine Brian dreaming, because he's the worm in the world, the thing that always goes wrong, the terminal disease that waits for everyone. Leave him in the treehouse. He's full of heartache and sickness, and he's bent on more murder. There's a woman floating by . . .

And since he introduced an octopus when he conjured the good professor's suicide, I can give you, as an added and hideous bonus, one live Pacific octopus. You only have to look, and you will see . . .

Dark water, deep water — down — a surge of foam, fresh water, a river — green — boulders rushing out of darkness — down — rolling and roiling — the song of a river surging into the sea. Then the beach, past the startled bullheads — further — deeper . . . Down we go, over the rocks. Beyond the bull kelp. A seal pup nudging an object, a naked foot.

I discovered the roll, and it was sweet, the movement in liquid space. I can't say I'm unhappy. Neither can I say that I am happy. On the second day of my death I floated. I think it was the second day. The tissue of my body swelling with water and rot. Later, I sank again. I was going down — into the real world at last.

She passes an underwater cave full of orange, purple, odd colours. Anenomes. Sea Pens. Her body settles on the rocks among the kelp and brown seaweed. The crabs arrive quickly. And the sculpins. An eye, a tasty treat at one hundred feet. They suck the meat off a finger. A sea worm slithers into an ear, a blue crab into the pubic hair, another crab, a hermit, into the mouth. This is not disgusting. They are only animals looking for easy access to meat. Like us.

In a few hours the appendages are stripped clean from the bloating corpse. There are no lips or ears or labia or fingers. This is a body gone to rot and hunger.

What would you say if you were a dead body?

You can feed on me.

I'd suspect it takes time to reach this state.

A while. I denied everything at first. No! No! I'm not dead.

Wannna bet?

Yes, you're right, I'm dead, but it's not a matter of being dead. It's a matter of being. There is no choice. You roll and roll, and after a while it isn't so bad. I wish I had eyes to see the sculpins. Oh, the sensuality of being fed upon. Life into life. Animal into animal.

Tell us what happened?

Nothing happened. I am dead. Once, I was alive. Now I'm twisting on the ocean floor, and I have no eyes, though around me lives a deep green life. Coral. Urchins. Plankton. Feelers touching unfeeling flesh. It's all gone.

What's gone?

Life is gone. What's that? I don't know any more. I wanted to touch and be touched. I wanted. I wanted. I was given lots. And I gave lots. The men, they also wanted — and gave everything they had — so little — to me, and I took it, and I gave them everything I had. It wasn't enough. I wanted to be happy. Charlie gave me love, then sorrow, so much sorrow, so much thinking. I didn't want to think, not that way. I wanted to be alive. And the others, they were worse. They thought I had a secret vitality, and tried to steal it. They were petty.

The worst pettiness was the last. He couldn't bear it, so he killed it. The 'it' was me. Insignificance. That's what it means; and despite what he may think, God, any kind of god or devil, had nothing to do with it, and I didn't have a say in the idiot game of my death.

You do now. Tell me what you know?

Nothing. There is nothing to say — no more — I'm living the life of the fishes. Everything you ask is meaningless. These questions are stupid. I am just waiting for the scavengers to clean me up. Soon, the large ones will be here. My mind is full of worms, my fingers that touched can never touch again, my breasts are eaten back to the ribs. Where are the toes? Gone. And the currents seethe around me as a big creature moves in, long and deadly like a machine, except it's alive, full of tentacles and suction cups, drawing me softly towards its beak.

I never wanted to be in this story. You are cruel. Let me go.

And so we shall. Let her go. We return to the cabin in the trees, where we can sit silently with Brian and Charlie. Both of them overflowing with sorrow and horror.

It was still light outside, and raining, when they heard footsteps on the ramp. Festus lurched in, the drenched parrot on his shoulder. He had a carton of eggs in his hand, but he stopped suddenly, confronted by the tear-stained men seated at opposite ends of the room, gaping at him as if he were a ghost. "Am I interfering?" There was almost too much innocence in the way he asked.

Charlie waved a helpless invitation with his hand. "No, come in. It's fine."

The parrot shuffled its feathers, and bobbed on Festus's shoulder. "Awkkk, it's cold." It flew towards its perch beside the stove, almost landing on the stovetop before it felt the heat radiating upwards, and ended up clinging to a shelf above it with a lot of squawking, flushing a mouse from behind the stove. The mouse dashed across the windowsill, startling Brian. The same mouse? Or were there hordes of them using the window as a highway across the treehouse?

"Stupid bird," Charlie said. "You'd think he'd have figured the stove out by now."

The bird fluttered to its perch, studying everyone with misgiving. "Roll that rock, watch that hawk!"

"I came by," Festus said, "to see if you needed anything tomorrow. Groceries . . . ?" He regarded the cardboard-covered window by the door.

"Brian picked them up a couple of days ago."

"I brought you a dozen eggs from the new hens."

"Are they fertilized? You still got that killer rooster?"

"Yup, the only real chickens on the island. They're on the scratch and the mash. No commercial pellets around our farm."

Taking the carton, Charlie smiled kindly, while the parrot eyed it with suspicion. "Thanks. I guess we can eat that, though Brian will tell you I should consider them morally dicey. My friend here has been educating me about the ethics of the world."

Brian shrugged. "How was the big city?"

"Very big."

"We've got food enough here, if you're interested in dinner." Charlie said.

Festus, too aware of their mood, went gruff, and began to swagger in front of the men. "I'll be leaving. You look like you don't need me."

"Today," Charlie said, "is a bad day."

***

Hours later, Charlie blew out the light.

In his bunk, in the dark, Brian wanted more — sympathy, or at least understanding, for kicking Rita off a cliff; the awful indignity of it — for both her and him. It was an accident. No, it wasn't, but yet . . . Most of us never kill anyone with our spontaneous cruelties. He did. Though it *had*, sort of, been planned. Who would ever forgive him? Who could forgive him for all the destruction he'd caused in his lifetime?

"Charlie? Will you forgive me?"

"I did that within a few hours of when you first showed up."

"I miss Rita."

"So do I."

"Charlie — are you going to murder me?"

"Only if I think you're going to murder me first."

"Time for bed," the parrot cooed softly in the darkness. "Time for bed." It dragged out the word bed like a plaintive hymn to a long-lost love.

Brian couldn't sleep. 'It's all revealed now, and he hasn't eaten the orange.' Or, if he did sleep, he wasn't aware of it. The parrot kept grinding its beak in the darkness, the noise jangling him. It wasn't supposed to be like this. He thought he was dreaming. He thought he was awake. Charlie was as quiet as a rock. There was an unearthly scream; then another; a peacock in one of the maples at the edge of the clearing. It sounded like a cat being strangled.

Watch out for that Brian, he is beginning to dream too much. He's going too deeply into this world of waking and sleeping. Going to bed, getting up, the nights and days running through our story —the one where half our life is unconscious, and the other half is unconscious, too.

***

Okay, let's take on our dreams. Dreams are used in lazy stories as symbolic allegories which explain everything about the characters. If the reader can understand the dream, the reader can understand everything that happens in the story. Lots of luck. You're reading the wrong story.

This is a real dream, without answers, full of suggestions, and phony forked paths that can lead the reader who wants to read too much into dreams, happily in all the wrong directions — or the right ones. Yes, it's a dream and merrily, merrily, we all go down the deepening stream. Live through it.

When Brian woke up he knew right away that he hadn't woken. The air held the stillness of a dream, a scary one. He half-expected the rock; instead, there was an unnatural light, a neon sign peeking through the jungle.

He followed the path for several yards until it forked, one branch leading to a dark, shrouded valley, lush with unknown plants and crying animals, the other to a fifties-style neon sign — THE MUSEUM OF US. He took the path to the sign.

There was dust everywhere in front of the building. The grass had been stamped down and ground into the earth. The sign had once said THE MUSEUM OF CONSPICUOUS CONSUMPTION; but most of the neon tubes in the last two words were burnt out. The edifice resembled a large mushroom cap resting on the ground, the neon sign curving over its surface. Yet another toadstool, a smaller version of the main structure, grew from its side, complete with two stacked signs. ROADSIDE ATTRACTION seated crookedly on top of TICKETS SOLD HERE. There was a photograph of a man below them, encased in plastic laminate, with the inscription: "Another presentation by Homer Entertainment." Brian approached the ticket booth. It was dark inside, but the thing at the window appeared to be a crocodile.

A crocodile? Yes, well, you figure it out. It's a dream, and a dream's logic doesn't have anything to do with what we see when we lie to ourselves with our culturally conditioned vision of life programmed into us since birth. The best thing about dreams is that they are what they are. Besides, you haven't seen anything yet.

"How much?" Brian asked.

"Everything you've got," the crocodile replied.

Brian groped around in his jean pockets. They were empty. "I haven't got anything." He rummaged in his shirt pockets. They were also barren.

"That's fine," the crocodile said. "If you've got nothing; then that's everything you've got, isn't it?"

The crocodile nudged the ticket forward with its snout. Brian, anxious about those teeth, grabbed it before the creature could snap at him, and walked through the shiny turnstile, past the racks of T-shirts adorned with gravestones and missiles. There was a souvenir counter. The woman on the other side of the low, glass case was naked except for a rough leather loin-cloth, and she was very hirsute. She had a pushed-up nose and thick brows. She rested her elbows on the counter, her hairy breasts flattening against the glass surface. "What can I do for you?"

"I want to go inside."

"You are inside."

"This is it? This is the museum?"

"No, this is just inside."

"Thank God." Brian rested his hands on the glass counter top. He was almost nose-to-nose with the Neanderthal woman.

"Can I sell you a plastic missile?" she asked. "How about a miniature working saw-mill, or a subdivision?"

"No," he whispered, "it isn't as simple as that."

"Wanna bet? It's only your thoughts that are complicated."

He rested his head on his hands, empty, exhausted. "No, it's not even as simple as that. I need it to be different."

"How about me, then? You can have me. I'm very raunchy. I could show you ecstasies you never imagined."

"You're sweet, but it isn't as simple as that either. Sex is boring. I want to go inside."

She shrugged, undisturbed, as if he were merely another dull customer. "There's the tour guide."

Brian looked over his shoulder at the sloth wearing dark sunglasses and a name tag dangling on a string around her neck. "Oh no." The sloth put her magazine away, and very slowly crawled onto all four feet. She slothed down the stairs without once looking behind to see if Brian was following.

The stairway opened into a monstrous, domed room, diffused light coming through the opaque roof. The sloth, as she eased along the overhead walkway, recited with her torpid, slothlike voice: "This is the first room of the museum. All the other rooms are the same, only different. Once you've seen one, you've seen them all. If you look to your right, you will observe a somewhat rusted diesel motor. It works. In fact, our plentiful monarch butterflies enjoy spinning in the wind from its fan — as you will notice. The growing monarch population, unfortunately, has presented us with a problem which our trained specialists are analysing at this moment. The males have an ugly tendency to rape the females when the females are not ready to mate."

The notion of butterfly rapists was almost more than Brian could choke down. He was clinging to the rail above the chaos. The wrecked airplanes, the car flashing its lights among the swamp cabbages; the huge, dead June bugs — as big as cows — lying like iridescent, mechanical wreckage under the wide-leaved palms. A thought struck him: "If this is part of Homer Entertainment, who was Homer?"

The sloth studied him with displeasure. "Samuel Homer, our founder, set aside from his many incomes the funds to support this institute, creating a foundation named after himself. But we prefer not to discuss him."

"Why?"

"He died in prison, after being falsely charged with sexual assault."

"Wow, that's grim."

"You will observe," the sloth droned on, "the predominance of insects, what we term 'opportunistic species.' They have the greatest ability to withstand environmental shock. Like people and racoons and coyotes and rats, the other opportunists. Cockroaches — they survive anything."

"I've met a few in my time."

The sloth paused near a gigantic banana plant hanging its produce over the rail, and began to eye the fruit. "But of course," she said, "none of this has anything to do with the real reason why you are here. Listen."

Brian found himself focusing on the ragtag landscape below. Beyond the airplanes and the prefabricated houses among the yuccas there was a tall palm. It stood far above the mess, shrouded by a swarm of hummingbirds. A great green ball fell. There was silence. Then a deep crack as the coconut hit the ground, and the air reverberated, distorted, striking him like a shock wave. He hung onto the rail, overwhelmed by the sound of that single coconut dropping. He stayed there for hours, a victim of that sound, his fingers wrapped so tight around the rail his knuckles glowed red. He opened his fingers, slowly, one after the other, watching the digits come alive. He turned to the sloth. She was up in the banana plant, taking her time, peeling a banana.

"Well?" Brian asked. The sloth ignored him, intent on her snack. Brian assumed that was the end of the tour. He passed under her, and found himself beside a grizzly bear in a too-small guard's uniform. "What a zoo," Brian heard himself say. Fortunately, the grizzly was more interested in a beehive than Brian, and he slipped by while its great claws slowly raked at the hive and the bees swirled around its skull.

The next room was a desert, full of succulents and parasitical plants, and a few hares. A road runner, which somehow resembled a parrot, zipped by him on the path among the dry rocks that led up to the rock. Yes, the rock. He knew it would be here. Along the side of the display was a line of machines, humming and vibrating and moving; computer robots — they were making a car. At the end of the line was an assortment of wooden Indians with forlorn expressions, as if they'd been purloined from cigar stores in frontier towns, and regretted it.

He approached the rock. It was singing. He wanted to know the words. The song bored through his skin, reverberating off his bones. He passed around to the other side of the rock where the monarch butterflies congregated on the ground in a swarm that was the shape of a man.

Brian clapped his hands. The swarm rose as one, like Lazarus rising from the grave, keeping the shape, winging in unison towards the assembly line. The figure beneath the rock was Charlie, very dead. "Bend down and kiss him goodbye," a female voice commanded.

"Goodbye." Brian touched the waxy, dead lips with his own.

Then he was running along the pathway, out the room, into the hallway, past the women hanging on strings, lascivious women, displaying their sex as if they were souvenirs from the shop at the entrance. There was another woman, behind him, her hair in curlers and a scarf; she was vacuuming maniacally, attempting to catch his feet, clean every trace he left behind. "Mother? What are you doing here?"

"I'm not your mother," she said.

The line of hanging women evolved into boys with big, white, perfect teeth. They were riding on surf boards towards the ultimate wave. Standing on the nearby shore, watching them were older men, all bald, holding charts and notebooks, making bids as if they were at an auction.

There was another man in the aisle, a wicked man who screamed like a hawker in a stadium: "Ice cream, peanuts, condoms." Brian stopped for a moment, facing the vendor, while the woman vacuumed around his feet. "Safe sex," the man said, "I'm selling safe sex, if there is such a thing."

Brian jerked away, and ran down the hall. There were windows full of exhibits. Twenty-five or more plastic palm leaves. Stuffed, dead mice. A row of distributor caps from cars. Carnivores mounted in attack positions. Piles of broken television sets, every screen shattered. And parrots, aww the parrots, all dead, with questioning looks in their glass eyes. Fourteen sculptures of black women in chains — suffering. One of the windows revealed mason jars filled with poisons, each one tagged, the cards relating details about fatal dosages. A poisoner's paradise! In the middle of the mason jars stood a stuffed white peacock, a faint brown stain on its chest. Then he was outside, on a path, flapping the palm fronds aside, until he came to the fork again, the one he'd taken to the museum, and he paused, gasping for breath.

Around him there was the smell of rotting vegetation — a world mysterious with life; a jungle filled with the cries of dying animals.

21

Brothers

NOT FAR AWAY ON ARTEMIS ISLAND, someone else was having trouble sleeping.

A grey light in a dim room, curtains shivering above the desk where the shadowy, inert computer sat.

Janwar struggled against his own dream, its subject forgotten already, but his teeth were clamped hard, and his jaw hurt. Wren was next to him, asleep, her face blank. He would be catching the ferry in a few hours. He should have been sick, except his stomach felt surprisingly stable, and he remembered the months, or was it years, he had awoken ill — gone in three, life changing weeks. Janwar studied the curtains on the window, remembering her arrival, long after dark. He'd woken as he felt her sliding in next to him. They spent hours making love, whispering incomprehensible things that were like code words or bird songs — their bodies growing hot, dangerous to the touch — half asleep, loving, pushing into each other; he thought he dreamt of spontaneous combustion.

That grey light like her skin. The sunrise was approaching, the morning hour of the birds awakening, and she was at his side. Everything was self-evident, yet there was business to wrap up, loathsome work he felt obligated to finish — conversations with Mother . . . Internal Affairs . . . a woman who disappeared . . .

He slipped from under the covers, and sat naked at his desk. He realized with a thrill he hadn't started his computer yesterday. The beauty of Wren's sleeping body was beyond description: this naked woman in his bed in a wacky health spa on a crazy island. "It's too beautiful. I don't deserve this."

He moused off the screen saver and logged onto the net. Out there, beyond this nest, existed a world of confusion and danger and enchantment. He still needed it. He had to talk to someone. There was an email in his box. Kirsten.

"Inspector Singh, I felt guilty about forgetting to check that licence plate, so I put in a few hours overtime yesterday. The place is always quiet on Saturdays, and it's easier to get stuff done, and I had nothing else to do. The Miata was rented on May 17th to an Orion Ambrose Laud, mailing address Box 4414 Station A, Vancouver, V8B 0M4, home address 4244 West 74A Avenue, Vancouver. It was rented on a monthly basis, the first two payments made in advance, using a Visa gold card. It is now overdue. I hope this will be of some use. Kirsten."

Irritation invaded Janwar's thoughts, collisions of emotions. His heart went out to Kirsten when he read "nothing else to do." At the same time his eyes focused on "May 17th." That was a day after Rita Norman's disappearance. He skimmed through his notebook. He'd written down Brian. Orion? What kind of name was that? Had he got it wrong? Did it matter? In less than two hours he would be on the ferry.

He studied Wren, so grey against the pastel sheet, like the sky against the sea. This place was turning him into a poet. That's all he needed. He began typing.

"Kirsten. Your diligence is appreciated. I was under the impression it was Brian not Orion. This might sound like a quibble. Since you will be in the office before me today, can you proceed further? Past history, credit and finances, institutions where he studied, books written (he's a writer). Also, the street number sounds odd for Vancouver. I was not aware the city planners utilized numbered 'A' or 'B' streets. That's a practice common across the river, in Surrey. I want to know more about this man. Besides, this might be an opportunity to bolster our liaison with Vancouver City Police. Since they are so territorial, our queries will give their officers a chance to feel useful. Thank you. Janwar."

He logged off and pushed the mouse away. There. It probably meant nothing, yet busy work always cleared his head. 'Orion? How could he get that wrong? A pen-name?' He found himself sliding in beside Wren again, the heat of her body a warmth he hadn't known since he slept with his sister when he was a child. Janwar let his hand rest on her belly. It was like a warm skillet. She slept hot, the way he'd heard climbers slept after they'd spent too many years in the mountains, freezing in sub-zero weather, their bodies adjusting their interior thermostat to survival on the cold, high grounds of the planet.

His hand, alive with its own intelligence, slid down her belly, slowly, to the dark hair between her legs, where it rested. There was more than an hour before he had to take the High Road to the city.

The High Road? How wonderful that a simple road name can also signify a way of life — what we can't reach, yet drive along to catch a ferry. Let's call that a mystery, too. And is this road leading to Brian? Is it leading to, or away from, love? Or is it leading to Coyote? The real man behind the legend? The dead man still alive? How did Coyote die in that cement factory? Right. Here's a story for you, as far-fetched as what you might read in your daily newspaper . . . or in a slim paperback picked up at the airport. What does it matter where they come from? They're all stories.

The tenement's entrance was dark, the painted steps slippery with a slimy and disgusting object that reminded Coyote of the placenta of a sheep. The door, scratched and gouged, and then repainted several times, was open. The lights were shattered in the hallway, the only illumination the ghastly red of the EXIT signs. An ill-looking, dark-faced girl, perhaps ten-years-old, sat on the first landing. She eyed Coyote with an expression close to hatred while he side-stepped her and climbed the stairs.

They creaked constantly, floor after floor, until it nearly became a game, attempting another step without signalling his arrival. Room 666. His contact had a sense of humour. When he knocked the door groaned open, so he stepped inside. The suite was dark, empty except for a beat-up desk, and a bed under the window — half-illuminated by a neon sign flashing in the window but out of the line of vision — the only light. There was a man behind the desk. Charlie shut the door and stood silent beside it.

The shadow behind the desk spoke. "Are you the one."

Aw, the unadulterated melodrama, the sadness of strange human beings in unforgivable rooming houses — the joke.

Charlie never wanted to star in cheap Hollywood films about heroes and failures, yet here he was in a forlorn slum with a forlorn man. This is what you get when you run up against the edge of life. Worse still, this is often what you get when you don't run. Right. This pathetic little room of sadness could also be what you achieve solely by being born into modern America. And life is equally strange in the suburbs. Awkward, stupid things can come in through the window, via the door — a wife or a husband with knife in hand. The weird kid down the block. They come in like the wasp seeking the sole allergic victim in a room. It comes in everywhere. And it just keeps on coming . . .

"I'm the one, and I have the money. Do you have the plans?"

"I got them."

Charlie said: "I have a second offer."

The man leaned back in the shadows. "Yes?"

"I have another envelope. Double your money. You helped build the place. The plans are nice, but what I really want is for you to tell me the easiest way to shut ChemCity down."

"Double the money?" the voice rasped. He sounded like decades of unfiltered cigarettes and bourbon.

"For fifteen minutes of your valuable time."

The head turned, facing the invisible sign. He'd become recognizable, yet he didn't care. "This is an apartment where I screw women I shouldn't be screwing. It's awful isn't it?"

"Yes, it's awful."

The face turned back into the shadows. "People live here all of the time."

Coyote nodded.

"Some of my women like it here, screwing in a dangerous place. It turns them on. I've only had one go screaming out the door. Mind you, a few never came back."

Charlie remained silent.

The man leaned forward, into the light. "Graveyard shift — there's maybe a couple dozen employees on the entire site. Go to central planning; substation II, room S-111. The site is numbered on one of the sheets: C-17, I think, or C-18. Whatever." The man pulled out a pen and shuffled through the papers. "There, it's marked. I've thought about that room for years. One of the things I never liked about the engineering is the flush valves to the cement module — the cement sub-plant, though it's big, it is a minor side-business, but the water pipes used to flush the cement lines through the entire plant. The staff use them for flushing different modules, besides the cement. Many of the modules are multi-use, you know. Well, if somebody mucked up real bad, the wet cement could back into the flushing system . . . "

It took longer than fifteen minutes, but the shadow didn't appear concerned. When he finished, he turned back, towards the neon, his face red and blue. "Why are you doing this? If you don't mind my asking?"

"You must know. You worked on the construction. You've been doing the talking about it — after all, I was asked to contact you. Besides, you only have to drive by ChemCity and look. The place is evil."

The shadow moved around the desk, the unrolled plans glowing in the neon light. "Sure, that factory is evil. And I did help build it. Now here I am, twenty years later. Like a boy who's built a sandcastle. The tide has been a long time coming in. It isn't just the money. I'd have never done this for the money, but you told me what I wanted to hear. They've ruined the river through that little town. Anybody there who's smart drinks water out of a bottle now — and the air, I hate to think of the kids breathing it. ChemCity was one of my first real jobs: I was only an assistant then — the guy who made the changes in the blueprints and copied them out again. But I kept these. Maybe I wanted to nail the place myself, one day. When are you going to do it?"

"Next week."

"I'll be waiting." He scooped up the two envelopes; then dodged out the door. "It's really not the money. You'll never believe that. But it's time I changed my life. I'm giving up this room." He creaked noisily down the stairs. After he was gone the building grew quiet, eerie. There was a thump in the room above the apartment, and the soft crunching sound of falling plaster beside Coyote. He didn't stay around to find out what was going on up there.

✳✳✳

Charlie left town. It was almost six months before he read a small article in a business magazine about ChemCity initiating an employee relations program due to a high staff turnover. It included piped-in muzak, subdued 'relaxing and natural' lighting, and, most interesting of all, prizes for the best costumes worn on Halloween. Yes! Trick or treat.

✳✳✳

"We're ready!" Charlie folded up the blueprints and threw them into the fireplace. He lit a match, touched it to a corner, and watched the flame eat the paper.

Tom contemplated the blaze. "I'm really proud that you let me come along."

"You gotta behave yourself and do what I say."

"Oh, I will. I will. I'll do whatever you say. I'm going to be a ninja at last."

"You're not going to be any ninja. You're too old for that kind of stuff. We're only going to shut the place down and get the hell away. But it's big, and I need you to keep an eye out — that's all."

Tom was dressed in his best ninja black, Charlie had decked himself out as a hayseed farmer, complete with straw hat and corncob pipe jutting from his overalls pocket, and a .357 magnum pistol bulging in the big hip compartment. His black Zorro mask seemed a little odd, though.

They left the motel where they'd registered two days ago under assumed names, and drove the ten miles to the wire perimeter, past the strip malls and the housing complexes. Though ChemCity had originally been built in an industrial park in a small town sixty miles from Chicago, it had merged with the monster city's suburbs in the intervening years.

Since it was Halloween, they weren't the only costumed drivers on the road.

ChemCity was an extended series of enormous structures — domed, square, smoke-stacked — tubes and pipes and ramps leading from one module to the next: everywhere, on the grounds, a faint white, chalky dust, eerie in the evening light.

"Tom, this ain't only a cement factory. That's a by-product, a sideshow. This place is so evil it makes hell look sweet. They manufacture everything but napalm. They probably make that, too."

"I like the decorations."

Charlie had to admit the goblins and witches adorning the highway side of the fence and a few of the buildings gave the site an eerie yet cute touch. The conglomerate's corporate board, after receiving another hefty fine for environmental contamination, were attempting to spruce up the company image, both with their staff and the general public. "It's scarier than it looks."

Charlie pulled the Jeep off the road, into the bushes beside the fence. He gave Tom the clippers. "Cut us a hole, but watch out for the poison ivy. It's all around the fence." The wire mesh was easy. No alarms. There wasn't any need for them; nobody had ever broken into a cement factory before. Tom was so excited he'd already begun to sweat in that ridiculous black outfit. At least he avoided the poison ivy.

A ninja followed by a scruffy, masked farmer in a straw hat rushed down the path through the dark yard and entered the first building. It was empty. Nothing. No-one. A ghost module, obviously unused for years. They crossed the floor, leaving an unfortunate trail of footprints in the dust that filmed its surface. There was a ramp leading to the second module. It was empty, too, and then the third. "Where the hell is everybody?" Charlie said, his voice echoing.

They found the sub-station. This is where things began to turn bad. There was a man at one of the computers arrayed around the glassed-in control room, his face rotting grotesquely in the soft glow cast by the terminals. He was alone. Charlie was about to move closer when he heard footsteps. He pushed Tom behind a duct and followed him. A woman, dressed as a nurse, entered the room, offering the rotted man a clipboard, which he took without looking at her. He signed the papers, pulled out his copies, and handed her the board, along with his coffee mug. She took it, gave him a cheeky curtsy behind his back and left. Charlie smirked as she left through a door at the end of the catwalk. "He won't be so important in the morning."

Tom nodded.

Yet this was trouble. The engineer had told him there wouldn't be anyone in the sub-station at night, maybe the occasional staff checking things out, drifting over from the main control centre and the first modules — but instead, those buildings had been empty. "It's all backwards. We have to wait."

"We're not finished yet," Tom said, wrapping the length of black cotton around his head, so that he was completely masked except for his eyes.

"What are you doing?"

"I'm a ninja."

"You're not a ninja. This hasn't got anything to do with ninjas. We're going to leave, hide for a while. We can come back later." But Tom was already gone. He slunk along the catwalk like a refugee from a Samurai film. "Tom! Come back here." Charlie couldn't raise his voice. The man in the control room might hear him through the doors. "Tom, you're not a ninja. This is the twentieth century. Come back. Besides, you can't win a prize. That's only for company employees."

Yet he had to admit Tom was beautiful to watch as he slithered noiselessly through the glass doors before he stood up calmly behind the man facing the computer screens. Tom touched him on the shoulder and the man slouched unconscious.

Charlie was impressed, but he knew things were going to hell. "We gotta get out of here," he muttered. He stepped out of hiding, onto the catwalk, and entered the room. "What did you do to him?"

"The touch of death." Tom beamed proudly.

"The touch of death! You killed him?"

"Oh no! He'll just wake up with a headache in a few hours."

"Where the hell did you learn that?"

"There's a lot of things I know that you don't. The touch of death is very tricky. Bruce Lee was learning it when he died. I think he did it to himself, accidentally."

"Bruce Lee? Aw cripes. We gotta get out of here. I told you no heroics, and already you're pulling goofy stuff."

Tom's shoulder's stiffened. His grey eyes shone wetly. You're laughing at me."

"I'm not laughing at you."

"Then do it, and let's go."

Charlie grabbed Tom by the arm and yanked him across the control room. "This is all wrong. You can't hurt anyone!"

"Charlie, I could never do the things you do. I'm the warrior. You're the brains."

"I don't want any warriors! Listen; all you have to do is keep a lookout." He held Tom up against the glass, and wagged a finger in front of his nose. "Stay there."

He had to reverse the flow of the cement in the control room and open the by-pass valves. Once it backed up into the ducts; that would be it. They'd freeze up for eternity, encased in their own cement. But there was still one other valve, the main junction in module 2. That would convey the cement in the pipes out of this building into at least half the others. "Trust me. It'll be simple. Beautiful things are always simple. So don't get complicated on me."

"I'll follow you to hell, Charlie."

"I'm not going to hell. I don't believe in hell."

The staffing change signified there'd been updating since the disgraced engineer had last seen the place. Either that, or Charlie had been betrayed, which was a possibility. There should have been two wheel valves. Facing him were three. And the computers were not where he was told they should be. Lost on the engineering that propelled the plant, he did what anybody in the same situation would do; he turned all three wheels. He glared at the computer screens in disgust, and began hammering levers and buttons. The fourth button he touched set off a hidden tape machine and soft muzak ushered through the building. A tacky, watered-down version of a familiar song, which depressed him. "Crumbs!" He kicked the machine, and the volume increased. Had he piped it into the rest of the buildings? "I want to give them cement, not muzak!" He threw more switches; then looked up at Tom.

"I like that tune," Tom said.

"Let's get out of here. I don't know what's going to happen, but it should be interesting." The engineer had fed him a line. It wasn't fair. Charlie wanted his money back, not only for himself, but the others. It had been hard work forging the secretive connections that lured Coyote here. Another great scheme gone off the deep end. He dashed out of the room and down the corrugated ramp, hurled the door open and faced the nurse. She gazed at him in shock, full coffee cup in hand.

He confiscated the mug, drank a mouthful, and passed it back to her. She took it like an automaton. He realized his pistol was pointed at her belly. When did he pull that out? No wonder she was standing there stiff as a statue. He holstered it in the overalls. "Sorry, I like mine black. I hate cream and sugar."

She still didn't move, her face expressionless.

"You better get out of here. The whole place is liable to fry in a few minutes."

"It is?" she said, hesitating. Her eyes widened further as the ninja appeared at the farmer's side. "You guys don't work here, do you?" She appeared so lost, so frail, Charlie took the cup from her hand. It was the gentlemanly thing to do.

"Nope."

"Thanks for telling me," she said, before she rushed down the stairs, not looking back. Charlie didn't know what to do with the coffee, so he drank it down and passed the mug to his brother.

Tom squinted, sweating so badly that dark stains were showing under his arms and on his chest. "You drank it all. I'm thirsty."

"It's not good for you. Let's go." Charlie marched down the ramp; this was so screwed-up he was beginning to enjoy it. An alarm rang. At first, it sounded like a wake-up call on a clock in a different room. Then it chimed through the entire building. Outside, too?

"Let's vanish."

Tom followed him along the ramp, clutching the coffee mug. There was a distant whump, and a wave of hot air rushed towards him. Charlie flew over the rail, landing on the floor below the ramp while dust spewed onto him. His back, it hurt — he couldn't breathe. He crawled behind a boiler. There was blood beside the suspender hook on his overalls. A cut on his chest. "Cross my heart and hope to die." There was another explosion, this time atop the boiler, and pieces of metal and more dust flew. He rubbed his eyes — the dust? It was full of fibres. "Asbestos. I'm going to get cancer!"

Tom was on the ramp, looking over the broken rail. The ramp itself was intact, but the weight of the cement was bursting the smaller pipes. What a mess.

"Tom, come down here. Jump!"

"Are you okay?"

"I'm fine. Jump!"

A man in a fireman's suit raced down the wobbling catwalk, a small tool box in his hand. Tom looked up at him. "Hi."

The man stopped. "What's happening? Who are you?"

"Stand back. I'm a ninja."

"A what?" He stopped, confused. Tom twisted, and flung himself into a sublime reverse axe-kick that struck the astonished worker's red fire helmet. The man flopped like a rag doll onto the ramp at his feet. Tom stood alone in the weird, dusty light flooding the damaged ramp, a hero.

Another song, a pseudo-rap piece, began to clink out a monologue to an eccentric drumbeat.

It sounded familiar.

There were shouts, men racing up the stairs, a group of them. "Who is that clown? Does he work here? Did you see him kick Herb?"

But where-O-where are the snows of years ago?

"He looks like a ninja."

"A ninja? What's that?"

"Hey mister, what are you doing?"

Down below, on level one, behind the boiler, Charlie was horrified. "It's Villon! They've murdered Francois Villon's poem!" They'd turned one of the greatest lyrics in history into an Americanized piece of crap muzak!

Another group appeared at the opposite end of the ramp. A second, higher-pitched alarm rang, howling out its idiosyncratic rhythm under the drum of footsteps on metal while the surrounding pipes groaned. "Tom, get the hell off that ramp," Charlie hissed from behind the boiler. No-one, including Tom noticed him. There was an almost unearthly pause as everyone froze in position, nobody wanting to make the first move.

The song meandered on, a river of nonsense.

Tom swaggered in front of the first group. A weapon appeared in his hand, a small metallic star. He flung it at the pipes above. Steam and gooey stuff splattered everywhere. He jump-kicked the first man, punched the second, and dropped the third with that beautiful reverse axe-kick. By the time he was finished, all three lay on the catwalk. He was still holding the coffee mug, now bloody. The last line of the song on the loudspeakers stuck in a loop, playing over and over.

Satisfied with the mayhem he'd created, Tom turned to face the second gang of workers. He held up the mug, as if asking for alms, and waited. *But where-O-where are the snows of years ago?* They advanced more slowly than the first group, hard-faced, almost delighted, like they'd been waiting for a fight ever since coming to work at ChemCity.

Tom turned, saw the door into the tube, and spun the wheeled handle, opening it.

"Tom, don't go in there!" Charlie's voice was drowned by the rumble that began to his left. The building shivered. Bits of dust and metal fell on him. The pipes were breaking up. The men at the end of the cracked ramp suddenly fell to the metal grating, hanging on, as if they knew something.

Tom stepped backwards into the tube, gave a cavalier wave with the mug, like the Crimson Pirate making his escape, and pulled the door shut on himself.

"Tom . . . Tom? . . . Awwww . . . " And that horror of a broken recording kept repeating itself.

One of the men on the rippling causeway, leaped to his feet, and cranked the wheel, sealing Tom inside.

Charlie stepped onto the empty floor below, shrouded by the dust and the roaring. A thunder swept through the building, the roar of wild materials released. The ramp tilted and the men clung for their lives. The big pipes bent like snakes under the weight of the cement rushed through them, down the tube that Tom had entered.

"Don't — please don't . . . " Rivets popped, pipes cracked, cement oozed onto the catwalk. The roar was punctured by the sound of metal flying. Charlie was in a shooting gallery, metal and bullets echoing. Bullets? There was an old man in a uniform on the floor, shooting at him or shadows. The old man was firing in several directions. At first Charlie considered letting off a few shots of his own, but he ducked behind the boiler; then slunk backwards like a dog that had touched fire.

At the second module, he found the valve. At least that was where the man had told him. He turned the creaky wheel that would flush the other substations. He was in a dream now, unthinking, unfeeling — blank . . . He fled the modules.

Reaching the car he paused to listen to the distant reverberations. He couldn't have done a better job if he'd known what he was doing — and Tom was gone . . .

***

"That's how you killed your brother." Brian set his tea bowl on the table. It had taken weeks to arrive here, and now the story seemed insignificant, pathetic. This must mean it was time to move on.

"That's how I killed my brother. I'd become the monster I fought."

That's the way we kill all our brothers — running for a dream, recklessly, intent on our own path, unaware, until we turn back and see the body lying by the side of the road where we have travelled.

"And you gave up being Coyote."

"I never much had the heart to break anything again. You have to remember ChemCity was the first time people got hurt. Not only did Tom die, he broke a few men's bones."

Charlie leaned back in his chair, his blue eyes reflecting the light thrown by the prisms in the window. His hand fell onto the ceramic bowl containing the last three oranges, and he rolled them around, unconsciously. He picked one out and began to peel it. "Want an orange?"

Shaking his head, Brian casually checked the bowl. The brown-spotted orange was still there. This was becoming fun. "No, I'm not hungry. You've killed my appetite again. If nothing else, I'm going to lose weight here."

"Shhh," Charlie held a finger to his lips. The room grew hushed. Outside, a quail was calling its instinctive three note song. Chi-ca-go . . . Chi-ca-go . . . His eyes misted, and he coughed an ironic laugh. "Bad music. Bad music," he said wistfully. "And I can't get it out of my mind."

***

Tell me where, in what country
Is Sharol, the beautiful Californian,
Or Marilyn, or Martha Washington
Who sewed together our flag?
The echo that speaks when it hears
Voices beside a fresh brook.
A beautiful woman, more than human.
But where-o-where are the snows of years ago.

Where have all our men gone?
The Kennedys and Jesse James?
Thoreau growing his beans
And demanding to know
Why we need to know so much
When very little was plenty.
But where-o-where are the snows of years ago.

Janis, white as lilies,
Who sang with a siren's voice?
Beautiful Bette, Jane, and Joan,
And Dorothy who killed the Terminator
In a battle for the future?
Where are they, the beautiful women?
But where-o-where are the snows of years ago?

22

JANWAR ARRIVED AT HEADQUARTERS AT 1:30 ON MONDAY, after a light lunch from an expensive organic fruit stall on the highway. Eating properly was going to put a dent in his budget. He should have returned Sunday since his holidays were officially over, but it was too hard to leave The Last Resort. How these weeks had changed him. His meticulous efficiency had gone right out the window.

Everyone was at their desks. When he opened the door all heads looked up, each one stony and silent. There were no greetings. Kirsten's sharp features fixed on his. There was an ironic coolness in the way she watched him approach her desk. And the silence was nearly deafening by the time he reached her. Not a chair squeaked. "Hello. Did you get my email?"

"No. What email?" She spoke with ostentatious efficiency. "I came in early, as it happens, and worked on my report from Saturday. Not a great deal of info there yet. I have a letter for you from Blake."

"I sent you an email early this morning. Blake?"

"The computers were all down until lunch. Programming glitch. I had to type out the report downstairs. Yes, the letter is from Blake. Nearly everyone has a different version, tailored to the individual, myself included. This is yours."

Janwar took the sealed envelope as if it were poison. "Thank you." He turned towards his office, tearing open the envelope, followed by the gaze of a dozen staff.

Inspector Singh:
I am officially tendering my resignation from the force this morning. There is nothing more to be said about the matter. I have spent thirty years proudly doing my work, and doing it well. The record is there! I want you to know that I supported you (but you should already know that). I tried to keep abreast of the times. Obviously, they have surpassed me, and maybe that's good. Let new, fresh minds lead the way. So be it. I wish them well. You will be one of them. In fact, I'm sure it won't be long before you assume the position I used to hold, and will possibly navigate it with more skill. The charges which led to my recent demotion are baseless, as you are aware. While I may be tactless, on occasion, I have always performed my duties impeccably. I had the greatest faith and respect in you, and was proud of your work as you surmounted the handicaps of your colour and social position. I was a little astounded by the viciousness of your private correspondence passed on to Internal Affairs, but I also have had my sins with a loose lip. You and your partner have no class and, in all honesty, I wish I'd sent her back to her kitchen before she tainted the

whole department. Alas, the bitch got me. (Right. I don't care what I say any more. Fuck you, too). I trusted you. I thought we were trying to work together for law enforcement in this country. I never expected I'd be betrayed by a social-climbing back-stabbing little Hindu. At least, I've got my house on the beach and a pension they can't touch. I'm going there this morning. Good luck. You'll need it in these "advanced times," asshole.

yours sincerely,
Ex-Chief Inspector Robert Blake

He opened the door into his office, unconsciously slowing down as he read the letter again. He crumpled it up, furious, mashing it into his hand, and slammed the door. The panel shattered, and the glass falling to the floor echoed through the department. Nothing but silence remained. Kirsten, at her desk, looked away smugly. Yet, there was a sad edge to her triumph.

There was blood on the letter. He noticed it remotely; and the hushed room. A piece of the falling glass had sliced his hand. Almost instantly, he realized how well-loved that cranky, awful man had been. And he had to admit, despite this scrunched-up crap he held, he was one of those who continued to love him. "It's nothing," he said too loudly. "I broke the door. I shut it too hard. I'll pay for it. Kirsten, would you mind calling maintenance." The quiet room ripped at his guts as the other members of Homicide contemplated him through the empty window. "I want all of you to know I'm innocent." That was an embarrassing, stupid thing to say, and he retreated to the mess on his desk: three weeks of reports, interviews to be proofed, court dates that needed booking, requests for information, staff memos . . . He studied it with horror. Is this what he'd done with his life? He'd left Wren on Artemis for this?

Kirsten popped her head in the door. "Maintenance will be here in fifteen minutes."

"Good. Thanks," Janwar said, standing lost behind his desk. "Where's the report on Orion Laud?"

"You're holding it — in the hand that isn't bleeding."

The blue file cover, when did he pick that up? The small cut reminded him of the gouge on Brian's hand. Then he remembered the cardboard taped over the window near the door of the treehouse, wondering at the time if someone had broken into Charlie's home. That's how they almost always did it — breaking a window beside a door. Had he been there only a few days ago? It was a lifetime. He shrugged his shoulders, abashed. "I'm sorry. I'm a bit distracted."

"I can tell."

"Good work. Thank you." He skimmed through the short report, aware that she remained standing at the door. His heart went out to her. He couldn't stand this silly battle of wills, and he knew she couldn't either. "That's fine. No. This isn't right. The man's not twenty-four-years-old. At least thirty-five I'd say." He looked up. "Find out all you can about him. Check everything. Place of birth. Family. University attendance. Subjects studied. Income. Credit cards. Vaccinations. I don't care what. Books he's written. Pen names. Fingerprints, if there are any. Everything I asked in my email, and more. I want to know if he had any contact with Rita Norman. There's an odd quality about him."

"Done." She didn't move from the door. "Anything else?"

He stared at her, helpless. "No."

"Are you going to complain about me to Internal Affairs."

"Did everyone really get letters like this?" He held out the bloody, crinkled remains.

"I don't know what you received but each person in the department got one, including the secretaries. Most were nice goodbyes. Short and sweet. There were a couple of raunchy ones. Mine, of course. I've already sent it along to Internal. I assume yours was pretty choice."

"No-one will ever read it. A private goodbye."

"Are you going to Internal about my quoting you without permission?"

"No. There's hardly any point, now, is there?"

"You still admire him, don't you?"

"Yes. And you as well, perhaps more. But you know that. Will they go after his pension?"

"There hasn't been any talk about that so far. It's too early. I doubt it. They'll want to keep this quiet. A couple of the letters might be abusive but they're not illegal. He's smarter than that — he's gone to the beach. It would be too ugly to chase him — and pointless. But how about me?" she asked.

"You?'

"Sure, you might be hated around here today, but you're the big wheel now, and everyone knows it. You're the one. You're going to be Chief Inspector within the month."

"Judging from the way things are going, that's not so far-fetched, especially if the brass ignores the feelings of my co-workers the way they usually do with these appointments."

"So, where do I stand?"

"Kirsten, I don't have time for this."

"Neither do I. I work better when I know where my feet are."

"Your feet are underneath you. I just let slip my feelings a moment ago, and I'm afraid that's all you're going to get. Don't rub it in. I never held anything against you. I've got work to do, and you also. As far as I'm aware we are a team, and I have great affection for you, despite how gruesome it has turned out. Does that make my feelings clear enough? Until informed otherwise we'll work together. I'll do my best to rectify the situation at a later time if it's awkward for you, but I said I won't be going to Internal. I've got miles of paper to wade through and a bleeding hand. And I need a cup of coffee. We've got a man who's different on paper than he is in person. We have missing women, and deaths unaccounted for. Let's get to our job."

Kirsten's cold, black eyes grew warm and eager with anticipation. "I'll know everything about this man by the end of the shift, and I'll bring your coffee right away — with lots of sugar."

"Thanks, you're very kind, but I've cut out the sugar."

She shut the door cheerfully, the broken glass crunching under her feet.

Janwar parked himself at his desk. His stomach felt good. Now that he thought about, he wasn't interested in any coffee. He wondered if there was any chamomile tea in the office, and if he dared ask. That truly would finish off his reputation.

Why was it always so awkward with Kirsten? The way she had turned his out-loud musings on the need for a coffee into an 'assistant, go fetch me a coffee' scenario was classic Kirsten. Perhaps strong people push the envelope unconsciously. She sure was a force of nature. And she wasn't going to remain a corporal for long.

He watched her through the broken door, loading the coffee machine. The easy grace with which she moved. Watching her made him feel glad to be alive in this world, and it made him want to be with Wren.

Before him lay a hell of a pile of papers to slog through, and he'd better get busy — once he stopped the bleeding.

✳✳✳

He made notes. He wrote memos, and letters for the secretary to type. He was polite, and he politely ignored the maintenance woman as she replaced the door window, after he explained that he'd slammed it too hard. She received that information with a curious look. He signed her chit good-naturedly, but the morose woman wasn't falling for his performance. Were the maintenance crowd friends of Blake's, too?

It was near quitting time before Kirsten rushed back into his office. "Hey Janwar, I've got some amusing information."

"Amusing?"

"That guy you wanted me to track? He's invisible. I can't find any books, any pen names, but I did discover that all his credit cards sprang into existence within the last six months. He's paying on them, he's paying on everything except the car rental which is overdue now, though they didn't sound worried about it, since they've got his gold card number. I checked out the withdrawals and payments. They follow a pattern. He's got three cards. Although the figures don't quite add up. It appears he's withdrawing cash from one card to pay the installments on the next. There's a few extra withdrawals, probably for spending cash. The address given to the car rental company doesn't exist. This fellow is very good. His bills for the charge cards are going to a post office box. There's absolutely nothing else, no university records, no job history — he's a ghost. I don't know what he's working on, but he ain't legal. Give me another day and I'll nail him to the floor. However, if he's as professional as this looks, it means he'll be dumping car and cards any day now — usually they don't hang onto them this long."

"I'm impressed, Kirsten. Good work. There's not enough time to make the ferry today, and this isn't worth a helicopter or plane. We've only got a fraud artist, so far, and we don't need any budget scandals, considering recent events. I'm going back to the island tomorrow to find out more about Mr. Laud."

"Do you want me to accompany you?" Then she froze. Her enthusiasm draining from her face. She'd caught his expression. It was as if she could read his mind.

"No, that won't be necessary." This trip meant he might have to spend the night there again. If it didn't, he'd make sure it did.

"You're going without backup? We've stumbled upon a serious fraud artist — maybe worse."

"You can accomplish more here. I want to know everything about him. Keep looking."

"Anything you request, Janwar. Say hello to Wren for me." Then she was gone. She knew everything. Had she set him up, too? — knowing he'd fall for her friend. This made him recall another of her sly remarks: "And remember, the Wren sings like a canary." Had they been talking all along? No, he was becoming paranoid. And he'd only been at the office a few hours.

* * *

The night was sleepless. He watched the stars through his apartment window, and was full of desire. He had to get up and go, though it was pointless to leave so early. Finally, at two in the morning, he gave up on sleep. He slipped into his car. The gates to the locked apartment parking area climbed slowly as he held his finger on the remote.

Venus, the dawn star, glowed above the horizon. He wasn't going to Artemis — he was going home, a joy he hadn't felt for years. Everything else, his career, his mother and her expectations, had become insignificant.

* * *

As he stuffed the receipt for the ferry into his laptop case, Janwar remembered the file on the disk found at Rita Norman's. He hadn't finished reading the last 'fire.' It was such indecipherable, 'artistic' writing there wasn't much point, but he had nothing else to do, sitting in his car while the ferry crossed the strait to Artemis. He pulled out the laptop and turned it on. The tract hadn't gotten any better since his last read. He skimmed through to the last few hundred words of **"The Final Fire:"**

then out of this maelstrom comes the singular duty to make the real fire the one fire the final fire back to

simplicity the beginning of the nothing in the vacuum
before black holes and before quarks and prions
before the real womb the mother of the mothers and
the holy moral urge to kill everything even oxygen itself
and thus the fire to end it all because every kind of
destruction is necessary and good a return out of that
complexity to a finer simplicity without birds and songs
and life of any kind so that all the diseases and plagues
may be seen for what they are the premature returns of
god in the form of death the friend not the enemy but
the friend of the earth father of aids and hepatitis and
liver disease and buboes and cancer and any shoddy
weapons in a storm it can find even wars and
malnutrition and crop damage all little efforts against
the overwhelming tide of evil the complexity that is
slowly running existence into ugliness so that all good
must be practised every waking moment and that
means squashing ants and torturing flies and poisoning
water and strangling little babies and eviscerating
whores and rewiring electrical transmitters into lethal
weapons for this the great war against the monster of
ecology we must fight until nothing remains but the
perfect rock as close to god as we can ever return
unless annihilation is truly perfected and it can chain
react backwards through the stars sinking every particle
into the dream which is all that perfection ever was
because they must be hung from doorknobs and have
their feathers plucked and buried on the side of the
road nor will we weep for fat whale-boys who fall
suddenly from the heart and the newest tree poisoned
in the alleyways of educational institutions while gut
shot deer pant their last on mossy meadows or old

women have their fingers burned off before they die
screaming and raped by the new politics that must
inevitably win oh you lucky crusaders of murder
sweetheart stalkers in the night who know the task that
real evolution demands the random effects of the
search for the night when the song of the planets strikes
up like a giant musical band emanating from a black
hole's heart or all of us reverberating on the end of a
tuning fork as we invent the night over and over again
perfect perfect perfect night blowing all into beautiful
smithereens and becoming once more the vacuum
in the beginning . . .

SO ENDS THE FINAL FIRE AND STARTS THE FIRST FIRE

Janwar sat with the laptop propped between himself
and the steering wheel, his jaw gaping. "Oh mother of
mine! Oh father of mine! I have been really stupid this
time. I have neglected my duties, a few minutes of
reading! Oh mother. Oh father!"

The ferry made its sharp turn around the deep water
of Point Nopoint, and the terminal at Artemis came into
view like a picturesquee collection of toys in a primitivist
painting. The trees above Mecca shone a dark, green jade.

Snapping the laptop shut, Janwar felt more eager than
he had ever felt before, yet stunned at the same time by
the implications of what he'd read. He had a trail now.

The ferry nudged the pilings and slipped into position.
The ramp lowered, and the red-vested landing man
unclicked the chain that opened up the island to the
passengers. Janwar smiled, temporarily distracted by
thoughts of The Last Resort. He dropped his hand onto

the ignition kcy. There was nothing. He tried it again. A faint click.

He tried again. Nothing. Cars began moving off the ferry. The one in front of him. Janwar tried once more — that same dead nothing. The man in the safety vest approached.

"Is there a problem, sir?"

"I'm afraid there is."

The man surveyed his car with the trained eye of a professional, an islander who'd seen this before. "Don't worry, we'll get you off the ferry, one way or the other."

***

Desperate, Janwar reached for his cellphone while the ferryman guided the other cars around him. Kirsten answered on the first ring. Her voice was clear and there was no interference.

"Kirsten?"

"That's me. Janwar? Good morning. Where are you?"

"On Artemis. I've developed car trouble."

"Do you need help?"

"No, I'm fine.'

"That's good because it's worse."

"Worse? What do you mean?"

"Orion Laud died when he was four-months-old. You're chasing a ghost with a gold card."

"Kirsten, there are other developments. That file on the disk, the one titled Cry Murder."

"Oh, I tried reading that a couple of times, but it was such pseudo-poetic gibberish it made my eyes cross."

"I finally read the end, myself, only now. There is another killer, not the accountant. Nor was the document written by Rita Norman. It's someone else, most certainly a man. An artistic type. He mentions the doorknob hanging of the Sweet Water woman, Rose. Also, there was an older woman, a few years ago, her hands burned — it was listed as a sexual assault and thrill murder — a particularly loathsome one. Chavez. She was a writer. There's a copy of the file in the top drawer of my grey cabinet. See if you can find it. Chief Inspector Blake always thought she was tortured for information. I think she belonged to a shadowy ecological organization with a violent reputation. Check out eco-activist connections with Rita, and the other student, Rose . . . I can't remember her last name right now. It's gone out of my head. Go deeper. I have this feeling about the Sweet Water connection. Also, that anti-whaling crusader, the fat young man who died of a surprise heart attack two years ago. Weren't there accusations of foul play . . . ?"

"Wait a second. Wait a second. You're going too fast for me. What's this all about?"

"I believe we're pursuing a madman who stalks ecologists."

"You have got to be kidding!"

"No, I'm not. Read the passage shortly before the end of the document."

"But I don't understand. Why would Rita Norman hang around with a person like that?"

"She didn't know. She never read the document. I'm betting it was put in the disk box by the same person who removed the address book."

"A clue? A game? Oh hell!"

"This could be a man who thinks he's too smart for us, who's playing. Check to see if there is any record of papers or similar disks in the personal effects of the others."

"Oh wow! Oh wow! Do you think it's your fraud artist?"

"That's an extreme leap."

"Do you want me to send a chopper? Did you take your gun."

"Yes, of course I took my gun. Don't be ridiculous about the helicopter. The department is in enough trouble over its outrageous expenditure on the drug lord case last winter. And with this Blake affair going on? I'm not going to stick my neck out and authorize a helicopter to apprehend a charge card defrauder. We'd never live it down. We have no connecting link, except Charlie Baker, and that's too distant. Besides, there's only one ferry off the island today. He can't go anywhere without my knowing about it. I'm fine."

"This call is being recorded, sir. I want it known that I don't agree with your decision. I don't understand this. After all, commercial fraud isn't even our department. Plus his address is Vancouver, and you know what the city police are like about territory."

Enraged, Janwar glared at the phone. "Kirsten, this is a straightforward matter. Please spare the melodrama for those it will impress. This is not a Hollywood film, and I don't need helicopters or nuclear missiles to back me up on a credit card fraud. I am going to get my car running, and I will inform you of the results of my interview with Laud. I'll bring him to the Sweet Water detachment. They can book him there. Meanwhile, you check on as many leads as you can after reading your copy of that file. Now we know we have another serial killer out there. That's our big leap for today. Thank you." He hung up.

He'd hung himself up. Kirsten was right — she always was, and he'd been so awful to her. Once, he'd had a high impression of himself. Not any more.

As for Brian or Orion or whatever he was called, this was no fraud artist. Janwar was chasing something mean and scary, and he didn't know how Brian would react to his return. That thick, high-cheekboned face kept invading his thoughts; Brian's grey eyes watching him. There was a creepiness about the way he sat beside Charlie Baker, the way held his body — trying to control the space around him.

Now Janwar had refused help. He was in trouble. He also wanted to see Wren again, though it was barely a full day since he'd been away. And what was going on in that treehouse?

✳✳✳

The cars and the foot passengers from the ferry were long gone, while the line-up for Sweet Water remained perched on the impossible hill above the terminal, the drivers impatient.

A rusty brown truck with a kayak rack on the roof, spirit catcher hanging from the inside mirror, and a 4-point deer skull mounted as a hood ornament, came rolling down the chute. It turned around in front of the store and backed onto the ferry. This was a tow truck?

A scrawny man emerged from the truck. "Peacock Jim, they call me, and I'm the healer for sick cars on this island, among other things. I also run the road crew. Transportation is my destiny. What's your need, mister?"

"The starter is dead."

"A lot of us have that problem. Don't worry. Have you ever read the sutras? First, I'll get you off the ferry; then we'll figure out the rest. Don't worry, it's karma. It happens to everyone sometime — somewhere . . . " Peacock Jim hooked the car up and hauled it over to a clear space between the store and Mecca. Then he climbed out, opened the hood with an air of authority, and began to rummage about inside.

"Try the key," Jim shouted as he slid into his so-called tow truck and revved its mis-timed motor. He'd hooked up jumper cables to the battery. There was nothing.

Janwar leaned out of his window. "Sorry. There's nothing. The ferry crew already tried to jump it. I think the starter is dead."

Peacock unrolled his long legs from his truck and jiggled the cables. Nothing again. He rummaged around for a while behind his driver's seat and pulled out an electrical tester that looked like it was invented shortly after the wheel. Janwar started to laugh nervously. This was all too much. "I believe I could do better with a rock and a tinder stick." Peacock Jim didn't pay any attention. After a few more minutes he slammed down the hood and walked up to the driver's window.

"It's your starter."

"I would have never known." Janwar couldn't believe his mouth. What was taking over him?

"You're in deep doggie-do."

"I guessed that also. But I have to get to Charlie's place."

"You know anything about cars?"

"I had a job working on them in my university days, mostly tune-ups and brakes, but times have changed, and I'm not up to date."

"Neither am I, but that doesn't make any difference. Not here on this island. Most of the vehicles are near ancient, except for the rich retirees from the prairies who drive new SUVs. I don't fix their cars on general principle. At least this car's no spring chicken. It probably has a few dead relatives on the island. We might be able to do a remove-and-replace."

"You think so?"

"Old Jake's got a similar model in his back forty. Belonged to his kid. Why's a cop driving a beater like this?"

Janwar leaned back in his seat with a sigh. It was his sister's car, left behind when she disappeared. More baggage from the past. "I've come to wonder that myself in the last few years. It's a beautiful old machine. I like to work on it."

"Sounds like my truck."

Janwar examined the rusted-out tow truck. It needed a lot more work than his car. "If Jake's starter won't fit, what then?"

"Enjoy your stay on the island. The nearest garage is in Sweet Water, and this week they've got a brain-damaged mechanic, paid for by the government on one of them work-sharing programs. Their real mechanic has gone wilderness canoeing in the Yukon. He makes enough money gouging tourists and government programs he can afford that kind of holiday. I hear Wren has extra room at her resort. I'm sure she could fit you in if you need a place to stay."

"That might be an alternative, but right now I have urgent business."

"There ain't much business that's urgent on this island. What kind of business?"

"It's not your concern. Are you busy today?"

"Naw, my crew is occupied ripping up the Low Road. They're going to be at it for another week at least. You want to hire me to set your starter problem right?"

"That might be a good idea, considering my circumstances."

"I was waiting for you to ask. I don't have much interest in my road work. Climb into the truck and we'll see what Jake's got in that field of wrecks behind his house. Hang on a second. I'll get us a coffee." Before Janwar could speak, Jim was gone into the crowd at Mecca.

While he waited he deciphered the obscure, faded, psychedelic lettering on the purple door panel of Peacock Jim's tow truck — KARMA WRECKERS.

Knowing that news of his return would be everywhere within the hour, Janwar wryly regarded the assembly of long-haired farmers, and tourists amid the stands under the arbutus trees with a serenity he wouldn't have comprehended three weeks ago.

***

Returning from his morning walk, a habit he was beginning to enjoy, Brian saw that Festus was on the deck with Charlie, talking. "What's happening, guys?"

Charlie and Festus looked down from the deck bench, like two birds on a branch. "Our friend is back," Festus said.

"What friend?"

"The cop. The Sikh Inspector. He left the island yesterday and rushed back today, arriving on the early ferry."

"The cop? What's he doing?"

"Peacock Jim is taking care of him. His car broke down. Dead starter, according to The Lady of the Rings."

Charlie studied Brian; then turned to Festus. "He's not come back to Wren? They've got moony eyes for each other, don't they?"

"More than that, I hear," Festus said, importantly. "But that isn't what Jim told Mother Mingus at her food stand. He said the cop was here on urgent business. That got everybody moving their mouths real fast. I went down to collect mom's pottery orders — the morning mail off the ferry — thought I'd pick up a few more details because we got it all garbled from old Boomer who's practically incoherent these days. We're gonna have to retire her, or at least steal her moonshine still. She's sampling too much, mom says."

"So what's going on?" Brian asked. It gave him the creeps the way the child talked — so precocious and sure of himself.

"Who knows? The word is that Peacock thinks any cop on urgent business needs spiritual guidance. He's going to islandize him, take him to visit Jake again, perhaps go for a little tour of dead cars, finish up on the south end after the last ferry leaves in the afternoon. That should give anybody who figures they could be urgent business for the police a chance to sort themselves out. That's the word Boomer is spreading."

Festus stared into Brian's eyes. "Peacock, despite his being a Buddhist, he's a nephew of Jake's, and he don't much like police either. The betting pool at Mecca is putting heavy odds on this cop spending his night in the arms of Wren at the resort. Though no-one's saying anything to her. If she catches on to Peacock's spiritual teachings, there'll be hell to pay. Meanwhile, everybody's starting to get real curious about you, Mr. Brian."

"Stay for breakfast?" Charlie asked.

"Naw, mom's got a pile of orders she'll be excited about. I want to take them home. I'll come back in a while to help you with that fence."

***

They ate an omelette Charlie made with fresh tomatoes, cheese, green onions, dried mushrooms from a jar by the stove, and the eggs Festus had brought yesterday. Brian sat at the table while Charlie expertly sliced and diced and mixed the omelette in his brown bread bowl. Little was spoken. Charlie poured it into the two small cast-iron frying pans that had been hanging on the wall, each a perfect portion size, and set them on the propane stove.

They ate with efficiency. The omelette was delicious but the air was filled with thoughts of Rita and the cop's mysterious return. Charlie waited for Brian to react. He didn't.

Brian finished his plate and pushed it away with a jauntiness that was new. "Either I'm becoming used to your cooking or you're getting better. You sure know how to distract an unhappy man, Charlie."

***

Hungry, that's what Charlie was when he returned to the motel from ChemCity. He stuffed his costume into his suitcase and, dressed only in his undershorts, buttered three slices of bread. The day before he'd discovered a bakery near the motel. The old Ukrainian proprietor, a

gnarly man with a grumpy sense of humour, made a
beautiful looking pumpernickel-rye loaf.

The knife shoved its load of butter across the bread.
Hunger. Food. He took a big bite. He kept picturing Tom,
grinning crazily, frozen in that cement tube, clutching
an ugly, white ceramic mug until he rotted away, leaving
nothing but the mug and bones behind.

The dark tangy bread had a sharp aftertaste he was
almost beginning to like, despite the mould that had
grown overnight on the crust, or maybe because of it.
Charlie's teeth sank into the bread; the butter stuck to the
roof of his mouth. He was crying, hunched against the
kitchen table, chewing methodically, the two remaining
slices in front of him on the yellow arborite surface. It
tasted worse when his tears fell onto the butter. He kept
chewing. There were streams coming down his face now,
making the bread soggy.

The cheerful baker, recognizing that Charlie wasn't a
local, had passed off a stale loaf on him.

There was a name, ergot, the mould that destroys rye;
the source of LSD. "Ah today, of all days, I should dance
the tarantella."

Charlie booked out of the motel an hour later, drove
to the next town, returned the rental car, dumped all his
assumed identification in a garbage can, the clothes in
another, and caught a bus to Chicago where he boarded
a plane to Vancouver.

The raid made a splash in newspapers across the country
for the next few weeks. The brothers had accomplished a
lot of damage. The cement, backing up into the flushing
system, had generated havoc in twenty percent of the
complex (It was revealed that another employee had

feared the same scenario as the former engineer-assistant and installed interrupters between the five major operations). There was water damage, busted pipes, entire lines frozen solid with cement. But this time there was no punning note in the wreckage. There was silence.

The media focused on the end of Coyote. The body was never discovered, buried in a massive bulldozed hole with all the ruined machinery and cemented pipes — his gravestone a field of grass, half dead from the pollution emitted by ChemCity.

Despite a report by a disgruntled assistant in chemical analysis that there was more than one man, Coyote's death was gleefully reported. She was discounted as being hysterical, confused by the onslaught of events, like the nightwatchman who'd shot a few round at God knows what. The media was not interested in the truth, especially when they had a dramatic and neat wrap-up to a long history. They described with intricate and mostly invented detail the story of the last battle. How, in his ninja costume, he overwhelmed several men while using exotic weapons and oriental fighting techniques until he was cornered. Then, giving his enemies a cavalier wave, brandishing his small white fighting club, he stepped into the pipe and self-destruction.

So Coyote died. There were a few more raids, easily recognized as copycat crimes, stunts pulled by Sons of Coyote, but the energy was gone. Coyote had become history.

***

Washing up the breakfast dishes, Charlie finally turned to Brian. "So what're you hungry for? What do you want?"

"That's easy. Simplicity. Pure simplicity."

Charlie dried off the pan and hung it beside the others.

"Hmm, simplicity, I loved it once. That was my problem. Now I've finally learned to accept complexity. Think of all this diversity around us, millions of cells combining and recombining with such a vicious beauty — the great rush of desire at the heart of everything, hopeless desire. It's gorgeous."

"Complexity isn't so great, it's just complex!"

And this is where, sometimes, I agree with my monstrous other self — Brian and his twisted little fantasy — 'Cry Murder' — well, perhaps only the main theme. One day, out of the mud and scum of the hot mineral mass, a cell was born — alive, perfect; within it, a confusion, a striving to continue itself. That cell wanted to survive. It had, oh most wonderful of all, a desire to make more cells. It used any method it could to perpetuate itself, multiplication, separation, mutation — attacking anything in its environment that interfered. Thus began the awesome process of devolution — the complication of that first perfect organism, the specialization into creatures more varied yet weaker than the original, a dissipation, until it becomes us, an end product, a self-destructive dinosaur, the excrement of evolution, and we, in our wisdom, translate devolution as evolution, and call our decline, progress — proclaim our weaknesses are our strengths — performing the most twisted revision of history conceivable.

"It occurs to me," Brian said, "that if you were a real ecologist, you'd shoot yourself."

"And save you the trouble?" Charlie smirked. "I wonder about that. I ask myself every day — should I stay alive? Maybe I never had the courage I thought I had, but my body wants to live, the way a lion or a wolf does. And I guess that's real ecology. I kill and I eat. But now I limit the extent of my damage. That's why I'm jealous of the rock — it's what it is. It doesn't have the disease I have. It isn't self-conscious. It's a rock, a beautiful, living, inanimate, wonderful rock."

"I could never write a story with a rock in it."

"No, probably not. You'd give it a name and a cute voice and meaningful pronouncements which would affect the way we live."

"That's not the rock you're talking about. That's not rocklike, right?"

"You're learning, Brian."

"I'm not interested in learning any more." Through the window, Brian watched an intruder enter the lower field. "Here comes Festus again." The boy dallied under a plum tree, studying the limbs. He picked a plum and stuffed it whole into his mouth. He wrestled with it for a moment, his face contorting, before he magnificently spat the pit high into the air. "I don't know how you can tolerate knowing that his stepfather beats him up."

"His stepfather is a good man."

"Really? You're in favour of beating kids? My father used to beat me."

"I don't know where you got that stupid idea about his stepfather. Nobody knows who his real father is. Elvira ain't talking. She's been through a lot, lost her husband and first child in a car accident before she came over to the island a dozen years ago. His stepdad is a wonderful man, though he does have to work off-island too much. The kid is working out all right; you can see the pain in his eyes, but he's learning to deal with his genetic crisis. The problem with you, Brian, is too many assumptions."

Assumptions, ahhh, deadly assumptions. Now we're getting somewhere. Another product of our logical facilities, and our cultural conditioning. Like Brian, we base our actions and lives on assumptions and more often than we'd want to admit, we die for them.

Right, we've returned to logic; the process by which we tell ourselves we think, and the methods we use, mathematical or non-Euclidean and intuitive, to get ourselves into trouble. Induction. Deduction. Reduction. Empiricism. Analytics. Metaphysics. Semiotics. Deconstructionism. Bleccchh! A million years of practice, and where has our thinking got us? We pollute ourselves, crap our bed, We murder everything in sight, upset the entire nest, and then congratulate ourselves for our natural supremacy (especially if we believe in 'Manifest Destiny'). We call this progress? Until a few hundred years ago we didn't put the planet at risk with nuclear weaponry, ecological terrorism, or 'good business practise'. Now, at the rate we're progressing, or devolving, we should arrive at zero within the next hundred years. Is that where we belong? Is my 'Bad Brian' right?

I'm off the track, again, sure, Festus, repeating myself, too, only from a different angle. But this is a big part of what your story is about. And if you don't like it, or my asides, you can go fuck yourself.

That's right. Read another story. You set me off. You started me down the river. This story is as much for myself as for you. If you're not interested, you'll find more than sufficient material to bolster your culturally conditioned world-view at any book or video store. Yes, I am angry. Helplessness always makes me angry.

Charlie stood up. "I've got some serious fence mending ahead of me, five rotten posts. I think I'll take advantage of that kid while he's floating about. He can fix anything."

By the time Brian followed him to the garden, the pair were checking out the fence posts like professionals.

"Well, mayor," Festus said, "I think you're right. They're kaput."

Charlie nodded. "It should be worth five bucks a post to you."

They started walking up the hill again to get the tools. "I'd do it for you for nothing, but since you're offering . . . "

"How come you call him mayor?" Brian asked.

"Because he is the mayor," Festus said.

Charlie winked mischievously at Brian.

"The mayor?"

"Sure, everybody on the island calls him the mayor. We don't have elections here. That's for city folks. But everyone knows he's the mayor. They can take their problems to him."

"I haven't seen any islanders here except you."

"That's because islanders are an independent people." There it was again. That wry awareness too mature for a child — his syndrome speeding him towards old age. "Anybody that's got serious problems usually works them out for themselves, yet we all know we can come to Charlie, though nobody ever does. That's why he's the mayor."

Charlie handed the boy a shovel. "Enough island politics, Festus. You don't want to confuse the man." The cheerful pair followed the fence line to the posts. Brian didn't offer to help. Instead, he wandered up the hill and sat down in the grass near the rock, and watched them dig around the old cedar posts and insert new ones from a pile by the gate.

At one point, Charlie cranged his hand between the shovel handle and a post; then hopped absurdly around it — like a fake Indian war-dancing in a bad western, his complaint floating through the meadow: "Gawd, it throbs worse than a sick bird's arsehole!"

The old man hadn't been in the same mood earlier. On his way out for his morning walk, Brian had seen Charlie beyond the clump of water hemlocks, beside the pond. The morning air was so rank with the smell of mice even Brian could detect it. Brian circled around, out of sight. He didn't have to ask Charlie why he was crying, throwing little pebbles from the bank into the dark, murky water where a water scorpion clung tenaciously to a cattail. Rita. That was good — he was feeling the pain, and Brian wasn't finished with him yet.

Charlie was turning into easy prey — he'd been so obvious studying him as Festus delivered the news about the cop — expecting Brian to show discomfort. Aside from not wanting to give the old man any satisfaction, there wasn't any problem. He was clear — nothing to trace. Maybe it was Charlie the cop suspected. Nevertheless, it was time to move. He'd catch the afternoon ferry.

When he looked up again, they were almost done with the posts. That was quick. Or was it? The sun had moved a distance . . . He was sweating, and there were curious pangs in his stomach, as if he were hungry already, despite having no appetite.

Paranoia surged through him. "Did he get me first?" Charlie bumbled happily along behind Festus, dragging the mattock until they reached the gate. Charlie leaned the mattock against the fence, and the two began to talk, their faces close. The boy looked up the hill in his direction. Then they talked a while longer. Festus left, giving Brian a funny wave while Charlie re-entered the vegetable garden.

He couldn't have been poisoned. The only thing he'd eaten, the omelette, Charlie had also eaten, and Brian had sat right beside him, watching him mix and cook it. The two frying pans? The dried mushrooms! Were they magic mushrooms? Psilocybin? Charlie had said he didn't do drugs any more. On the other hand, he consumed cheese, eggs, milk, the wine at the beach — perhaps he was backsliding? Brian passed an awkward several minutes trying to decide whether he was stoned.

That was one of the things people had told him about their first trips — they could never decide whether they were high or not — at least not until they were over the deep end. 'Am I high? Is this natural? Am I having a religious experience? Am I vindicated?' Why had he always avoided hallucigens? Were they a test, a proving ground where the demons of self could be released, exposed? That was too dangerous. Now he regretted it. Or did he? What was he thinking about?

The sky was such a religious blue. The meadow vibrated with life. The treehouse was like a living animal. Charlie was perched on a stump in the vegetables, meditating, the way Brian had seen him atop the treehouse on the first day, and then again, just recently with the hummingbirds. Only this time the old man was surrounded by floating butterflies, hundreds of them.

'They're drinking his sweat,' Brian thought. He was suffused with joy. 'Yes, this is good. The world is beautiful again.' The crickets rolled their castanets over the meadow. A distant bird called from among the big-bottomed cedars by the swamp. He looked back and the butterflies were gone, the old man rigid and silent and alone on his stump. 'I'm hallucinating!'

He found himself facing the rock. It was floating above the ground. There was a gap almost a foot wide between its base and the dirt below. Brian's chest seized up. He tried to forget his heart pounding. The paranoia again. The rock was motionless, frozen in space . . . "Are you God's will?" he asked.

The rock was silent.

"This is real, isn't it?"

The rock remained silent.

"Are you God's will? You can answer me. You are, aren't you? I've known it all along." He sat mutely, beside it. His heart was going faster and faster. He had to talk. "I'm also God's will. I knew it as soon as I looked over the edge of the cliff and saw Rita in the river. Actually, that's not completely true. I knew where I was going as soon as she told me she thought this old boyfriend of hers was Coyote. That's not true either. You know that. I hunted her to find Charlie. I had to burn an old lady's hands to find her. But I wasn't looking for her then, only him. You know that too. It was a long game, wasn't it. Because I fell in love with her." He had trouble finding the words. "You could never understand the sorrow, the absolute sorrow of seeing her dead. It was different with her . . . He sat down with a resigned thump beside it.

The air radiated energy around the rock, an aurora. Was it going to speak? Would it answer him? "Okay, I knew I was God's will long ago, and it was inevitable that I put her out of her pain, like the others. Oh, isn't there too much pain? And then, this is the best part, now I'm going to avenge her by killing the man who had made her into what I had to kill. I knew I needed to be very careful and tricky, because this Coyote had to be a smart man. And he is. I like him. I hope you will have mercy on his soul."

Then the rock spoke.

It began as a low hum that came from the back of Brian's head, a deep, consistent pressure, growing louder. No, it wasn't inside his head. It was inside the rock. It increased in volume, spreading across the meadow, into the trees, around the world — a huge, deep energy that emanated from every molecule. A nucleus of power so strong it pressed against him and through him where he sat, until he understood the rock was everything he always thought it should be. A pure, beautiful simplicity. He wanted to worship it, worship anything. He just wanted to worship.

He compressed his palms against his temples, fearing and yet loving its force, squeezing his eyes shut as it pierced him. The power of life singing like one long, drawn-out word. The word was Yes! And it soaked into his bones like a mantra. Yes to everything!

When he opened his eyes, the rock was on the ground again, the sound ebbing; a hushed tide flowing through him, making him rise, almost involuntarily, to his feet, his knees stiff. He had been sitting for a long time. His eyes were streaming with tears. He had never felt so happy. 'I'm not stoned. Maybe I am? Who cares? This is it; I'm alive!' And he wished he could die now, that the world would be perfect, if only for a moment. The guilt had gone away. He turned towards the treehouse and the vegetable patch, clenching and unclenching his hands, while Charlie sat with his back to him, seated among the stupid butterflies. They were back! They were real, after all.

"I've eaten mushrooms." It wasn't so bad, or was it something else? Acid? Did the old relic still have LSD around? The paranoia rushed through him again. Then he relaxed, almost enjoying the after-effects of the emotional flood.

An urgent need to urinate overwhelmed Brian, and he unzipped himself, leaning back into the sun, shooting an impressive arc into the air as he staggered around in a semi-circle, spraying the oregano, into the wind, his own pantlegs and shoes, a bit on the rock, until he fell hard onto his back, the geyser subsiding into a tiny pumping fountain. 'Wow, had that ever felt good, except now my jeans was stained.' He decided every man should piss on God and the fate that takes us all, at least once. Every man should eat mushrooms.

To Brian's left, at the meadow's edge a pair of peafowl played a game of tag, hiding behind bushes, jumping out at each other like bogey men, and then fleeing . . .

23 The Dance of the White Peacock

BY NOON JANWAR AND PEACOCK JIM had already toured not only Jake's back pasture, but several other junk-heaped fields around the island. At least they had escaped Jake's without any deep diving into the whiskey bottle, although Jim insisted he needed a couple of quick shots to 'prime up' for the next phase of the search, almost daring Janwar to tell him he could no longer drive since he'd drunk more than the legal limit.

As far as Janwar could surmise, the likelihood of finding a dead Chevrolet with a live starter that would match his was equivalent to Peacock Jim's crew fixing all the potholes on the road, each one of which he was learning too well since the springs and shocks on the tow-truck had long ago given up the ghost.

Every few minutes Janwar was wearing his turban down to his nose after jamming his head into the ceiling of the truck when it hit a deep hole. Worse, Jim happily struck them at high speed with an unerring accuracy, declaring this was merely the world of illusion, *samsara*, so what was the difference?

Meanwhile, Janwar imagined Kirsten had quietly gossiped to a superior or two that he'd rushed off alone in his old beater to Artemis, instead of a departmental car

— for a take-down on a fraud artist and possible serial killer.

Jim decided to stop for lunch at Mecca, and it was there he admitted, reluctantly, after several minutes of interrogation by Janwar, that maybe they weren't going to find a starter on the island, after all. Their best bet was to take Janwar's apart. If it was the brushes, there was a chance they could match them up, or at the very least, Jim remembered a trick of his father's when the same thing happened on a trip north to Vanderhoof. They were "miles away from nowhere," but the old man took the starter apart and wedged foil from a cigarette package between the spring and the brush, and that had given the motor a half-dozen more starts — enough to get them to a garage where they could order a rebuilt starter.

The question settled over lunch — a vegetarian repast from the Instant Karma Thai Noodle And Western Organic Greens Nourishment Stand run by a tiny old lady with a moustache, Mother Mingus — they soon had the starter out and the pieces lying on a tarp beside the truck in a spot Peacock Jim had found behind the store. It was the least visible spot on the entire knoll, one where they didn't have much of a view of ferry traffic, yet were close enough for every passer-by to stop and offer advice on their way to or from Mecca's assorted craft stands and food stalls. Since Jim didn't have the capability of talking and working at the same time, Janwar finally began fiddling with the pieces himself, cleaning them up and reassembling the starter while Jim supervised and explained what they were doing to anyone who cared to stop and listen, male or female or dog.

The news that Jim was giving the royal tour to a police officer gained him instant forgiveness for his creature-from-the-lost-lagoon stunt on women's night. Now his sense of mischief was being put to useful purpose, and he'd become an island hero by lunchtime — though Wren might think otherwise if she heard of his latest caper.

* * *

At the treehouse, there wasn't much for Brian to pick up, his alpine pack, a pair of dirty socks lying beside the bed, and two more vials at the bottom of the canvas bag, both larger than the one he'd buried in the swamp. He changed, grateful he'd washed his clothes beside the pond a few days ago, though not well. His spare jeans felt greasy, but at least their crotch wasn't soaked. That was mortifying. Fortunately, Charlie hadn't seen anything — he didn't want to give the old goat the pleasure of knowing how spaced he'd become at the rock. He stuffed everything except the vials in his packsack — there were more angles to play yet. Catching his reflection in the small mirror above the sink, he saw he was grinning uncontrollably.

* * *

Corking the half-used second vial, he took a last look around the treehouse. It was so comfortable, so human; the affectionate double-bust of Charlie and the woman, Elvira, the mother of Festus, was touching. He wished he'd met her — it could have been interesting. Life is full of lost chances — the grey woman performing Tai Chi on the beach. He was feeling wickedly normal again. There was the bowl, the raku dish with the lonely orange. He picked it up.

The mouse — the one that had kept dashing back and forth on the windowsill, distracting the parrot and Brian over the last month — stood on its hindquarters, waving its puny claws, as if saying goodbye, before it vanished.

Adjusting the packsack on his back before he shut the door, he gave the room a last lookover. He felt sad and powerful at the same time — a tightness in his stomach. The place was alive. He wished he could have explained things better to Charlie, but he had done well enough. Besides, words were nothing compared to action. That bloody grin wouldn't leave his face.

Charlie hadn't moved from his stump overlooking the garden. The parrot was on his shoulder. The world was clean and beautiful. The cauliflowers were humming. Brian entered the shelter under the treehouse. Ignoring the firewood and the well-equipped wall full of tools fastidiously placed on hangers, he considered the droning refrigerator.

When he returned to the ramp, after shutting the cellar door, he thought he saw the old man's hat flicker. No, he hadn't moved. He was meditating, the parrot dozing on his shoulder.

He came up behind Charlie on the stump. "I'm leaving now," he said, tossing the orange into the air and catching it.

"Good idea. It's time for you to go." Charlie refused to avert his gaze from the garden. Was he trying to tell Brian, without words, that he would miss him? "We all gotta go out there sooner or later. Besides, despite your complaints, the way you eat I'd have had to send you to the store for more groceries. Young people eat like horses. The older you get, the less you consume."

"You can have the last orange." He flipped it to Charlie who turned and snatched it effortlessly out of the air without looking at Brian.

"Thanks. I'll enjoy it."

"Someone should. I'd hate to see it go bad."

"Waste is a crime."

Brian had to tell him. "I've talked to the rock."

"And did it talk back?"

"Yes, it did."

"What did it say?"

"You'll have to ask it."

Charlie snorted. "I might get to miss you, mister."

Brian turned away. "I can't say I'll see you later, because I won't." That sounded too melodramatic. He wished they hadn't gotten into such a magic moment with the orange. "Will you forgive me?"

Charlie was thoughtful. "The same way as I forgive myself — Tom — Rita — the bureaucrats eating up the world, and all the fools who believe in something."

The old man was unrepentant. Brian liked that. There wasn't much else to say. "God bless you, Charlie."

"I don't want his blessings. I got my own."

"Well, goodbye then."

"Goodbye." Charlie remained motionless. He looked intimidating on his bench, surveying the vegetables and the hillside, the strait on the horizon.

The beautiful sadness . . . the beautiful . . . the sadness . . .

Brian slid back the cracked, aged dowel in the wooden latch, closing the gate behind himself. He considered the latch. "Doors . . . doors . . . always opening and closing . . . " He picked off a big thorn from the rose blooming beside the gate.

On the path, Brian lost sight of Charlie briefly; then saw him through the wild roses again. A cluster of monarch butterflies had returned, floating about the figure in the straw hat while the parrot snapped at them. Damn! He would never know if those bloody things were real. They must be. He didn't feel so stoned any more, until he walked into a blackberry bush. Cursing, he untangled himself, disconcerted, but the old man couldn't see him because of the brush lining the path. Brian began walking faster. He felt powerful, clear-thinking, immaculate. The road lay ahead, the parked Miata, the peacock standing on its hood, fanning a tail full of indigo eyes.

***

A warm afternoon calm settled on the meadow after Brian's footsteps faded away. 'There he goes. Do I deserve this, all this pain in a lifetime? No one does. Was I so monstrous that I needed this punishment?' Then he listened to the garden. It was growing. If he worked hard enough at it could he hear the root maggots chewing on the broccoli? The broad leaves were wilting, which meant the tiny monsters were spreading, that his liming and hilling more dirt around the stems had been useless. Unconsciously, he clutched the orange in his hand.

He lobbed it into the air, catching it, pitching it higher each time, while the uneasy parrot on his shoulder watched. There was a brown spot on the orange, one that had set it off from the others, a circle near the end that reminded him of the widening gap in the ozone layer above the north pole, and he was annoyed by the notion — that he now thought in terms of ecological cliches. 'Everything is breaking down. This is not the world of my dreams, or my childhood, the one I was born into — or is it?' The orange smelled faintly of urine, and more . . . "That boy's been reading too many mystery stories." He took his pocket knife out, opened it, considering for a moment the blade chipped by Brian's adventure with the oysters. He pressed the blade against the rind, and sliced the orange in half. The parrot, expecting food, danced on his shoulder. There was the faint smell of almonds, and a murky area inside the sweet flesh. He sniffed at it. The parrot backed away on his shoulder. Charlie turned over the two halves in his hand until he found what could be the tiny puncture mark made by the needle. "We don't want to eat that," he said to the bird, standing up. He found a shovel, dug a deep hole beyond the perimeter of the outlying vegetables and dropped the orange into it. The parrot hissed, annoyed by the burial of a treat, while Charlie threw a sod on top.

Charlie packed the ground tight with his foot, then scuffed the grass around until it looked undisturbed. "You know," he said to the parrot, "there's so many different kinds of people, and I think they're all variations on dumb. Most are truly dumb, the ones playing in the rye field, running towards an invisible cliff through the high grass. They're the best. I'm jealous of them. They don't think about where they're going. They only go. Then there's the ones like this kid. Smart. Street-smart. Clever. But in the end, dumb, real dumb, wanting to make everyone safe or kill them. And then there's us, who think sideways to the rest of the world. We're just differently dumb."

The parrot squawked and flew from his shoulder into the trees. Too much philosophy and not enough food.

Charlie had things to do. At the gate he noticed the thorn wedged into the cracked dowel. He bent down and sniffed it. Nothing. Gingerly, he pulled out the spine and smelled it again. Nothing. He dropped it outside the garden and squashed it into the earth with his boot. "Thanks for the note, Brian." He walked directly to the ground floor shelter. Okay, where? Refrigerator, of course. He opened the fridge. A quart bottle of milk sat forlornly inside. He took the lid off the bottle. Almonds. It smelled like almonds. That city kid couldn't smell his way to a barn if the manure was on fire. There was a trick here, wasn't there? And clues? He took it outside, poured it onto the ground under the ramp, and scuffed the soil and milk together into a dark patch.

Upstairs, in the treehouse, everything was normal. With a sense of urgency, he began pulling jars off the shelves. The tea first. He smelled every jar. Lentils, chick peas, navy beans. Nothing again. Then he stood back for a moment. The mushrooms. Already, the jar was slightly fogged with condensation. He unscrewed the lid. Almonds. He nodded. Brian was having fun, telling him a story. What was the ending? He screwed the lid on tightly and set the jar on the table; the world carries more than its weight of cyanide, yet it is easy to smell — did Brian think the odour would dissipate? Charlie couldn't understand this amateurish business. Did he want to be caught? The cyanide had to be a distraction from the real thing. There had to be one left, the real one. Would he find it and live?

This petty hide-and-seek was such a shame, Charlie thought, because he had already won the war. He surveyed the room again.

The vegetable knife. An old carbon steel blade he'd rescued from the island dump when he was a child, possessed by his recycling delight at an early age, despite his parents' dismay, though they had to admit the knife always cut better than their expensive, stainless steel blades. It had been a precious memory that had survived his family, and the burned down cabin. The blade lived, the handle charred. He'd made a new hilt out of a deer's antler discarded after the winter's rut.

Charlie picked it up. He didn't know why — his luck? Or was it a payoff for the weeks he'd spent studying Brian. He examined the thin line on the blade. It looked like a tiny cloth or sponge had been drawn from tip to hilt along the grey carbon-steel. He stepped out onto the deck, examining it in the direct sunlight. The old rain barrel he kept for emergency plant watering was beside him. It was so seldom used it was full of mosquito larvae, and tadpoles had recently hatched in it, beginning to feed on the larvae. He swished the knife around in the water and then wiped it off with a raggy handkerchief from his back pocket before returning it to the cabin's table.

He climbed the ladder, wondering what other traps, and how many, Brian had set. There was a sense of disgust in him, the knowledge that he would have to take every bit of food in the house and dump it, sterilize every sharp object. Check for anything. The cyanide was a decoy. He hated the waste, and he hated the ugly feeling that he wouldn't sleep well for days, suspecting death traps everywhere. Should he burn it all down? Begin again? Cleanse his life with fire?

***

"Kirsten, this is Janwar."

"Good to hear you're still alive."

"Please don't be flip."

"Sorry. I'm worried for you." The affection in her voice was apparent. "I've found more interesting stuff in the last few hours."

"Yes?"

"Your connection is fading."

"Sorry, I'll walk around towards the bluff. It might be better up there. How's this?" Below, the marvellous water of the strait lapped against the black rocks. An arbutus shaded him. It was too beautiful to talk about murder and fraud.

"You're fine now. The woman with the burned hands, Eileen Chavez, was a long-time activist, rumoured to belong to a radical fringe group known as EarthHouse, possibly involved with ecological sabotage. Her murder was particularly brutal. It was years ago, as you know; the file was in your cabinet like you said. No unusual personal effects like the disk were mentioned, or noticed. The door knob girl, Rose Hopper, was also an ecological activist. She'd been on two anti-whaling cruises with the fat boy. The same with Rita. I mean ecological stuff. No whaling activities for her. I haven't got much on the anti-whaling guy himself, except for a number of reports he was perfectly healthy, despite his weight, pushing 350 lbs. What a tub. Oh, and he wrote a back cover blurb for Chavez's book, according to an editor at the publishing house, so they possibly knew each other. Alas, he was cremated too quickly. A bureaucratic foul-up at the morgue — sent him off to the funeral home without an autopsy. I've no idea how that happened. So it does look like we might have someone stalking ecologists, but not a lot to go on yet. Wild world, eh?"

"It is that."

"And on another subject, scuttlebutt has it we are no longer called the 'token twins' in the department."

There was a long pause before Janwar said: "That's good news."

"I wouldn't go as far as that. The 'toxic twins' is our new handle."

"Great. It's about what I expected. I have to go. We're still trying to fix my car. Call you back soon."

He turned and saw a man dancing. No, it was a tall boy — on the rocky knob of Mecca's bluff, a place that had been empty earlier, which he'd thought strange. It should have been a choice location. Now he understood. It must have been reserved for him. Janwar stopped to watch. The boy was darkly tanned — he had platinum blonde hair and startling black eyes, frightening eyes. He was naked except for a small cloth around his waist and crotch. There were bright carpets and cloths at his feet. The dancing was odd, jerky, almost Egyptian, and it possessed a grace impossible to forget once seen. He had to be the Day boy Wren told him about, the child of the mushroom-eaters. Instantly, he understood Charlie Baker and his generous offer, watching this odd Egyptian dance with veils and batiks.

The boy leaped and posed and drew his fingers across his eyes, admired, yet treated casually by the local crowd who tossed an occasional coin or bill into the wooden bowl beside his magic carpet. The sight was unearthly enough that Janwar stood beside his car, mouth open, and his heart went out to the island. He was destined to join the unique lifestyle offered here — this loving, dancing, weird home of the wonderful.

* * *

Brian sat behind the wheel of the white Miata, a bit sweaty after the walk from the treehouse. He turned the key, distractedly, not noticing the failure of the ignition lights. With the motor running, he sat there, admiring the scratch marks on the hood made by the peacock before he'd chased it away. He'd have to take the High Road because of the roadwork; that was a nice, simple, meaningful-enough answer for today. The scratches on the hood were no problem. After all, it wasn't his car. Nor was it traceable. Or his license. He wasn't as stupid as Charlie insisted. On the other hand, Charlie might not be as smart as he thought he was, especially if he discovered the cyanide and thought he was safe. The old fool.

He turned off the ignition, climbed out of the car, opened the trunk, and removed the solar battery, carrying it up the path, stumbling, until he reached the overgrown junk pile. It wasn't that heavy — Brian realized he was walking at an angle and had a hard time correcting it. Those bloody mushrooms! The old man had caught him off guard with them.

The peacock was there, fanned out again, this time on a porcelain sink. He didn't have the heart to chase it away. And his stomach was churning. He should have used the outhouse before he left. There was a great dump binding up in his belly. Or was that the mushrooms? Did he really have to use the outhouse?

The battery might be worth a lot of money; yet that wasn't why he'd come here. The stark lucidity of the air haunted and invigorated him. He was proud of himself for returning the battery, though he couldn't resist wiping it clean of fingerprints, overcome by more paranoia again — pointless, because he'd probably left prints everywhere in the cabin. The flashes of paranoia were beginning to grow on his nerves. At least the police didn't have any copies of his prints, so he was safe. He hated being such a fetishist, always thinking things like this out; still, that was how he'd survived so far, how he'd become an avenger. God's will. He wanted to smile at the trees and the sky. "I have to get myself under control. I have to leave with dignity. He's got me stoned, the bastard."

Charlie had probably eaten the orange already. Festus only showed up every few days. By the time he or anyone else found the old man's body in the garden it would be ripening, and everyone would assume it was old age, a heart attack. If they did suspect Brian, and his sudden departure, or stumbled on the mushrooms or the rotting milk, or his backup, or even if the cop was actually coming back, and that wasn't a cooked-up scheme between Festus and Charlie to scare him into leaving — Brian would be impossible to trace. "After all, 'My name is Legion for I am many.'" He kicked a few leaves over the battery to make it look as if it had been there a while. He was filled with many fears. The worst was when he realized he was being watched, and it wasn't the peacock. His heart skipped; a maniacal energy almost overwhelmed him. That omelette had put him on an emotional roller coaster. He glanced around. It was the parrot, above, concealed in a scrub alder. Birds! Stupid birds, they were everywhere. "I'm a killer, not a thief," Brian said, jerking his middle finger at the parrot. He wished he had a slingshot. Congo growled, lifted a pathetic, threatening claw, then followed him, fluttering from tree to tree, down to the road where Brian climbed awkwardly into his car again, after undoing the clamps and folding the softtop behind the seat.

The world was good, so good, clean of his past. 'I've never felt like this before, as if my mind has been washed.' He noticed the cold eye of the parrot in the low branches overhanging the car. He gave a jaunty wave to the bird, expecting it to say something perfect, meaningful, perhaps about rocks.

"Bye, asshole," it chuckled, and winged its way up the path, the laughter floating behind long after it was gone.

"You're going to die a lonely bird," he said. Time to get out of here. He drove the low, white sports car out from behind the brushy Ocean Spray half-concealing the driveway. He was on the High Road now, refusing to let the parrot deflate his mood. If anything, he felt better. He stepped on the gas, trailing a stream of dust along the straight, flat stretch, the sole unpaved section — passing a burnt-out farmhouse, then a row of dilapidated cabins, and a pasture with a congregation of crows. One was perched on a stump, while the others stood in rows like students in an auditorium, listening to it declaim.

"Kill the parrot!" he screamed at the crows as the car sped past, his hair swept back by the wind. He felt so good, alive. Was he still stoned?

Remembering, he pulled an empty vial out of his pocket and hurled it into a clump of salmonberries alongside the road as he sped by. Then the other vial, with a tiny discoloured sponge in it.

Poor Rita: she had a knack for dangerous men. Well, that was cleared up now. He was glad he'd come for

Charlie. A lot had been clarified — not only his guilt for her death, but the past, the others.

Murder! We condemn it, yet we also praise its ecology.

The evisceration of a thousand salmon when the eagles hit the creek at spawning time is natural, along with the epic carnage of volcanos and typhoons, or a man slaughtering other men to protect his country. They never achieve the moral hatred of our society. But what if the serial killer thinks he or she is an ecological function? Do we criticize the mink in the tern rookery? Is the murder of a murderer good because his murders are not? How can a society say murder is wrong when it executes those who kill? Oh murder, I don't understand you and I'm constantly surprised by you, resent you and reject you, and sometimes I fear you are more right than I am, that you are natural — like a child's twisted chromosomes . . . "

They weren't so important, those others. One hung up in a closet — a suicide note on top of her laser printer — that was Rose, whom his mother still asked about. His most stupid escapade — and introducing her to Mother — what was he thinking? Thankfully, Mom didn't read the papers, and he'd never bothered telling her about Rose's lamentable passing — that would have really got the old rosary going. Then there was the one with her head dented by an odd bit of plumbing from a renovation in a lane behind the dormitory at the university. She was boring. Stupid whining woman — like the hitchhiker dumped in the bush near Wawa, or the hooker with her stomach opened up in the hotel room. He'd done that merely to muddy his trail, make it appear a different modus operandi. That's not entirely true. He'd always been curious about what a human being looked like inside. And the fat blonde boy with the missing thumb, who resembled the whales he supposedly protected, when he wasn't out scoffing pork chops on the lucrative lecture circuit. Heart attack. So it goes. And the old Chicano woman he held to the fire for a single lousy lead, but it was a good lead — Rita, and the door to Coyote.

Here, on the island, this was different. It had meaning. He would have taken the kid, too; unfortunately, it didn't work out. That's alright. Charlie was his first real man. The whale boy didn't count for much. Too effortless. Too stupid. At least now he didn't feel like a sexist, or a creep only picking off the weak. He felt like a hunter — a real warrior. Murder is so easy. Why didn't more people try it? Maybe they didn't have the fortitude, or the desire. Besides, murder wasn't the point. He had far more to prove, far more to work out, which is why he'd taken his leisurely time with Charlie. Melodramatic knives or guns would have been boring.

There! What have I done to myself? He's about as awful as a man can get, isn't he Festus? As dangerous as a force of nature or a disease? But have I answered your question, told your story? No, not yet — there's more.

The car floated over the crest of the hill, the pasture far behind, and into the first curve. When he pressed the brake pedal, it felt mushy. Was he still stoned? Had he been stoned at all? What the hell was in that omelette? 'I'll have to get this checked at the garage in Sweet Water.' He cruised along the straightening road. 'I must be low on fluid; but there's no warning light?' He'd dump the machine when he got back to Vancouver this evening. It was time to get rid of it. Time to switch names again, too.

Ah yes, the hook, the awful hook that makes us believe in our dreams and refuse to acknowledge what's coming at us even as we swallow it. Is this straight, unadulterated stupidity? Is it dumb bad luck? Or is it a combination of both?

Maybe when he reached Vancouver he'd draw enough cash for a down payment off that fat Amex card in the safety deposit box, and buy something fancy —that "Lil Red Truck" in the car lot on Kingsway, if he could beat the price back a little.

He arrived at the last, long curve, and braked; there was nothing. 'Son-of-a-bitch!' He hammered it to the floor. Nothing. He jerked at the emergency brake. 'I'm not going to let this destroy my mood!' The wheels began to smoke, and he found himself entering the chute to the ferry dock. He couldn't see the dock although he knew it was soon. The slate walls rose above him. 'I should have signed that petition.' The grin was frozen on his face.

Oh Brian — Oh Brian, my lovely monster, ugly shadow of myself; at last I can begin to weep for you, the same way I can weep for the bullet-riddled cougar after it killed forty-three sheep on our island and plucked a child from the wooden steps of a movie theatre . . . Now say hello to Inspector Janwar Singh and the low end of the High Road.

The snap of his emergency cable parting rang against the under-carriage with an awful clarity. "Aww, you're not going to do this!" He squirmed in his seat, the car drifting out of the long curved section of ravine and facing the ramp to the ferry. He could pull towards the side, try to bounce off the vehicles lined up along the road, but the rear one was a truck, its high back-end at head level. Besides, he was going too fast now, and he was suddenly about to become public news, the last thing he needed. 'To hell with it.' He wasn't going near any truck.

"Charlie, you bastard, I'll get you for this. What a stupid amateur! The brakes! How hokey!" The ferry hadn't arrived yet. The blue sea at the end of the ramp was inviting. A chance. This show wasn't over yet! He thumped on the horn to warn everyone out of the way.

He would let the car race straight down, and leap out as it went over. It would be like jumping off the wharf. Give a tourists a real show. But he had to leap as soon as the car became airborne. If it rolled or twisted when it launched, he'd be finished.

Abruptly, almost obscured by the store, the startled face of the cop jerked up from under the hood of an old Chevrolet. 'Shit, he's here!' It was true, what the kid said, only worse.

One hand on the wheel, he unbuckled his seat belt, wondering for a moment when he'd put it on, holding the car on a straight course, whistling past the gaping tourists and the clueless truck driver with a Styrofoam coffee cup who barely jumped out of the way and splattered himself with coffee while the car swept by. Then the car was on the ramp. Brian stood up partially on the seat, one-handing the steering wheel, waiting for the car to catch air. A sign loomed in front of him, attached to the steel cable stretched across the ramp. "Restricted Zone." The Miata flashed beneath the cable.

To his left, on a creosoted piling, the old white peacock flashed its tail in a big fan. There were a hundred eyes in that eight-foot tail — faint brown shadows in the harsh white of the feathers, each eye watching the events below as the king of birds lifted first one clawed foot before lowering it, and than the other, performing a slow dance of power as ancient as the natural world.

Brian felt the contact at his waist, heard the loud twang, before he spun around, leaving the car.

He was sitting in wet junk, his arms out like a gorilla's, propping him up on scraped knuckles after he'd bounced and rolled onto the ramp; he was gawking at the chute, the tourists, the truck driver, the High Road. A lazy June bug crawled across the corrugated metal in front of him, and a fly was stuck in a splatter of blood. 'Where do all these bugs come from?' Festus was standing outside the grocery store, sucking on a black chocolate bar, watching. Brian had time for another thought: God and flies mixed up together. The wet stuff was his entrails. Only half of him was here, the other — gone . . . He fell back, rolling leadenly onto his side, his bloody thumb jamming into his mouth.

The car soared above the ramp behind him, a white bullet plummeting towards the dark green ocean, his lower torso and legs spread-eagled on the seat. The car hit the water with a smack, sending out a starfish of foam that held it momentarily, before it descended, leaving nothing but the foam and a dwindling stream of bubbles.

Beneath the surface, clinging to the wharf pilings, the scarlet anenomes, the banded feather dusters, and the horny-surfaced barnacles contracted, sucking tentacles and necks into their protected bodies. On the ocean floor the urchins waved menacing spines, and a Pacific octopus inhaled itself into a hole among the rocks; each creature disturbed by the shock wave that signalled intruders and trouble.

***

Charlie lowered his binoculars. High on his pedestal above the treehouse, where his view encompassed not only the road and the ferry terminal, but beyond, island after island riding the water. The parrot flew up, anchoring itself on a branch near his face. They were almost eye-to-eye.

It has nothing to do with simplicity. The danger always lies in what you don't anticipate. The simplest things — they can kill you, but confused dreams are worse. Brian? Why should he have suspected his brake system was tampered with? That is not the question. Whether Charlie wanted to scare Brian, perhaps give him a little thrill, let him know it's not so easy to walk away from murdering the one you love, threaten him, or kill him, doesn't matter either. That is also not the question. The act was done, and Charlie would have to live with it, as he had to live with the other consequences of his life, as he'd been doing for so many years, That is, if it was Charlie who fixed the master cylinder for the brake system. The deed is more like what a smart kid would devise, not a sabotage performed by a wily old veteran. Who knows? What do you think, Festus?

Myself? I think the peacocks did it.

Or, maybe it was the parrot.

Right. Who did it or whether they meant to do it is also not the question. This story began with a request for a story. And a question that made me question the world. So what is the answer? The answer, time after time, is that the question is meaningless.

All I can give you is your life and your story, thrown back at you — yourself, your friends, your family, your neighbours, seen from a new angle — myself deformed into different variations, young and murderous, old and saddled with history, and as an unreliable narrator who lies (yes!). It's your world reflected in a distorted mirror. Strange isn't it? — as strange as the world we wake into each morning, as strange as a coyote yapping on a grassy island hill. You asked me for a story and I gave you one that asked more questions — that's what stories can do.

Everyone has performed their set pieces in this mystery, enough has been said. Now you have to figure it out. What's my favourite answer? — confusion, gorgeous confusion — the beauty and horror. Jokes and mysteries. I'm not going to say anything more, nothing, except perhaps — Thank You. That's for you, boy, a man now, and alive since you are reading this. That was the promise made, that if you lived, I would release this story when you turned twenty-one. And Thank You to whoever else has made it this far, all you readers, Thank You for running with me.

The last words are courtesy of the surviving members of our cast. They might be more help than I have been, at least on the obvious questions.

On the branch by Charlie's head, the bird surveyed the distant activity by the ferry dock, and gave an ecstatic bounce, wagging its beak, as if this were the funniest thing it had ever seen. Then it said: "I'm a killer, not a thief."

Charlie shoved the parrot away, and it flew squawking and cursing into the forest. He glassed the ferry terminal again. There was a crowd around the remains on the ramp. A blanket had been thrown over Brian's torso. People always want to hide the dead. In a few minutes, the sun hooked itself on the distant ridge of Vancouver Island, and the sky began to prepare for its nightly light show.

For a long time, he sat on his perch as the last light spread its fingers over the water, invading the treehouse, giving the vegetable plants within the garden darker, longer, intense shadows. Time passed. The evening wind came up, and the crickets began their sundown songs.

The cop would be coming here soon, for sure, but everything was legal, if eccentric. Brian was writing a book on organic lifestyles, and had stayed with him for a while — research. If it turned out he was a wild card that wasn't Charlie's problem. Yes, it was safe, if murder can ever be called safe. What Charlie didn't know was that all the tadpoles in the rain barrel on his front porch were floating, one-by-one, to the surface, belly up.

***

Festus took the path to the treehouse via the shortcut from Mecca. The boy climbed up the ladder and sat down beside Charlie, wordless, watching the remote activity at the wharf.

Between them, in the silence, there was the unmistakeable bond between an old man and a young boy. One, his skin withering, looking back on the decisions and chances that ruled his life, remembering his vanished powers, the times he won and those he lost. The other, tight, full of energy, eager to make the run, confident he will win, yet recognizing the evidence: the partial remains of a body at the bottom of a hill, the feel of his own mutant flesh, the relics of hazards in the old man's eyes — the expression that said: 'I used to know everything. I don't any more.'

"Prince," he said to Festus,
" . . . beautiful as a merlin.
Know what he did when he departed.
He took a big shot of bitter drugs
when he left this world behind."

Charlie heard the distant roar of the Coast Guard hovercraft from Sweet Water approaching the coastline — an electric water spider skidding across the strait. Upon its arrival at the wharf, a squad of yellow-suited divers holding lamps went over the side, eager to get the job done before the advancing twilight became darkness. He studied the radiant patterns beyond the ramp — writing hieroglyphic codes with lanterns under the ocean.

Festus watched the old man lower the glasses. He didn't have an idea what to say. There wasn't much he could say, but there was a question. "Why are the tadpoles in the rain barrel dying?"

Charlie raised an eyebrow. "They are?" Delicately, he reached around and pulled the handkerchief out of his back pocket. He threw it over the side of the treehouse, so that it fluttered down into the salmonberry bushes by the back window in the cellar. The treehouse would be getting one hell of a cleanup job tonight. Or should he burn it down, after all, and begin again?

The lone figure of a man appeared among the wild oregano in the meadow. He'd got his vehicle running at last, despite Peacock Jim's help.

The cop gave a silent wave, head down, as he trudged through the fragrant clearing. He reached the ramp, walking up it with a bitterness in his posture that made both Charlie and Festus nervous. He stopped outside the door. "How do I get up there?" he asked loudly enough to be heard on the roof, not bothering with a greeting. He glanced over at the slimy rain barrel, noticing it was full of dead tadpoles.

"There's a ladder inside the treehouse."

In a very short time he clambered onto the roof. For a moment, he was stunned by the view, absorbing it, silent. Then he fixed his attention on Charlie, so unnerving the old man with the obvious anger in his thin, small frame that Charlie, for one of the few times in his life, was at loss for words. He could learn to appreciate this cop.

Janwar sat down beside Festus, beneath Charlie on his throne. He rested his head on his hands and stared at the distant ferry terminal.

Finally, Charlie broke the silence. "It appears we've had a spot of trouble."

"It does. He killed Rita Norman, didn't he?"

"That's a possibility."

"His real name isn't Brian, is it?"

"I have no idea."

"I could haul you in fast."

"Yes, you could."

"But what I want is the truth?"

"The truth — well, now that's a question. Actually, it's an entire story."

Janwar seemed to settle down, regain his composure. He was silent again for a while, watching the wharf. "Did you kill him?"

"No, but it had crossed my mind."

"Do you want me to arrest you?"

"No. I'm an innocent man."

"Innocent?"

"As innocent as any man can be."

"You killed him, didn't you?"

"I didn't have anything to do with him going off the wharf."

"Then, who did?"

"Maybe he killed himself."

"I doubt that."

"Maybe I killed Brian," Festus said.

"You?" Janwar turned to the boy.

"Maybe Brian killed himself?" Festus grinned, playing on Charlie's words. "Why don't we just call it a mystery?"

"I don't think he was Brian," Charlie said, interrupting before this went too far. "I don't think he was writing any book. I think he was a weirdo. He learned I was an old lover of Rita Norman's and came up here for some godforsaken secret reason I never could understand. Maybe he thought this would be a good place to hide out, take advantage of an old man living outside the grid. Then he had a car accident. He's dead now. Your case is wrapped up. Check him out. I think you've got your man. You're a hero."

"I am not a hero. I've spent the entire day being taken for rides by one of your friends who could end up charged as an accessory. What in hell's name is going on around here?"

Festus spoke with a slow, quiet confidence surprising for a child. "None of this is our fault, not anyone's on the island. It just happened to us. That's the way the world works."

"What do you know?"

"I know he came up here to kill Charlie, and Charlie is a friend of mine."

Charlie looked down at him with an expression akin to fear, or sadness.

"That's okay, Charlie. I dropped over to borrow the metric wrenches and I didn't want to disturb you, but I heard him when I was in the shop under the house. I knew he was a creep, I knew what he intended."

Charlie nodded distantly.

"What will they find," Janwar asked Festus, "when they take that car apart?"

"Not much — a faulty seal in the master cylinder, the warning lights dead because two wires in the electrical harness shorted out — the short caused by the jury-rigged installation of the car's stereo." Festus spoke mechanically, like a manual. Charlie was speechless.

Janwar turned his attention to Charlie. "Brian said he was doing a book on coyotes. I think he was hunting ecologists. Do you know anything about the man called Coyote?"

Charlie examined the sky; then Janwar — for a long time . . . "If you're talking about who I think you're talking about, didn't he die many years ago?"

Janwar looked at Festus. "How old are you?"

"I'll be twelve next month."

"Are you aware of the Young Offender's Act."

"I am."

"What do you know about it?"

"I can't be charged with any crime unless I am twelve-years-old. You can't touch me. Maybe you could get social services to put me in a home, but you won't. You shouldn't."

"And you, Charlie, you didn't put him up to this?"

Charlie turned to the boy. "Oh Festus, anything could have happened. You could have hurt someone else, or brought him back to us, here . . . "

Festus pursed his lips stubbornly. "I was unlucky when I was born. I've been lucky ever since."

Janwar had never seen the lines so clearly, the awful triangles of fate. There wasn't any need to stalk this old man, nor the kid, both of whom he felt he wanted to know better, in different circumstances. There was a quality about the old man, a fatherly comfort when he sat beside him. He liked it.

He was going back to Vancouver where he would resign his commission once he had wrapped up his current duties; then he would tell his mother what he'd done. He would tell her about his sister, too, and give her the phone number if she wanted to use it. Then he would go down to the *gurdwara* and polish the shoes of the devotees for a month while considering his life, paying a little of his debt to a great community. After that he would return to the island — to Wren, if she would accept him.

So many years on wrong roads. It would take a lot of learning to catch up to what was in his heart. It was a queer heart, out of kilter with the rest of the world. It belonged on this odd island, not in the police force. Kirsten was the chosen one, not him. He knew it as soon as he opened the letter from Blake. Once she was older, had matured, with a few more years under her belt, she would break through the chain of white men dominating the force. That would really drive Blake nuts on his beach. Janwar felt a rush of love for her. Things could have been, should have been, different; but they weren't, and both their courses were set now.

"I'm beginning to understand your story. The man knew of you through Miss Norman, and thought he could hide out by posing as a book writer and taking advantage of your legendary hospitality, Mr. Baker. Then when he'd heard I was back on the island, after I'd initially come up here on a false lead concerning you, he panicked and fled in a vehicle that failed him on a dangerous road. You could say I've solved another case, and that will look good on my record. I'm going to have it all wrapped up and closed before I retire from the force, perhaps to this island. Do both of you understand that?"

Festus beamed, looking his true age. "That's my kind of story! Exactly the way I thought it worked out."

Charlie was quiet for a few second. "I'm impressed. You must be a fine cop."

"I don't believe I ever was a cop, but I know a good story when I encounter one."

"Well then, you might make a good islander."

"I hope I do. If anybody else questions you about the matter, I would appreciate knowing it. And don't embellish your story. Simplicity is everything. You should count your blessings, we should all count our blessings. There are a number of missing people, mostly women, whose fates, I suspect, were changed by this man."

"A number . . . ?" Charlie lowered his head.

"More than one. Five at a minimum. That could be an underestimate." Then his expression changed, as if this were not a topic for decent men. "I'll take my leave now. It's growing dark. Thank you for your cooperation. It will be appreciated by my superiors at RCMP headquarters." Janwar rose to his feet and found the ladder. He climbed down into the treehouse, descended the ramp, and crossed the meadow, an elated jaunt to his stride. He was returning to the arms of Wren.

Hawww! I'm a cheater. I'm not finished yet. One last song, one last little breath in a world that is closing, because, like everyone who sees the end ahead, I want to continue forever, retain my voice. But I will no longer exist after the final page. After all, I am only a story. Goodbye. Yes, that's it. Goodbye clouds and salamanders. All of you. Strange hills and strange days, floating thistles in a high wind. Killers and killed. Rocks. Beautiful diseases. Cauliflower. Dead tadpoles. The holy root maggots — goodbye — goodbye — my children, my loves, my dreams, goodbye . . .

Down at the terminal, the divers surfaced. They had hooked a cable around the car, and began winching it to the surface, where they cinched it to the side of the wharf. Heavier winches would have to be brought over to haul it out tomorrow.

Calm settled once again upon the island — an environment where sea anenomes show off for scuba divers, where the arbutus and the last of the Garry Oak orchards cling to the rocky bluffs, where the people live like the odd creatures they are in an astonishing universe.

Through his binoculars, Charlie watched the dim shapes of the divers bring the remains to the shoreline; they were going to put the two halves together, an oddly touching gesture in the face of death's brutality. They carried the mess to the hovercraft while other men hosed down the ramp, and the ferry, which had been waiting in the bay for hours, approached its terminal.

The raccoons arrived quietly on the lower deck, where they found the compost bucket brimming with choice fruit and vegetables, since Charlie had been too distracted to empty it for days. Each chose what appealed most and climbed up onto the chair beside the rain barrel. Ignoring the dead tadpoles, the mother and her two kits, washed the discarded tea leaves off their evening snack of plums.

The hovercraft's motors roared to life again. It turned and sped out of the bay, south towards Vancouver, its searchlight playing across the ocean under the deepening indigo sky. Charlie lowered his binoculars. The boat fused into the glassy black surface, gone, out of sight. With an old man's fussiness, he tucked the binoculars into their case. The resentment in his dry mouth had a taste like almonds, bitter almonds.

Below them, the three racoons deserted the ravaged compost bucket and scampered into the nearby brush where they would fold up together, later in the evening, forming a little pile, slowly breathing out the last of their poisoned lives.

Charlie was silent on the rooftop for a long time. Finally, he spoke: "It wasn't necessary. He was already dead."

"Huh?"

"There was more than psilocybin in our omelette this morning, at least in his portion. You killed a dead man."

The boy's eyes lit up, almost gleefully. "Truly?"

"Truly. He would have got chest pains tomorrow morning, general discomfort in the stomach. Within a few days he'd have had a heart attack. And if he managed to get to a hospital, he wouldn't tell them where he'd come from, not after all his little traps here. Nor would they find anything in his blood unless they knew what to test for. He'd merely be another overweight, hard-drinking, heavy smoker who didn't realize he had a bad heart. Knowing how to murder is easy. Living with it is the difficult part."

Festus glanced shyly back at him, fearful this time. The look in those eyes knotted Charlie's heart. The old man studied the boy. "Oh, my lad — what has come looking for us, and what have we done — what happened?"

Charlie snorted, and tried to hold back the flood, his eyes brilliant with water. The more he sobbed, the shorter and jerkier the noise. Then almost imperceptibly it transformed into a subdued, choking laugh. And for a moment he was rocking on his seat near the surprised boy, holding his belly like a modern Ho-tei, the future Buddha, a figure sometimes known as one of the seven gods of happiness — the crazy laughing bodhisattva, refusing heaven until he can take everyone and everything with him.

He gradually became an old man again, over-seeing his garden and the darkening landscape beyond as he settled into silence. When he spoke at last, his voice was ironic and wistful. "Now you can tell your story, Brian — make it a mystery."

And the night full of shadows finally came down, the beautiful night, invading, possessing, reclaiming its share of life on earth, clamping the blue dark world in its invisible claws.

ACKNOWLEDGMENTS

This text would not have been possible without the writings of Gary Snyder and Edward Abbey, supplemented by the sometimes extreme writing of factions in the Deep Ecology movement. And *Animal Liberation* — Peter Singer's extraordinary book, which haunted me, along with his examinations of several other difficult mysteries that he has attempted to resolve. This complex, controversial thinker is a lively philosopher of our time, unafraid of dangerous questions.

I have used statistics from other books, *The Deadly Additives* by Linda R. Pim, for instance, but it should be noted they are dated according to the era of this novel. In most cases, today, a least a decade later, the situation is worse. As always, statistics mean little; the life behind them is everything. *Deadly Doses: A Writer's Guide to Poisons,* by Serita Deborah Stevens with Anne Klarner, was the source of much information on various toxic compounds.

All speeches by Congo, except three or four, are courtesy of the parrot I've lived with for twenty years — my companion, Tuco. Though the character of Congo is different and not nearly as clever, he couldn't have existed without Tuco, who is an endless source of inspiration, and orders me to work every morning. And that's no story.

I have attempted not to give any detailed accounts of ecotages or exotic poisons, except for historically known or obvious or historic actions, in the interest of safety for all and for my own conscience. I have also distorted RCMP procedure intentionally, creating a non-existent homicide office. They have a tough enough job without my help.

Artemis Island is based on the characteristics of a half-dozen islands in this fabulous archipelago known as the Gulf Islands — so that none may point at their neighbour. Sharp readers will notice I've also had the nerve to toy with natural blooming cycles and the behaviour of the horticultural world in this particular climate.

I have done my best to seek instruction from elders and the original sacred texts of the various faiths featured; all errors of religion are my own. While it might appear that Festus is a victim of Hutchinson-Gilford's syndrome, his troubles and his 'cure' are unique to him.

Wherever possible, in attempting to create an authentic and true atmosphere, I've been telling a story. So, of course, I am solely responsible for all failings. The narrator of this book, as I state in the text, is not me. He developed in the course of its construction. But believe what you would like to believe. None of the other characters is based on anyone I know. Anybody who thinks they are one of the persons in this book must have rocks in their head. It is only a story.

I thank the Canada Council and the B.C. Arts Council for their generous support during the long gestation of *Coyote*.

And finally, I would like to dedicate this novel to Peggy and Seán, who demanded it. They held me to the fire, insisting on a story. I've done my best to give them one.

Does a dog have Buddha nature?
This question is the deepest of all.
If you say, "Yes,"
Or if you say, "No,"
You lose your own Buddha nature.

To which Joshu replied: "Mu!"